MW01698591

18 Truths

Jamie Ayres

A Division of **Whampa, LLC**
P.O. Box 2540
Dulles, VA 20101
Tel/Fax: 800-998-2509
http://curiosityquills.com

© 2014 Jamie Ayres
http://jamieayres.com

All rights reserved, including the right to reproduce this book or portions thereof in any form whatsoever. For information about Subsidiary Rights, Bulk Purchases, Live Events, or any other questions - please contact Curiosity Quills Press at info@curiosityquills.com, or visit http://curiosityquills.com

ISBN: 978-1-62007-446-6 (ebook)
ISBN: 978-1-62007-447-3 (paperback)
ISBN: 978-1-62007-448-0 (hardcover)

TABLE OF CONTENTS

For GG, the real Olga Worontzoff. You are one of a kind. I'm sorry I never learned to count in Russian, but I hope this makes up for it in some small way. xoxo

Prologue

"For, after a certain distance, every step we take in life
we find the ice growing thinner below our feet,
and all around us and behind us
we see our contemporaries going through."
—Robert Louis Stevenson

Truth: Every morning when I woke up, the biggest truth I've ever faced landed like a grenade in my heart. I never said this when I had the chance: I love Olga Gay Worontzoff with all my heart, soul, mind, and body.

Okay, maybe not body because we never touched outside of handholding and hugs, and usually because tears were involved on her behalf, not in an "I want you" kind of way at all. But I digress, which happened a lot lately since there wasn't much to do here other than have silly conversations with myself.

Now, where was I?

Oh, false: It's better to keep your feelings to yourself so you don't ruin your friendship. What a bunch of crap. I couldn't believe for twelve years I freakin' ate a pile of that shi—

Um, I mean, crap. That was one of Olga's favorite words, a word I used a lot these days as I worked on my language.

It was all I thought about in Juvie. No, not sh—crap. Although maybe if I had said a few less 'bad' words, then maybe I wouldn't have ended up here. But I seriously didn't think the Big Man Upstairs cared so much about that stuff as he did people. Otherwise, he would've sent me straight to Hell like I probably deserved.

But, like I was saying, every morning I woke up after another weird dream that usually involved me yelling at Olga to hurry, like I was the white rabbit and she was Alice, and then my truth hit me again like a ton of bricks. I was dead, and I never once told Olga I loved her, was *in* love with her.

And now? Too late.

I didn't know if she survived the freak boating accident on Lake Michigan that involved lightning and hypothermia and took my life, but even if she didn't, she was in Heaven. I knew this because she was an angel even on Earth. But me? I was stuck in Juvie, one of the four realms of the Underworld, reserved for teenagers like me who were undecided about the whole God thing at the time of their unfortunate demise.

I squeezed my eyes closed, trying to shut out my agony. Here was another truth: there were tears after death, at least where I resided. Sean and Kyle would probably revoke my Man Card for admitting I cried, but I figured I had nothing to lose at this point. Okay, that was only half-true. I could still lose my soul.

Even if this part of the Underworld was temporary until judgment or whatever, there was a terrifying finality to it. I tried to focus on Godly things to get me through, but Olga filled my thoughts instead. Not always the PG version either.

Truth number three: I regret dying a virgin.

Most people thought I wasn't one. In a twisted turn of feminine power events, this girl Denise, who I had dated for three weeks during the beginning of junior year—an all-time record high for me—claimed we slept together after we broke up. I didn't dispute the rumor because One, we did get about as close as you can get to sleeping with someone without actually doing the deed, and Two, why would anyone deny something like that?

I climbed off my cot in the darkness and stood. It was always dark here, with very little light. I paced around, going stir crazy once again.

I can't take this anymore.

My roommate yawned luxuriously, and I was thankful for the sound of something real. I threw my pillow at him.

"Wake up, Sunshine!" His real name was Bo, a seventeen-year-old like me. He died in a car crash, so cliché.

Bo reciprocated my gesture, and a pillow fight ensued. "I was having a *really* good dream, Conner."

Truth: all good things must come to an end.

"Sorry," I told him. "But breakfast waits for no man."

The Underworld would be unbearable if I didn't have some friends here, but one thing I had always been good at was making people love me. I just sucked at loving them back. Loving someone required faith, something I obviously never had; otherwise, I wouldn't be in this predicament right now. But I did have faith in Olga. Her friendship was like a good rock ballad, something I used to sing myself to sleep with to keep the nightmares away.

Bo and I headed outside. I never imagined the Underworld while I walked among the living, but even if I did, it wouldn't have come close to this. Juvie kinda felt like being shipped to a boarding school for rednecks. You might be a redneck if… your parents send you to a boarding school where you live in tents. Yep, there was a bunch of tents for us to stay in. When I first arrived and met Bo, I observed, "Man, this place is intense."

Ha ha ha! In tents=intense. Well anyway, he laughed and that pretty much sealed the deal on our bromance.

Everybody had a roommate in Juvie, an accountability partner as Leo stated. Leo was our angel headmaster, in charge of the two thousand teens housed in Camp Fusion. Juvie was divided into many camps with one angel in charge of each. My home at Juvie was just one small fraction of this plane. And if you thought two thousand teens were a lot to handle for one angel, then you haven't met Leo. Besides, there was a lot less opportunity for sinning here, so two thousand-thirteen- to-nineteen-year-olds camping together wasn't such a big deal. Since we were still fully human, with um, human desires, Leo said the same commandments we should've followed on Earth applied here.

There wasn't much else Leo explained to us though, only that we weren't fit for Heaven or Hell, so we were in a holding cell of sorts. We'd forever remain the age we were when we died, had daily assigned chores, and still attended school. Although there wasn't much separation of church and state here. In fact, most of our studies focused around religion.

Bo and I made our way past the community bathrooms on our left, the red barn with animals in it to the right, and then headed down the path lined with fields of wild flowers. The actual school sat on a pristine lake that was always the perfect temperature for swimming despite the absence of the sun to warm it. Old oaks and manicured hedges lined the sidewalk leading up to the school's front entrance. Just inside, to the left of the foyer, was the cafeteria.

I opened the glass door and called, "Honey, I'm home," like I owned the place, because that was how I rolled. A year ago, when I stepped into Camp Fusion High for the first time, my arms and legs felt like Jell-O. I was terrified at the uncertainty of what might go down in Juvie. Plenty of time had passed since then, and I'd regained my title as Most Popular. Oh, sure, I went through all the phases before finally acclimating myself to this new environment—shock, disbelief, bargaining, guilt, acceptance. Waking up in a place like this had been a complete mindfreak. I still hadn't made it around to hope yet. Hope would be seeing Olga again, and that was never going to happen. I'd heard of heartbreak, but I never knew your heart could literally break into a tiny million pieces, repeatedly, with each remembrance that the one thing you lived for was gone forever.

Damn, this sucked. I still couldn't believe I'd never told her. I thought about that lame question teachers used to ask us as an icebreaker on the first day of school: "If you only had one day to live, what would you do?" I'd always come up with some bullsh—crap answer. Seriously, Leo should create some sort of shock collar for me to break my cursing habit. Must be the sailor in me.

If I could just have one more chance, I knew exactly what I would do: tell Olga I was in love with her. Hell, if she walked through the cafeteria doors right now, I'd probably drop down on my knees and ask her to marry me. Forget about the no marriages rule in Juvie.

I wondered if she had a man now, if she survived. She had to survive though, right? I should've had a lifejacket on. I remembered bits and pieces of that day. Maybe my submission to all things reckless had angered God and that was why I died. Olga had tried to save me, and I remembered that, too. She probably thought she failed, but then again, if I would've died a few years later, I wouldn't have been a teenager anymore and would've been sent straight to Hell, so in a twisted way, she *did* save me. I still wasn't very comfortable with this God stuff, but Bo told me that was okay. He said if we could just trust we were all here for a moment and that was real and something had to cause all that—then that made a great first step.

I had a while to figure it out, I supposed. I sought out God in my studies—though we didn't have teachers here; class was more like homeschooling ourselves. There were plenty of books…Olga would've been happy to know that. I was pretty sure her idea of Heaven included an unlimited supply of books and coffee.

So, I tried to figure out the God stuff. I mean, He was real, obviously. But Leo told me my job now was to get to know Him, and I had no idea how to do that. I mean, the Dude didn't even visit! I just wished I would've had my, "Luke, I am your Father," moment a little sooner in life. Then, if Olga was in Heaven, I would've been there with her. Pretty much, before I died, the only religion I knew had been Star Wars. I didn't claim to be an expert on much, but nobody could deny my status as a Jedi Master when it came to all things created by George Lucas.

I figured if Darth Vader could overthrow the emperor at the last second and still be saved, then maybe that was what Juvie was all about. God wasn't through with us yet. We all had a little bit of Luke and Vader in us; we just had to choose which one we were going to listen to the most.

Bo took a seat at the picnic table and poured himself a bowl of cereal. "What's eating your brain? You've been quiet since we stepped in here."

"Star Wars," I answered through a mouthful of chocolate chip pancakes. Piles of food mysteriously appeared on the tables at mealtimes, but then they also magically disappeared after an hour, so you had to be quick.

"Dude, that horse is dead. Time to put the stick down."

The orange juice I sipped squirted out of my nose a little as I let loose a laugh. "Look around, dude. Reality has absolutely no place in my world."

I got sidetracked by the sight of Julia eyeballing me from across the table with those big baby blues of hers. She had the look of a girl who knew she was exceptionally beautiful and knew that you knew it, too.

"What?" I mumbled.

"You have bed head."

Julia reached over and smoothed down my hair. We'd been going steady for four weeks now, my new record. Our courting was proof we weren't trying to create a Utopian Society here by any means. So far, our relationship had been filled with happiness and disappointment, confusion and clarity, and all the other things, good and bad, that made dating interesting.

She leaned away from me, shaking her blonde-streaked brown hair as she plopped back down on the bench. Her yellow sundress gave her an angelic glow, but this one was no angel, which was what I liked about her. Julia was about as far away from Olga as I could get, so there weren't many reminders about the girl I lost when we hung out together.

"You sleep well, handsome?" Her waggling eyebrows seemed to suggest to everyone else at the table that we fooled around last night before our midnight curfew.

"Sure," I agreed, but my tone conveyed otherwise. Last night was the first time we advanced past kissing and rounded second base, so I should've had sweet dreams and all that. I didn't know why, but I felt so guilty afterwards. Okay, so I lived in the Underworld and was much more aware of sinning or whatever. But that wasn't really what bothered me. It felt like I cheated on Olga, which sounded crazy since I was never gonna be with her.

"Aw, what's wrong?" Julia asked in her annoying, puppy dog voice.

"I dunno," I answered, bringing my best analysis of the situation I was in to the table.

Julia shot me a dirty look, but Bo intervened and started telling her about the weird dream he had last night. We all had weird dreams here, and we told them in detail, almost like ghost stories around a campfire.

I got so lost in deep thought about my Olga dreams that my brain had to travel a few dimensions back to present when the food disappeared and Julia called my name.

She stood behind me now, wrapping me in a hug. It didn't even come close to producing the warmth Olga's arms had once held for me, but it was the best substitute I could find here.

Stretching my arms above my head like a cat, I stood and faced her. "You're hot," I said ruefully.

She laughed. She had a nice laugh.

"How do you view our relationship?" she asked.

The weight of our four-week courtship settled upon me at last. Here was Julia. In an otherwise miserable existence, she'd brought a little light to my life of late. But she wasn't Olga. She was a carefree indulgence on my part. Did I hope my attraction would bloom into something more like love at some point? Sure, but I wasn't holding my breath.

"I'm crushing on you, girl. You know this."

My answer possessed a nugget of truth, but her eyes flashed for a second and I was pretty sure I pissed her off. Clearly, she viewed me as more already.

"It's just that, like, it feels like there's this invisible wall between us. Can we talk about the accident?"

"No," I deadpanned.

"Conner, please. You've never opened up to me about it, and I think it would help us grow closer. I told you my death story."

She talked about dying a lot. She was an artist and into painting all these watercolors depicting her drug overdose. In truth, I'd experience never-ending shame if I died from swallowing too many pills. What a stupid way to die.

"What's there to dissect? I took my annual first spring sail on Lake Michigan with my best friend. Lightning struck me. I wasn't wearing a life jacket, and the voltage and hypothermia formed a deadly combo, inducing cardiac arrest."

Truth: just the thought of that day made my throat close up. I knew now how wide, high, and deep this galaxy was, but this conversation had a way of making me feel claustrophobic.

Julia eyeballed me again, probably trying to gauge my mood to see if she could push me, but all I gave her in return was a glassy stare.

"Why does it take so much effort to even make cracks in you? Why do you act this way? We're here to heal. You can't do that by bottling everything up."

I felt my body bending away from her without actually moving. "Ugh, Julia. I don't know. Maybe I can't let myself move on because I don't know what happened to Olga. Did she die too? Is she in Heaven? Did she survive the accident? Is she happy if I'm gone? Because honestly, even though people here constantly surround me, I feel alone and I don't know why that is other than my best friend isn't here with me. And that's what keeps me up at night, all the dreams about her. But there's also not a damn thing I can do about it, is there? Because nobody likes to give us real answers around here."

There was a gleam in her eyes, like she understood. "Thank you. I just wanted you to acknowledge the elephant in the room. You've put Olga on this pedestal, and I'm never gonna live up to your hero. I'm tired of competing. You can't date a memory, but you can date me."

I couldn't help myself. This was my Achilles' heel—I couldn't stand to have anyone angry with me, so I leaned forward and kissed her forehead. "You're right. And I do want to date you, okay?"

On her tiptoes, Julia pressed her forehead into mine and we saw eye to eye, literally and figuratively. I'd become that good at lying—able to look someone in the eye and still bear false testimony. Our lips touched briefly, and as we hugged, I promised myself I'd truly focus on Julia. I'd focused all my thoughts on Olga, and it was time to get them back… because she wasn't coming back.

"Oh, looks like we have an audience, honey."

I twisted to get a look at what she saw behind me.

"Olga?" I whispered. I dropped my hands from around Julia and turned to face Olga completely.

"Olga?" I repeated, this time at a regular volume but my voice cracking. Then I shouted, "Olga!" and ran to her.

It turned out that my first impulse wasn't to drop down to my knees and propose. Instead, I touched her. I wanted to make sure she was real. Lifting her off the ground, I swung her around and around again.

Truth: God, if this is a dream, I don't want to wake up.

CHAPTER ONE

"You can't change the truth,
but the truth can change you."
—Anonymous

One month ago…

Growing up, when I thought about spirit guides, I thought of the Native American legends and Disney movies portraying bears, horses, and wolves who offered advice and comfort to the heroes in stories. I definitely never imagined *I'd* become a spirit guide, or that they were even real.

I crossed my legs again, the torn vinyl seat cover scratching against my thigh, and flipped through the same *Stone Soup* children's magazine for the fifth time. If I didn't occupy my hands, I might break down the light brown door where Dr. Judy waited with a black hole, ready to suck away the future I spent the past year building for myself.

"What's taking so long?" Nate asked in a not-so-quiet voice, brushing a muscular arm against my own, sending chills down my spine.

Behind us, a secretary sat at a desk in the receptionist area, noisily working over a piece of gum like a cow chewing his dinner, and I could smell the cinnamon flavor from my seat.

"Shh," I answered him, trying not to blush—something I should have been able to manage since I'm dead, but nope. Amazingly, our bodies were carbon copies of when we were alive. The only thing really changed was that we could walk through walls and appear at random places, just by willing ourselves to go there, which was pretty stinkin' cool.

"Why?" He trained his blue-green eyes on me, making me itch to go back in time to twelve hours ago.

Back to Lake Michigan, him serenading me with the *Summertime* song he wrote about us, strumming his guitar. Back before we knew we'd been dead for the past year.

Pretty much back before everything suddenly became so complicated.

"They can't hear us, remember?" He gestured around the therapist's office waiting room.

I uncrossed my legs and snatched glances at the other people in the waiting area. One teen girl like me clenched her hands together in a worrying knot. A man with a Detroit Lions ball cap pulled low sat next to a tiny elderly woman wearing a blue scarf around her neck, looking lost and frightened. I blinked back tears, thinking about my parents visiting *my* therapist for grief counseling.

When I say therapist, I do so using air quotes in my mind because Dr. Judy isn't a real one—she's a spirit guide like us… well, like we were going to be. I wasn't even sure what the job entailed, but Nate and I were about to find out. Dr. Judy was our spirit guide after we died, we just didn't know it until today. *Or that we were even dead!* I was having a hard time processing that truth.

I studied Nate, the weight of the world on his shoulders, making him slump in his seat. Yup, it had been one of those days.

"Do you know any good jokes?" Nate asked with a half-crooked smile. "Because I could sure use one right now."

I took his hand in mine and squeezed. "We both could, but nope. Witty sarcasm is more my thing."

Nate leaned toward me and pressed his forehead against mine, his coffee colored hair slipping over his left eye. I felt his breath on my lips, the fresh scent of spearmint washing over me. Somehow, everything about Nate reminded me of my favorite things.

I sighed, not wanting to disappoint him. "What did the ocean say to the sand?"

His eyes lit up. "What?"

"Nothing, it just waved."

Snorting, he shook his head.

"Well, whaddya expect? The only jokes I know are from popsicle sticks."

He clung to me, and I held him tight, reveling in the feel of all things safe and good wrapped up in his tanned arms.

"What are you thinking about?" Even the sound of his voice soothed me, like gentle, peaceful waves rolling into the shore at sunrise.

I shifted uncomfortably in the thinly padded seat and lifted my hands, running them through his silky hair, then letting the strands fall to his shoulders. "I'm just thinking how this place used to be my safe haven and now it just feels like, I dunno, a black hole sucking away my future. We don't have a future anymore."

For the past year, Nate and I had been in a state of Limbo, completing a list of tasks Dr. Judy suggested so that we could learn our life—er, death lessons—and find true happiness again before entering Heaven. Apparently, I accidentally killed myself when I took a bottle of pain pills while feeling guilty about Conner, my best friend, who died in front of my eyes. I was unable to save him and blamed myself for his death.

Nate unintentionally killed himself while drag racing another kid from his school at the end of his junior year, all because he was upset about having to move to Grand Haven, my hometown. He found out today the other kid died, too.

After discovering *we were dead* and all this other stuff, entering Heaven seemed selfish when we left a wave of destruction here on Earth. Both of us had just witnessed, for the first time, our families grieving for us because of our stupid choices. Becoming spirit guides and helping others with unfinished business seemed fitting considering our circumstances.

Nate placed a finger under my chin and tilted my mouth to his. His lips were warm and soft. Usually, I wasn't a big fan of PDA, but we remained invisible to the 'living' people in the waiting room. Being in spirit form had its advantages.

"Olga Gay Worontzoff," he whispered after slowly breaking away from our kiss.

The worst thing about my life when I was alive, up until Conner's death, was my horrible name—named after my grandmothers, of course.

"As long as we're together, we'll always have a future." Nate's words scorched my ears, warmth spreading through my insides.

I sat up straighter and placed my hands on his broad shoulders, giving them a squeeze. "You're right. This is still just so hard to take in. I like my structure, ya know? And suddenly, my life has entered this frenetic pace where I don't even understand what's happening or—"

Nate's watch beeped, making me jump. We could roam Earth—the real one, not the fake one we'd been living on during our alternative timeline for the past year—one last time until midnight. At first, we just wanted to visit our families and friends. But not being able to interact with them was too depressing, so we spent most of our hours walking around the town we loved so much. I felt caught in some twisted version of Cinderella. At the stroke of the clock, my remarkable fortune would return once again to unfortunate circumstances. I mentally kicked myself. I should've known the past year was too good to be true.

Dr. Judy opened the door to her office. "Oh good, you're here." She seemed surprised, like we had a choice in the matter. "Are you ready to go?"

I slid my hand down to Nate's and held it as we stood together.

"No," Nate answered.

"You can't stay here." Dr. Judy eyed us cautiously.

Nate nodded his head. "We know, but we hoped to speak to you about becoming spirit guides."

She frowned at us for a moment. "Well then, come on in."

My eyes wandered to the waiting room, then to Dr. Judy, who followed my questioning gaze.

"Oh, I get to pick when they can and can't see me. One of the perks of the job."

She ushered us in and closed the door. The room still came equipped with the furnishings I'd grown accustomed to: two wicker cushioned seats, a desk and a leather chair, and a recliner. I didn't know why, but I expected her office to look different now.

As usual, she took a seat behind her desk in the middle of the room, and Nate and I sat in the two chairs in front of her. "First, do you understand what you're saying? What you're signing up for?"

"Sure," I said. "Spirit guides… we help people, or spirits, or whatever. We nudge them in the right direction, like you did with us. Only, we can't tell them they're dead. We have to *trick* them, let them believe they survived their accident and are still among the living." Okay, I might've delivered my answer with just a tad bit of resentment.

Dr. Judy gave her head a small shake, and I didn't blame her. Even to myself I sounded too immature for this job.

"It's so much more than that. Let's start out with a few things you need to know." She folded her hands on top of the mahogany surface.

Her tone sounded world-weary with a touch of skepticism. I wondered if this was how I'd sound after dealing with ghosts caught in the in-between for a few years. Even if I did get sick of my new profession, it's not like I could tell my boss to take this job and shove it.

Dr. Judy sighed loudly, drawing me away from my thoughts. "This is no cake walk. Spirit guides, unlike angels, do not possess any special powers. We answer to the angels, and they in turn answer to God."

"So you think we're not… capable?" I chose my words carefully, because I didn't want to hurt Nate's feelings. He'd already been hurt enough today.

Dr. Judy hung back in her leather chair and gave an exasperated sigh. "I didn't say that. In fact, I think you're more than capable, despite your young age. I was very impressed with how you progressed in Limbo, as was my boss. So I do think I could pull some strings with my rank and get you an assignment even though you are teenagers. But first, I want you to understand what you're signing up for. A spirit guide, unlike an angel, was once a human being, like me and like the pair of you, if you become guides. They lived their life, performed their tasks and died, then crossed over to the other side, but not into Heaven. We're part of the Underworld, a region that is beneath the surface of the world. It's where departed souls go who aren't allowed in Heaven. We're connected to the Heavens and the Earth, but we have four distinct regions down here."

Four? She'd only mentioned Limbo and Hell to us at our meeting earlier today. My creeped-out level raised a few notches. "So we're not in Hell, but we're not far from it?"

She held up her slender hands. "Relax. Yes, the Hell of the Damned is one of the regions, but you're not in danger of being sent there. Well, not right now anyway. Hell is in the deepest part of the Earth, existing solely as a state of torture. The chance for redemption there is lost. The other three parts of the Underworld are intermediate states. Right above Hell is Purgatory."

Nate peeked at me from the corner of his eye. "But you said we're not there either."

Dr. Judy shook her head, her wavy butterscotch hair slipping over her shoulders. I'd always admired her hair. Even though she wasn't an angel, she sure looked like one. My appearance was far from that description. With my long red crazy curls and fair skin, I looked like the vampire chicks that were all the rage these days.

"No, you're not," Dr. Judy answered in her sweet voice. "Purgatory is like a waiting room for Heaven. There are good souls in there, but they weren't Heaven-ready for various reasons, but they also didn't have any unfinished business. Neither do the souls from Juvie."

I put my elbows on my wobbly knees and dropped my head in my hands. "Say what?"

"Juvie is also for souls who aren't eligible for entry into Heaven yet, but not because of their choices, but rather for lack of choice. Unclean souls of teenagers are there."

Dr. Judy waited patiently as we tried to digest all this.

I felt like I was drowning. Is that where Conner was? He'd been my best friend since kindergarten; if he happened to get some God into his life during the twelve years I knew him, I would've known. We told each other everything and were hardly ever apart until high school when his girlfriends began to steal away his time from me. But to my knowledge, he was sort of an agnostic. He took a very scientific approach to the world. Whenever I told him God loved him and had a plan for his life he'd say, "Prove it." Likewise, when his band mate Kyle argued with me that there was no God; Conner would also respond with, "Prove it."

And if I was honest with myself, my motives for wanting this job weren't as pure as Nate's. I couldn't shake the feeling Conner needed my help.

"So Olga and I didn't go to Juvie either because we believed in God."

"Correct."

I exhaled with relief, glad Nate still had the presence of mind to ask more questions. To be honest, Nate and I hadn't talked much about God this past year. Not that I was surprised he believed in God, because we did talk a lot about having *faith* that things would work out in life. Plus, he'd attended church with his parents every week just like I went to Catholic mass with mine. In retrospect, I didn't have to question him at all about having a spiritual life because I just *knew* from the way he acted… unlike some people in my life. Like Tammy.

Tammy. I hoped becoming a spirit guide meant I could go visit my friends sometimes.

But first, I needed some more questions answered. "Okay, we're not in Juvie. But you did state at our meeting this morning that we've been in a state of Limbo for the past year. What does that mean, exactly?"

As I looked up, Dr. Judy fixed her gaze on me. "That's right. You're in the realm closest to Earth, called Limbo—a place of alternative timelines mimicking a person's experiences on Earth. This place is for souls who need to go through the after-death purification process, for those who accepted God into their lives and were sealed for the day of redemption, but then died while backsliding, or falling into sin, and therefore, they could not ask for God's forgiveness and receive His grace."

Her explanation made sense. I committed suicide, albeit not intentionally, and Nate decided to drag race when he was upset. We definitely didn't have that whole dying with grace thing down. Still, I wasn't happy about being tricked with the alternative timeline thing. It would've been nice to receive this information a year earlier, even if Dr. Judy claimed we were both too depressed to hear the truth back then.

"So," Dr. Judy continued. "Spirit guides like me help people in Limbo find their joy, peace, and grace again. Then they are free to move on to Heaven. There are very few cases in which people actually choose to stay here."

I exhaled. "But you stayed here, right?"

Dr. Judy's mouth dropped open, then closed, and we all sat silently for a few seconds. "More like sentenced. Limbo or Purgatory wasn't a choice for me, so the angels told me I could become a spirit guide to avoid Hell."

The hairs on my arms stood up. Hearing about this type of stuff in Sunday school class was one thing; it was another thing to find yourself living it, so to speak. "Do you mean you were told the *truth* from the start? That's not fair at all!"

"Life isn't fair, Olga. Build a bridge and get over it."

My posture stiffened at her sudden coldness.

"Sorry, I didn't mean to snap at you. It just gets monotonous explaining these things day in, day out. But I know you still have a lot of questions, so go ahead. I'll try to be patient."

I cleared my throat. "So, the souls in Limbo are the only ones eligible to enter Heaven now?" I asked, still trying to comprehend all of this. "Well, I mean, as soon as their purification process is done?"

Dr. Judy rubbed her tiny forehead. "Yes, and as spirit guides we continue to learn and spiritually advance while helping others learn the life lessons they never had a chance to learn while living. Since we were once human ourselves, we are well aware of the problems they're facing. We were concerned with similar matters not so long ago. "

She had that faraway look in her dark green eyes, and I wondered what she was remembering, if something haunted her like Conner's memory haunted me. The wrinkles around her mouth were set deeper than I remembered.

Nate grabbed my hand. I looked down and noticed his knuckles were white despite his tan. To know he was scared of something for once felt oddly comforting. "Once we receive our assignments, how will we know what to do?"

A smile stretched across Dr. Judy's face. "Prayer. It plays an important part in the life of a spiritual guide, for more than one reason. You should know that since we're in the Underworld, there are even more demons and temptations here than on Earth. You are closer to Hell and they want those lost souls for Satan just as much as we want them for God. You should perform a protection ritual every morning when you wake up to safeguard yourselves against undesirable encounters with them. If you're not choosing to move on to Heaven, there's always the chance of being damned to Hell *if* you are led astray. That's the most important thing you need to understand here tonight. If you take the oath of a spirit guide instead of going to Heaven, your soul will not be safe until Jesus returns. And no one knows when that will happen. It could be tomorrow or in five thousand years."

"So, this is our mission, should we choose to accept it? And this message will self-destruct in sixty seconds?" Nate sounded grim, but I also detected this weird hint of anticipation in his voice.

Dr. Judy tilted her head to the side, and I squeezed Nate's hand.

"Um, yeah, we don't have much time to decide this, right? I mean, you told us our time was up at midnight and we've already been here a half hour."

She glanced toward the wall clock. "I have my next appointment in fifteen minutes. So yes, you must decide quickly."

I rubbed my chin with my free hand. "Now, when you say appointment, I assume it's with someone in Limbo, since it's so late here on the real Earth. But that's the thing, how are you counseling my parents and stuff when they're not dead?"

She nodded curtly, like she expected my question. "Just as there are different levels of rank among the angels, even among the demons, spirit guides are part of a hierarchical system as well. Some are limited to this plane, which is the case for all newbies like you, but some can go back and forth. I operate on a higher vibrational frequency, so even though I'm not human when I'm on Earth, people sense my presence and perceive I am."

Again, I felt impressed by Dr. Judy. Nate twisted in his chair and lowered his head to mine like he did in the waiting room. "Now that we know what the stakes are, I won't blame you if you back out. You didn't kill anybody else. You should move on to Heaven."

My gaze darted to Dr. Judy, wanting her to back me up that Nate really didn't kill anybody, but she busied herself by flipping through a book on her desk.

"You so didn't kill that kid. The car crash was an accident."

Nate shook his head, and I knew there was no use trying to get through to him at the moment. I hesitated before saying aloud I still wanted to be a spirit guide, beginning to reconsider the wisdom of going straight to the pearly gates. Heaven would be so wonderful and probably make me forget all about Nate and Conner. But I didn't want to forget.

"I'm all in. Wherever you go, I go. Remember what Dr. Judy said earlier? Our souls are tied together."

He paused. "I'm flattered, but are you sure you have your priorities straight?"

"He's right, Olga," Dr. Judy butted in, her voice so calm it almost had the power to cure the hurricane-sized headache gnawing at my fried brain. "Yes, you were connected through your bond during Limbo, but you can choose to sever that bond at any time, much like a spouse can decide to get a divorce. There may be consequences, but your free will is still intact and your decisions are your own. Shouldn't you have some sense of self-preservation?"

I frowned at her, wondering what consequences she referred to, but then I decided I didn't care. Turning to Nate, I said firmly, "I love you. I'm not leaving you."

He leaned down and gave me a quick peck on the lips. I let out a silent breath of relief. I had started to worry he wanted to get rid of me. But this was the guy I did eighteen outrageous things with during the past year when I turned eighteen. Things like riding the biggest rollercoaster in the U.S., wedding crashing, firewalking, and hardest of all, going sailing again. Conner was struck and killed by a deadly combo of lightning and hypothermia the last time I was on a boat. He was the bravest person I'd ever known, and I was tired of being scared.

I met Nate's eyes and touched his face, my fingers lightly caressing his cheek.

"I love you," he whispered before turning his attention back to Dr. Judy. "We're ready to take that oath now."

Dr. Judy motioned for us to stand as she did the same. She held out a Bible and told us to put our right hand upon the surface and to repeat after her. I anxiously shifted from one foot to the other as she opened her mouth to speak, and we echoed the prayer.

"Heavenly Father, I surrender myself completely to you. I take a stand against all the workings of Satan. I put on the girdle of truth, the breastplate of righteousness, the sandals of peace, the helmet of salvation, the shield of faith and take in my hand the sword of the spirit. I put off my old human nature and put on the new nature of spirit and truth with courage. Blessed Holy Spirit, I pray you would fill me. I pray I would be a mighty spirit guide to pull down strongholds and cast down imaginations and every high thing that exalts itself against God. Help me to be aggressive enough to smash the plans of demons. Give me a spirit of love and a sound mind. I pray in the name of the Lord Jesus Christ with thanksgiving and humbleness. Amen."

Nate rolled his shoulders. "So, where do we go for our first assignment? I say, bring it on, Satan! I'm ready to kick some demon butt!" He yelled the words, not sounding very humble at all.

We turned our heads in unison as a loud crash sounded through the walls. A simple wooden cross hanging above Dr. Judy's bookshelf began slowly swinging back and forth like a pendulum. I gasped when the cross began to rotate in a slow circle, picking up speed until it spun on the wall like the arms of a possessed clock.

"Be gone, in Jesus' name!" Dr. Judy shouted. "Or I will call upon our guardian angels to torture you and drag you back to the pit of Hell from which you came!"

I did a double take, glancing back to the spinning cross on the wall, and searching for whatever Dr. Judy screamed at. Squelching the surge of terror rising up from my gut, I scanned the room, but found nothing.

Abruptly, the cross stilled, scraping the wall as it slowly slid back and forth, then eventually settled into its original position… as if I'd imagined the entire incident.

I turned to Nate, and he reached out and touched my shoulder hesitantly, his eyes wary as he asked Dr. Judy in a strained voice, "What the heck was that all about?"

She shook her head. "That is just one of the many demons I warned you about. Do not provoke them. They are more than ready to take on a newbie in a fight."

"But why couldn't we see anything?" I stared at the crucifix on the wall.

"Some can choose to make themselves invisible, so beware; you never know when you're being watched." The phone rang, and with a sigh, she stepped toward her desk to answer the call.

Nate wrapped his arms around my waist, holding me close. "You still want to become spirit guides after witnessing that little freak show?"

I didn't even hesitate this time. "Yup, you can call me crazy, but love makes you do crazy things."

He grinned, then leaned down for a kiss, but Dr. Judy's shriek made us both freeze.

"What do you mean she's dead?" she demanded into the phone, her face devoid of all color. "How did she die?"

I swallowed hard. Nate and I glanced wide-eyed from one another to Dr. Judy, wondering what was going on as she slumped into her leather chair and put her head on the desk, crying. No, not crying, bawling. Nate and I both moved to stand behind her, our hands embracing her shoulders, waiting. I could hear someone talking on the other line, but I couldn't make out the words.

Finally, Dr. Judy lifted her head and flashed me a devastated stare before mumbling into the phone. "No, Riel. I have two new recruits I want assigned to my daughter. You and Ash will be their case handlers… uh-huh… the teenagers… I know… I'll send them to headquarters now… thank you."

She hung up and just looked at the phone for a moment, like she was trying to will the call to not be true somehow. "My eighteen-year-old daughter is dead."

I crouched down and wrapped Dr. Judy in a hug. "I'm so sorry."

"How?" Nate asked.

My mouth dropped open slightly, shocked at his insensitivity.

He looked at me, then seemed to rediscover his common sense. "I'm sorry. I just meant that she's so young. Was it an accident like ours that'll mean she's coming to Limbo?"

Dr. Judy didn't look angry at his questions. She didn't look like anything but numb. "Yes, she'll be coming to Limbo. Grace will be your first assignment."

"Us?" I frowned in disbelief. "Are you sure we're qualified for this?" Becoming a spirit guide to your boss's daughter seemed like a pretty big first assignment, and I felt like there should be some job training involved first.

Dr. Judy stood up, walked to the other side of the room, and opened the door. The waiting room had disappeared. Now the entrance exposed a small pond, and an ancient building looking like Roman architecture stood across the way.

"Olga and Nate, I believe you've become spirit guides for such a time as this. You'll be my interns. I'm always here if you need my help, and I'll expect a daily report on your progress, but you must go now." She ushered us out of her office. "Oh, and please, don't make me regret trusting you with this." With those parting words, she slammed the door firmly behind us.

CHAPTER TWO

"Once we have eliminated the impossible,
whatever remains, however unlikely,
must be the truth."
—Conan Doyle

Shaking my head, I whispered, "I can't believe Dr. Judy's daughter is dead."

"Forget that. I still can't believe *we're* dead. I can't believe they're allowing us to become spirit guides and giving us her dead daughter as our first assignment!"

I didn't know what to say to that so I just held out my hand, and he took it, sliding his fingers between mine. In silence, we strolled around the pond toward a marble building with great white pillars that supported broad arches, heading toward our future. Ducks swam around a fountain positioned in the center of the water, which I found odd at first before realizing, why wouldn't God put animals in all parts of His creation?

I still can't believe I'm dead.

Learning I was no longer a mortal changed things big time, and made me question what I went through all my eighteen things for. But then I looked at Nate and found my answer. Now was not the time to backpedal. He had been my strong tower this past year, and now I needed to stay strong for him. After all, he'd not only learned he was dead too, but that he'd played a part in killing someone else. We had to fix our eyes on the path ahead of us if we were going to steer clear of eternal damnation.

When we rang the doorbell, a girl about my age answered. She stood a couple inches taller than me, and had a golden tan, straight blonde hair, and bright blue eyes. Immediately, I thought of Toe-touch Tammy. She'd remained my arch nemesis throughout high school, but during my after-death purification process, she became one of my best friends, even though I guess my Limbo wasn't real. Anyway, her looks were startlingly perfect, just like this chick. Already I started questioning if Nate would really want to stick with me forever when measured against beings like this one. I guess even death couldn't keep my insecurities away.

Ms. Perfect glanced at me, then Nate.

"Follow me." She sprung down the wildly long, vaulted-ceilinged hallway dotted with numbered closed doors, and we hurried to catch up before she abruptly stopped at the eighth door on the left. "Wait in here," she said before running off again.

A table with four metal chairs sat in the middle of the sterile room. Trembling, I took a seat.

"What is this place?" Nate rubbed his palms down the front of his jeans.

I tilted my head from side to side, noticing the gray carpet, the impossibly white walls, and the fluorescent lights that gave the impression we were in an interrogation room. My mind whirled with a thousand possibilities, but the sound of deep voices alerted me to the door.

A moment later, two angels walked—no, *flew*—in. Their arms and legs resembled polished gold, their faces like the lightning that killed my best friend. Radiating light bounced off their wings until they landed on the chairs and the wings folded into themselves, the brightness disappearing with them so I could actually see their more human faces. Both of them had the same long, surfer styled jet-black hair, no eyebrows, but their long dark lashes stood out as otherworldly over big blue eyes the color of the sky after a storm. Their lips, their noses, the shape of their faces, were straight, perfect, and angular. They were the most beautiful creatures I'd ever seen.

"Welcome, sons and daughters of faith," one said, nodding to us. Of course, his voice sounded like thunder. *Of course*! "I am Ash. I separate souls from their bodies at the time of death and carry their spirits to the place where they will live their afterlife."

"Wow," was all Nate said in return, and I met his gaze, unsure of what my own reaction should be.

The other angel chuckled and extended his hand, shaking first Nate's, then mine. Interestingly, his grip felt like a normal human handshake. Nate pressed his lips tight, seemingly disappointed.

"Are you guys, like, like the real superheroes?" Nate asked.

I fought the urge to roll my eyes.

"My name is Riel."

"Real? As in, for real?" Nate said.

Riel narrowed his dark eyes at Nate. "That's how it's pronounced, yes. But spelled R-i-e-l. Now where was I before I was so rudely interrupted?" He tilted his head to the ceiling and let out a sigh.

I couldn't stop my ogling. It was as if one of Leonardo's gorgeous paintings of angels had come to life. Yet, their looks possessed a magical realism too; humanlike, yes, but so beautiful one could've never possibly imagined what the angels looked like.

"I open the doors of perception to souls during their afterlife. The interceding prayers their loved ones send on their behalf help me determine the reality I should create, one that hopefully will inspire the lost souls to evolve. I was the one who determined your perceptions of reality during your after-death purification processes."

"Uh, thanks." I leaned closer to Nate, too afraid to grab his hand as I studied our new bosses. They were both dressed in loose blue slacks, almost like yoga pants, paired with long-sleeved white T-shirts… oddly casual attire for angels.

"You're welcome, Olga Gay Worontzoff. And no, Nathan Tyler Barca, we're not superheroes. It's true we are stronger than humans, but not omnipotent."

"But still, lifting-a-car strong?"

Riel ignored Nate and continued his explanation. "We're greater than man in knowledge, but not omniscient. We're more noble than mortals, but not omnipresent. We are entrusted by God to aid His children and we are holy, but we can still fall to the dark side, just like the humans."

Nate glanced at me and moved his hand over mine, resting it on my knee underneath the table. I already knew what he would say, but I tried to flash him a look that said *don't even.*

"So, not superheroes, but Star Wars fans, eh?"

Ash actually growled. "Contrary to what you may think due to Riel's bedside manner, this is not the time or place for jokes. There's a great unseen war raging beyond anything the pair of you can imagine. The war has been going on since the beginning of time, and you've just enlisted yourselves in it. There's no turning back now, so I suggest you pay close attention."

"Yes, sir," I said, anxious to please, but my response just sounded like I was mocking him. I cringed in my seat as I caught Riel staring at me. But he didn't look pissed off or anything. In fact, he flashed me a playful grin before continuing where Ash left off.

"Dr. Judy has put her trust in you, and I also think you are capable of becoming a master spirit guide; otherwise, I wouldn't have agreed to your placement in our program. You both did well with the tests I created for you in Limbo and your time there gave me the chance to know you well, even though you were unaware of my presence. In case Dr. Judy didn't have time to explain the purpose of souls being sent to Limbo, God wants His would-be chosen ones to live within Him more deeply than they desire to go on living falsely for themselves. Your duties as spirit guides will include helping departed souls realize their purpose. You followed your heart during your own Limbo process, and it will serve you well to keep doing so now. Your humanity will be your greatest strength."

I tried to focus on what he said, but all I could think in my head was *this isn't real* over and over again.

Ash shook his head in agreement. "Congratulations on all your success. Now, any questions before we go over the details of your first assignment?"

I thought about the difficulty of completing some of the tasks this past year, and tried not to panic. I hadn't known then that if I failed I'd go straight to Hell, and now I'd put my soul on the line again. I had worked so hard to get through the last fourteen months and just learned the whole experience was total bull crap. If I still didn't know how to deal with all that, how was I supposed to help someone else?

But maybe helping others was exactly what I needed to get past everything. Moving on with my "life" had been about me and getting to know myself. Mission accomplished. Becoming a spirit guide was about helping others. I mean, Conner had to be in the Underworld somewhere, and I could possibly find him! That was huge! I'd find out what happened to him, and helping Grace might prove the perfect opportunity to delve into my investigation of discovering where he was.

Ash flashed us a dark look. "You should know by now we live not just once, but every day of our lives, whether on Earth or during the afterlife. It shouldn't be a process for self-indulgence, but that's really what the past year has been about, has it not?"

My posture stiffened. *Oh my gosh! Can he, like, read my mind or something?*

"You need to learn that selflessness is the best thing you can do for yourself." Ash's expression soured, relaying subliminal messages to me, intentional or not. "It'll only come with the realization that everyone else is as special as you are. Taking care of others is the highest priority around here."

His words stung like a slap in the face, a wakeup call. The whole time I completed my list, I felt so proud the world had finally seen *me* for a change, well, the peeps from my hometown anyway. But the whole time I should've been seeing the world, the people in it. I mean, I guessed the eighteen tasks became much bigger than me, but none of that was real. Only the journey kinda was real because my actions were tied to my loved ones still living. Ah, this thought process proved so convoluted, even to me. I hadn't heard anything this confusing since I sat down in front of the television one night with Nate and his dad and tried to watch the final episode of *Lost.*

Ash cleared his throat, snapping me out of my thoughts. "We know you've *chosen* to become spirit guides, but heed this warning. On Earth, you hear the expression *'you're an angel'*, all the time. But it's overused. There's a lot more to being an angel or spirit guide than a bell rings and someone gets their wings. You're lucky because you'll get to work together instead of alone. You are bound in spirit now. One's success will be the other's success. It also means that if you fail, you'll cause the other to fail as well."

Until today, I'd never thought about being tied to someone spiritually before. Was I really mature enough for all this heavy? I sure hoped Dr. Judy meant it when she said we could come to her for help. Taking me on as an intern may turn out to be more than she bargained for because I *loved* to ask questions. And even though I'd wanted nothing but more freedom this past year, I didn't think the likes of Nate and me should be solely in charge of someone else's destiny. I let out a big sigh. Geez, this proved much more complicated than the "pass-pass" or "fail-fail" system for group projects at school.

Nate flashed his teacher's pet smile, seemingly unfazed by all this. "Maybe you could tell us a little bit about what you're looking for us to do with Grace?"

Okay, maybe he worried, too, but he hid his anxiety better than me for sure. My gaze met his, instantly calming me.

Riel cleared his throat. "I'll make this simple, so you'll understand, Lover Boy."

He snapped his fingers and the fluorescents went out. A panel in the wall slid open and images of a ragged, teenish looking girl played on a large wall-mounted flat-screen monitor. I mean, she looked beautiful, but a hot mess. She wore a Motley Crew T-shirt and barely there shorts, smoking something out of a pipe.

"This is Grace Newton," Ash announced. "She was killed tonight by a police car, of all things. She just walked out of her house, onto the street that met the end of her driveway, and laid down. The cop never saw her, killing her instantly. We've been watching her for a while; scared she might do something like this based on the reports her guardian angel sent us."

"Why did she do it?" My voice came out barely a whisper.

Ash advanced through the next few slides of Grace's downfall. The last one landed on what must've been her bedroom, looking like a hurricane went through it, photographs scattered on the floor like tree debris. My eyes focused on a picture of Dr. Judy.

"I think you've just seen the answer to your question," Ash said, fanning a hand toward the very photo I studied.

"Because she never healed from losing her mother, and…" My voice squealed, my thoughts too horrible to finish.

"Yes," Riel concluded for me. "As you can imagine, there was a multi-dimensional frenzy to retrieve her soul. But we got it."

Ash handed Nate and me a backpack.

"School supplies?" Nate asked, shaking the bag, his eyes wide.

"Good thing we didn't pack it with explosives. You might've just been blown to bits. What a pity that would've been." Riel smiled at me, a playful grin. "And, not exactly. You don't need to worry about graduating. You need to worry about warfare. You'll find binoculars, a Bible, a crucifix necklace to wear that's been anointed with oil, Grace's case file, the roles you're playing in this after-death purification process, a copy of your Spirit Guide Insurance Policy, your daily meditation guide, cell phones, a tranq gun, an Angel Phonebook with who to call for specific problems, your Limbo passports in case someone needs to see your ID, Spirit Guide For Dummies 101, etc.—"

"Hey!" Nate snapped.

Since he looked furious, I had to cover my amusement with a question. "They make a Spirit Guide for Dummies book?"

"He's just joking on that part," Ash said.

"Not really."

I detected a teasing note to Riel's voice, but I wasn't positive, and frankly, I didn't have the presence of mind to try and figure him out right now. Even though all the stuff the angels were showing us was cool and all, it was hard to wrap my brain around. Plus, a big part of me had felt lost since learning the truth, like I'd never recover my childlike sense of wonder and my ability to find joy in the things I experienced each day. I knew I should be thanking God for giving me a healing light for my darkened spirit, but the last twenty-four hours had been rough, and I kinda dreaded the work ahead of me. Sighing, I pinched the bridge of my nose, wondering how I was going to figure out when to use all these new tools. Back on Earth, it took me forever to learn how to use my Smartphone. The only reason I figured out anything was because Conner showed me.

Ash unzipped the front pocket of my backpack, revealing a pencil pouch. He opened the nylon bag, pulled out a glue stick, and popped the cap, exposing a toggle switch. "Now that you're spirit guides, we won't be following you like we did during your Limbo tests. We'll be working on other cases. You can still report to headquarters each night to sleep if you wish, and we're around then as well, should any problems arise. However, if during the day there's an emergency and you need immediate help, hit this switch."

"I thought the Angel directory tells us who we should call if we need help."

Ash nodded. "It does, but think of the directory as like calling the police station for a non-emergency. This switch is like Angel 9-1-1."

"Okay, so that's pretty cool," I said to Nate.

Riel blushed.

I didn't know angels blushed, but the pink stood out beautifully on his pale, polished skin.

"Thanks. I invented it," he explained.

"Yeah, it's all cool and everything, but it's summer. We won't be in school." Nate tilted his head back slightly and lifted one eyebrow. "How do we approach our assignment?"

"Actually, you will be in school." Riel turned sharply away from Nate and focused on me only. "Grace was a senior, but failing her classes. If still alive, she'd attend summer school in order to graduate, so that's what she'll do in her alternative timeline."

Nate sighed. "Aw, man. I thought I was done with school. I hoped we could at least enjoy the summer in someone's Limbo."

Riel glowered at Nate before flashing a lascivious smile. "Would you like me to arrange another place for you to go?" He snapped his fingers and the room dissolved.

Falling, falling, falling, like I rode in an express elevator.

The light faded into nothingness until it was just a pinpoint above me, and then there were stars winking in the sky.

Rain pelted my skin, leaving me nowhere to hide. I was on a sailboat.

So cold, so alone.

Conner's dead body was draped across the hull, the number thirteen on the sail flapped in the violent winds.

"Conner!" I screamed, my echo the only sound answering my cry for help.

The full moon loomed like a ghost in the darkness, illuminating the fact there was nothing else around for miles. Just the open sea and me.

My head fell upon Conner's chest. A rapid erratic heartbeat. I didn't know if it was his or mine, all I knew was the sound of fear. I cried for him, like I'd done a million times before. I could cry another Lake Michigan with my tears.

"Conner," I screamed again, louder, sharper.

A yoke of guilt bowed my shoulders and sent my gaze to his pale face. I touched his cheek, fearing he wasn't real and was real at the same time. A familiar feeling swelled in my chest: frustration. The air filled with the ravings of the unfairness of our wasted lives, cut too short. The sky darkened with each breath I took. As the arms of despair wrapped around me, my eyes grew used to the dim light of my own personal hell. There was no escape hatch, no rewind button. Once again, I was stuck.

Then up, up, up, almost like Peter Pan leaving the Jolly Roger.

My hands flew to my chest, and I blinked the water from my eyes rapidly. I gasped for air, trying to recover. Headquarters felt like such a warm, wonderful place, sunlight pouring through the rectangular windows high on the walls. This didn't comfort me though. I felt nervous for reasons I didn't understand.

"What the heck?" Nate sputtered.

"More like Hell." Riel didn't bother to mask his irritation, and I ventured to guess that was normal for him.

I swallowed hard as I glanced from Nate to Riel to Ash.

Ash looked back at me with a smile that wavered.

"I thought flames licking your skin until you're nothing was Hell." I turned my gaze back to Nate. "Were there flames in your Hell?"

Nate opened and closed his mouth and shook his head. "No. Much worse."

"Let's review lesson number one." Riel glared at us.

I didn't think I liked the thought of Riel teaching us any lessons, but I doubted I had a say in the matter.

"I open the perceptions to reality in Hell, just as I do in Limbo."

"Sounds like a lot of responsibility for one person," Nate said, grabbing hold of my hand.

Riel gave a slight nod of his head. "For a *person*, it would be impossible. But yes, for me, it's still a lot of responsibility. You two would do well to remember who you are dealing with." A smirk slid up one side of his perfect face.

"So where you just took us, that's our own brand of Hell, if we were sent there?" Unable to look Riel in the eye, I studied my shoes. I only asked out of curious habit because honestly, I already knew the answer, even if I didn't want to.

"Ding, ding, ding. And it's all yours should you fail to accept this mission, so your boyfriend better think about that next time he wants to so eloquently state his objections to an assignment I give you."

Nate dropped my hand and put his arm around my shoulder. "Are you gonna ramble all day, or tell us about the roles we're playing?"

I looked at Nate for a long beat, admiring his bravery, albeit *stupid* bravery. I just loved him so much; how could anyone not?

"All the details are in the backpack, Mr. Barca," Ash told him. "As always, this mission is not to be taken lightly. Your souls and the souls you're trying to save are all at risk. But this one is even more serious. Dr. Judy handpicked the pair of you for her daughter. Be careful out there. The enemy wants Grace's soul even more than most since she's the daughter of our head spirit guide."

My mind flashed to my own Limbo, and my heart sunk. How could I reconcile keeping such a big secret from Grace? Nate and I were both so upset over the ruse. Taking a deep cleansing breath, I told myself there'd be time for panic attacks later. Losing my cool in front of our bosses, especially Riel, wouldn't be the best idea, and I had a major shortage of those already.

Riel popped his wings out, ready to leave, and I found looking at him difficult again. "Your assignment begins next Monday when the summer session starts. Grace will be recovering in the faux hospital for the next few days anyway. Take the time to study all the information I've given you and formulate a plan of action. You'll also have training sessions Monday through Friday of this week from eight to five. Ruth, the girl who let you into headquarters today, will lead you through those classes as sort of an initiation process. Good luck."

Riel gave me a hard look. His sharp features startled me with their beauty, even in all his fury. I returned his stare, hiding a thousand insecure feelings behind one wide smile.

CHAPTER THREE

"I want a do-over."

Dr. Judy crossed her arms over her chest. "There are no do-overs in life once you're dead. All your friends have that YOLO saying backward. It should be YODO because really, you live every day, but… You Only Die Once."

I looked at Nate. A grim expression twisted his mouth and I wondered if he was thinking what I thought. Where's the candid camera? Because this had to be a joke.

Dr. Judy wrung her hands. "So, sorry, but no do-overs. And there are no shortcuts in the after-death purification process. There are things each person must accomplish here before they can move on, and you have. Congratulations."

I watched Nate's gaze travel around the room, to the couch against the wall, to the shelves filled with books and puzzles, finally to the chairs we sat in. "But why not just tell us from the start this was all fake? I mean, no one likes to feel duped, you know? Why not just tell us the situation we were in from the first time we met here?"

Dr. Judy smiled at Nate, and Nate stared at her.

"Those are the rules of this realm. I don't make them, but I play by them. My guess is many wouldn't care about their success if they knew they were dead. Just like you two at the start of this process. Many wouldn't care about their soul at first and the risk of truly dying as a consequence of not completing their mission. Think back to the beginning—you were both very depressed spirits."

"Hey? You listening?" Nate's nudging elbow penetrated my flashback.

"I don't buy into their philosophy," I muttered, the memory of Dr. Judy telling us about Limbo dissolving as I found myself back in my spirit guide seminar, my purple pen still poised over my journal to take notes.

"What do you mean?" he whispered, glancing at our instructor, Ruth, who was typing something on her computer in the far corner of the room.

I jerked my head toward the television screen, to the training video we were supposed to be watching: "Telling Your Assignment About Limbo: How To Break The News."

Today was Memorial Day. I should've been relaxing at Grand Haven Beach with my friends. Instead, I was remembering the most pivotal day of my 'life.' The day when Dr. Judy finally revealed we were dead. I replayed the events over and over in my mind like a broken record, her words a sad song in my head. We were healed. We could move on to Heaven. I'd finally let Conner go. Only now, sitting here in this room, I felt like I'd gone from healed to freaking out faster than I could even say Limbo.

At first, when Nate and I learned the truth and met Ash and Riel and got our cool new book bags, everything seemed almost fun. But not now. Not after forty-eight hours of trying to process the indescribable truth that we were dead. Indescribable—what an apt word. There truly weren't any words in the English language that I could use to describe the wonder and awe of everything that'd happened to me. No matter how great of a writer I was, there were just no words.

Mostly, I thought of Conner today. I thought my eighteen things taught me how to detach and let him go, but now I felt this need to find him in the Underworld. A need so strong I could barely stay in my seat. In many different ways, I felt like I was in worse shape now than I was after my 'suicide.' I cringed, just thinking of the stupid word. Being in that place where I could look at myself with love and forgiveness wasn't possible anymore. How could I ever face myself in the mirror again, knowing the wreckage I left behind on Earth?

Truthfully, the suffering I experienced from the news of my death felt so deep, I didn't think I'd ever heal from these fresh wounds. All of the life lessons my eighteen things list taught me seemed totally pointless.

My gaze wandered to the clock on the wall; only a half hour left and our first day of training would be over.

Sighing, I tried to focus on the words coming from the screen, instructing me on my responsibility to tell my assignment the truth about what happened to them once they were healed. I squeezed Nate's hand beside me, glad I didn't have to do this alone. I doubted if I could go through with our plan. Maybe he had what it took to be a spirit guide, but not me. But I also didn't see any way out of this.

Nate slipped an arm around me and smiled. Smiling back, I reminded myself to maintain my composure despite dealing with my own emotions. There were a lot of people depending on me now—Nate, Dr. Judy, Grace, Riel and Ash, and maybe even Conner.

The video instructed us to deliver the news to our assignment as straightforwardly and succinctly as possible when the time came—no technical mumbo jumbo. We had to be prepared for their reaction. There could be screaming, yelling, and crying. They might throw themselves on the floor. They might try to flee the area in denial. They might physically grab us and demand to know how this was all happening.

Wondering why I hadn't thought to do all those things when Dr. Judy delivered the news, I realized none of it mattered. Very quickly, I was realizing there were no words of comfort that could make them feel better, that nothing I would say could really help. Sure, I could apologize and answer all their questions. But even with the experience of being in their shoes at one time, I felt a sense of helplessness, knowing no matter how much training I received, it'd never be enough to deal with these things, over and over again for all of eternity.

In life, you learned from experiences. What did we learn from death? I thought back to the life list Dr. Judy had me write this past year. Turning the page in my journal, I made a T-chart. On one side I wrote "List" and the other I labeled "Lesson." I tried to narrow down what each 'thing' taught me. Fire walking/Becoming fearless. Trying out for the cheerleading squad/Taking chances. Getting a record deal for the Cantankerous Monkey Squad/Following dreams. Doing whatever the Magic 8 Ball said for a day/Having adventures. Start telling people what I really think/Being true to myself. Starting a blog/Finding my passion. Letting go of guilt/forgiving myself.

Tearing out the page, I balled it up and shot the paper into the trash. Unfortunately, the past year was a lie, total crap. The truth was we don't control anything, so why even try?

The video droned on, listing bullet points from today's session. Reminding us that every 'assignment' was different, that things may happen very quickly and we may need to make decisions very fast, or they could move at a snail's pace, but the important thing was to establish a rapport with the assignment right away. They don't know us from a hole in the wall; they don't know their soul is at stake. *Yeah, and to make matters worse, we have to tell them everything will be okay, only to tell them a year later that they're dead and their loved ones are grieving! But hey, all of that is okay, because* you *get to move on.*

I felt like puking. I needed time and space to process my feelings. I wanted to go back to that moment two days ago so I could run up and down the hallways, just to let out all my frustrations. But now I had to respect Nate's needs and be a model student, because those were the only two things left that I knew how to do. Even doing that would be hard, but if I shut off my heart; if I went back to autopilot and stuck to the script in this video when working with Grace, then maybe I would be all right, given a little time. *Fake it till I make it.*

But how could I ignore that feeling of guilt that was back in the pit of my stomach, weighing me down? How could I forget about Conner, knowing I could possibly get to him now, knowing there was a chance I could locate him in the Underworld? How could I help Grace when I didn't even know what *my* next step should be? The training video hadn't covered these things. I was just supposed to be strong, stoic, and move on.

And I was so sick of hearing those words: move on. I remembered the encouragement whispered by my friends: It's not your fault you waited too long to administer CPR to Conner. You did everything you could to save him.

Yeah, I went through the stages of grief and moved on.

But how could I have been healed from something I never knew happened? After all this time to find out I'd killed myself, discovering what I'd put my parents through, my friends. How could I ever help Grace or any assignment 'move on' toward the light of a happy tomorrow and reconcile the truth of my past at the same time?

The lights came on, the video now over. Sitting straighter, I rubbed my eyes, trying to shake off the anger stirred up by my feelings. Yep, it was Memorial Day, all right, but I didn't want these memories. I wanted the ones where I could practically smell the suntan oil and feel the soft sand beneath my feet, as if remembering hard enough might magically transport me to the beach with my friends.

"Well, that concludes day one of training. Any questions?" Ruth asked, her voice sounding wearier than this morning.

She already knows I'm going to suck at this.

Ruth's standard-issue training guide uniform made her look like a yoga instructor, and her calm demeanor matched the style. Since the pants and long sleeved shirt were both white, her in-your-face beauty stood out even more. Listening to someone that perfect-looking made my mind wander to my fake friendship with Tammy. At the thought, I teared up.

Nate's big, soulful eyes locked on mine, giving me his puppy dog stare while frowning. Finally, he turned toward Ruth to answer. "I think we have plenty of questions, but we need some time to process."

She nodded. "No problem. I'll see you here at the same time tomorrow. Feel free to come with any questions or concerns then."

Nate and I thanked her, gathered our book bags, then shuffled out of the room together.

"You okay?" he asked as we made our way into the hall toward our living quarters.

Without meaning to, I let out a slight snort.

Nate raised his eyebrows, his pecan-shaped eyes holding all the colors of an ocean, the place I'd most like to be right now.

I wondered if he knew me at all if he even had to ask that question. Opening my mouth to say so, I quickly bit my tongue. I really didn't want to have this conversation right now. But if I said I was okay, then it'd be the first lie I ever told Nate in our dating relationship. And I hated to deceive him, but if there's anything my after-life had taught me, it was that some truths were left unsaid.

"I'm okay."

"Here you are." Ruth handed me a cup of coffee that smelled like caramel and cinnamon.

I gripped the mug with both hands, the warmth spreading through my body despite the terror plaguing my every thought. "Thanks." After taking a few sips, I asked, "How long does it usually take *people* to adjust to their life as a spirit guide?"

She shrugged. "Depends. Although I mostly deal with training angels, some people I've trained only took a few days, others took a few years."

"What do you think the difference is?"

Patting my shoulder, she said, "Confidence. You have to believe you can do this. Now, are you ready?"

I spent the day learning the basics of hypnosis, how the process worked. Now Ruth was going to put me under as part of my training. Nate would experience the same training session but without me in the room, since hypnosis was a very personal matter.

"Pay attention to the tone of my voice and language so you can integrate my techniques into your own hypnosis," she reminded me. "I'll start with the most basic induction and then move to a more progressive approach. By the end of today, you'll have the ability to relax yourself and others deeply in minutes, no matter the emotional state."

Over the next hour, Ruth tried to put me under hypnosis, but the process didn't take. "Is there something wrong with me?"

She smoothed a hand over her hair. "We're all broken, Olga. Some people just have a harder time relaxing than others. With your photographic memory, I'm sure you know the hypnosis script by heart now. But the most important thing to know before I release you today is not necessarily if you can hypnotize someone. It's can you stay calm in crisis?"

After Ruth muttered some words, a demon materialized in the room.

I stepped back, staring in horror. "What are you doing?" I screamed, eyeing the dark creature before me, his red eyes sparkling with amusement. He stood at least a foot taller than me and wore a black robe. His face was a skeleton, whiter than Riel's skin, nothing remotely human in his glowing scarlet eyes at all.

"Training you. Remember, look up."

Taking Ruth's advice literally, I pinned my gaze on the ceiling but saw nothing.

The demon took advantage of my momentary distraction by lurching forward and grabbing a hold of my crucifix, choking me with his thin, skeletal hands. I closed my eyes for a heartbeat or two, praying for Ruth to fight this battle for me. When she didn't, I realized her advice to look up wasn't meant to be taken literally. I narrowed my eyes at the demon and stretched a hand in front of me. "Satan's angel, I command you, in the name of the Lord, to leave my presence, and I bring the blood of Jesus Christ between us."

The demon didn't listen. Instead, he tightened his grip, paralyzing me. My eyes pleaded with Ruth, letting her know I was in trouble, the only thing I was capable of. I couldn't even open my mouth to speak. My lips felt like somebody had glued them shut. Then, I forced myself to breathe in and out through my nose like Ruth instructed during hypnotherapy, and pictured the fear wearing away at my face disappear.

Closing my eyes so I couldn't see the demon again, I prayed silently, asking God to give me the strength and faith to pass this test. I wasn't sure what would happen if I didn't, but I knew I would trade in several years of staying in a cold room of steel and concrete over having to redo this particular exercise. I opened my eyes and focused, finding my words enough to shout the same prayer as before. This time a strange feeling swelled in my chest, and I knew I really meant the words. My crucifix went slack, and the demon popped out of the room, like it was never there in the first place.

Ruth pulled me toward her in a hug. "Well done, Olga, well done. In fact, you defeated that demon in record time. Looks like I won't have to give you detention for your lack of faith after all."

"Day three of our training session will commence outside," Ruth announced. "Follow me, please."

"This should be interesting," Nate whispered to me on our way out.

A knot formed in my stomach. "Not sure if interesting is the right word, but I guess anything will be better than yesterday."

We ended up at a grassy knoll behind the headquarters building, where Riel waited in a tree for us. He popped his wings, then flew to the ground with the grace of, well, an angel. He stood across from me, dimming his brightness so I could actually look at him. "So, I heard you fought a demon and won. Do you think you'll have the same results with an angel?"

"Um, excuse me?"

He grinned at me. "I'm here today to aid Ruth in instructing the pair of you in hand-to-hand combat."

"I thought our fights would be more of the spiritual nature than physical?" Nate questioned.

Riel nodded. "They are, but that doesn't mean you won't get into a few scuffles along the way. Even though you don't feel pain in Limbo, there's no guarantee you won't find yourself in another dimension. The first thing you need to know is to keep your hands by your faces to protect yourself at all times. It will save you the hassle of being knocked unconscious."

When I didn't do anything, Riel reached for my hands and positioned them in front of my face. His touch was warm and made my heart beat faster for some reason.

Nate copied my movements, then faced me.

"Oh, am I fighting you?"

He answered me by hooking a foot around one of my legs and yanking me forward, knocking me to the ground while he cushioned the fall underneath me. We both vibrated with laughter.

Riel lifted me to my feet. "Obviously, Nate can't be trusted to play fairly. Change of plans. I'll fight you, and Ruth will take Nate."

Nate sat up, flicking pieces of grass off his pants. When he stood, the movement was stiff, and his mouth held a scowl.

But Riel didn't notice because his gaze remained locked with mine as he circled around me.

Beads of sweat dotted my forehead. "So, you think *this* is playing fairly? You're an angel!"

"The fallen angels you'll be up against will hardly care if it's a fair fight."

I shook my head. "What's a girl to do, then?"

He grinned. "Try to outsmart your opponent."

Going for the element of surprise, I swung my arm, aiming for his face.

Ducking easily, he laughed. "That's the best you could come up with?"

I glanced at Nate, but it didn't look like he would be giving me any pointers on fighting later. Ruth already knocked him to the ground. At least Riel showed me a little mercy by giving me a chance.

Lurching forward, I tried the run-like-a-bull approach, but Riel easily popped out his wings and flew behind me.

"Cheater."

"Human."

An idea formed. I decided to ignore his rule about guarding my face for a moment to loop my hair into a ponytail. Afterward, I pretended to throw something over Riel's shoulder. Just like a stupid puppy, he fell for the oldest trick in the book. As soon as he turned his back, I pounced on him, figuring if he went anywhere this time, at least he wasn't getting away from me.

Punching an angel just seemed too wrong, so I settled for digging my claws into his arms as hard as I could. Riel yelped before beating his wings twice, completely knocking me off. Before I could even hit the ground, he caught me in his arms.

"Much better."

I was too breathless to reply.

Ash suddenly appeared beside us, startling a scream out of me. "Sorry to frighten you, Olga. Riel, the throne has requested our presence at once."

Very gingerly, Riel set me down and whispered, "Too bad. This was just starting to get fun. We'll pick this up another time."

Faster than I could think Awesome Angel Abilities, Riel and Ash were gone.

Nate rubbed a hand over his face. "I hope that means we get a free pass for the day."

Ruth's eyes glinted. "Not totally. I want you to use this *free* time to start studying for your written exam tomorrow. The test will consist of two hundred multiple choice questions, as well as two essays. You'll both need a ninety percent to pass."

She headed toward the back door of headquarters, but Nate called after her. "What are we studying, exactly?"

"I would've thought it obvious. Your Spirit Guide Handbook. You received a copy from Ash the day you signed up. Or as Riel lovingly refers to it, Spirit Guide for Dummies 101."

Ruth departed without another word, leaving behind a hazy cloud of vague instructions.

Nate looked over at me and grinned. "You want to study in my room?"

I undid the ponytail I created in haste earlier. "Unfortunately, I think that's a bad idea if we plan on studying."

A few minutes later, we sat on a bench by the pond, our instruction manuals spread across our laps. "The Spirit Guide Handbook is your key to understanding the mysterious Underworld. Questions will invariably rise on your journey to aiding lost souls to find healing, and this book will help you unlock spiritual treasures, revealing greater insight into God's holy plan for His children."

Nate groaned after I finished reading the introduction. "I'm confused already. What's with all the big words?"

Ignoring him, I kept on reading. "Today, you learned the truth. You now know more about the world God created than ever before. Yet, there is still much to learn. The ins and outs of being a spirit guide is a subject of enormous scope and depth, covering a full range of history and reaching the most mundane aspects of people's lives to their most sublime thoughts and aspirations. We will describe in clear terms the…"

The words meshed together, hurting even my brain, although I normally loved to study. By the end of our study session, we'd read twenty-five chapters ranging from "Developing A Religious Need In Your Assignment For A Positive Transformation" to "Manipulating Situations in Time and Space For Spiritual Satisfaction." We had to pull an all-nighter, and even though I now had an interesting compilation of answers to hundreds of questions I'd been dying to know about religious concepts and beliefs, I somehow felt less prepared. The amazing spiritual and historical context of our handbook only demonstrated to me even more how wide the universe is.

"Congratulations, you got a hundred," Ruth finally said to me, handing back my test. She'd taken painstakingly long to grade my answers. She moved to stand in front of Nate. "I know you stayed up all night to study, Nate, and your hard work paid off."

"It's not a ninety percent though," Nate said, looking down at his eighty-nine-point-five percent.

"We like to round up here at the Spirit Guide Training Academy. Showing grace is what we're all about." Ruth looked like she struggled to hold back a smile. "After lunch, the rest of our day will be filled with some more educational videos and going over any questions you might've had while studying."

I nodded. "All right. What about tomorrow? It's our last day with you, right?"

"Yes." Her phone beeped, and she slid the device out of her pocket. "Ah, here's a text from Riel now. He said he'll have a special test for both of you tomorrow, a final *final* exam of sorts that will involve you taking part in a simulation he created."

I'd dreaded the last day of spirit guide boot camp for many reasons, but especially now. Videos and reading were two pastimes in the middle of my comfort zone, but I was certain 'simulation' wouldn't fall under that category.

Chapter Four

Sorry I'm late. The Throne called me for an emergency," Riel told us at eight-thirty. We'd been waiting for him a half hour.

"No worries," Nate said. "We're very flexible, as long as it doesn't cut into our lunch break."

Riel ignored him and continued. "The scenarios you're training in today aren't real. They will be figments of your imagination created by me. I fashioned them out of your experiences, much like your after-death purification process. When you've passed both of the tests together, then you'll be card carrying members of the spirit guide club."

All it took was one snap of Riel's fingers, and Nate and I were in a NASCAR race, with Nate in the driver's seat! The green flag already waved high in the air, and Nate stepped on the gas faster than I could've ever imagined. It felt like we were flying. For the first lap, I couldn't stop screaming.

Once I calmed down enough to gather my thoughts, I realized Nate's test was perfect because he hadn't driven since he died in his accident over a year ago.

Then I heard Riel's muffled voice coming over the headphones in our helmets, giving directions to Nate to fly high, then stay low, then to catch up with the number eighteen car because he'd made a deal with that driver to help us if we could keep up. Nate flew around the corner, the turn hugging us. After surviving the steep incline of the track, I laughed out loud when I realized the driver of number eighteen was Ash.

I slid up the visor portion of my helmet and waved to him through the mesh covered window, black specs from tire rubber flying through the little holes. Screwing up my nose, I caught a whiff of octane. The smell wasn't like gasoline, making me gag. This fuel held the scent of raw power and made my eyes burn, flooding them with tears. I immediately slid my visor back down.

During the next two-and-a-half hours, the forty-three cars on the track rumbled with uncontrolled rage, thunderous applause vibrating in my ears. The drivers often ran in one to three packs, sometimes only inches apart, while traveling over 200 miles per hour. Nate and I didn't chat. He conçentrated on driving the ride from hell, and I prayed harder than I ever had before, my chest heaving with adrenaline. Somehow, I felt horrified and exhilarated at the same time.

Just as I feared, "The Big One" came at the end, and we were one of the five cars involved in the crash. All I saw was a blur. Another car rounding turn one lost control and hit us. Suddenly, we fishtailed wildly. Everything seemed to happen in slow motion as our car went completely sideways. We ripped through a thick cloud of smoke before skittering into a wall. Then the car went airborne a good fifteen feet above the track. Gravity did its job when the vehicle came down, end over end in an endless barrel roll. The car crashed against a guard rail, spewing flames and smoke with exploding pieces of machinery littering the track. The atmosphere remained eerily quiet for a moment, like a graveyard. The only sound came from wind flapping the race flags around the track, then the scream lodged tight in my throat finally let loose.

"Nate!"

The smell of burnt rubber made me choke. I couldn't imagine anything being left of the vehicle, and as the smoke cleared, it revealed little more than a rolling cage with four flat tires.

Nate and I slipped off our helmets. He looked up and muttered a few choice words to the man upstairs, but to my surprise, not the using-Your-name-in-vain kind. Instead, Nate thanked God.

I gave him a few seconds as I surveyed the crash, the paramedics nowhere in sight. I squelched my panic though since I knew this was all part of the scenarios that Riel set up. *I think*.

"Are you all right?" I yelled, my ears still ringing from the sounds of the crash.

He held up his gloved finger. "Just give me a minute to catch my breath."

I undid my safety harness and crawled out of what was left of the car. Nate followed suit.

Holding onto him, I didn't loosen my grip as I said, "For the first time ever, I'm glad we're dead." My voice sounded thick as I held back sobs.

Nate smiled, actually more of a grimace, like he was in pain. It'd have to be the emotional type though since our bodies couldn't hurt in this realm. He leaned against the barrier, still intact, and sighed heavily. "Why do you say that?"

"Because if we were alive, we would've just died, and I haven't had nearly enough time with you. At least now, no matter what happens, we'll always have each other."

He frowned. "I'm not sure about that. Do you really think I passed that test?"

"Well, Ruth told us yesterday that our tests would be about the fear of being out of control. But you can't control something that's out of control."

Now he smirked. "You mean like fate? Destiny?"

"Exactly. Nobody knows what's going to happen—not in a car on the way home from school, not on a sailing trip, not during a thunderstorm, not when you swallow an entire bottle of pills, not when you turn down Heaven to become spirit guides."

Nate's face looked like he had just walked out from underneath a dark cloud into the sun. "So control is an illusion. The only one who knows those things is God, and He's the only one who can control anything, so I need to hand over my control to Him."

I grabbed him by the front of his safety suit and gave him a lingering kiss. "You got it! But like Victor Hugo said, we also have to have courage for the great sorrows of life and patience for the small ones. We can't always be waiting for the other shoe to drop, thinking the worst. Can I ask you something?"

He wiped the sweat off his forehead and seemed to hesitate as his eyes searched my face, but then he nodded.

"Why did you really want to become a spirit guide?"

He raised his bushy eyebrows. "I wanted to still feel needed."

"What about what you need?" Even to me, my voice sounded slightly irritated.

"Olga, you're all I need. Don't you know that?"

He pinned me against the barrier, kissing me forcefully. We both slid down to the track while he let out a half-hum, half-moan. His mouth on mine was like the first sip of coffee in the morning, awakening every part of me. Our kiss slowed, taking our time as if we were only on a pit stop from a relaxing Sunday drive.

Then, suddenly, the ground we were on was no longer made of asphalt, but sand. Nate lifted himself from my body. I scrambled to my feet and brushed myself off, noticing as I did that we weren't in our driver suits anymore. I wiped my hands on my jean shorts and T-shirt and studied the water and sky, a breath catching in my throat.

"Looks like we've arrived at your simulation safe and sound," Nate said, a grin on his face. "Welcome home."

"Mhmm. Let's head to the pier. I have a feeling that's where we need to be."

As we strolled down the beach, I enjoyed the picturesque setting while residents and tourists swam, sunbathed, and ate leisurely picnics, ignoring the approaching storm. I thought of how anyone would be hard pressed to find a safer suburbia than our town of Grand Haven. Yet at this moment, the rasping breaths in my chest had me feeling like an asthma attack was inescapable, even though I knew my respiratory condition died when I did.

Light rain began to fall on us, and lightning flashed in the distance. This was most likely the source of my terror—a sixth sense for the coming storm. The lightning strike that caused me to lose Conner made me step outside of myself during the past year. Experiencing a trauma like that ultimately helped me better understand my place in the universe. The accident made me feel smaller than ever, but also freer, more capable of change, more capable of creating my own destiny rather than the one my parents had laid out for me. Before Conner's death, I didn't think I believed in fate, but as Nate squeezed my hand, I knew I did now.

"Are you scared?"

I shook my head. "To death."

He laughed. "Where do you want to take refuge until the storm passes?"

I lifted my eyes to the sky, stars now twinkling in-between the rain clouds, a round moon illuminating the lighthouse at the end of the pier, where some kids—well, more like people my age—jumped into the water.

Squeezing my eyes shut, I knew the next part was going to be a whole lot of no fun. "I don't think I'm meant to look for shelter right now."

My heart beat so fast I couldn't feel anything else. When I opened my eyes, every thought I had focused on those stupid, stupid people as I dropped Nate's hand and instinctively ran toward the spot where they jumped. Jumping off Grand Haven Pier into Lake Michigan wasn't like jumping off a diving board into a pool. Only the best of swimmers should even attempt the stunt, but the act was still prohibited and even more dangerous during a storm.

The waves were big, at least two feet, and choppy. As I searched for a lifeguard on duty, I knew of course, there wasn't one. This was *my* test. Someone shouted "help" and the cry sounded achingly familiar. I didn't have time to think as I slipped off my shoes and dived into the water. At least the water wasn't as cold as the last time I attempted to rescue someone in Lake Michigan. The water temperatures were in the sixties during summertime. No hypothermia to worry about, I kept reminding myself.

I was still numb inside, but outside I was a force to be reckoned with. I couldn't let another person die while I tried to save them. As I got closer, I realized the guy could pass for Conner's twin if he'd had one. He tried to push toward the shore and tired himself out, then went under, but I couldn't get to him yet. I was an experienced swimmer—maybe too experienced, given my history, and I'd been caught in the undertow numerous times, so I knew the best thing to do was swim parallel to the shore, then test for a weak part in the current. Still, panic wasn't hard to come by when waves pounded against me like we were in a fist fight.

"Hang on," I shouted. A rush of lake water filled my mouth, and I coughed the fluid up, then clamped my lips shut so I wouldn't choke before I saved him.

Finally, I had my chance when the undertow let up. My numb hands cut through the water, legs kicking frantically. This wasn't real like when I tried to save Conner, but the whole simulation felt real to me. I shuddered. What was the worst that could happen if I didn't fake save him? *Oh, I'd probably be damned for all eternity.* I could not panic The stakes were higher than ever. I needed this. The overwhelming desire was strange, the need to save this person. All the while, I knew I was really trying to save myself, so one day I'd have the chance to be able to save Conner again.

I couldn't give up, even though my limbs begged me to. I kept pushing as I saw the boy slipping underwater. When I finally reached the spot where he was a moment ago, I sucked in a deep breath and kept my eyes wide-open as I sank below the surface. Luckily, the bright pier lights shone down on the water, otherwise, I wouldn't have been able to see a thing. Riel had changed the simulation from sunlight to almost total darkness in a matter of seconds.

Luckily, the guy hadn't sunk deeper than about eight feet. I swam with long, powerful kicks and grabbed him by the shoulders.

My eyes bugged as I got a close-up of his face and realized they'd used *my* Conner in my test, not just some lookalike. A wave of shock and fear paralyzed me. Hysteria revved up inside me like a flywheel, and I let Conner go. Watching him float to the top, I fought nausea. Could I puke under water? Hyperventilate in a panic attack and drown? Conner's face stared down at me, shimmering through the water, an ethereal light surrounding him. Getting farther away, his body receded until becoming a point of light, like a fading bright dot at the center of a turned-off television, and it was not until I touched the bottom that I noticed I'd let myself sink. The depth must've been thirteen or fourteen feet here, and this realization scared me into action.

Launching like a torpedo, I slammed my arms and legs against the water full-force until I reached him. I held him up underneath his arms, my hands claws on his shoulders, and lunged toward shore, throwing my whole body into a swim I was certain could win an Olympic medal. Quivering now, my teeth locked in a titanic rigor, but not from the cold. I chanted in my head, *I am weightless. My arms are fast, my legs are strong. I can do this all day long.* I knew the power of believing was the key to this test. I heaved forward with adrenalized strength. The drizzle increased to a steady rain, water spraying down on me like a shower. I turned around, looking for a lifebuoy, for anything to appear, but it didn't. No easy way out. Waves pounded over us, and I started to choke and buck and thrash—a scream tearing loose from me—as I struggled for air. One last wave crashed over us, and then I busted to the surface, fake-Conner in tow.

Nate ran out to meet us, knee deep in water, then carried Conner to the sand and laid him there before turning to me.

"Olga?" He gripped my arms, maybe a little too harshly. "Are you okay?"

My head snapped from side to side, examining Conner's face, then Nate's.

"Nate, meet Conner."

My voice was icy with control even though I breathed harder than any asthma attack as I flipped him over on his stomach. I straddled him, pushing down on the middle of his back with both hands. Water gushed from his lips, and I repeated until the flow stopped. I was a girl possessed, a spirit guide in training on a mission, as I flipped him over onto his back, then immediately delivered CPR breaths. I was all thumbs when I tried to rescue him last year, but not this time. I ran my own reality show now—driven, hopeful, believing that what didn't happen before could happen this day.

Remembering what I did wrong before helped me now. To onlookers gathering around us, it must've looked like a senseless frenzy, but I controlled the chaos here. I took his pulse. Nothing. Still not breathing. I screamed and slammed my fist down on his chest, desperately trying to wake him.

I wouldn't give up. I slapped his face. "Fight!"

"Hey, what are you doing?" Nate shouted.

I ignored him and gathered all my wits and strength to remember the steps on how to save a life. Step one: open Conner's airway, tilt head, and put my ear to his mouth. Step two: listen for air flowing, look for chest movement. None. Step three: pinch his nose, and start mouth-to-mouth again, big enough to make his chest rise. Step four: watch his chest fall. Repeat.

My muscles strained tightly with the déjà vu feeling, but this time I knew the outcome. Because this time felt different, like the kiss of life instead of death. When I checked for a pulse, there was one. Water tickled my feet as a wave crashed against the shore, and I laughed. Water didn't feel scary in this moment; it felt like the soft hand of God reaching out to me.

Conner's body convulsed, coughing violently, and it was like watching a rebirth. But not his. Mine. Our eyes locked, inches apart, and I felt his breath on my face, so thankful it wasn't his last. Not here, at least. I shook all over as a sound escaped my lips, something between laughing and crying.

His eyes were so intense on me, his voice was a hoarse whisper. "Olga, you saved me."

That brief statement set my teeth chattering beyond control. I wanted to say something, but my voice twisted into a sob, and I wept quietly as the ambulance pulled up. This was the part I missed before because I had been knocked unconscious by the sailboat boom. I watched as the door crashed open. They loaded Conner on the stretcher, packing heating blankets around him and placing a clear oxygen mask over his mouth. I stood up, staring at his gray face in the moonlight. I grabbed his hand, running my fingers over his, and somehow, he felt warm.

"I never told you this, but I love you."

This might've been surprising for Nate to hear, after all this time. This moment, I knew it wouldn't be enough. No trace of the words I just confessed registered on Conner's face. I felt my heart break again. I wanted to stay with Conner now more than ever. Terror shot through me at the thought of going on without him, but what choice did I have?

It wasn't real. This isn't real.

When the ambulance pulled away, everyone clapped around me. Real or fake, I lifted my hands to the sky anyway and told God thank you, taking a deep breath of fresh salty air. In that moment, it didn't matter how badly my lungs burned.

Nate's shadow moved in front of my closed eyes before whispering in my ear. "You are brave."

I supposed courage might've been doing what needed to be done even though there was nothing in you that wanted to do it. "Maybe I am brave."

He pushed the wet hair back behind my ears with trembling fingers as tears streamed down my face. "Not maybe. You did it."

I grabbed his head in both hands, then pulled his mouth to mine. We locked together in a fierce kiss, fueled by passion and fear.

Then the whole world disappeared, and we were back at headquarters.

Gasping, I pressed a hand to my chest. Riel grabbed my other hand and pulled me to my feet. Reluctantly, he helped Nate stand, too.

"You're back just in time for lunch. Pleased, Lover Boy?"

"Did we…?" I couldn't finish my question, too afraid to hear the answer.

"Pass?" Riel titled his head, studying me. "Yes. Congratulations."

He patted me on the back, and the whole thing felt awkward, like I was his puppy and he was my master. He seemed to sense the uncomfortableness and pulled away.

"After lunch, Ruth will go over some last minute reminders in your exit counseling session. Enjoy your weekend. School starts on Monday."

Riel gave me one last glance before popping his wings out, and then he was too beautiful to behold, so I looked away.

Chapter Five

The next night, I sprawled out on my bed at headquarters and studied the contents of my backpack. Nate sat across the room in a desk chair, doing the same thing. His iPod Touch blared *Some Nights* by FUN. I nodded my head along to the lyrics, which seemed very fitting for our situation since the self-deprecation the song spoke of threatened to overwhelm me at any moment.

Nate happened to have his iPod Touch in his pants pocket when we were brought into this other realm, which was lucky because his playlist was his life. I felt very grateful for the music at the moment. I watched him, studying every inch of his body. He sported a pair of jeans and a T-shirt which featured a storm trooper on the front, the words 'Do not conform to this world' written underneath the image. Our closets at headquarters were magically filled with clothes just the right size and style for us. Apparently, God was a fan of Star Wars too, which made sense considering how popular the series continued to be over the years.

Nate's chin dropped to his chest, and his coffee colored hair covered one eye, his tanned fingers scanning the pages. I ached for those fingers to touch me in the same way. As if he sensed my ogling, he looked up at me and smiled. I smiled back, which was all it took for him to amble over to where I rested on the bed. He dropped to his knees on the carpet and gently pushed me backward. He lifted my T-shirt until the fabric rested just above my bellybutton and then pressed his lips to my navel sweetly.

"Nate, we should really keep studying so we're prepared."

The truth was I couldn't stop thinking about finding Conner. No way could I tell Nate that after all he had done to help me this past year and with all the guilt he felt over his car accident. I didn't want to lie either. So, as the saying went, silence was golden.

He sighed. "I only study when I can't think of anything better to do, and this, this is definitely something better." His lips traveled just above the waistband of my jeans before turning his gaze toward my face. "I really wish we could've had kids one day. You would've made a great mother. You know that was my Hell, right? When Riel took us there for a moment that first day we met him? I sat on your bedroom floor and watched you swallow an entire bottle of pills, and I couldn't stop you from hurting yourself. You didn't care about anything else."

His face remained stern and constant. I could count the number of times on one hand when I'd seen him so serious. "What was your Hell? Did it have to do with me?"

Regarding his expression, I knew I should tell him the truth, but I couldn't. Somehow, the truth would change us, and I didn't want that. "Yeah, mine was about losing you, too."

He nodded his head. "I figured as much. It's our greatest fear, isn't it?"

Tears pooled at the corners of my eyes, but of course, he mistook my sadness for another reason. The impulse to kiss him took over. Pulling him onto the bed with me, I enveloped him in a sea of passionate kisses on his mouth and neck before trailing more down his shoulders, arms, and hands. I took in his warmth, his smell, letting his closeness calm me. My hands slipped through his fine hair as he mimicked my path of kisses before kissing my navel again. I flashed him a mischievous smile, beckoning him to come closer with my index finger. He slid on top of me, elbows resting on either side of my shoulders, pressing his forehead to mine.

"How far do you think we can go before they stop us?" I whispered.

He gave me a look of pure hunger.

I licked my lips, and then arched upward, bringing my mouth to his. The spark between us had never felt so strong, and I began to think that maybe emotions came more easily in this realm. I felt like my whole life I'd been riding a bike with training wheels, and now I'd advanced to driving a motorcycle. And our free will still seemed to be intact because nobody stopped him when his hands roamed over my body… and mine his. Except the thought that my impulsiveness was really an evasion, a camouflage for the truth, put an end to what I'd started.

"I don't mean to be a party pooper, but maybe this isn't the best way to prepare for our first assignment."

His lips moved against my skin as he spoke. "I know. Maybe it's how we can celebrate after our first 'A' plus?"

I laughed, something I didn't think I'd done since arriving at headquarters.

"Sounds like a plan." I brushed my cheek lightly against his. "Are you scared about starting our new job?"

He shrugged. "Kind of, I guess. It has this video game feeling to me, like Zelda when Link is returned to the Temple of Time and meets the mysterious Sheik, who guides Link to rid the five temples of Hyrule from Ganondorf's monsters and—"

I held up my free hand and giggled. "You lost me at video game. English, please."

A moment of silence followed. "I don't know how to explain my fears really… but in those games, the storyline makes it so easy for the creators to throw in a twist or two. Because everyone's thinking, 'Oh okay, we just have to collect the five elemental gems from the five temples, then we'll be done,' but BAM, nuh-uh! You never get past the third temple before there's a plot twist! So, like, what are those angels gonna throw at Grace and us on her Limbo plane? Riel and Ash are kind of snippy, don't you think? I get the feeling they don't particularly like humans, especially Riel, but I always thought angels were like our servants, so that doesn't make sense."

I wanted to tell Nate to shut the hell up, because hello! Certainly, they could hear us with their angel superpowers or whatever. "Maybe that's why they don't like humans, because we abuse their help. Anyway, we're not humans anymore, remember? They probably don't have human emotions, and perhaps it's time we stop thinking like humans, too. Look toward them as a good example."

He wet his lips and gave a jerky nod of assent. "Yeah, but to me, just the fact they're more powerful and more intelligent means they have less vulnerabilities and makes them emotionally different than us. Oh man, I hope there's a killer battle between the demons and the angels or some junk like that during our assignment! That would be so cool to watch. Like something out of the movies!"

Punching his shoulder, I shouted, "Nate! Remember what Dr. Judy said? Don't tempt the demons like that."

"Fine, fine."

I stared at him, not in the least bit amused but unable to stay upset with him for even a second.

"Well, I should go to my own room for the remainder of the evening or the party timeline will move up considerably." He shifted his body off the bed and gathered his things, pausing at the door. "I don't know if I've told you lately, but I love you."

Closing my eyes so he wouldn't see the tears forming again, I nodded yes.

"Even so, I love you."

"I love you, too," I muttered, and I opened my eyes just in time to see him walking through my wall—something I didn't think I'd ever get used to.

I glanced at the clock on my desk. 11:58 p.m. Earth time. A week ago, we were entering Dr. Judy's office for the last time as her patients; now we were her interns.

Time didn't matter, since I didn't need sleep anymore. I still doubted my qualifications for my new position, but the good news was pulling an all-nighter to prepare would be a piece of cake now. I opened up the folder labeled 'Role Playing' on the tab and studied the character I needed to portray for Grace's limbo. We got to keep our same names, same personalities. The alternative timeline would take place in Black Mountain, North Carolina, and I wondered if that's where Dr. Judy made her home on Earth or if her family had since moved. At nine years old, I had visited Ashville with my parents on vacation, and I thought Black Mountain was nearby. The town certainly sounded familiar. I skimmed over some notes on the area, but this induced boredom after five minutes. Then my gaze landed on the cover story for Nate and me, my eyes bugging when I read the part about us pretending to be twin siblings.

What the heck?

The typed document stated that since the community was a small town with only about two thousand people, two teenagers from different families moving there at the same time would seem too contrived. We needed to work together though, so pretending to be siblings equaled the best solution.

Based on our recent make out session, I wished some acting classes had been part of our spirit guide training. No way would I be able to pull off this one.

CHAPTER SIX

"The truth is rarely pure and never simple."
—Oscar Wilde

Nate and I headed through the nearly empty hallway of Charles D. Owen High School together, bags over our shoulders, inhaling the scent of bleach, pine sol, and fresh paint. My shoes made quick scuffs on the tile as we found our way to the classroom using a map Ash had given us. I hadn't felt terror like this since Conner died. Today, just like that fateful day on the sailboat last April, someone's life was in my hands. More than life actually, her very soul! And just as no amount of boating safety classes could've prepared me for that lightning strike, no amount of spirit guide sessions with Ruth could've truly prepared me for what lay ahead.

But turning back now wasn't an option, so I rubbed my arms to get rid of the goose bumps and plowed ahead.

Grace was registered for two classes this summer: Algebra II and Biology. Nate and I enrolled in both with her, although we posed as incoming seniors wanting to get used to our new school before the fall semester started. At least playing a goody-goody was right up my alley.

The atmosphere in 13-A was a hive of activity, sounding like a frenzied mob at Discount Mart at the stroke of midnight on Black Friday. Students swooped in with traveling coffee mugs in hand, their phones buzzing with early morning text messages as the teacher shouted at them to put their stuff away. I slid into an old fashioned school desk and hung my backpack on the chair. Nate and I both sat next to each other in the back row to keep an eye out for Grace. As the teacher reached my seat, I took the syllabus with cold fingers, wishing I'd spent every moment studying for my real assignment instead of making out with Nate. The late bell blared, and still Grace didn't show. I listened to the teacher give announcements and watched Nate gaze out the window, a look of concern on his face. Quietly, I tore a piece of paper from my composition book and scrawled, 'What do we do now?'

I handed him the note when the teacher turned his back to write something on the whiteboard, the steady clicking of the wall clock making me anxious.

Nate read my note, then nodded out the window, and I saw her. Grace perched on the edge of a bench in the courtyard, wearing an oversized T-shirt and sweatpants, despite the heat. Her complexion was pale and not in a flattering way. Some sunlight would do her good, but if she cared at all about her future, she'd be in class right now.

I knew from reading about role playing that because all of this existed just for Grace, we could simply get up and walk out of class without even so much as a hall pass, so Nate held the door open for me, and we left. We found Grace flipping through a trashy magazine, tears streaming down her face.

"Is everything all right?" Nate asked when we approached her.

She jumped like a scared cat, then looked at us for a long moment. Her hazel eyes held golden flecks that were mesmerizing to look at. Finally, she broke down in sobs, cradling the magazine to her chest with her sickly pale arms. If we looked up emotional wreck in the dictionary, Grace's picture would be next to the definition. At least I had managed to keep myself mostly together during my Limbo state. I struggled, but nothing like this. The only thing that wasn't completely wrecked was her shiny, chestnut colored hair. Even in a messy bun, I could tell she had very long locks. As I sat there staring, no supernatural ideas on what to do flooded my mind, but of course Nate looked as calm as all get out. He dropped down on the bench next to her and hugged her as she continued to quake.

After a moment, she tried to regain her composure, but putting her mind at ease proved a losing battle. I tried to recall something, anything, from the Angel Code of Conduct to help her, but I came up empty again.

Out of options, I simply handed her a tissue from the pack I kept in my bag.

"I'm not… usually… like this." She blew her nose a few times.

I handed her another Kleenex. "It's okay. What happened? I mean, you don't have to tell us, but we're here if you feel like talking."

She shook her head slowly, sadly. "I wanted Red Velvet Cake."

Nate raised his eyebrows at me.

I cleared my throat. "Um, wanted Red Velvet Cake for what?"

"For my eighteenth birthday last Friday. Mom used to make that cake every year for my birthday. It's the little things I miss most about her, and my homemade birthday cake is one of them."

I paused, clasping my hands behind my back, thinking about what to say. "So your mom is…?"

"Deceased," Grace finished for me. Of course, I knew this, but she didn't know we knew.

"I'm very sorry to hear that," Nate said, patting her back lightly. "When did she pass?"

"Three years ago. She was a drunk. One night, on my fifteenth birthday, she drank too much and never woke up again and—" she broke off, turning her face away.

"And what?" I asked, wanting desperately to know what her next thought was, still reeling from the knowledge that Dr. Judy used to be an alcoholic.

But the momentary heart-to-heart between all of us snapped.

Fast as a cougar-strike, Grace jumped up. "What do you care? Who are you anyway?"

"Who am I?" I asked, trying to search for an answer, because I didn't quite know anymore. "I'm a girl, like you, who suffered loss. But when I didn't think I could get out of bed one more day, I had friends, and my b-brother, to help me." I stumbled on the brother part when looking at Nate, almost calling him my boyfriend. "And it looks like you could use some friends now."

Grace didn't respond. She picked a leaf off a nearby Red Oak tree and shredded it to pieces.

"You want to get out of here?" Usually, I didn't think skipping school was a good idea. I'd gotten the perfect attendance award every year until Conner died. But today, ditching classes seemed like the right plan.

"And go where?" Her gaze bounced from me to Nate to the surrounding area. "This is Black Mountain. You drive five miles and you end up right where you started. Not exactly a lot to do here. Besides, I don't even know you."

She stood, digging in her purse, looking for something. I assumed she searched for her keys, anxious to get away from me.

"All the more reason we should hang out today. My brother and I are new in town. We could use a friend as much as you."

Grace backed up a step. "I never said I needed a friend. I said I needed cake."

"You know, I saw a shop called Hey Hey Cupcake on the way to school. We should go there and get you a red velvet cupcake." Even I could hear the desperation in my voice, but I crossed my fingers, hoping she'd say yes.

She smiled. "They do have really good cupcakes." Finally, she found her car keys in one of the front pockets of her purse. "But I'm driving. Dad would kill me if he knew I got into a stranger's car. Besides, you scare me."

I nodded. Technically, the license I'd obtained a few months ago didn't count since the test happened during my Limbo timeline, and Nate had never gotten his back after the accident either. And I didn't blame her for being scared of me. Truth was, I think I would've bolted by now. Grace had no reason to trust us. Not yet anyway.

We headed to the parking lot together. No campus security stopped us from leaving, not that I was surprised. None of this was real.

As she drove down the highway, *All Apologies* by Nirvana blared from her stereo.

"Wow, George Lucas called. He wants his sound system back."

"Excuse me?"

"Olga is a huge Star Wars geek," Nate informed her from the back seat. "I'll apologize now for all her references."

I turned around and stuck my tongue out at him like a good sister would. "I just meant you have a really nice stereo for an older car."

"The stereo is a recent upgrade, a birthday present from my dad. Music is the only thing I care about these days."

"Well, here's a fun twist for your viewing pleasure." Nate leaned forward, resting a forearm on each of our headrests. "I was the lead vocalist and guitarist for an indie rock band when we lived in Michigan."

Grace raised an eyebrow. "You don't say? What was the name of your band?"

"Cantankerous Monkey Squad."

She snorted. "That's a pretty ridiculous name."

"That was Conner for ya." My stomach clenched painfully at my unexpected use of his name. I tried to hide my pain, but Grace didn't seem to miss much.

"Ex-boyfriend?"

I nodded in agreement because she was a stranger who didn't know any better and because the idea of Conner as my boyfriend made the pain go away a little bit. Then, I remembered Nate. He had slumped back down in his seat.

After a few seconds of silence, except for Kurt Cobain's lyrics about screwing everything up, I couldn't take the heavy anymore. "This song is kind of depressing. Do you mind changing it?"

Grace rolled her eyes. "Fine. Here, take the wheel."

"What? I can't take the wheel! That's the first rule Mom told me when she taught me how to drive. The driver always keeps both hands on the wheel. Two and ten o'clock."

"Well, my mom wasn't around to teach me how to drive. Taking my hands off the wheel now."

I shrieked as she let go and then opened her center console. "I know I have the new Coldplay CD in here somewhere. Is that upbeat enough for our seven minute drive?"

Trying to keep my hand steady, I gave a tight nod.

"You look terrified. Are you always this high-strung?"

Was Grace teasing me already? Maybe this was a good sign. Friends tease each other.

"You know, the rule isn't two and ten o'clock anymore." Nate's voice was carefree again, apparently over my Conner comment.

"What?"

"My Driver's Ed instructor told me they changed the hands thing to nine and three o'clock after the invention of the air bag."

"Good job, Mr. Know-It-All. You want a prize?"

"Hey, I just didn't want you giving our own kids the wrong information one day."

Grace, having already loaded the Coldplay disc, took the wheel back, but abruptly jerked it to the side at Nate's comment. "I thought you guys were brother and sister?"

I gave Nate an incredulous stare.

"Um, we are. I didn't mean kids we'd have together… just the kids we'll have one day with our spouses."

Grace nodded, seeming to buy the cover up. "Right. I'm never having kids."

"Why not?" I asked, although I already felt certain of her answer.

"Well, first of all, every child deserves a grandma to spoil them, and mine won't have one. You know what? Bump all of that, every child deserves a mother to love them. I can't even love myself."

I tried to search for some wisdom I'd read in my eighteen years of life to help her, but I came up empty.

"It's not who you are that holds you back." Nate's words startled me out of my thoughts, making me jump a little. "It's who you think you are not."

Grace laughed as she pulled up to the cupcake shop and parked. "Who are you? Some modern day Confucius or something?"

Now I laughed. "You have no idea."

"It's from the last book I read, *Seeds of Greatness* by Denis Waitley. I can loan it to you if you want. The book is full of good stuff, if you don't mind all my highlights and notes in the margins. I've probably read the book forty times by now."

This roused a low chuckle from Grace. "Okay, sure." She turned her attention toward me as we strode through the front doors while two blonde haired ladies greeted us from behind the counter. "Do you like cupcakes?"

"Are you kidding?" Nate gasped. "Olga lives on sugar. She tried to convince her boss at the bookstore where she worked in Grand Haven to pay her in candy instead of cash."

I shoved him sideways. "I did not! Although, that's actually not a bad idea."

"What can I get for you?" the lady asked, peering at us over the bakery case.

"The biggest red velvet cupcake for my friend the birthday girl here, and I'll have… Mmm," I murmured, viewing the display. "What's the 24-karat cake?"

"Five pounds of carrots and cinnamon frosted with cream cheese, no nuts and no raisins. Would you like me to cut you a slice?"

"Sounds just novel enough to be fabulous! Make sure you cut the slice big enough that it could count for my daily serving of vegetables."

Nate elbowed Grace. "See what I mean?"

I batted my eyelashes at him. "Can you pretty please get the Black Mountain Cup-uccino cupcake so I can try some?"

"She means eat most of it," he told the lady. "But go ahead and box one of those up, and a Bonita Margarita, too."

"Will this be for here or to go?"

"To go, please."

"Where are we going?" Grace and I both asked at the same time.

"Jinx!" she called. "You owe me a coke."

"Will you settle for me buying our cupcakes?"

"That'll work too." Grace smiled warmly, and I could see the Dr. Judy in her. Then, she turned back to Nate. "So, where am I taking us next?"

He shrugged. "You tell me. I'm new here and despite the smallness of Black Mountain, you have to admit the town is beautiful. There has to be at least one cool place where we can go hang for a while."

Grace slowly flipped through a catering menu, stroking the glossy pages as if lost in thought. "Robert Lake Park at Montreat College is nearby. Mom and I used to picnic there all the time."

"Is the park free?" Nate asked, emptying his wallet since he wouldn't let me pay for the cupcakes. With the added three coffees he'd ordered, the twenty bucks he'd found stuffed inside his spirit guide back pack last night was almost gone.

I still had my twenty, so I waved the bill in front of his face, but he shooed my money away.

Grace cocked her head to the side.

Oops. We'd have to get better about not flirting with each other in front of her, or she may think this was turning into a Star Wars flick. Luke and Leia kissing still made me want to puke in my mouth every time I watched that scene.

"All the parks are free around here," Grace said in a quiet voice. "And Montreat is actually open past seven."

"Bonus," said Nate, holding the door open for us as we said our thanks to the cupcake ladies. "We can go wild and crazy then."

Another seven minute drive was all it took for us to reach our next destination. The wilderness of the park was breathtaking. Winding paths circled narrow streams all around us. Perfectly crooked branches sprouted from regal trees taller than I'd ever seen before. I lifted my face, letting the sunlight dance across my skin through the shadows. Bees hummed in and out of the flowering plants and a pair of pigeons greedily fought over some seed hanging in a birdfeeder. I inhaled the minty smell of shrubbery while following Grace, smiling at the sound of my feet sliding through the leaves. She led us to the top of some rocks above one of the shallow rocky mountain streams winding throughout the park. On our way up, she tripped among the bundles of craggy roots, but luckily, Nate caught her before she fell. I shoved the curly hair out of my eyes, ignoring a pang of unnecessary jealousy. Still, I mentally checked out her style as if she was potential competition. She had an edge to her. Her black sweatpants were paired with a loose gray T-shirt that, interestingly enough, had a white lightning bolt down the middle of it. The leopard print Converse sneakers looked brand new, not broken in enough for hiking up hills.

Once we completed the trek, we dipped our feet into the cool water while munching on our cupcakes and chatting amicably. "So, what brings you two to summer school?" Grace asked, balling up her cupcake wrapper and stuffing the trash inside her empty coffee cup.

I plunged my fist into the lush grass and released the blades to the wind. "We'll be seniors this year, so we thought we'd get a jumpstart on our classes and get to know the school a little better before the halls were crowded with students in the fall."

Grace smiled like an indulgent parent would at the naivety of their child. "This is Black Mountain. School is never crowded. Gosh, I can't believe you guys are willingly wasting your summer away at school while I should've graduated already."

"Why haven't you graduated yet?" I hoped my question sounded sincere, but of course, I already knew the answer. The real question was if she trusted us enough to tell the truth.

"I actually tried to kill myself the night of graduation. I was already flunking out of school."

Again, I tried to act as though this was all news to me. "Why'd you do that?"

Grace smiled, but the gesture looked forced. "Which one? Kill myself or flunk out?"

Nate picked up a pebble and skipped the rock across the stream. "Whichever you feel like explaining."

She opened the front of her purse and applied some cherry flavored Chapstick. "I guess the two things are really tied together. I just didn't feel like my life was headed anywhere. I'll never attend college, so why bother with high school?"

My stomach twisted with the pain of knowing I'd never attend college either. "Why won't you go to college? If you graduate high school, community college will still accept you and if you keep your grades up there, you can switch to the university of your choice after two years."

Grace stood, then jumped onto a large rock in the middle of the stream, holding her arms out wide. "With what money, exactly? Since my mom died, we only have my dad's meager salary to live off of. He's late on payments all the time, so it's not like the powers that be would've given us a loan. I screwed up my grades way too much to ever earn a scholarship, so when my final year of high school came around, I didn't see the point in trying anymore."

I shook my head. "Wow. Pity party, reservation for one, please."

She grabbed at a low hanging branch over her head. "Excuse me?" Her voice was cold.

Nate's clenched jaw told me he didn't approve of my comment, but I had the feeling everyone had given Grace a free pass for far too long, and she needed some serious tough love now.

"If you can trust me for just a second, listen to what I'm about to tell you. There is a higher reason to this obstacle you're facing. I didn't think so once. Then my parents sent me to grief counseling after I lost Conner, my—"

"Your boyfriend?" Grace interrupted. "He died?"

Thankfully she stopped me, because I almost called him my best friend, and I needed to keep my story straight. "Yup, and I was right there with him when the accident happened. I tried to save him, but I couldn't. Afterward, I swallowed the entire bottle of pain pills the hospital gave me. So, my—our—parents"—I nodded toward Nate—"sent me to a therapist who suggested I write a life list of eighteen things to do the—" I paused. I couldn't say the year I turned eighteen, because that would contradict mine and Nate's cover story since I posed as an incoming senior, so I wouldn't technically be eighteen until October. "Um, before I turn eighteen. I felt so small and tired as I wrote my list. Things had been so tough in my life, and my faith was tested moment by moment. But the list revealed this quiet strength within me, and I can see that in you even though we just met. Maybe we can even do some of the items on my list together. It just might be the thing you need to bring some joy back into your life."

She scowled at me. "I bet you were a cheerleader at your old school."

I fought off tears, remembering my time with Tammy on the squad. "Actually, I was, and I'm not buying your whole misunderstood Courtney Love routine either. You're better than that."

Grace crossed her arms over her abdomen and looked away. "Well, enough about me, Olga! What are your hopes and dreams for the future?"

I studied her, a little hurt by her faux beauty queen cheerleading tone, but she wasn't getting off the hook that easily. The literary geek in me searched for an analogy that could make her understand. "Grace, you can be like this oak tree here that stands tall, roots firmly planted, bending with the wind, not against it, with roots that will never break, no matter how strong the wind. But growth has to start with renewal, your faith in life being renewed. Don't you think that's what your mom would've wanted for you? Maybe something she didn't have at the time of her death."

Grace turned toward me, repulsion written on her face, and I knew I said the wrong thing. "Yeah, that's pretty much my philosophy on life, too. Just trust that everything happens for a reason and whatever doesn't kill you makes you stronger." Her voice dripped with sarcasm.

"I'm sorry. I don't mean to—"

"I wasn't done talking! Let's get one thing straight. You are not my mother, so quit trying to act like one. You've never even met my mother."

Well, I had, but now wasn't the time to bring up that small fact.

"How could you possibly know what she wanted for me?" Before I could answer, she continued her tirade. "My mother died from alcohol poisoning on my fifteenth birthday, so even if you did know what she wanted for me, I frankly wouldn't give a damn. So, I don't want to hear your cute little anecdotes and life lessons. I don't want to hear your words of encouragement. There's no surprising strength deep inside me. There's only the hurt of right now, and right now I want the hell away from here."

She splashed through the creek, grabbed her shoes and purse off the bank, and bolted for the hills. "Sorry, but I can't do this. You'll need to find your own ride home. I gotta go," she called over her shoulder to Nate.

I looked helplessly at him, and he jumped off his rock. "I'm going after her. Um, I'll call you later."

I watched them race down the boardwalk, past the playground full of children, my mouth dropped open in shock. He left me here?

Now what?

Chapter Seven

Nate never showed up to headquarters the rest of the day, and he either avoided my calls or turned off his phone. My stubborn streak prevented me from searching for him and Grace. Around ten o'clock, I gave up and went to find Ash or Riel, figuring they'd still be up and roaming about somewhere.

I inched down the hallways of headquarters, passing one closed door after another until I eventually came across a boardroom with glass windows. Riel occupied the front of the room, speaking to a dozen angels seated around a long, oval table. When he spotted me, he said something to his peers and they disbanded around him. I stood outside the door, watching him while waiting. He was so beautiful to behold that it made my eyes hurt, but I couldn't make myself look away. He stuffed a couple of papers into a briefcase before heading toward me, the last one to exit.

"To what do I owe this pleasure, Ms. Worontzoff?"

"Um, I was wondering if you could help me with something."

He stared at me for a moment. "I can't read your mind, so you'll need to spit the words out for me to know what you're wondering."

I smacked my forehead. "Oh, right." Knowing he couldn't read my thoughts made me breathe a huge sigh of relief. "It's my friends, the Jedi Order gang. I know I'm practically a ghost now, but they're the ones haunting my mind. Dr. Judy said Nate and I wouldn't be able to travel back and forth to Earth like her since we're newbie spirit guides, but I just thought… isn't there a way for me to see them? I mean, I don't want you to put me in some fake Limbo for a play date or anything. I just want a peek at my real friends from time to time, to know they're all right."

He gave me a gentle smile. “Sure. Come in here for a minute.” He reentered the boardroom, picked up a small remote from the table, and aimed it at a projector on the ceiling.

A light flashed across the front bare wall as Riel typed in a series of code on the connected laptop, and a moment later, a video of my friends at Lake Michigan appeared. “Is this happening in real time?”

“Yes. Here, let’s listen in.” He pressed another button, and we magically had volume. After setting his briefcase on the floor, he pulled out a chair and motioned for me to sit, then hopped up on the table, winking at me. In this setting, without his wings out, he looked almost boyish and charming, like he was just another guy my age with untidy hair.

I shook my head and fixed my eyes on the wall.

“Whoever invented waffle cones was pure genius,” Kyle mused, shoving the last bite of chocolate ice cream into his mouth.

“No one related to you then,” Nicole said, handing him a napkin.

Tammy rolled her eyes. “Yeah, the person who invented the fat now clogging your arteries is a genius. Don’t you guys care even a little bit about eating healthy?”

“Mhmm. What do ya’ll say to a game of soccer to burn off these calories we ate today?” Sean asked, throwing a ball into the air and bouncing it off his knee, sending the sphere straight to Tammy’s head.

“Dude!”

Riel laughed beside me. “Oh, that had to hurt. And from what I can tell, she doesn’t need any more blows to the head.”

“Hey, now,” I told him before realizing too late I probably shouldn’t reprimand angels.

He held up his hands. “Kidding.”

We both focused our gaze back on the wall.

“Sorry!” Sean yelled. “But it wasn’t my fault. You guys felt that gust of wind, right?”

“Shut up, Dr. Horrible.” Tammy massaged the back of her head. “How we playing this? Kyle and me against you and Nic?”

“Game on,” Kyle agreed, scooping the ball off the sand. “But beware; I played on a winning soccer league for three years in middle school.”

“Played?” Sean let out a hoot. “All I remember is you sitting on the bench, loser!”

Seconds later, Kyle scored the first goal, and Riel and I both cheered, high-fiving each other.

"Oh yeah! Who's the loser now, big guy?"

"Must've been that wind again, except it helped this time, made the ball soar right over the line." Sean pointed to one of the sticks they had laid down to mark the goal lines.

"Wind? Whatever, man. Just admit it; I know how to work balls."

A snort escaped Sean's lips. "I'm gonna leave that one alone."

"Come on, guys, we playing or what?" Nic yelled down the beach.

Riel and I watched them play for another few minutes before he spoke again. "You know, you were lucky to have them. Most people can't find one true friend in their whole lifetime, and you've managed to make five in your short span of eighteen years… says a lot about the kind of person you are. If you're going to have success as a spirit guide, you need to start seeing yourself as others see you, as I see you, as God sees you."

"Which is?"

"Have you ever read Psalm 139 in the Bible?"

I gave a shaky smile, not understanding his question. "Bible?"

"Yeah, you know, that religious text of sixty-six books sold all over the world for hundreds of years that are supposed to be like a set of instructions for your life?"

I punched him in the arm, forgetting again that he was an angel, not to mention my boss. "Very funny."

He opened his briefcase and retrieved a Bible, flipping the book open to Psalms. "Read it."

I raised my eyebrows.

"Please. With a cherry on top."

"Okay." I glanced at the live feed of my friends just in time to see Tammy score a goal and punch the air in victory. Smiling, I read the verses about how God's character goes into the creation of every person. I understood what Riel tried to show me. When I felt inadequate and worthless, I had to remember God's spirit at work within me.

"I wrote a song about those verses. Your journey through Limbo inspired me." He popped out of view and returned in a flash, guitar in hand. "Would you like to hear it?"

Great, just what I need. Another man in my life serenading me with a guitar.

I nodded, because if I opened my mouth to speak I knew I'd cry.

"It's called *Face of Love*."

He strummed his guitar for a few moments before the lyrics came, his deep voice changing to a gentle whisper.

"Deeper oceans drying day by day/Memories of many drifting away/But even if you settle on the far side of the sea/Even there my spirit will guide thee/I wish you'd have as much respect for yourself as I do for you/You won't believe that you are precious but it's true/I keep speaking words of grace/But you turn away your pretty face/No matter what you do or where you go/My loving presence you can hold/Picture perfect face of love/Smiling at you from above/Blind to all your imperfections/Death no more, only Resurrection.

"I tell you, you are dearly loved and you don't answer/You let your thoughts eat away at you like a cancer/Wake up, look out, let me in/A battle wages for your soul and you have to fight to win/You're broken inside, but you're not insane/Devils trying to trick your brain/Away from me, you bloodthirsty men/How vast is the sum of them/Everything you search for/It's just beyond this door/Brilliant light shines at the end/Come, walk home with me, my friend/I search your heart and your mind/There's no foulness for me to find/So let's travel on the everlasting way/Leave all the garbage down by the bay.

"I know what you're thinking now/But don't worry, I'll show you how/I'm a lover of society/I'll make you see how I see/I watch you in wonderment and draw you closer/Are you listening, or are you a poser?/I'm the one helping you breathe/Since the day that you came to be/Search me and I will offend/But isn't it worth it to be made whole again? Picture perfect face of love/Smiling at you from above/Blind to all your imperfections/Death no more, only Resurrection."

Tears streamed down my face when Riel set his guitar on the carpet, then leaned over me, smoothing my hair. "Olga," he said my name as if it was fragile, which only made me want to cry more. "I've spent a lot of time studying humans since the dawn of creation. You're one of the most beautiful people I know, inside and out. But you have to believe that. You have to love yourself before you love anyone else, or there's no way you can help others."

His smile was tentative, but the way he looked at me… it felt like God's stamp of approval.

I nodded, not knowing what to say, then turned my attention back to my friends as Nic fell swiftly to the ground, tripping over her own goal line.

"Bahahaha! Epic fail!" Kyle laughed, until he tripped over the same branch, his cell flying from his fingers. "Ah, my phone!"

"Oh, I see how it is," Nic said. "Your friend falls, you laugh. Your phone falls, you panic." She patted the back of her shorts. "Crap! I lost my phone! I lost my phone! Everyone spread out and find it!"

Riel and I watched as Nic worked herself into an escalating panic as the minutes ticked by without any sign of her phone. Up until a week ago, losing my cell would've caused the same reaction. Funny how death tended to put things into perspective, making something that was basically the center of my life seem so trivial now.

As if Sean could hear my thoughts, he told Nicole, "Relax, Babe. We've already lost two best friends this year. Losing your phone isn't the end of the world. I'll buy you a new one tomorrow."

Nic placed her hands on his chest and shoved him. "That's why I need to find the darn thing, you idiot! It had some pictures of Olga and me that I never backed up on my laptop!"

I snatched the remote off the table and muted the volume and the screen, fighting back tears once again. "Um, thanks for that. I'm gonna go to bed now."

Riel reached for me, but I ran from the room as fast as I could, not that he couldn't catch me if he wanted to.

Even though sleep wasn't needed to survive, I went to bed with the thought that slumber would be a welcomed break from everything that happened during the past four days. Instead, I tossed and turned, analyzing all the reasons why I hadn't heard back from Nate. It's funny how one little unreturned text or call could turn a bad day horrible. Maybe cell phones did still rule my life. Whatever the case may be, seeing Nic freak out over her cell phone because of lost pictures of us convinced me I didn't want any more sneak peeks at my earthly friends.

I stared at the ceiling and sighed. All the quiet just gave me a chance to ponder all those existential questions I thought I'd already had the answers to. *What is suffering? What is happiness? What is weakness? What is hurtful? What is worthwhile? Can something be both or neither?* All the life lessons I thought I'd learned the past year went out the proverbial window. I had to reject the standard wisdom and search for answers myself because I was someone with an impossible choice. Someone who absolutely must have two conflicting things. Conner was the one thing I couldn't walk away from. I'd learned that lesson the hard way, and now I had the chance to change everything. But I also loved Nate. I knew no matter what, I barreled toward disaster. My heart was broken again, and I didn't know how much I could take. Already, I felt like I was on the edge, hanging on by my fingernails.

At some point, I'd need to stop being polite around Nate, and start being real about why I became a spirit guide. Keeping secrets from him was like emotional claustrophobia, and I squirmed with discomfort at all the thoughts swirling in my head.

CHAPTER EIGHT

After a few hours of tossing and turning, I got up to attend the sunrise service at 6:00 a.m. They held the service at headquarters daily, but we were only required to attend two days a week since all the spirit guides and angels operated on different schedules. So I dressed in my long denim skirt and my blue top with the sequined heart in the middle, and shuffled down the hall to the chapel room, scanning every corridor for Nate. *Maybe he's already in service.*

Riel's voice boomed from behind the podium as I took my seat. *Great, I'm late for my first sermon as an official spirit guide. I'm certainly making a nice impression around here.*

"Not many of the prayers recorded in the Bible are long. Most prayers are pleas going straight to the heart of the matter. Even our Lord's model prayer to his apostles is brief and simple enough for a child to learn."

Riel stared right at me when he said the word *child.* Looking around the room, I could definitely tell I had that market cornered.

"Jesus prefaced that prayer with the following instruction in Matthew six, verses seven and eight: 'When you are praying, do not heap up empty phrases as some people do; for they think they will be heard because of their many words. Do not be like them, for your Father knows what you need before you ask him.'

"When the Bible speaks of praying without ceasing, have no fear. God's Word makes it clear it's the quality of our prayers, not the quantity of our words that matters to the Lord. Praying without ceasing means living with a sincere heart. You don't need to be in chapel, kneeling, head bowed, hands folded in prayer, speaking with an eloquent tongue, for God to hear you. Prayer is like our secret weapon, always available in our Jedi tool belt."

Riel's words washed over me from the pulpit. I knew this message was meant for me because of the Star Wars reference, but I wondered why Nate wasn't here. We both said we'd attend Wednesday and Sunday morning services together.

"We need to make prayer an everyday practice. Request God to give you strength to stand against personal attacks and temptation, courage to overcome fear, and discernment for the voices speaking to your spirit. You'll need it." As Riel spoke those last three words, he looked directly at me again. "Let us pray with confidence to the Father in the words our Savior gave us."

We all recited the Lord's Prayer together, and this time the words took on a whole new meaning. I'd addressed God as Father my whole life, but I never knew how much He loved and cared for me until I learned I was dead. Imagining God cared that deeply about a human being blew my mind. I mean, there were over six billion of us on his planet, but through Riel, He still orchestrated the entire Limbo experience for mine and Nate's well-being.

I found myself announcing the phrase 'Your kingdom come' with such conviction. Never had I yearned for God's spiritual reign so much… to have all my friends and family together again. Then death wouldn't matter. When I prayed 'Your will be done,' I realized I couldn't resign myself to fate any longer, but that it was up to me to help accomplish God's purpose in the state I was in now. 'Give us our daily bread' made me see that I must trust God daily to provide what He knows I need. Did He know I needed Conner? Because Conner was definitely on my mind when I recited the last part about temptation. I knew God didn't lead us into temptation, but He did allow us to be tempted. That's why Dr. Judy told Nate and me to guard ourselves against Satan every morning.

Riel stepped down from the podium and made his way to the head of the aisle for communion. We sang a song, prayed again, listened to Ash's concluding blessing, and then it was time to go.

I stood and followed the crowd toward the lobby. I wanted to chat with Riel again, but it seemed everyone did, a long line forming in front of him.

Settling for a wave instead, I practically ran to Nate's room to check on him. I didn't bother knocking, but instantly regretted not doing so. I had grown accustomed to seeing Nate in all sorts of disorder—especially after a hard-core Cantankerous Monkey Squad performance where he'd sweat out half of his body fat—but today was different. He lay on top of the tangled covers, brown hair matted in clumps on his forehead, arms and legs flopped wide across the bed in a Jesus-on-the-cross pose, fully dressed in yesterday's clothes, Vans still on his feet and covered in caked mud.

I stopped dead in my tracks. "What the heck?" I yelled, glancing around his room, searching for any answers to the million questions running through my mind.

He jumped up. "What time is it?"

I narrowed my eyes. "Um, time to call your girlfriend back."

He headed to his closet and pulled his dirty shirt over his head, then changed into a clean white one. "Sorry about that. I was just busy with Grace."

"Oh." I felt like someone punched me in the face. I held back tears. I wasn't the crying type, nor was I the jealous or yelling type, but here I was doing all three. I blinked a few times, took a calming breath, and stared up at him.

His pale blue gaze met mine, his expression all too serious, which sent a spike of anxiety through me. "It wasn't like that."

I bit my lip. I didn't remember accusing him of anything. I fumbled to think of the right words around my excessive swallowing, still fighting the urge to not yell. "Um, maybe I should go."

"Olga." He grabbed my arm as I walked by. "She needed my help. I was just doing my job."

"I know what your job is." Even I could hear the anger in my voice.

He released my arm and turned to his closet again, pulling a pair of dark jeans off a hanger. "I knew you were fine. You can take care of yourself."

Already, I felt like he didn't need me anymore. But I refused to shed any tears or give myself away, because I still needed him.

I cleared my throat. "Well, you're right, I can take of myself. But not everybody can… like Grace, and Conner."

"Conner?" He snorted, and I imitated the sound right back to him. Then he sighed, slipping out of his shoes.

"I've actually been thinking about trying to find a way to see him."

He raised his eyebrows. "You don't say." He pulled his pants off then, not bothering to change his boxers before pulling on the fresh pair of jeans.

Maybe for the first time, the sight of him in his boxers didn't send my pulse into overdrive.

All I could think about was that he didn't change his underwear. *Gross.* I looked away for a moment, but not for long. I could never keep my eyes off him for long.

"Yeah, I mean now that we know we're in the Underworld, I figure Conner is here somewhere. I'm betting on Juvie. Maybe if we searched Dr. Judy's office"—I paused as a wave of irritation moved across Nate's face.

He studied me for a moment, then turned his attention to putting his shoes back on, brushing off some of the dirt and making a huge mess on the floor in the process. "I can't deal with this right now. I'm meeting Grace for breakfast, and then we have school."

My cheeks were hot, I could feel the anger there, but all I did was give a tight nod. "Okay, but can you at least tell me what you think of the idea first? Will you help me search for some information?" My gaze pleaded with him to understand.

"You want to know what I think? I think your judgment is impaired. You'll compromise our entire mission!"

He grabbed his book bag off the floor.

I tried not to look too alarmed at his response. "Whatever. We'll talk more about things later, I guess. But shouldn't I come with you to breakfast? I thought Grace was an assignment for *both* of us."

"She was—but I don't know—you're ready to go into a realm you're not supposed to be in. Now, you won't get a lecture on ethics from me when it comes to helping someone you love. But it's obvious you're not thinking clearly, not focused. The Grace job may be better suited for a solo."

I laughed, hiding my hurt. "This is total crap! I got one shot, and now you're saying I'm out? Where were you two all night anyway? What happened to you?"

Nate sighed heavily and slumped down, his back against the wall. "Grace landed us in jail, faux jail, I guess. The whole thing was stupid, but it all felt so real, so when they gave me my one phone call, I dialed my parents' number." He barked out a laugh. "And Grace and I stayed up all night talking about things we've done that our parents will never forgive. I asked her, how about drag racing on your way home the last day of school? And the worst thing isn't totaling Dad's Monte Carlo. It isn't going down to the county jail after a hospital visit, booking me, throwing me in a holding cell with a bunch of other criminals. It isn't staying there the whole night and trying to sleep on a hard wooden bench like the one we're on."

I placed my hand on his shoulder, but he shooed my touch away.

"It's not being stripped naked and giving up my clothes and possessions and putting on an orange jumpsuit. It's not going up in front of the judge who sets the bail and punishment. It's not the car ride home with my parents."

I felt a weight in my stomach as he looked up at me guiltily. Breathing was difficult, and I didn't know how he managed to continue.

"The worst part is being spared from experiencing any of that! Instead, you find out you're dead, and you killed another kid in the accident."

"You said all of that to Grace?"

He hesitated a moment before answering. "Not the part about being dead." He stood up and gripped my arms, his breath a whisper against my cheek. "I'm sorry for judging you. I shouldn't be here either, training to be a spirit guide. Why did I think I could ever do this? Losing control over my own destiny is one thing, but to ruin others? There's no way I can help anyone else after what I did."

Wrapping my arm around his shoulders, I told him, "You helped me, more than words could ever express."

Nate shook his head and shoved my arm off his shoulder, then waved his hands frantically in the air. "That was before I knew what was really going on!"

He kicked the wall with his shoe, fists clenched.

I moved in front of Nate and shoved him. Hard. "Snap out of it! Do you even remember all the things you said to me during the past year? Did you actually mean a single line you fed me?" My adrenaline spiked, perspiration erupting all over me at once. "You used to know about mercy, about promises, about forgiving others and ourselves, about having a little faith. Now you're just somebody looking to throw a pity party. It's like Grace has warped you with her negativity after one day! You need to pull yourself together and lead by example when *we* meet our assignment for breakfast. We can't let her bring us down. We have to bring her up. Otherwise, you fail. Otherwise, I fail, too."

I sucked in a deep breath, wondering if I'd gone too far. Ever since Conner died, I tried to jump into things with my heart before my head could tell me no. But that was before I knew *I* was dead, *Nate* was dead.

There was nothing I could do about that though. Maybe I didn't want to be alive anyway. Maybe I would've never gotten over Conner's death without Nate, and I couldn't have met Nate unless I died. I'd made mistakes in my past life that I was determined not to repeat. I felt alive when I hung around Nate, and the time had come to return the favor. He had brought the passionate side out in me, but one look at him now painted a different picture. Nate looked… destroyed, but he was also nodding.

"You're right. I'm so sorry. I'll see you later, okay?"

Any delusion I had about getting through to him vanished as I watched him walk out the door without me. At least I managed to hold back my tears until he was out of sight.

CHAPTER NINE

"Many of the truths we cling to
depend greatly upon our own point of view."
—Obi-Wan

The air was hot and humid this Saturday night, flavored with the scent of cocktails, chocolate covered strawberries, and smelly gourmet cheeses. Grace had invited us—well, she'd invited Nate, but I was part of this so I had to tag along—to a charity ball at the Biltmore Estate in Asheville, the largest privately owned home in America. Her dad worked for a nonprofit, and his organization was one of the beneficiaries of the event, so we all got in for free. The function was held outdoors with live music and dancing, wine tasting, hors d'oeuvres, and an elegant dinner, the cavernous grounds lit up with thousands of twinkle lights that blended in with the stars above. It was just the right setting for the charity date auction, featuring Asheville's most eligible bachelors.

Riel had dressed Nate and me for the event, and for a guy who spent his time in robes, he'd done a really good job. My white spaghetti strapped dress cascaded down to my ankles and would've dragged across the ground if it weren't for the four-inch gold heels I wore. With a golden sash tied snugly around my waist, Nate had told me before we left that I looked like a present that needed to be unwrapped. Then, he scooped me into his arms and kissed me. The small show of affection was the only attention I'd received all week from him, and I hoped he wouldn't be able to keep his hands off me when the event ended later. I certainly couldn't keep my gaze off him. He looked completely 'rock and roll' in his striped black and white blazer, slim fitting black button down shirt, black pants with a leather belt featuring silver bling embellishments, and military style lace up boots. He looked beyond gorgeous, and our ensembles made me long for the prom night we never really had, even though this event was way fancier than our Grand Haven High School dance.

All in all, the evening wasn't half-bad, my straightened hair even remained frizz-free as the three of us boogied on the dance floor to the jazz band. Another guy managed to steal a brief dance with Grace, offering me some sweet relief. As Nate spun and twirled me around, my face hurt from smiling so wildly. I couldn't help but continue to think of our prom, the disco ball rotating above us when we professed our love for each other the first time.

All too quickly, Grace's dad swooped upon us, shouting over the music about a bachelor who didn't show up.

"Oh, you should totally do it!" Grace said to Nate. Before he could reject the idea, she pulled her dad and Nate aside and volunteered him.

As Grace and I sat on the lawn while Nate was carted backstage, I thought our time alone together might be a good opportunity for a girl talk. "Truth or dare?"

She shook her head. "Neither. I don't play games."

Oh, really? Then what are you doing with my boyfriend? I plastered a smile on my face. "Oh, come on. It'll be fun."

Grace's returning smile seemed forced as well. "Usually, I'd go with dare, but I'm too tired. Hit me up."

"What was your latest wish?"

She chewed her lip. "To die."

"Grace."

"What? Why does everything I say seem to put you on edge? If you don't want honesty, then don't play."

"Good point."

"And I don't want any of your encouragements either."

I raised an eyebrow at her. "Fine. My turn. Truth, please."

She sighed, and I wished she didn't look so absurdly vulnerable. If Nate's track record stayed true to form… I sighed, too. He was a sucker for the bird with a broken wing.

"Okay, name your dream job."

I blinked at her. If she only knew about my real job and how there was no way I'd ever have another one. "Um, a writer."

"Nice. What do you want to write? Love stories?"

Shrugging, I said, "Probably not. I haven't had much luck with love. I mean, I've only ever had one boyfriend."

Grace dug in her purse for something and eventually pulled out a tube of lip-gloss. "Oh, right. The guy that died?"

My eyes held back tears from the effort of keeping another part of my life a secret from her…the moment that ultimately landed me here as her spirit guide in the first place. "Yes, that guy. What about you? Have you dated much?"

She fluffed her long chestnut hair so that her locks tumbled about her shoulders in subtle waves, and I wondered why she acted like she was getting ready for a date. "I've actually never had a boyfriend. I've gone on lots of dates, even made it to date number three with the same guy once and snuck him into my bedroom through my window."

She's like the female version of Conner. A quivery sensation rippled through me like it always did when I thought of him, which lately was more and more. I took a deep breath and focused on Grace. "How'd that turn out?"

She laughed, and I noticed she had one of those really nice musical laughs. "Well, Dad heard something and knocked on my door to investigate. I shoved the boy into my closet, but Dad insisted on checking in there, and when he did, the guy went flying past him, straight out my window."

Nodding, I said, "I hope your bedroom was on the first floor."

Grace retrieved a compact from her purse and checked her reflection in the little mirror. "Nope, second story window. He broke his arm."

"Ouch."

Pressing some powder on her face, she said, "Better than dead, and six feet under is exactly where he'd be now if my daddy got a hold of him that night."

I winced at her choice of words. "Sounds like a great dad. Are you guys close?"

But before she could answer, the auctioneer introduced Nate as one of Asheville's most eligible bachelors and opened the bidding at ten dollars.

Grace jumped to her feet. "Ten!"

I yanked on her black and white polka dot chiffon mini dress. "What are you doing?"

"Bidding! I volunteered him for this thing, it's the least I can do!"

"Do I have fifteen?"

Crickets. *Seriously? Was Riel just messing with this Limbo experiment, because my man was a catch!*

"Take your shirt off!" Grace yelled.

The auctioneer's lips curved instantly into a devilish smile. "Oh, we have a request from your bidder. Do you have six pack abs under that suit? Because if you do, I think we'd all like to see them."

Now that got the crowd going, everyone hooting and hollering.

"Are you serious?" Nate asked, tapping the buttons on his black shirt.

"One hundred percent!"

"Oh my gosh, I don't think I can do that." His face turned beat red.

"Come on, it's for charity!"

The crowd started chanting, "Take it off! Take it off! Take it off!"

Slowly, Nate unbuttoned his blazer, then his shirt, and tossed both of them to stage left. A lean, muscular body, nicely defined biceps, and a tanned set of abs proved he could make any girl swoon.

After that display, he didn't need any help from Grace. Six other teenage girls were already engaging in a bidding war, and the price quickly escalated to ninety-five dollars.

"One hundred dollars!" Grace called out as the other girls checked their purses, frowning.

"One hundred dollars going once, one hundred dollars going twice? Sold to the pretty girl in the retro style dress in the back. Congratulations."

"Why did you do that?" I asked her as everyone applauded.

She shrugged. "I don't know. I thought it would be funny to see him sweating on the stage in front of everyone. Tell me that wasn't priceless when the moderator made him take his shirt off!"

I cleared my throat. "No, I mean, why did you bid on him? Do you like him?"

Grace rolled her eyes. "Please, you guys are so into Star Wars, I was doing those poor girls a favor. Any one of them would've been bored out of her mind. A girl can only hear the words, 'Han shot first,' so many times before she finally snaps."

A wave of irritation washed over me. "I hear ya, I do. But I just don't think you're at a place in your life right now where you should be going on dates with anyone, no matter how innocent your intentions."

And just like that, awkwardness tore through the air like a bullet, punctuated by the piercing stare Grace shot me with. "You know what? You really need to relax. Why don't you drop out of Biology and take a yoga class or something?"

"Excuse me?" I said after a long pause.

"You're excused."

"Grace, you don't—"

"Stop! *You don't* get to sound so sad after saying my name, and you've used that tone with me every day this week. Yeah, I told you a few things about my life. But quit pretending like you know how to save me."

"I'm sorry." I bit my lip. "But I know what it's like to lose someone you love, and I—"

"Just leave me alone, okay? You can go Oprah someone else."

As I watched Grace walk up to the stage to collect her date—*my boyfriend*—I tried to think in what circumstance this could be construed as positive. I couldn't think of any.

A few minutes later, Nate led Grace back to our blanket on the grass. "Of all the tomfoolery these rich snobs think up, this one is my favorite," she told him. "So, are you ready?"

"Ready for what?" I asked.

She gave me a cold stare. "For our date."

"Now?" I shrieked, feeling a rush of panic. "But what will I do?"

Grace gestured to the crowd. "Look at all the hot single guys out here. I'm sure you can find something, or someone, to occupy your time." She sighed. "Olga, there are lots of fish in the sea. This world is swim or sink. It's time you put yourself out there."

"I don't like swimming," I muttered dryly, which was true. What I really wanted to retort was, *Oh, who's Oprahing who now*?

But I bit my tongue.

"Whatever. All I know is I plan on getting my money's worth tonight." She studied Nate's profile, looking him up and down. "Your brother is quite the catch. Shall we?"

Nate held out his arm, and she placed her hand on his bicep. At least his clothes were back on.

"It's getting late, Nate. We should head back home."

I wished he would say something, agree with me. Instead, he just stood there, one hand stuffed into the pocket of his pants, the other hand clenched in a fist as Grace kept a firm grip on his arm while checking her cell phone.

"Gosh, what are you, his mother? It's like, nine o'clock. Relax."

Looking at Nate only, I asked, "Can I please speak with you for a moment, alone?"

"Sure." His deep voice sounded low and serious, and slightly uneven. "I'll be right back," he told Grace. His hand on her back felt like a slap across my face.

We walked a good hundred meters away from Grace before stopping behind a tree, out of her line of stalker vision.

"What's up?" His blue eyes danced like flames in the night, giving my stomach butterflies despite my anger.

"So, you're going through with this date?"

The band switched gears, the music slowing. Nate calmly reached out and grabbed my hand, pulling me toward him and swaying us hypnotically to the steady rhythm. "Hey, quit acting like I did something wrong. You're my girlfriend. I love *you*, nobody else." He grazed my forehead with a kiss that was full of brotherly love, then leaned back to look at me.

I rolled my eyes, resenting the fact that I even needed his reassurance, resenting the fact that I couldn't melt properly at the touch of his body against mine because of our undercover status.

"Oh, come on, Olga. What do you think is going to happen?" A quick smile teased his mouth. "She paid a lot of money for a date with me. What's the difference if I go now or later?"

"A lot of money? This isn't even real." Whispering instead of yelling took all my strength.

"Exactly. So don't make this into a big deal. We'll sit and talk just like we have all week long. She's finally beginning to open up to me. I can't waste this opportunity."

"No."

"Thanks. I'll catch up with you later. Don't wait up for me."

I didn't mean the no as an agreement. I meant the no as in 'you-can't-go,' but I quickly realized I didn't have a say in what he did anymore.

He bent down and kissed my forehead again, whispering, "I'd never do anything to hurt you."

Watching him walk away, all I could think was that hurting each other was all we did these days.

Chapter Ten

I sank down to the grass, listening to the wail of the wind picking up. I didn't know what to do. No amount of life lessons from bucket lists had prepared me for this. Three weeks ago, I'd learned I was dead, but I thought I still had Nate. But ever since he'd met Grace, he'd barely managed to return my phone calls or texts, let alone spend any real time with me. Oh sure, we'd see each other at school, pass each other in the halls at headquarters while he came and went. Each encounter brought more tension between us. Each time he ran off to be with Grace, I felt more uncertain about the status of our relationship.

The night of the charity auction, I'd stuck around for a while, enduring a quiet dinner by myself, concentrating on eating my food properly without spilling any on the dress Riel gave me. Afterward, I watched Nate stroll leisurely around the grounds with Grace from afar. When they took a private carriage ride, I'd finally had enough and vanished back to headquarters.

Just last night, I'd wandered into his room and lay on his bed, trying to chat with him, hoping to seem provocative to him once again. Instead, he seemed irritated by my presence, to the point that I left after a painful half hour.

How had I managed to lose the two guys I cared about most in this world? I didn't know which one stung worse: not being able to save Conner, or watching Nate willingly slip away from me.

Actually, the worst part was thinking about both of them all the time. I loved them both so much; I was finally realizing that, not glossing over that fact. Maybe the distance from Nate is what it took me to acknowledge that

I didn't just love Conner; I was still *in* love with him. And I had no idea how to rectify those feelings. Not that my emotions mattered, since one boy hardly wanted anything to do with me these days, and the other, I still had no idea how to find. I was too depressed to form a plan, and there was no Jedi Order around to pull me out of my funk this time.

There's always Riel. I stared at the horizon, laughing at the thought.

Delusion was taking over. I shook my head. Sighing, I listened to the bossy voice of my conscience and got to my feet. I couldn't waste time and energy sitting under a tree feeling sorry for myself. My instincts would see me through the end of this; intuition had brought me this far. Somehow, I'd figure out a way to locate Conner, with or without Nate. The little devil on my shoulder also reminded me of everything my instincts caused me to lose, but I shrugged off the condemnation. I had to focus on the positives, not the negatives, if I was going to survive the day. Plus, two negatives equaled a positive, I told myself. So even if I lost both of the great loves of my life, I'd truly be free to become a kick-butt spirit guide and help others through their problems instead of creating my own. A sense of purpose drove me forward once more.

Thank you, God, that even though I stumble, I will not fall. Your loving hands are there to hold me up.

I rounded the corner of headquarters and envied all the spirit guides eating and drinking at the outdoor tables together. Why hadn't I thought to make any friends here yet? I started toward one of the small crowds, but then I heard the pounding of feet from behind, and I turned to see Riel. His face was always white, but this time the color seemed paler, full of concern.

"Olga Gay Worontzoff, what are you doing?"

My heart lurched. "What do you mean?"

He moved forward, coming to stop mere inches from me. "I've flown all over these grounds looking for you. You haven't been in your room. I didn't see you in Grace's Limbo plane. I've been worried you got in over that curly red head of yours."

I swallowed hard. "Why would you worry about that?"

He looked at me wearily. "I've noticed you and Nate haven't spent a lot of time together. I asked him about Grace, and he said she had become a solo project of his. I wanted to make sure you were okay."

I raised my eyebrows. "Oh, right. As my boss, I guess you're required to check up on me from time to time."

"Not just as your boss." His eyes searched my face, and they looked like they could see through to my soul. "As your… your friend."

A feeling of great sadness washed over me. I needed a friend, but I didn't want anyone's pity. "Well, anyway, I guess you should assign me a new case soon."

Before I knew what was happening, in one swift motion he caught me by the waist and took to the sky with his wings spread wide, holding me securely in his arms.

"Riel!" I shrieked, grabbing onto the front of his robe as he glided through the clouds. Somehow, we were already at airplane level height. "What are you doing?"

"I'm cheering you up. Nothing like an early morning flight to clear away the sadness!"

We soared over headquarters, the nearby storage facility, the pond with its fountain and quacking ducks, and the rolling green hills. The wind tore through my hair, and I thought of my old dog, Daisy, who used to love riding around town with her head out the window.

Sunshine, flowers, the fresh breeze, all of the things I was grateful for when I was alive were still here in death. As Riel kept flying, I realized the headquarters campus was far wider than I ever imagined. There were fruit trees bordering a garden full of vegetables, rose arbors complete with walking trails, sparkling trees with brightly colored hammocks stretched between their branches, a cozy brick courtyard surrounded by potted plants of all descriptions, a long dock beside a serene fishing pond with a fire pit and wrought-iron picnic tables to the side, yard swings on wooden stands with awnings positioned for shade, cushioned plastic lounges, and an open barn with horses inside. Everywhere I looked, angels and spirit guides of all cultures were joined together enjoying God's creation just as humans did on Earth, maybe even more so. It's definitely not what I'd pictured Heaven being like. When I was human, I just thought the Heavenly realm would be this place where harps played all day while we reclined on some clouds. In truth, headquarters was like a busy city, but held the added radiance of a rare jewel and the glory of God.

I looked up at Riel to find him staring down at me.

"What are you thinking about?" he asked.

"How I never knew any of this was here. I just thought I was at headquarters to do my job."

He dipped us lower to the ground, and my hands instinctively tightened on his robe until he deposited us gently onto the fishing dock. “Have a seat,” he said. He sat, pushing his robe to the side with a flourish and dipping his feet into the pond as his wings folded in on his back.

I squinted my eyes at the sun and wondered how to casually chat with an angel. “Are you a fisherman?” I asked, sitting next to him a little closer than I was used to, my feet dangling but not touching the water.

He laughed, and I realized it was the first time I’d heard him truly laugh. The sound was musical, like wind chimes swaying in the breeze. “We’re all fishing for something.”

I dipped my fingers into the pond and rubbed some water over my face. In the distance, a plunging waterfall fought its way down a mountain and crashed against giant rocks at the bottom. “Why is all this stuff here?”

Riel kept his eyes on me, like he was trying to figure something out. “Why not? You humans don’t seem to understand that you’re dead a lot longer than you’re alive. Doesn’t it make sense for our Creator to take the same things you enjoyed about Earth and place them in the afterlife?”

The breeze played with my red hair, dancing like flames against my back and shoulders. “I guess.”

“You want to go for a swim?”

I glanced out at the water. “We don’t have our bathing suits.”

Riel’s smile widened as he splashed me. “Come on. You’re dead. Live a little.”

Holding his gaze, I smiled back. “Funny. I didn’t know angels had a sense of humor.”

“I joke around all the time,” Riel mused, straightening his back.

I pointed at him. “More like ridicule.”

“Didn’t your mother ever tell you it’s not polite to point?” He winked at me, and then before I knew it, he stood up, lifted me from behind, and launched me into the lake.

The water felt just right. Actually, the cold fluidity of water on my skin as it seeped through my clothes felt more than just right. Still under water, I watched some minnows scuttle between the rocks at the bottom. The lake was their safe haven, and it held that same feeling of refuge for me, too.

The moment I surfaced, Riel jumped in and yelled, “Cannonball!”

After wiping the splash off my face, I turned to him. “What was all that about?”

Shrugging slightly, he said, "You looked too serious. I was trying to help. Did it work?"

"Yes." I looked at him sideways and added thanks as an afterthought.

"No thanks needed." We bobbed around in the water together. "Promise me you'll try to enjoy yourself a little bit more. In fact, why don't you take the week off before I give you another assignment? You've been through a lot."

More than you know. I smiled as I inhaled the peaty smell of seaweed and listened to the gentle lapping of water hitting the shoreline.

"Hey, you want to race?"

He regarded me with a smirk. "Oh, I feel such pathos for you, thinking you could actually race me with even the slightest chance of winning!"

"Ha! You forget our Creator endowed me with much logos, so maybe I know a way to outsmart you like Tortoise did with Hare."

Riel circled me in the water like a shark about to attack its prey. "I suppose if I possess much ethos, then I should just let you win."

I laughed, a deep belly laugh, and something inside me melted. It wasn't just the fond memories of high school English lectures making me feel all warm inside. Maybe I had been wrong about Riel. This whole time, I'd assumed he didn't feel the same things humans feel. But if that were true, then why was he looking at me like he cared about me more than I cared about myself? It seemed impossible that he could feel so much toward me… given his high rank and my inferior status.

"I don't want your pity, but I forfeit. I know a lost cause when I see one."

He popped his wings out, floating just above the water.

I shielded my eyes. He shone brighter than the sun.

"Have it your way then."

His hands clamped around my waist, surprisingly warm. He launched us into the sky again, the reflection of his wings against the light and water blinding me for a second. After a few blinks, I looked below to everything blooming around us, and I found it suddenly easy to focus on the blessings in my life, surrounded by paradise. When we landed outside of headquarters, I was air dried and renewed, as if I'd left my worries up in the clouds.

"I have some work to get back to, but don't be a stranger." Riel breathed the words over my cheek. "And I want you to meditate on chapters thirteen and fourteen in the book of Corinthians. Love should run deeper than romantic feelings. God's love never gives up, never fails, and never runs out on you. Remember that."

I reached out for his arm and stopped him. "Riel? Are there ever any meteor showers around here? I mean, is that something you could orchestrate?"

For a moment, he just stood there, studying me. "If it would make you happy," he said finally.

I nodded.

"Done. The shower will run from nine to ten tonight." He spun around and walked through the door.

All day I ruminated over the love chapters Riel told me to read. The whole time I formulated my plan. I left a note on Nate's door, inviting him to meet me outside of headquarters at eight o'clock sharp for a romantic rendezvous. I didn't realize how much I'd expected him not to show up until I was so surprised when he did. But I felt inexpressibly happy to see him walking toward me.

He wore army green cargo shorts and a gray T-shirt that said 'Reckless.' His face appeared groggy, but a look of joy spread over his features when he spotted me.

He held up the invitation, waving my card in the air. "Well, this was unexpected."

"What's surprising is that you didn't already have plans tonight."

Flinching at my comment, he said, "Actually, I did. I'm probably ruining someone else's night by being here with you."

I took a step back, away from him. "Meaning Grace, right? Look, you didn't have to come." The picnic basket I held suddenly felt a thousand pounds heavier.

Closing the distance between us, he grabbed my hand. "Yes, I did. I missed you."

I shut my eyes—it'd been so long since we touched. "Me, too."

He leaned down and kissed my cheek. "So, where are you taking me tonight?"

"I'll show you."

Picturing the lake I visited with Riel earlier, I blinked hard and a moment later, we arrived on the dock. I set the picnic basket down so I could gesture the appropriate "Ta-da!" with my arms spread wide.

His gaze was on me, questioning. "What's this?"

"Apparently, there's a big old world right here at headquarters we haven't explored yet."

He beamed at me. "Cool."

We stared at each other for a long minute, and inside I felt like we were saying all the things we wanted to say but for some reason couldn't. My heart rate elevated when he leaned down to kiss me, sliding his hand out of his pocket and resting it on my hip. I lifted my own hands to his arms, his muscles tight and defined under my grip. I opened my eyes because this pressing need to look at him took over, and, startled to see his eyes open, I accidentally bit his bottom lip.

"Hey!"

"Sorry. Are you hurt?"

"We don't feel pain anymore, remember? Well, at least not the physical kind."

"Do you always kiss me with your eyes open?"

He flung an arm around my shoulder, steering us down the beach. Bending his head, breaths fluttered against my ear as he whispered, "Sometimes I just can't stop myself from staring at your gorgeous face."

I shoved him lightly. "Stop lying."

Nate frowned. "If you don't love yourself, how are you ever gonna love me?"

My conversations with Riel flashed in my mind. "I do love you. So much."

He shook his head. "Then do me a solid, and repeat after me. I am a generous, kind, smart, loving and yes, beautiful, human being."

Out of all those adjectives, human being seemed the most wrong. But I didn't feel like repeating him anyway. Instead, I hurtled myself at him, my lips immediately finding his. I closed my eyes and kept them closed when I kissed him this time.

When he pulled away, I wondered how everything could feel so miserable and magical at the same time. Nate studied me for a moment, his ocean blue eyes wide open, like fire melting my heart. My lips crushed against his once more, the usual tenderness gone as my hands slid under his shirt to trace the hard skin there. I sensed the passion pressing us closer as his arms went around my neck, his hands gripping my hair, startling me. I wondered if spiritually binding meant we were allowed to…ugh, I didn't want to think, I just wanted to do. I'd prove to myself and to him that I still loved him, no matter how much I still thought about Conner. I broke my lips away from Nate's, then trailed kisses down his neck.

Nate moaned, then chuckled. "You don't usually, wait, change that to never, attack me like this. What's gotten into you?"

"Attack?" I felt discouraged by his choice of words and pulled away a little to study his face. Maybe he hadn't been enjoying himself as much as I had.

He kissed the top of my head. "I don't want to feel like I'm taking advantage of a bad situation." Another kiss, on my eyelid this time. "Things have been… off with us lately. I think we should talk, don't you?" And one last kiss on the tip of my nose.

Why did it feel like the kiss of death?

I nodded, letting him lead me back to the dock in silence, wondering why he was acting so mysterious all the time. What kind of boyfriend stops a heated make out session? *One who's not into you anymore.*

"Shall we?" I plopped down next to the picnic basket, then pulled off my sandals before lightly kicking the tips of my toes in the water.

He sat down next to me on the edge of the pier, but not close enough for our bodies to touch. I tried to chalk that up to meaning nothing, but knew it meant everything.

"What's wrong?" I asked him.

"Nothing." Nate frowned, then looked at the basket. "What's in there, anyway?"

Carefully, I unpacked our dinner, setting it out on cloth napkins I laid behind us. "We have some baguettes, some cheese, and some ham for the main meal. One hundred percent pure milk chocolate squares for dessert, and—"

"What are you playing at?"

I leaned back. "Huh?"

"Oh, like you don't know chocolate is a natural aphrodisiac."

Laughing, I felt my cheeks flush. "Whatever. I have a sunset picnic overlooking a beautiful lake surrounded by mountains, followed by a meteor shower. Do I really need chocolate to sweeten the deal?"

He smiled, his gaze scanning the lake. "Nope, you don't."

"But if I did need more reinforcements, I also have this." I pulled out a bottle of wine. "I've never drank any. Have you?"

Nodding his head, he said, "Yup, but where'd you get that from?"

I unscrewed the cap. "Swiped it off the communion table. There's hardly any of it left anyway."

Nate shook his head like I just said the most insane thing ever. "Do you *want* to go to H-E-double hockey sticks?"

"Whatever. It's not a big deal."

"Isn't thou shall not steal like the seventh or eighth commandment?"

I waggled my eyebrows at him. "And that's not the only commandment I may break tonight."

"I guess I should shut up then, if I know what's good for me." He grabbed the bottle and took a swig, then handed it back to me and made a sandwich. "Here you go, my lady."

A deer sprinted across the grass in the distance as I took a bite. I couldn't think of a more perfect setting to reaffirm our feelings for one another.

I expected Nate to fix himself a sandwich next, but instead he picked up a stray pebble on the pier and skipped the rock over the lake. Once. Twice. Three times before he blurted out, "I'm sorry. I'm sorry for being so distant."

I grabbed the bottle of wine and took my first sip, wondering if I could get drunk… if alcohol could still have the same effect on our bodies here. "Yeah, but why have you been trying to put so much distance between us? I thought you were looking forward to being spirit guides together."

He sighed, and then turned to face me. "Over the past few weeks, ever since we learned about Dr. Judy's secret, it just seemed like there were two different sides to our relationship. I mean, I was looking forward to spending forever with you, no matter what forever entailed. But when I would hold your hand, hold *you*, look into your eyes… I didn't see the same kind of love for me I saw before." He paused for a moment, his face a wrestling match of competing emotions. "There's all this heat between us that wasn't there before, like just a minute ago and all those nights at headquarters in your room during our week of training, but it feels like a distraction, like you were letting yourself go so you wouldn't have to think about something."

I played with the cap on the wine bottle. "I thought you were having fun."

"I was. But I also know when there's something on your mind, and it hurts me when you keep things from me."

The ugly truth slapped me in the face, daring me to tell him how I really felt about Conner. But I sat there and watched Nate's face change right before me, expecting the worse, and I just couldn't do that to him. So of course, I put up my best defense and took the attention away from me. "That system works both ways you know. You leave me in the dark about everything these days."

He lifted his hands in the air, palms facing me. "Believe me, I know. I feel so much better now that I got that off my chest. You know I'm a bit weak, so with that on my chest, it was pretty hard to breathe."

And there went his defense mechanism: sarcasm. And it was confirmation he was holding back information from me, too. I just didn't know if his restraint had to do with Grace or something else.

We mainly just sat in silence the rest of the evening. Well, not exactly silence since he'd brought his iPod with him and proceeded to play the entire Imagine Dragons album while we watched the meteor shower. As I listened to *Radioactive*, their song about waking up to a new age, I kept thinking how this new age felt very familiar. The first date Nate and I had was watching a meteor shower at his house. That date ended badly, because losing Conner had still felt like the apocalypse, and I just couldn't deal.

Tonight, just like that first 'date', I ended up crying myself to sleep alone in my room.

History loved to repeat itself.

CHAPTER ELEVEN

"It's no wonder that truth is stranger than fiction.
Fiction has to make sense."
—Mark Twain

All night I tossed and turned, worrying about where Conner was and what he might be doing and what I didn't say to Nate the night before. At school, Nate still sat with Grace in our math class. I guessed since he took her on as a solo mission, and I'd be reassigned to someone else by next week, I didn't need to bother with school anymore. I knew most people wouldn't, but most people didn't actually enjoy Algebra II and Biology like I did either.

During our ten minute break between classes, I bumped into Grace while leaving the bathroom.

"Hey." *Stay cool. Don't act like a jealous girlfriend.*

"Hey." She coughed and shuffled to a stall.

"Wait. I was wondering, do you want to grab some lunch with me after school today?"

The way she looked at me, I could just tell she didn't like me. "Um, Nate and I are actually skipping Biology and going to take a nap in the park, and then we're going out to eat. I'm really tired and hungry after last night."

Last night? The way she said those words gave me chills, alarming me to a truth I didn't want to hear about.

"What happened last night?"

She slowly opened one of the bathroom doors. "Nothing. We were just out all night. I told him we're allowed two absences during summer session, so we're taking the second one today. No biggie. I'll see ya later."

My chills disappeared, an angry heat spreading through my core as I pictured them out together, and then him keeping that little tidbit from me.

I marched into the hallway and spotted Nate waiting on a wooden bench by the lockers. "Where were you last night?"

"Excuse me?" His eyebrows squished together.

"I went looking for you after our date." Two could play the lying game. "You weren't in your room, and I couldn't find you anywhere."

His gaze darted everywhere but me. "What are you, the RA of the spirit guide dorms now?" He laughed, like the whole thing was a joke, but he stopped after a second when he noticed my silence.

Finally, I said, "Maybe I am. Had to find something to occupy my time since you won't let me help you. Are you gonna tell me where you were with Grace or not?"

Grace materialized in the hallway as if on cue, but thankfully maintained her distance.

"Can we do this later? Grace and I made plans, and she's waiting."

"You know, I'm getting really tired of that excuse. Are you just sick of me or something?"

Nate stood up. "I'm sick of you acting like I killed your dog every time I run into you."

I shook my head. "My dog died a long time ago."

"You're missing the point."

Grasping his chin between my thumb and forefinger, I forced him to look me in the eye. "No, what I'm missing is *you.* I mean, what is up? You're not acting like yourself at all."

He closed his eyes, completely shutting me out. "And you are?"

The bell rang, and Nate reached into his pocket. "Here, this is for you."

Watching him go, I wanted to crumple up his card and hurl the envelope at him without even reading his words, but I just stood there, biting my tongue.

Deciding there was no point in going to Biology, I instead lounged on the same outside bench where I first met Grace three weeks ago and opened Nate's card.

Olga,

Thanks for the date last night. You've made the last year of my 'life' the best ever. I want to do the same for you. You are the main reason I do everything. I don't care if our whole year was real or not, I'll never forget all the things we did together. No one has touched my life like you have. I hope that I can always be a part of your forever. I know life, and even death, isn't fair. Remember when we listened to Demons by Imagine Dragons last night? The song spoke of hiding the truth to shelter someone he loved. I want to protect you so badly, Olga. I'll do anything to accomplish that task. We all have our secrets, our demons, don't we? Lately, I feel like you only show the best parts of yourself to me and hide the worst. But remember that I will always love all of you, with all my heart.

~Nate

What the heck? His words were so cryptic and sounded a lot like goodbye. I couldn't decipher his hidden meaning, and I was too jacked up to sit around all day thinking about things I didn't understand.

Sighing, I unzipped my backpack and took out the Daily Meditation Guide, hoping for inspiration. Today's scripture came from the book of Psalms, chapter twenty, verses four and five.

"May the Lord grant you your heart's desire, and fulfill all your plans… May the Lord fulfill all your petitions."

Underneath, there was some blank space to journal on, so I uncapped my pen. For a moment, I hesitated over putting my plans down on paper, but then I figured God could probably read the journal of my mind anyway. After all, He knew me better than I knew myself, right?

I think it's funny this verse is my meditation today. It's like a sign showing me that finding Conner is what I will do. From the time I was a little girl, God has given me the desires of my heart, no matter how childish, like getting a new bike for Christmas. Over the years, I had a good family, a good education, good friends, and good coffee. What more could a girl ask for? But it's time to let go of denial and acknowledge the vast empty hole in my heart that is exactly Conner Anderson shaped. I thought Nate had filled the void, and in many ways, he did, but it was more like instituting a restraining order with a fifty-foot perimeter. He kept my heartache at bay, but his love wasn't a cure. The problem was always there. I'll never fully let go of Conner. Maybe knowing what happened to him will fix that problem, maybe not.

This past year with my list of 18 Things, Nate taught me how to get out of my hiding place and experience 'life.' And I think becoming a spirit guide is about that even more in some ways. I still don't know the details of everything here, so I have to step out in faith, and God is always pleased with that, right? He wouldn't want me to give up. I can't just sit here and waste time. Yes, I still have a job to do, but I can't just wonder what happened to Conner in the meantime. I can't be like that hamster my parents got me for my eighth birthday, running in a wheel with no forward progress.

And yes, there will probably be groaning and great gnashing of teeth to get to where he is. Yes, the path of least resistance has better coffee and chocolate, but I'm willing to give up some of my comforts to find him. I just hope I don't have to give up Heaven, or Nate. Anyway, thank you, Lord, for the blessing of your faithfulness in always hearing my prayers, even when You choose not to answer them in Your infinite wisdom. Above all else, I believe You are good and kind, and won't punish me for my curiosity when You are the One who made me who I am. I don't want to be who I was, a coward, so I'm moving forward today. I hope I have Your blessing.

I scanned over my entry, stunned I had so much to say, my writing overflowing to the next page. I didn't even notice the tear running down my cheek until I finished reading. Conner was the one constant desire in my life from such an early age, and the time to get him back had arrived.

After returning the meditation guide to my bag, I took out the cell phone issued by headquarters. The phones on Earth looked identical, only this was a smarter version of the smart phone. Actually, the cell was somewhat mind-blowing. Instead of a 2D flat display, the screen was 3D, letting me reach in and touch stuff and grab the app I wanted to use. Ash said Earth was usually ten years behind the technology in this realm. If only we had an advanced Google search or Facebook page that could help me locate Conner in the Underworld. Using voice activation instead of punching in a number, I simply said, "Call Dr. Judy."

When she picked up, relief flooded through me to discover her number was the same one I had for her during my after-death purification process. "Hi there, Dr. Judy. Olga Worontzoff here."

"I know."

"Um, right. So, how are you?"

"I was just about to ask you the same question. Nate's been updating me on Grace, but I haven't heard anything from you. Is everything okay?"

"Well, that's kinda what I'm calling about. I was wondering if I could get some advice on my love life."

Total lie. Although I could have used some tips in that area, my intention to snoop in her office for information about Conner trumped all my other needs.

"Sure thing. I'll always be here for you. I just had an appointment cancel. Can you be here in an hour?"

"That's a good question. I'm not exactly sure how to get to your office anymore."

"Just make your way back to headquarters and ask them for door number three hundred twenty-nine. The entry will pop up on the other side of the pond in front of the building. Just knock and I'll open for you."

As I made my way back to headquarters, I felt like I had lost my mind. There were so many convoluted thoughts running through my head. Like, Nate was a good guy, and he didn't deserve what I was about to do to him. But Conner and I were supposed to be together forever—that was my plan since I met him at five years old. I didn't even know who I was anymore or what I was doing or why I was doing it. Because I was dead, and I knew in my heart Conner lived in the Underworld somewhere, and I needed to find him.

I knocked on Dr. Judy's door and heard the lock slide open. She greeted me with her usual smile plastered across her face when I stepped inside. I walked over to the window. Shifting from one foot to the other, I wrung my hands, realizing the town I looked out at wasn't Grand Haven.

"What Limbo town are you counseling in today?"

"Toms River, New Jersey, near where that massive hurricane hit on your birthday last year. Why don't you take a seat?" Dr. Judy clicked the door shut behind me.

On the other side of the glass, rain poured down, fittingly, and I ignored her offer to have a seat to watch the weather instead. After a few minutes, I thought her office had sprung a leak, before realizing I'd been crying. I wiped my tears, knowing Dr. Judy could do little to comfort me this time.

"I know it's going to take some time to get adjusted," Dr. Judy said from behind me. "How are you holding up?"

"I'm good. I'm fine. I'm okay." A surge of adrenaline percolated through me as I turned away and spotted the two tall filing cabinets on either side of the wall behind her leather chair. Maybe they held some answers for me. My heart pounded a million beats per second. Sweat coated my forehead. Jumbled thoughts clouded my mind. As I took a seat, I imagined this was what a meth addict felt like.

Dr. Judy didn't look like she bought the whole 'I'm fine' bit, her forehead creasing in a look of genuine worry before her permanent smile flashed across her face. "So, are you really here because of your love life? I figured you and Nate would be solid now that you don't have to figure out that messy business of where your relationship was headed when he left for his band tour and you left for college." She raised an eyebrow. "I assumed when you called that you must have a lot of questions for me since you found out you died." She widened her ultra-calm smile. "We never did have our proper round of twenty questions that day I told you and Nate. I think you were both too shocked, which is usual. Most people just move on to Heaven and forget about any questions, though."

I scoffed. "I wish I only had twenty questions. Try a million."

"Well, hopefully I can answer some of them. All I ask for is a little patience."

"Don't tell me to be patient when you're the one who didn't tell me for a whole year that I was dead."

She reached for me, but my hands flew up, warding her off.

I gave her the you-owe-me-big-time glare. "You know how it is. Learning you're dead. You've been there before." Tears sprung to my eyes right on cue. "It's like a death sentence all over again. I haven't just lost Conner. I've lost everyone I loved."

"Through your own actions," Dr. Judy said under her breath, but I still heard her.

"You're not helping."

Her face flushed. "Sorry."

"Anyway, I've mostly been too depressed to get out of bed again after our last session. For a while, being in the classes and simulations for spirit guide training made me feel like my old self again. And getting our first assignment gave me hope, knowing it was possible to help someone else through the same experiences I went through, especially when it turned out to be your daughter. Knowing all my pain wasn't for nothing. But I don't know how to get through to Grace, and Nate has mostly taken over our assignment. I need your help to make this work. She told us that you were an alcoholic, that you drank yourself to death."

Dr. Judy let out a long sigh and walked toward the door, her shoulders slumped. When she turned and looked at me, it was as if her whole life flashed in her eyes. "I wasn't a good mother, and I've blocked out most of Grace's childhood. Time moves differently here. My life on Earth seems so long ago even though only three years have passed." She wiped a hand over her face. "I don't know if there's anything in my memories to help you connect with Grace, but I'm desperate to help my baby. To tell you the truth, the numbers aren't impressive for the success rate of spirit guides helping teens through Limbo. They're prone to hellish behavior and continuing states of crisis."

I gestured at her impatiently. "So you've given Nate and I a case doomed to fail for our first mission? Come on, there has to be some advice you can give me, some tidbit of wisdom."

"I wanted you on the case because you're the only teen spirit guides we have. I thought you'd relate to her the best. And I can give you something better. Would you like to try hypnosis on me?"

I recognized the total look of reckless urgency fueling her. "I thought you told me once that hypnotherapy was cheating."

She stepped toward the reclining chair in the corner by the window. "To deal with grief and guilt, yes. But not to retrieve memories to save your only child. Everything is fair game to help with that."

I took a deep breath. "But I don't know the first thing about hypnotizing someone." Technically, that wasn't true, but I still didn't feel qualified.

"Didn't Ruth teach you about hypnosis in your spirit guide training?" she asked over her shoulder.

I bit my lip. "She tried to put me under as a way of teaching, but I resisted. Then there was, like, two pages about hypnosis in our textbook. I think our written final exam only featured three questions on the subject."

"Well, for someone equipped with a photographic memory like you, it should be no problem."

She didn't look me in the eyes, so I couldn't gauge if she was joking.

"You seriously want me to put you under?"

"There's a script in my desk, the second drawer on the right. Read from the paper in a soft, soothing voice until I'm asleep. I'll still be in charge of what I say, but you can ask me anything, and I want you to. Whatever you might think of to help. I want to make up for my past mistakes."

I tried to protest again, but Dr. Judy raised her hand for silence, and reclined in the leather chair.

"These memories you're retrieving are painful, that's why I've buried them deep inside me. It's not everyday someone goes prodding around my psyche, so I might seem delusional. It's your job to make sure I keep digging for more information until you have what you need. Do you understand?"

Her green-eyed gaze met mine across the room, but I didn't speak. I wanted to question her about why she would let me do this to her—wanted to point out she acted more like the hormonal teenager than I did in this moment. But as I moved behind her desk, a horrific plan came to me. While under hypnosis, I could try to gather information from Dr. Judy about the real reason I came here: Conner. Hating myself, I pulled open the drawer and found the script right on top.

I forced out the words, calm and smooth. "Now, I want you to imagine a wave. A wave of relaxation just like on a boat." I stifled a groan, thinking about Conner and the accident, and laid the script on the desk before continuing. My trembling hands couldn't hold the papers steady. The daunting task looming before me seemed like too much to handle. But then I remembered my plan to retrieve the information I needed. "The same type of wave you feel on a boat. Feel this wave with each deep and fresh breath of clean air you take. As you fill your lungs, you feel a wave of relaxation going from your head to your toes, just like on a boat, your body relaxing with each wave.

"Now feel the wave again. This wave of relaxation you felt before. The same type of wave you feel on a boat. As you sway from side to side, you feel your body going deeper and deeper into hypnosis and relaxation." *Finally, hypnosis. I'm so over this boat analogy.* "You feel a wave of relaxation going from your head to your toes, and this makes you want to sleep. Sleep now. Sleep now.

"I will count backward from ten to one and you will go down a flight of stairs covered with a thick, deep carpet. When you get to the bottom, you will fall into a deep state of relaxation and hypnosis.

"Ten—you feel your body sinking into deep rich carpeting. Nine—you feel your body sinking more into this plush, deep, rich, carpeting. Eight—your body sinks now into this thick, plush, deep, rich, carpeting. Seven—let your body sink and feel yourself going into a deep sleep. Six—your body is sinking more and more now. Five—let your body and mind sleep now. Four—sleep now. Three—continue to sleep now and feel your body sinking into this thick, plush, deep, rich, carpeting. Two—sleep now. One—sleep.

"Now, I want you to lift your head, and tell me where you are."

When those green eyes opened to me, I hesitated. Dr. Judy helped me so much in the past year, but I reminded myself what brought me here in the first place.

"I'm frosting Grace's cake for her fifteenth birthday. The lights go out." Dr. Judy shook her head and closed her eyes.

"How are you feeling, Judy?" I knew how I felt: terrified. From my one real conversation with Grace, I knew this was the day Dr. Judy died. The air was cold in the room, and I wished Nate were here with me.

"I'm afraid they're going to get Grace."

I stared into the whitened face of the most responsible adult I knew and wondered what the heck she was talking about. We were entering uncharted waters here, and I knew I should say something to comfort her. "Nobody can hurt Grace, Judy. This is just a memory. She's safe. Tell me who you're afraid of."

Her face twitched like she was asleep, but caught in a terrible dream. Her grip on the arms of the recliner tightened, her knuckles turning white. "The demons. The angels. God. Everyone."

Now I really didn't understand. Mouth open, I forced my breath in and out, trying to remain calm for her. "Judy, listen to me." My voice echoed around the empty room. "I want you to take me back to an earlier time. To your time on Earth. You were remembering Grace's fifteenth birthday. Start again from there."

"I am. I don't want to investigate the noise." She shook her head, illustrating her point. "But I have to. Three creatures in black robes with long unkempt hair and dreadlocked beards hiss at me in the backyard. A thick fog falls around me, a subtle shade of purple. The ground trembles. A shadow falls over me. The creatures stomp in my direction. Their black eyes glisten. The red hole of their mouths opens and sucks the life out of me, paralyzing me. They're carrying me away." With eyes still closed, her breathing became heavy to the point of panting. "Please don't hurt me... don't." She whimpered, her hands shaking. "I don't want to go."

"It's okay, Judy. It's all right. I'm right here—this is only a memory. No one can hurt you now. Where are the creatures taking you?"

Dr. Judy gasped and pressed a hand to her chest.

"They lay my lifeless body on my bed, force goblets of wine and an entire bottle of pills into my mouth. They set me up, but I opened the window for them to do so because of my choices. I conceived Grace in sin, with someone, something, I shouldn't have been with. Then I was so depressed over cheating and over missing this creature I shouldn't love, that I drank until I became an alcoholic. The pain of existence without him was too much. I had to numb the pain." She curled herself into a ball on the chair and hid her face.

"I thought alcohol would help weaken the power of my memories. Any time I remained sober, I felt so ashamed and wanted to forget everything. I didn't want to die, but I didn't know how to live. I wanted to find a way to move on, to relinquish my guilt and anger, and find closure. But guilt and anger were the only two emotions I could feel after being so abruptly abandoned by the one I loved." She made a guttural noise. "Will you make it stop? The guilt and anger?"

"Yes, I'll make it stop," I lied, repulsed by what I had to do. I couldn't make any sense out of her memories and how this information could help Grace, so I had to make sure this hypnosis session wasn't a total waste. "But first you have to do something for me. You have to tell me where Conner Anderson is."

"No…" she groaned like she was in pain. "I don't know that information."

"Can you tell me where to find that information?" I looked to her filing cabinets once again, wondering if I should try to rummage through them in search of answers.

"Yes, if you make it stop."

Pulling out a piece of paper and pen from the top desk drawer, I nodded, although I wasn't sure why since she couldn't see me. "Yes, I'll make it stop." Keeping my voice calm took every ounce of effort I had left in me.

"There's a guarded storage facility behind headquarters. Usually, it's off limits to me. But once, after I first died, Ash brought me there as they tried to figure out where they should place me. They knew my… complicated past."

"Tell me what you see there that would help me find Conner." Detouring into her past wasn't an option right now. I knew how cringe-worthy my actions were, but I didn't have time to dwell on that.

"First, I take the elevator to the seventh floor. Ash punches in the password on the keypad. The pound sign, then two-two-one-three, followed by an asterisk. Upstairs, I see a computer. Riel is typing, but I can't see what's on the screen."

I narrowed my eyes, willing her to see something, anything. "Judy, think back to what Riel did before typing. Can you see anything he or Ash typed on the computer that would help us?"

"No, Ash is leading me past the computer, but I'm slipping in and out of consciousness."

"Go back and try again, Judy, slowing down this time and concentrating on the keyboard."

"I still can't see the keyboard. But I see four names scribbled on a piece of paper. Michael, Gabriel, Ash, and Riel. There are words, numbers, and symbols next to their names. They seem to be passwords."

"That's good. Now, tell me what the passwords are."

"I can only see one. E-d-e-n, pound sign, number two, colon, number eight."

I repeated the password back to her, making sure I wrote down all the information correctly. Then I tried to untangle all the emotions inside me before continuing. If my memory served correctly, Michael and Gabriel were the two archangels mentioned in the Bible. If Ash and Riel were the only ones outside of them who had clearance to this storage facility, then they were even a lot more powerful than I thought.

"All right, Dr. Judy. One more time… is there anything you see on the computer screen now?"

"It's all my fault, all my fault." Dr. Judy sobbed. "Riel is mumbling a message to Simon. He thinks I don't know how they communicate across planes, but I know all about their angel power. He says he will wipe my memory of this night. I'm glad. I want all the pain gone. I know I did wrong."

I glanced at the clock. The hour was almost up. "You've done lots of good over the years, Dr. Judy. Like right now, you're helping me. Please, tell me what's on that computer screen."

"I see maps of the Underworld. Then I see a bright flash of red when the Alpha File 120 pops up."

A map of the Underworld seemed exactly what I needed. *But what was the Alpha File?* Unfortunately, I didn't have any more minutes left to find out. I looked down at Dr. Judy's notes on how to bring someone out of hypnosis. "Now, in a moment you will wake up and feel refreshed and content."

"No, I don't want to wake up. I want to feel like this forever."

I tried not to panic. "If you ever want to feel like this again, then you must wake up. Is there anything else you want to tell me before I count to five?"

"Don't forget about the Alpha File 120."

"Why would I want the Alpha File?"

Dr. Judy gave a little sigh. "Because then you would know everything and could use the file to help you get what you want."

Again, I had no idea what mumble jumble she referred to, but I seriously needed to get out of her office. "Okay, I won't forget about the Alpha File."

"Alpha File 120. There are one hundred twenty-one Alpha files, but you need that one. Don't forget… don't."

"Right. Alpha File 120. Got it. Now, I will count from five to one, and when I get to one you will be wide awake, feeling happy and refreshed as if you have slept for eight hours. Five—feel every muscle in your body relaxed. Four—your body feels good and ready to wake up. Three—you feel as if you just bathed with fresh spring water. Two—you are getting ready to wake up. One—wake up, wake up."

Dr. Judy opened her eyes and looked at me, her face pale. "Did you get what you needed?"

I nodded slightly, fighting tears. "Yes, but can we chat about the session another day? I think I need some alone time to… process things."

"Of course. I have another appointment soon anyway." Her gaze bounced from me to the door, seeming just as anxious to get rid of me as I was to leave.

I slid out of her usual seat and grabbed my book bag before I had to tell any more lies. "Okay, see you later, Dr. Judy."

Awkwardly, I hugged her goodbye.

Chapter Twelve

I didn't feel like eating lunch, or sitting around headquarters thinking about Nate. Instead, I decided to spy on him. Googling lunch restaurants for a small town proved easy enough, and I stopped at the first place that popped up on my computer screen. Cheshire Village Town Center housed a little eatery called Morning Glory Café, and that's exactly where I found Nate with Grace sitting under a colorful umbrella on the patio overlooking a pristine pond and towering mountains. I knew after I drank seven cups of coffee this morning that I'd do something stupid. Spying on Nate, betraying Dr. Judy's trust… I'd done nothing but shameful and reckless things the past twenty-four hours. Maybe I should just continue my streak. Run up to Nate and blow our whole cover by accusing him of cheating on me. Getting everything out in the open would be such a relief!

Of course, I could just have that conversation with him at headquarters, without blowing our cover and without landing in hot water with Riel and Ash. But I wouldn't do that either. Ugh, I wanted to take my love back from him so badly. My thoughts bounced back between him and Conner so much that sometimes I wondered if I loved either one of them at all. Actually, I didn't wonder; I wished, I hoped, I prayed; because then I wouldn't feel this pain.

If I could stop myself from loving either of them then I would, but that's the trickery of love. You can't stop yourself from falling, and you can't stop loving someone once you start either. In fact, the more I tried, the more that truth became evident. Mine and Nate's old connection might be lessened. Mine and Conner's connection might be lost for eternity. My levels/types/depths of love for them might change over time, but the brutal honesty was my heart was forever lost to them both.

Hell, I might just lose my whole soul over them, as well.

I didn't know how long I'd been spying from the front steps of an antique and vintage shop, a few doors down from the restaurant, when a guy approached me, soundless and graceful as a cougar. His catlike gait was unsettling, like he would shift into a crouch and pounce on me at any moment. Maybe another day the thought would've been appealing because he was young and handsome, probably just a few years older than me if judging by the defined muscles peeking out from his ribbed white tank top and baggy jean shorts. But the smile he flashed gave me the heebie jeebies, as Mom would've called it. Something in my gut told me not to trust him.

He sat down behind me, leaned back, and rested his elbows on the step above. For a moment, he just studied me with lifeless charcoal eyes and I studied him back. Taking in his midnight colored hair, he reminded me of a raven. Immediately, I thought of Edgar Allan Poe's famous poem and took it as an ominous sign. My heart pounding, I felt a foreboding sense of doom, like he didn't belong in the light.

"Nice day for stalking, isn't it?"

I sat up straighter, smoothing down my shirt. "Excuse me?"

He shrugged. "You're stalking your boyfriend and Grace. I'm stalking you. Riel sure did create a beautiful day for stalking is all I'm saying." He gave a knowing smirk and held out his hand for introductions. "I'm Sam."

I drew back slightly. A gazillion questions flashed through my mind, starting with who was this guy, and how did he know about Nate, Grace, and Riel? I knew from the moment I saw him that something was off, and I wasn't entirely sure I wanted to know what, but I pressed on anyway. "What are you doing here?"

With a raised eyebrow, he said, "Stalking you. Didn't we just go over this?"

My body tightened. "Okay, well, stalkers don't usually announce they're stalking you. So at the risk of repeating myself, what are you doing here?"

"I came to make you a deal, Olga. I can help you locate Conner, but first you need to give me something."

A tense beat followed as our eyes locked, and I felt like a volcano about to erupt. I didn't like this one bit. "Who are you?" I whispered.

He let his breath out in a low chuckle. "Sam. Geez, are you special or something? I'll have to inform Riel that he should stop new recruits from eating the paste and sniffing the permanent markers. You ask a lot of questions I've already covered."

I scooted up a step to meet his gaze, looking at him uncomprehendingly. "You know what I mean. Do you think all your smack talk is going to intimidate me? You already told me I got something you want, so let's hear what you came for."

Sam stretched himself out among the three steps, and completely lying down, put his hands behind his head. "Sorry, sweetheart. I was just having some fun. I like to work hard and play hard. You know what I mean?"

"Sorry, no."

He smirked a little. "Well, then you are in for a crazy rollercoaster ride."

I threw my hands in the air in mock fashion. "Wheeee! Now, like I said, let's hear what you came for."

Sam looked amused, and mildly annoyed. "You got lucky in Dr. Judy's office with her hypnosis suggestion. But those passwords are only the beginning of your questions, and only I can answer them. Well, I guess others could answer them, but I'm the only one willing."

Oh, crap. I tensed at his words, and prayed the movement was microscopic. He knew about Dr. Judy and the hypnosis, too? Examining my nails, I pretended to be clueless. "Whatever. I really have no idea what you're talking about."

I seriously needed to know how he just showed up and knew all this stuff, but I knew from experience with guys that playing hard to get was the best strategy. Okay, that was a lie. I didn't know from *experience* per se, but I'd heard.

He lowered his eyelids and looked at me through his lashes, his gray gaze pinning me in place. "You wanted to know who I am, and now I'll tell you. I'm a demon, and that means I'm also someone with the resources to help you locate Conner. But first you have to do something for me." He nodded to where Nate sat with Grace. "Oh, and the mission I have for you is for you alone. If you tell Nate, you may never see him again, unless you do something stupid to land you both in Hell."

By now, the color had most likely drained from my face, but I tried to act nonchalant. "Oh, I'm shaking in my boots. I'm pretty sure you don't have that type of authority."

Sam looked at me, his storm-cloud eyes narrow. "You know, I would prefer if we stopped these little reindeer games and focused on business from this point forward."

My mind raced as I wondered if I should hear him out, try to be rid of him, or run to Nate for help. Eventually, I conceded with a nod. "Fine. What do you want from me? The passwords?"

"You can keep your passwords. I already have them anyway, thanks to you."

"Thanks to me? I didn't give them to you."

His responding laugh was loud, a cackle even. "I can be anywhere I'm provoked or anywhere evil takes place. Therefore, I sat in a chair across from you the whole time, invisible to your eyes. But what I want is what those passwords can lead to. You can open doors we can't go through."

"We?"

"Demons."

I tilted my head to the side, studying his face. "Now who's the glue sniffer? You have to be out of your mind to think I'll go along with helping a band of demons." Privately, I was relieved I had the guts to stand up to Sam, but my control of the situation was only temporary.

He sat up and opened his arms wide. "I already saw you in Dr. Judy's office and how you manipulated her hypnosis. I've already seen your desperation. By the way, well done." He straightened his spine and gave me a golf clap. "I mean it, bravo! The question is, how far are you willing to go to see this thing through? You won't find Conner on your own, and your boyfriend won't want any part in helping you."

"Why should I believe anything you tell me? You're a demon."

"Hmm, demon, angel, tomato, tomahto, potato, potahto. Don't you realize you're just a pawn in this game? You get that Alpha File 120 for me, and you'll realize that for yourself real quick. Now, I'll give you thirty seconds to do the right thing. After that, my offer expires, and you can forget about ever finding Conner. You can forget about everything you've ever worked for."

"Wait. Before you start that countdown, I need some hardcore proof you know where Conner is to even consider your offer."

"I thought you might go there. You want your proof, sweetheart, you got it." He pulled a small brown package from the inside pocket of his vest.

After he passed the padded envelope to me, I blindly undid the clasp and dumped the contents onto my lap. Up until this point, my gaze had been locked on Sam's. Slowly, I lowered my head and gasped, my mouth falling open, then I silently scolded myself for showing emotion. There were three photos, all of Conner. *It's pictures of Conner!* I studied the images, my mind spinning. I could tell the pictures were recent. His blond hair was longer, in a full-blown Jesus of Nazareth way but styled in dreadlocks. He rocked pork chop sideburns he never had before. Plus, his wispy soul patch had grown into a small beard.

I wanted to pick up the photos and caress the glossy images, but my fingers froze. "Conner?" My voice was barely a whisper, my eyes wide with shock. The tears already came, but I tried to hold them back. I needed to study the pictures impassively, revealing nothing more to Sam, but in reality, remaining upright was a task in itself. I decided to ask a lighter question in search of confirmation. "How does he have long hair now? I didn't think you aged in death."

Sam shrugged. "You don't, but your hair, your nails, your waistline, all of those things can still grow." He pressed a button on his wristwatch. "Your countdown starts now."

Seconds ticked by as I fought for control. There was no time to process my feelings. I mulled the decision over feverishly, trying to think clearly through the shock gripping my brain. Proof existed that Conner was, in fact, somewhere near! I had to see him. It felt like my life depended on that truth, and possibly his for some reason. But could I trust Sam? One more look at him and my gut instantly told me no. But I couldn't afford to ignore his offer either. I only had a split second to decide. Stay with Nate, help Grace, and follow 'our' plan to be spirit guides—although one glance at the pair of them told me I wasn't needed on that front—or throw caution to the wind and follow my heart.

"I'll do it." My mouth made the choice before my brain did. I waited for the bolt of lightning that took my best friend to shoot out of the fake clouds and strike me dead, damned to Hell for good. Nothing happened, so I proceeded with my plan. "But I'm not handing over those files until after you take me to Conner. I have to make sure you follow through on your word first." I tried to look intimidating, but scary was sort of hard to pull off with my voice breaking on practically every word I spoke.

His gray gaze flicked up and down the length of my body. "Fine, I guess a situation like yours does call for some type of security measure." He shot me a crooked smile. "I have some security measures of my own. Meet me at the Lake Tomahawk Park clubhouse after school tomorrow. Don't be late, or there will be consequences. Understand?"

"I understand." Getting the words out proved difficult this time. The fact that I, the rational valedictorian, just made a deal with a demon, finally resonated with me. My decision to work with Sam was the darkest one I'd ever made, and the thought gave me the chills.

Light-headed, I closed my eyes so I couldn't watch Sam walk away. Our talk left me feeling like I was being featured on a controversial after-school special for spirit guides. Dropping my chin to my chest, I breathed in and out, very slowly. "Please, God…" I was in so deep now. I wondered if I'd passed the point of praying for some guidance and protection.

When I opened my eyes, my gaze darted to the pictures still spread across my lap. I gathered them up quickly, then bolted inside the antiques and vintage store. The lady behind the counter greeted me, and I asked if I could use their bathroom. She pointed toward the back of the shop.

After closing the door, I collapsed on the tile, clutching desperately to the photos of Conner. I reached out and touched him, mesmerized by his image. Then, I burst into tears, covering my face so my salty drops wouldn't ruin the pictures as I allowed myself to cry quietly.

"I can't believe it's him," I whispered, still reeling from the shock of seeing him. So many emotions flooded my heart: terror, relief, helplessness, shame, joy. Slipping the Morticia Addams ring out of my jeans pocket, I turned it over and over between my fingers. "Oh, God, I don't know how to do this." I looked down at Conner's photos again. "I don't know what to do. There are some truths I never want You to learn about, but You already know about them, don't You, God?" My heart sped up with the weight of everything resting on my shoulders. Out of nowhere, I felt weak and lightheaded, and I gasped for air. Chest aching, mind racing, everything around me crashing—it felt like this might be the end. One final moment of extreme terror… then suddenly, it melted away as I glanced at Conner's picture again. His voice in my head told me I didn't have time to sit in a public bathroom and wallow.

Even though it was almost impossible to take my eyes off Conner, I stuffed the pictures into the brown envelope, then into my backpack.

Grabbing onto the sink, I pulled myself up and checked my reflection in the mirror. A pale ghost stared back at me, my gaze pained. After splashing some cold water onto my face, I forced my expression to remain flat and exited the restroom.

After leaving the shop, my gaze immediately found Nate and Grace. He held a pen in his hand and wrote something on her palm. Marching, I followed the circular path leading to their table. The crowded porch filled the air with noise, and they didn't hear or see me approaching since they had their backs to me. When Nate grabbed both of Grace's hands and held them in his, I decided to hide behind a wooden pole and listen to their conversation.

"When we lose someone we love, when life is cut short, we often find ourselves asking why. Why her? Why my mom? Why now? After gut-wrenching sorrow, there has to be a glimmer of hope to move on. Discover what that hope is, and hold onto it with all your might."

Grace heaved a deep, agonizing sigh, and I peeked around the corner just in time to see Nate rubbing her back. She held up her palm, and I could see what he wrote as she read the words aloud. "Hold onto hope."

I felt like a stalker, like Sam, watching them from this vantage point. Remembering my pain after Conner's accident, my heart did break for Grace. I'd cry again now just from the memory of his death if I didn't have the hope of seeing him again.

Instead, I stood on a porch by myself, watching my boyfriend comfort 'our' assignment. In the distance, some jocks threw a football on the green, a couple shared iPod headphones, and trash skittered by on the brick pavement. *But none of this is real*, I kept telling myself, and I needed something real. I decided the time was now or never. I needed to break up this little love fest and tell Nate about my plan.

My throat tightened as I stepped into view. "Um, hey, bro. Fancy meeting you here."

Nate flashed me a smile that wavered at the edges. "Hey, Olga."

I ignored his lackluster tone, pulled an extra chair to the table, and lifted a colorful mug to the waitress. "Is it okay if I join you guys, Grace?"

"Uh, okay."

The lie was clearly written on her face, and for a moment, I felt sorrier for her than I did for myself. Part of me just wanted to blurt out the truth.

She was dead, and if she just got better, she could see her mom again, and I could have my boyfriend back.

Watching the server pour the black goodness into my cup, I tried to gather my thoughts for what I should really say. "Look, I've been worried about you. I'm glad you've had Nate to hang out with and everything, but one of the reasons I wanted to have lunch with you today is I also really wanted to apologize for what I said the day we met and at the charity function. I didn't mean to upset you."

Grace turned and looked toward the mountains. In that moment, Nate gave me a stare that seemed to say *why are you here ruining all my plans?* I pushed my hands in the pockets of my shorts and stared back at him defiantly. But then the wind mussed his hair and he lifted a muscular arm to straighten the strands with his long, elegant fingers, reminding me how much I just wanted his reassuring arms around me instead. I sipped my coffee, letting Nate win this staring contest.

"It's fine." Grace's voice snapped me out of me lustful trance. She raised her eyebrows at me. "Hey, are *you* okay?"

Right now, I no doubt looked like I needed a white padded wall and a strait-jacket. "Not really. Something important came up, and Nate needs to come home."

Grace tossed her napkin onto the table and stood. "No problem. I have some things to do anyway. You guys want to hang out tonight though? There's a concert in downtown Asheville I was thinking of going to."

I knew Nate would love that, but I shook my head. "Not today."

Nate glanced from me to Grace and back again before standing. "Right. Um, let me walk you to your car, Grace."

My heart pounded, just thinking about him escorting another girl to her car like the perfect gentleman. "We both will!" I knew I said the words with a little too much fake enthusiasm.

The three of us descended the steps onto the cobblestone path lined with specialty shops meant to attract tourists. *Like taking candy from a baby, if only it were so easy to lure Nate to me.* We were quiet enough to hear a pin drop. Perhaps they were lost in their own thoughts. I simply didn't know what to say.

Grace pressed a button on her keychain and headlights on a white Kia Optima flashed.

I just couldn't help myself from muttering a quip remark. "Hey, by the way, nice job on being Student of the Month at Gulf Middle School. I forgot to congratulate you that day we skipped school together."

I didn't know if I hurt her or Nate with the reminder of our faux friendship, but I did know I'd already succeeded in torturing myself.

Grace laughed. "Thanks. My mom put the bumper sticker on when I was in sixth grade. This was her car, until she died. I guess having a car waiting for me when I turned sixteen was kind of morbidly convenient."

I froze in place at her comment, and Nate move forward to open the door for her. Drawing in a sharp breath, I watched Grace get in, then Nate leaning forward and placing his hands on the roof of the car, whispering something in her ear before shutting the door.

I shuddered when he moved past me, still mute, and debated telling him anything at all. Then I dismissed my jealous thoughts when he looked back over his shoulder with those eyes I could get lost in.

I *so* despised the idea of posing as his sister. Our cover meant I couldn't run to him now and hold him like I wanted to.

I also didn't like dealing with demons, but doing things I didn't like seemed to come with the territory these days.

CHAPTER THIRTEEN

"Speak the truth,
even if your voice shakes."
—Bumper Sticker

Once Grace drove out of sight, honking at Nate as she left the parking lot, we both blinked. When we opened our eyes, we'd arrived at headquarters territory. One second—that's all it took to change everything. In retrospect, I longed for the necessity of walking or driving from Point A to Point B. It gave you a chance to clear your head before you said something stupid.

Unsurprisingly, Nate's mysterious mood toward me hadn't improved. "What's wrong with you? I already canceled the plans I had with her last night. Are you trying to destroy all the progress I've made? What if Grace needs me? I can't afford to botch this assignment for us."

"Seriously? Is that really all she is to you? An assignment?"

He frowned at me. "What? You still think this is some sort of hook-up thing? Because if that's what you're implying after everything we've been through—"

I threw up my hands. "I don't know. Maybe I am! I'm not sure of anything anymore. Honestly, sure isn't even a feeling looming on the horizon. I just want you to be real with me, and tell me what's going on, because I can tell there's something you're keeping from me. Like where you were last night?" I sucked in a deep breath, then forced the words out. "And I'm also ready to tell you what's going on with me. So, if you can stop worrying about your new girlfriend for like ten minutes, I'd like to have a serious conversation with you."

He shook his head. "She's not—"

I turned my back on him. "Whatever. I'm done talking about Grace. Weren't you listening to me? Because I don't admit you're right very often, but you were last night when you said there was something on my mind I wasn't telling you."

Nate came up behind me and spun me around.

"Look, I'm sorry, okay? Tell me what's wrong." He tilted my chin up, forcing me to meet his gaze.

"I went to see Dr. Judy after school today."

"Without me?"

"Yeah, and you really don't have the right to complain right now."

"Sorry. It's just the 'you fail, I fail' predicament we're in," he said, adding air quotes. "You have to give me a heads up about these things."

Predicament? I shook my head. Maybe he didn't mean to use that specific word and all its negative connotations. But I loved how he conveniently acted like Grace was 'our' assignment whenever it suited him.

"All I'm saying is you're being a little hypocritical right now because Dr. Judy said you'd been updating her on Grace's status—"

"Yeah, but just over phone calls and text messages, not going to—"

"Whatever! It'd still be nice if you kept me informed on things." I pinched the bridge of my nose. "Anyway, you want the gory details or not? Because, well, I hypnotized Dr. Judy today and discovered a lot of things."

"You did what?"

I explained the hour session with her, the details flying out of my mouth without any censorship. He watched me the whole time, never saying a word or even giving a slight nod of his head.

In the end, I met his gaze, praying mine appeared genuine. "I'm getting Conner back, and I'd like you to be a part of my mission."

He tilted his head for a moment, and then leaned closer, like he was trying to hear me better. "I'm not following you. Are you talking about those passwords you discovered from Dr. Judy? You think you can use them to locate Conner?"

"Yes! Don't you see? I can find him now."

"Yeah, and I can find the North Pole and Santa Claus, too."

"Don't do that. Don't be condescending."

He froze, standing as still as a statue. "So, it's been exactly what I've thought all along."

Blinking, I gathered the courage I needed to deliver my speech. I'd rehearsed what I had to say in my head a thousand times while waiting around for Nate these past three weeks. "It's just who I am. In this job, we're going to see people at their worst. People don't think of the meaning of life and why they're here and the point of everything. It's already so hard to make Grace see the light, and she was only eighteen when she died. Imagine how much more bitter people are in their thirties, forties, fifties, and so on. The number one rule Dr. Judy, Ash, and Riel taught us was don't let the darkness take us over."

I bit my lip and shifted my eyes to the woods, making sure nobody eavesdropped on our conversation before finishing. "And if I become the person who doesn't go after Conner, then I'm the kind of person who's stuck in the dark. I'm the kind of person who can't look herself in the mirror. I'm the kind of person who lets bitterness take over, and I'm the kind of person who won't be of any use to anyone. Because please understand this one thing: the only way I can truly move forward with you is to find Conner first."

Silence hung in the air, and for a moment, his crumpled face held the puzzled expression of trying to decipher what I'd just unloaded on him. This quickly changed to a look of contempt.

"How would you even know how to find him? You only have some passwords and no idea of how to use them."

"A demon told me." I shrugged to make my bombshell seem like less of a big deal.

He met my gaze, sucking in a violent gasp. "What? A demon! Geez, Olga, as long as you have a reliable source!"

"That's not fair… he had proof."

I forced myself to take a deep breath. I needed to choose my words carefully. Nate needed to understand how much I loved him, but he also needed to understand how much I needed to go after Conner.

"Nate, I understand how this whole thing seems insane and how making a deal with a demon could totally blow up in our faces. But I don't need another lecture right now. I need your help. I've never been more nervous or terrified in my whole life. My eighteen things didn't prepare me for this. Finding Conner is… well, if I'm being honest with myself and with you, he *is* the reason I took the spirit guide job instead of going to Heaven. And I've been so scared to admit that to you because I don't want to lose you, but more than that, I'm scared of not finding out what happened to him."

Nate stiffened like I'd just pointed the barrel of a gun between his eyebrows. "How could you even do this to me? Do you want to destroy everything we worked for?"

A tear slipped down my cheek. "None of this changes the way I feel about you. I love you. I want you to be my boyfriend. Nothing will change that. I just want my best friend back, too."

I felt sufficiently exposed, not to mention idiotic. My words sounded stupid even to me, but I couldn't help feeling this way. I reached for his hand, but he pulled his arm back. He didn't look convinced by my words of reassurance at all.

"I don't think you are in the best frame of mind right now. This plan has disaster written all over it." His voice was cold. "You can't blindly go into a realm you're not supposed to be in. You don't have the perspective you need yet. Let's give this new information the demon gave you a few days to settle. I think you'll see how crazy you sound after I help you decipher everything." He grabbed my arms, giving them a firm squeeze. "And then *we* need to take this to Dr. Judy. A demon trying to make bargains with us is new territory. She'll know how to handle things. You'll have to come clean with her about what you learned in hypnosis, but I don't entirely trust Riel and Ash yet, so we can't tell them about you almost going rogue. Dr. Judy is our best bet for an ally."

My eyes widened in horror. "No. I don't trust Dr. Judy either. I don't trust anybody."

His gaze met mine, leveled and dark. "Anybody?"

"Except you. That was implied. Otherwise, I wouldn't have told you all this." My heart stopped for a moment, waiting for his reply.

"Well, if you trust me, then I say we trust Dr. Judy. You don't even know what the consequences are. You have a responsibility."

Raising my hands in exhaustion, I said, "The only responsibility I have is to Conner. And Dr. Judy, or anyone in charge for that matter, won't help me find him! This demon is the only lead I have, but I can't do this alone. I need your support. Are you going to help me or not?"

"Just stop, Olga!" he yelled. "I didn't accept this job so I could break a million laws to find your precious Conner."

I flinched, and Nate's features softened. He touched my face, his fingers so faint against my cheek I barely felt them there.

"I hate to see you torturing yourself like this. Conner isn't *your* responsibility. The accident wasn't *your* fault. You need to accept that. God had another plan for him and for you."

I realized a new truth right then. Something happens when you find out who you are. That girl who took risks this past year? She wasn't the real me. It was one thing to say I'd moved on, let go of my guilt. But talk is cheap, and it wasn't enough. What matters is what we do when we're put through the fire. When demons aren't just externalized, but appear right in front of us, we see who we really are. Was I still that 'good person' from the past year if I was willing to sell my soul for answers? I didn't want to help the other side. I didn't want to let Nate down. I felt so out of control. Did my good outweigh my bad?

"Well, it's time for a new plan!" I let all my thoughts explode out of me, surprising myself. "I'm done with this spirit guide business. Conner is out there, and it *is* all my fault he's alone. And I'm just doing Jar-Jar Binks stuff here anyway."

Nate's muscles turned rigid down the full length of his body. "What's that supposed to mean?" The anger in his clenched teeth surprised me, the words slow and cold and precise.

I still didn't know what I was *supposed* to do, but I knew what I *could* do. I could make this deal with a demon, but run a counter mission of my own. I could cut Nate loose so he wouldn't get in trouble. That meant I had to hurt him, or he might never let me go. I took a deep breath and looked at the ground, because I couldn't look him in the eye and say what I needed to say.

"Jar-Jar Binks… the most annoying sidekick ever. That's what I feel like here next to you. An annoying sidekick only good enough to handle the kid stuff. I mean, what am I even doing here, Nate?"

"You're guiding souls to find the healing they need."

"No, I'm not. You are." I shook my head. "This was your path. I don't belong here with you anymore. Just admit it." I looked up at him and tried to make my expression unreadable, so he wouldn't sense the nausea in me, how sick the statement made me. I hated lying to him, but right now, I did exactly what I needed to do. And that was the truth.

"If that's how you truly feel, then no, I guess you don't." He sounded calm now, his expression all business, but I saw the hurt in his eyes.

Nate was the strongest person I knew. Seeing him look so sad tore me apart. The cold stare I faked lessened a little. I swallowed hard. "I'm sorry. I don't know how to do this without being horrible. I've never had to… to—"

"Dump someone before?" He shook his head back and forth. "Don't bother. Your message is loud and clear."

Hearing those words was a punch in the stomach. I pressed my hands to my abdomen and looked away, my lip quivering as I held back tears. Of course, I was the one doing the dumping, but I felt so lost. I was thinking one thing, saying another, and doing something else entirely.

Minutes passed before he spoke again. "I don't even know who you are anymore, and you know what? I don't think you do, either." His voice was light, not angry at all, but the tone was brittle, giving him away. "And you know what the worst part is? I've heard plenty of stories about Conner, and let me tell you about guys like him. He will disappoint you. I'd bet my ticket to Heaven that he hasn't been worried for you this past year. He loved you only for what you did or didn't do. I just love you for you."

I flinched at his words before looking up at him, balling my fists at my sides. "Nate, I love you, too. I always will. But—"

He held up his hand, signaling for me to stop, and then crossed his arms. "Because I love you, I will let you do what you feel you need to do. You won't have to worry about me interfering. You also won't have to worry about coming back to me because I'm done."

His words rang through the wind, my breathing suddenly ragged. I counted to thirty as we stood there, staring at each other, waiting for him to take it all back. At least something more along the lines of *I'm sorry I can't help you, but I guess if I love you, then I should let you go. Good luck.* Instead, he turned and walked away. My mind became a clanging cymbal shouting *Don't, Don't, Don't* over and over again. Even though I set the wheels in motion, even though I needed us to end, I couldn't comprehend what was happening. The words were all jumbled in my mind. Did I break up with him? Did he break up with me? I realized that I never thought he'd actually let me go. So much for happy endings. I should've known better for thinking those could happen to me.

For one moment, he turned around and looked at me, his gaze shifting slowly toward headquarters before finding my face again. I wanted to run to him, but my whole being went numb, my feet glued to the floor. Something flickered across his face as his own frozen expression melted. The intensity of his gaze overwhelmed me, making my legs wobble. I breathed in and out, unable to open my mouth and say anything, but praying he'd close the hundred yards or so between us and make his way back to me.

I watched him exhale, his chest falling. "Be careful, okay?" Then he muttered the three words I never thought I'd hear him say. "Goodbye, Olga Worontzoff."

I couldn't feel his emotion through the words, but nodded my head anyway. I would be careful. Being careful was my calling card. Careful didn't mean I wouldn't screw up everything though. In the end, I hoped he would see what drove me—my sense of responsibility for Conner, for not being able to prevent the situation which landed us here in the first place. Not my love. Even though I owned up to loving Conner, to myself at least, I knew he never loved me, not in the way I wanted him to. I suffered no delusions after feeling the sting of unrequited love for so many years.

Although, I also thought it would be Olga and Nate forever, something as sure as the quadratic formula. Now, I hadn't just pushed him away to keep him safe, I'd completely destroyed any future together. Did that mean I could be wrong about other things, too? I was usually right, but I did draw the wrong conclusion sometimes. I had thought Nate was different from all the other guys I'd known my whole life, but he gave up at the first sign of trouble. He was just like all the rest. He didn't even fight for me.

In retrospect, maybe I'd been wrong about how Conner felt about me, too. I shook my head. There was only one way to find out.

CHAPTER FOURTEEN

"I hope that real love and truth are stronger in the end than any evil or misfortune in the world."
—Charles Dickens

I'd always imagined that when I appeared at the pearly gates of Heaven, an angel would greet me and present a slide show of my life before God judged if I could enter or not. My friends and family who had gone on before me would gather around to watch with shocked expressions as they viewed moments they never knew about. Some of these moments would even be a surprise to myself, moments I forgot about, or wished I could take back, or were shocked that I'd participated in them at all.

If I ever made it to Heaven, I imagined that this moment would no doubt be at the top of that list. And yet, here I was, determined to follow through with my plan, and ready to make good on my deal with a demon.

People flocked to Lake Tomahawk Park this time of day, the sun high above us, scorching our skin from the blue sky. From my perch atop a picnic table, I watched some children kick around a soccer ball and some teens fishing at the lake. For a moment, I almost felt giddy with the potential of summer, until I remembered again why I was here. But I also wondered how this could all be here. Did the whole city exist for Grace to be in it? I pictured the town only existing in the places Grace went. Maybe the demon created this mirage. I shuddered, and not for the first time, I second-guessed coming here.

I scanned the park, searching for Sam. Couples strolled the circular path of the lake. Kids splashed in the pool by the clubhouse. Grace and Nate hung out at the swings, him pushing her high into the air from behind.

What the heck?

I bet all of this was here because they'd already planned to meet at the park today, and Sam knew that. I spotted him peering around a corner at me from the balcony of the clubhouse. After taking one more look at Nate and Grace and getting that "more than friends" vibe reaffirmed, I walked briskly toward Sam, climbing the outside stairwell with determination.

Determination, yes. But the thoughts of *what if my plan doesn't work* nagged constantly at my mind with each step.

I shook my head. No, my plan had to work. It just might cost me my soul in the process.

On the balcony, Sam lounged in a plastic chair, his pale hands clasped behind his head, looking creepy as hell. The wife beater and baggy shorts must be his standard attire, but today there were barbeque stains down the front of it… or blood. I hoped those red spots were from a barbeque lunch.

I took a seat next to him. Just a little over three weeks ago, I had my chance at Heaven, now I made deals with demons. My, how the mighty had fallen.

On the gritty cement down below, a two-year-old kicked and wailed in his stroller. Never before could I relate so much to wanting out. I swallowed hard, thinking, could I really do this? Once upon a time, I would've *never* entertained the thought of doing something like this.

But now wasn't a fairy tale, and I was far, far away from once upon a time territory. When Sam remained quiet, I leaned over the small white table between us.

"So, I'm here." My voice sounded hoarse with weariness, but I continued. "What's next?"

Checking his watch, he said, "You're here, and you're on time. That makes you reliable, not that *I* ever had any doubts." His gaze felt predatory. "Pain has made you strong, Olga. Your loss is our gain."

I looked at Nate and Grace on the swings. "Whatever. I'd say pain has made me weak, especially if I'm making deals with demons."

"In due time, I think you'll see things my way."

A big part of me wanted to yell at Sam that I'd never see things his way, but a bigger part of me wanted to get this meeting over with. "Look, just tell me what I need to know for this mission."

"There's a building behind headquarters."

I shook my head. "Right, a storage facility."

"You'll need the fingerprint of someone who has access to get into the storage facility." He paused and reached to the inside of his shorts pocket before holding out a zip lock baggie. "Inside the bag you'll find some tools to help you. That right there"—he nodded—"is an artificial gummy finger with Riel's fingerprint on it. Just slip it on your pointer finger and press the security panel to the right of the front door for a good three seconds."

"Couldn't I—and Riel for that matter—just walk *through* the front door?"

Sam thrust the bag into my hands. "You think they'd make access that easy? They have wards up to protect against that type of thing."

"How did you get Riel's fingerprint?"

"Those aren't details you need to worry about. Now, when you step into the elevator to go to the seventh floor, a machine will most likely automatically scan you for high-tech gadgets and hidden tools, so you'll have to stash a bag somewhere on the first floor with the rest of the things I'm giving you for your journey. Your cell phone won't be able to receive calls or send any messages. I can't give you a com link. If your mission is compromised in any way, there will be hell to pay. Literally."

"How do you know this? Why not just go in yourself?"

Sam picked a stick from a nearby plant and twirled the piece of thin wood in his fingers. "I'm sort of guessing about the tech scan, but we have something similar at demon headquarters, and I've heard rumors of the angel technology. Although nobody who goes in there seems to be allowed past the first floor anyway. Moreover, the reason we need you at all for this mission is that the wards I just told you about? Demons can't penetrate past them. We've never been able to enter or even see what's through the windows. Only four angels have access to the building, and they are untouchable. Even if we could touch Michael and Gabriel, they travel so fast across the universe, we can't even track their whereabouts. We didn't even know Dr. Judy possessed such knowledge until you hacked into her fried brain."

Swallowing hard, I placed my hands on the tabletop and leaned forward. "Why do you trust me with such an important mission? I mean, I'm flattered, but I'm only on my first spirit guide job. And as far as I can tell, I'm failing. Do you really think I'm capable of completing this task all by myself?"

Sam let out a long sigh. "Look, the fact that you're new is why we approached you. Plus, the Creator made you very intelligent. And your weakness is you care way too much about others to let this mission fail. Now, if you can focus for five minutes, I can explain the rest of the mission to you and get us both out of here. You still have the elevator code Dr. Judy gave you?"

"How'd you—"

"Squirrel!"

I jumped, expecting some rodent with rabies behind me, but nope, nothing.

"Oh, sorry. There's no real squirrel. There's no real anything here. I'm just referring to your short attention span. Do me a favor, sweetheart. Be like a camera and focus. Where was I? Let's recap. You'll scan Riel's finger, stash your bag of tricks, type in the elevator code, and an automatic tech scanner will activate when you push the up button. Once you're at the seventh floor, like I said, you're on your own. Type in the computer password you obtained from Dr. Judy to grant you access and download the Alpha File 120 onto your phone."

"What do you mean? I thought my phone wouldn't work inside headquarters." My gaze fell on a couple by the lake enjoying a picnic. I could not imagine ever wanting to eat again. This had to be at the top of my list for the craziest conversation ever.

"Probably not for calls, I've heard it's a dead zone in there." He paused, chuckling at his own lame joke. "But we're hoping you'll be able to download the file through your phone because it's an angel issued device. I'd give you one of our tech pieces, but I think the computer system would detect something off. Once you have the file, you'll need to escape the building. I have these to help you gain entrance and exit undetected."

He handed me a pillbox under the table. When I opened the small gold container, I found two white, oval-shaped tablets, each about two centimeters long. I kept my gaze downward, not wanting to give Sam the satisfaction of my terror. The pills I swallowed, the pills that took my life, looked exactly like these ones. Certainly, Sam knew that.

I narrowed my eyes. "How are these pills going to help me?"

Swatting a fly in the air, he seemed irritated I didn't show more emotion. "Place it on your tongue and the pill will dissolve instantly, giving you a full minute of invisibility. We're working on a prototype that will last longer, but sixty seconds is as good as it gets so far. I hope you move fast."

"I'll be fast enough. Now, are we done here, or—"

He held up a hand and edged in closer, his face a mere inch away. "Just to be clear, I'm the one in charge. Yeah, I'm giving you a long leash. Just understand I won't allow you to compromise our mission. Inside here"—he handed me an envelope—"you'll find your directions for locating the wormhole and for the dead drop. I won't be able to follow you to Juvie through the wormhole, so—"

"Juvie? So that's where Conner is?" My body went as still as a statue.

"Yes. But I'm not telling you how to get there. You'll need to hack that information for yourself when you're in the storage facility. Otherwise, I'd have no insurance policy you'll follow through with the Alpha File. The thing is, demons have free reign in the Underworld to mess with angels and spirit guides because you are mere servants, less than humans. But there are wards the angels put up, allowing only one demon at a time the permission for a twenty-four hour access pass to enter each Limbo plane, each Juvie camp, and each Purgatory cell. Even after we're in, we can only target those already contemplating evil.

"So, once you enter Conner's camp, I can't follow you because since you're using our entrance, they'll assume you're a demon. You can leave anytime you want, but I'm willing to give you your day with Conner as your reward. The next day, if you perform the dead drop as instructed, then it'll be as if we never met."

I took a deep breath. "You mean, I'll never have to see you again?"

"Nope. Disappointing, isn't it?" He licked his lips.

Ignoring how terrifying he looked with his vacant eyes in his vampire pale face, I asked a dangerous question. "What if I don't perform the dead drop and stay in Juvie forever?" After all, the demons wouldn't be able to get in then, would they? Would Riel and Ash come looking for me, or leave me for God to judge later?

He snapped the stick he held in his hand with more ferocity than necessary, and pointed both halves toward Nate and Grace. "Then they suffer the consequences of your bad decisions."

A vision flooded my mind of Nate and Grace locked in a cell, beaten and covered in blood. I sucked in a breath, trying not to hyperventilate.

"We straight now?" Sam asked, confirming my suspicion that he'd given me a taste of the future I could expect if I didn't follow orders.

I nodded, slow and careful.

"Good. I've kept the wormhole to Conner's part of Juvie open for you tomorrow, but it expires at sunset. That gives you until almost nine to complete your mission. Good luck, Olga. I'll say an extra Hail Mary for you before I go to bed tonight."

CHAPTER FIFTEEN

For the third time this summer, I skipped school. I was surprised the Tammy in my Limbo state never added that one to my life list.

I just didn't have the strength within me to face Nate and pretend to be his sister for three hours of summer courses, even if it would mean seeing his face one last time. Instead, I performed the everyday motions of a normal person. I woke up at seven. I took a shower. I dressed. I walked to the cafeteria. I ate breakfast. These felt like the last normal things I would ever do, so I savored them.

When I packed my backpack, nothing felt normal. Inside, I kept all the contents issued by Riel and Ash when Nate and I officially became spirit guides. The glue stick with the toggle switch could prove especially handy. Then I added all the stuff Sam gave me: the gummy finger, the pillbox, and the folder detailing my assignment.

The thought of leaving Nate a note crossed my mind, then uncrossed it. The less information he knew, the less he was involved, the better.

Instead, I opened my spirit guide meditation book and prepared to journal. Today's verse came from the book of Isaiah, chapter forty, verse thirty-one: "Those who wait for the Lord shall renew their strength, they shall mount up with wings like eagles, they shall run and not be weary, they shall walk and not faint."

I had to admit, I felt guilty reading these verses. Part of me wanted to hide myself from God, but I knew concealment proved impossible. So I poured my heart onto the page.

Lord, You know I'm tired. Your strength never weakens, and for that, I am thankful. I pray You would give me some of your strength for this mission today. On my own, I feel the weight of what I have to do, and it's crushing me. You've helped me to rise above so many difficulties already. I hope You're not too busy or too angry to help again. I do trust You, but I also trust You are giving me tools to accomplish a task. Trusting means following the prompts of Your Spirit, right? And I don't feel a 'no' from You in any of this. Maybe I should wait longer, be more patient for answers about Conner. But I care too much for him. I know You're all-knowing and see what's driving me. I have but limited knowledge, and I have this need to understand what happened to Conner above all else. I pray for Your mercy and protection, that my plan will work and the Alpha File 120 won't fall into the wrong hands. I hope I can save the fate of four souls today, not just one.

Thumbing through some more meditations, I searched for additional guidance, but my mind was already somewhere else. I stuffed the book into my backpack, zipped it closed, and slung the bag over my shoulder along with a navy parka incase where I headed was cold. On my way out, I passed Nate's room and on a whim, decided to go inside. Just as I suspected, he wasn't there. The time on the bedside clock read just after nine, and he'd done the responsible thing: gone to school.

I turned to leave and noticed my reflection in the full-length mirror. My sneakers, my faded jeans, the avocado colored T-shirt over my long sleeved white shirt, the crucifix necklace I wore, my French braid… all of these things made me look so normal on the outside.

On the inside, I felt like a hot mess. But my look was missing one thing. I grabbed Nate's army green hat off a peg on his wall. The hat featured a small cream colored cross on the left side. I tried the hat on for size and found wearing something of Nate's gave me courage. I shut the door on my way out, never looking back.

I tried to leave headquarters undetected, but heard Riel's voice behind me just as soon as I walked through the wall.

"Olga!" he called.

Great, I can't even leave the building without someone noticing. So much for my life as a super spy.

He teleported to the other side of the wall and stood next to me within the blink of an eye. "What are you doing here? Late to school today, or did you take my advice about taking the week off?"

I thought about lying, but figured the less I did of that, the better. "I just didn't go. Nate and I officially broke up, so Grace is definitely his sole responsibility now."

He nodded his head and took a step closer. "I'm sorry to hear that. I guess my little meteor shower wasn't enough?"

Tears sprung to my eyes before I could help myself.

"Hey, don't cry. It'll be okay."

"No, it won't, but thanks for saying that."

He put his arm around me and immediately, I felt warm and fuzzy inside. "We could go watch Mel Gibon's *The Passion of the Christ* in the rec room. That'll cheer you up."

"What? How would that help?" The words burst out of my mouth as a shout before I could remember to compose myself in front of my boss.

Riel laughed. "You'd be surprised. Nothing ever seems quite as bad after sitting down for 127 minutes to watch Hollywood's interpretation of the final hours and crucifixion of Jesus Christ."

I let out a long sigh. "You're probably right, but I don't think I can handle any more suffering right now."

"How about horseback riding then?"

I raised my eyebrows. "Horse riding? I dunno. I…"

Oh, crap. I couldn't exactly feign busyness, because then he'd ask about my plans.

"Um, I haven't been riding in a long time. I'm not sure if I remember how."

"Tsk, tsk. That's the downfall of being a teen in this world today. You're all too busy to enjoy the simpler things life has to offer." He scooped me up in his arms. "No matter. It's just like riding a bike." He eyed the backpack on my shoulder. "Are you bringing that with?"

I shrugged. "I guess so."

A few minutes later, I hung my bag on a hook in the barn while Riel filled a bucket of water for the horses to drink before our ride. "Will this be safe if I leave it here?"

Riel grabbed a brush, then started grooming the horse, gesturing for me to do the same to mine. "Why? Are you hiding drugs in there you're worried about?" He grinned over the back of the horse.

I tried to smile back, but it wavered, as I thought about Riel's fingerprint in my bag, more dangerous than any illegal substance. After grooming the horse, my gaze settled on my watch. Nine thirty. I took a deep breath, swallowed hard, pushed down the thoughts of all I had to do today, and picked up a saddle pad.

A half hour later, I looked toward a short fence on the trail and tightened my fingers on the reins. "Guess it's time to turn around."

"Nonsense! We just started. You just have to jump over the obstacles in your way."

"Says the angel with powerful wings. I guess you don't ever need to worry about falling."

"Not in the sense you're talking about," he mumbled.

His horse's white ears flickered at his comment, like he was more puzzled than me by his words.

I steered my horse toward the fence, and she threw her head back in excitement. "Easy, girl," I told her, patting her neck. "Any pointers for me? I've never jumped before."

"There's a first time for everything. Just hold on tight, keep your eyes on the prize, and have faith, knowing the horse can lead you to safety."

Certainly, there had to be an analogy about God and me in that sentence, but I still didn't feel confident about my jump.

"Here, watch me first." Riel nudged his calves into the horse's sides, urging him into a gallop. A brilliant smile lit his face as he rose up in the saddle, his black hair streaming behind him and the air rippling his robe.

I squinted in the sun-streaked sky, determined to learn his techniques of flying without literally flying. The whole process was breathtaking to behold.

"See, easy-peasy-lemon-squeezy," he said from the other side.

After a curt nod, I squeezed my legs and felt the horse's muscles gather as she lifted into the air, as graceful as Riel flying, and I could feel him watching me. There was a moment of suspense, where I wondered if we'd clear the obstacle, before we landed safely on the other side.

"Good girl," I whispered, caressing her neck. This time, I smiled genuinely at Riel.

As our two horses met, he said, "You're safe now." His tone implied we weren't just talking about clearing fences.

"Am I?"

Riel flicked his reins, trotting down the trail, and I did the same. "I know you're having a hard time coming to terms with leaving your life behind. But you can have so much more here. I hope you'll let me show you that."

We rode in silence for a moment. "It might take me a long time to realize that truth, but I am grateful for your help."

Riel looked at me, and his horse moved him closer. "My pleasure. You're amazing, Olga, whether you realize it or not. You have great instincts. You'll make a gifted spirit guide one day. I could see you taking over Judy's position when she retires."

I shook my head. "I don't think I could ever be even half as good as Dr. Judy. I still have a lot to learn. I couldn't help Grace at all."

"You can't think negatively," Riel reprimanded quickly. "No good ever comes of it."

I nodded. "Okay, well, do you have any tips for thinking positively then?"

He moved close enough that his horse stretched his neck out to nuzzle my horse affectionately, and his leg brushed mine. I'd literally been 'touched by an angel' a few times now. Usually, his touch brought some much needed comfort, but today I couldn't really feel anything. My body was numb and his eyes—the way he looked at me—confused me.

"Yes, spend more time with me."

My eyes focused on his, searching for the motive behind his comment. "Ya know, if I didn't know better, I'd think you were hitting on me." I couldn't believe I just said that aloud.

He laughed. "Well, an angel getting involved with humans in that way is frowned upon by our Creator, but not unheard of."

"Have you ever… been involved with a human?"

We were both silent for a moment, nothing but the sound of hooves along the path. "No, but I've known other angels who crossed the line. The consequences are, well, should be avoided at all costs. But as I'm sure you know, sometimes you can't help who you fall in love with." He cleared his throat. "So, why did you and your lover boy breakup?"

"Lover boy? For real, Riel?"

He smirked. "How long have you been waiting to say that to me?"

I exhaled a breath. "Pretty much since the day we met."

We both laughed. I wanted to check his face because his heavenly beauty was magnified when he laughed, but I could feel him watching me again, so I didn't.

What's going on here? He's my boss! He's an angel for Pete's sake!

"Yes, for real, I want to know why you and Nate decided to end things."

"We just couldn't… see eye to eye on some issues right now." My voice was barely a whisper. Admitting the truth hurt too much.

I felt Riel studying me, but I kept my gaze straight ahead.

"Do you think this split is permanent or more like a break?"

The effort of even thinking of an answer drained me. "I don't know. I mean, I never even thought breaking up was a possibility. So yeah, the split feels permanent, but I hope one day he'll see things my way."

I thought I heard the seed of a sigh in his exhale. Turning my head, I looked at him now, bits of sunshine dotting his skin, making me want to reach out and touch his stunning complexion.

"Come on, Riel, what are you thinking? I know you have a quip remark in there somewhere."

He bit his lip for a second. "You're right. You know me so well already. I was just thinking you sound like a typical girl for once, thinking you're the one who's right and he's wrong."

"Be careful," I warned him, although I knew I couldn't do anything to hurt him.

"No, I'm quite sure you *are* right, given what I know of Nate."

"Go easy on Nate. He's got a good heart." The words came out dryly, unsure of why I defended him when he left me hanging so easily.

Patches of clouds blocked the sunlight, and everything turned a shade darker as we cantered on, including Riel's talkative mood. After a few minutes of silence, he pointed to a trail off to the right. "That leads to another headquarters."

I raised my eyebrows. "There's another headquarters?"

He nodded. "About five miles down there's a creek you have to cross, then the trail leads up to a ridge. The building sits on top of the hill. Two other angels are in charge there."

My mind flashed to Michael and Gabriel, the two names Dr. Judy mentioned seeing on the piece of paper when under hypnosis. Suddenly, I felt like I knew too much information, and I wanted to turn around.

Luckily, from directly above came the sound of wings beating the air. Ash called down to Riel, telling him he needed him back at headquarters.

Riel sighed. "Give me your hand."

"My hand?"

"Yes, that petite little thing with five fingers attached to your wrist."

I switched the crop over to my right hand and held out my left. Obedience had always been my strong suit, but I wouldn't be able to claim that for much longer.

Riel's hand around mine felt strangely warm and right. A moment later, we popped into the barn. "You can teleport with animals, too?"

He smiled. "See, being friends with me has its advantages. Can you put away the horses?"

I nodded. "Yeah, no problem."

Hopping off, he brushed some dirt off his robe. "You want to have dinner tonight?"

I eyed my backpack. "Um, I can't. I have other plans."

"Another time then. Just remember, I'm always here for you."

Another second later, he disappeared as I grimaced.

I had a sinking feeling in the pit of my stomach that he'd renege on that promise soon.

CHAPTER SIXTEEN

"I believe that unarmed truth and unconditional love will have the final word in reality."
—Martin Luther King, Jr.

I crouched near the pristine wall of headquarters diagonally across from the storage facility. Peering around the corner, I held a pair of binoculars to my eyes and spotted the guard pacing back and forth in front of the entrance. The guard didn't look too intimidating, dressed in what looked like a choir robe, similar to but not as fancy as Riel's, and carrying a stun gun. I sighed before slipping back into hiding, then reached into my bag for my parka. I thought I might need the extra pockets the jacket provided. My pulse pounded in my ears as I slid my arms through the holes. I felt like I could run a marathon. Finally, I was being proactive and tackling my guilt and worry head-on.

I adjusted my backpack on my shoulders and moved my braid from front to back.

"All right, deep breath," I told myself. Conner's salvation was just a hundred yards away. Thirty more seconds, and I'd swallow the invisibility pill Sam gave me and break every rule in the book.

Out of nowhere, Nate strolled from… I didn't catch from where. *Had he been hiding some place, too?* I guessed he hadn't gone to school after all. Although it was afternoon now, so maybe he'd just gotten back. I wanted to call after him, for him to meet my eyes. Maybe he'd already forgiven all the inexcusable things I'd said yesterday. Maybe he came to help me. I watched him climb a tree to the left of the storage unit and yank out some papers stashed in the back waistband of his pants. Standing on the branch, he shouted at what must've been his highest decibel.

"Shadows! It's the thing I live in! For what purpose? I don't know!" He glanced down at his papers, and then raised his arms over his head. "What purpose does life possess? Protection. For fear of finding one's self. It's much easier to hide in someone—to live for them, become them. Stop! I tried, but night fell. And back into the shadows I went!" He threw the papers to the wind, ripped his shirt down the middle, and wailed.

From the corner of my eye, I saw the guard scurrying toward him. I had never seen Nate like this. The whole scene was so bizarre I didn't know whether to laugh or cry. I did know I should save my pill for later and sprint toward the entrance while I had the chance. I didn't have time to ponder if Nate's show was in response to our breakup, like he was having some sort of mental breakdown, like I would've if I had time to think about everything. *Breakup.* Just thinking the word made me want to fall apart and I couldn't do that now.

My hands trembled when I reached for the scanner and placed the artificial gummy mold of Riel's finger on the pad. A green light flashed, like the device was making a photocopy of his finger. Then, the door buzzed softly, and the lock clanged free. Trying the handle, the door swung inward, and I walked quickly through the airy lobby of silver filing cabinets lining the walls from floor to ceiling to my left and right. Good thing the information I sought wasn't kept in those, or I could've been here for a hundred years before finding anything.

After setting my backpack in-between two cabinets, I jabbed the code for the elevator and when the sleek silver doors opened a moment later, I stepped inside. Just as Sam predicted, a detection scanner roamed up and down my body, searching for anomalies. An automatic voice gave the all clear, and then I rode the elevator to the top seventh floor as *How Great Thou Art* drifted through the speakers inside. The elevator doors slid open, and I quietly cleared a set of frosted-glass doors.

The room seemed to be devoid of all beings, but one never knew, so I proceeded on tiptoe. The office inside was modern with vaulted ceilings, and the computers were set up along the nearest wall, a plush leather desk chair in front of each of four flat-screen monitors. I slipped into the first desk chair, the seat warm. Not a good sign. The heat meant someone had just been here and would probably return soon.

Pressing my lips together, I typed in the one password I had, holding my breath until it granted me the access I needed. I tapped furiously away at the computer. Any minute, a guard could burst in on me, and make my task even more difficult. There was another door at the other end of the room, but I didn't have time to investigate. My heart pounded with trepidation. I was trying to save Conner, but in the process, I could lose Nate, Grace, and myself.

Even as my hands worked the keyboard, I felt the hypocrisy of everything. Dr. Judy, Riel, and Ash all trusted me, and here I was using their trust to get what I wanted. My heart felt like it pounded inside my skull, beating my brain with toxic thoughts, even ones I had convinced myself I'd let go of. If only I hadn't been jealous and asked Conner to go sailing with me that day. If only we had worn life jackets. If only I'd cared more about my job to help others instead of undertaking this dangerous mission. If only I'd listened to Nate. If I'd just stuck to our plan, I wouldn't be in this mess.

I swallowed a lump forming in my throat. *Don't go there*, I thought. If I allowed myself to dwell on the reality of what was happening, I wouldn't be of use to anybody. As much as I wanted a hero on some white horse to ride in and save us all, that wasn't happening. Really, everything was up to a computer now.

Conner Anderson. His name was toward the top of the Juvie manifesto. *Thank God for the tyranny of the alphabet!* I bit back a wave of excitement and forced myself to take a deep breath. I couldn't let my emotions distract me. All my focus went into how to find him now. His life depended on it, and now a lot of others did, too. I clicked on a link and a satellite photograph of the four divisions of the Underworld appeared on the wall from a tiny projector mounted to the ceiling. Juvie, Limbo, Purgatory, and Hell.

It was all here. All the information I needed to know to infiltrate Juvie and find Conner, like my own personal MapQuest of the Underworld. I glanced around the room, paranoid, as I snapped pictures of the needed information with my cell phone. Most important, was a color-coded map with each tent—*tent?*—clearly marked. An area marked in green labeled 'Camp Fusion' displayed Conner's name. An eerie sense of calm settled over me, even amidst the disquieting silence of the room. My task was mind over matter now. I had work to do.

Next, I scanned the computer screen as lists of files from various folders scrolled in front of me. I had no idea what folder the Alpha File 120 was saved under, and the lists were never ending. Lists used to equal fun, but not anymore. The computer screen beeped, and a flashing red line appeared in the center. The Alpha File had finally popped up on the screen, but I had no idea what the beep meant. I hoped the sound didn't mean the system alerted the media any time the file was accessed. In any case, I clicked on the file folder and discovered there were 120 different Alpha Files, the last one being 120. I opened up the folder and tried to decipher the contents on the screen, but the words and symbols were all Greek to me. It didn't even look like an Earthly language. I plugged my phone into the computer to download the document and prayed for the best.

Thank you, God, for bringing me this far. Please don't let me fail this mission. Please let Conner be okay. Please let Nate and Grace be okay, too.

I froze suddenly when I heard a pair of voices on the other side of the mysterious door. I didn't have time to investigate. The words were too muffled through the wood surface, and the sound of all the computers working made eavesdropping impossible. A tiny window next to the mystery door provided the only other way of escape, but there was no way I'd survive the drop. Then, I remembered I was already dead. I wished I knew how that type of thing worked. I wished I had my invisibility pill, but I had to leave it downstairs in my bag in case the scan was able to pick it up. My knees felt weak, and I could hardly breathe while waiting for the file to finish downloading, praying I wouldn't be discovered. I didn't actually know if God heard these prayers though.

The computer screen flashed red again and beeped, signaling completion of the download. Trying hard not to think of the consequences, I reached out, disconnected my phone cord from the computer, and slid everything into the front pocket of my jacket. Then, without even thinking about why, I picked up a pair of black sunglasses with super dark lenses and two silver buttons on each side off the desk and slid them into my other pocket.

As I rode the elevator to the first floor, I hoped Nate was still down there for round two. When the doors dinged open into the lobby, Riel talking to the guard caught my eye. *He must've come because of Nate's commotion.* My pulse skyrocketed. I crouched behind the filing cabinet where I'd stashed my backpack and caught the site of Nate stepping into a clearing to the left of the building. His eyes swept over the inside of the lobby, and I could've sworn he saw me. I wondered if he was trying to catch me in the act and rat me out. As I pulled a tiny circular pill from my backpack, I knew I had to time my exit perfectly. When Nate let out a strangled cry, I swallowed the pill, activating the functional invisibility shield around myself. I ran briskly for the front entrance, emerging from the building and into the sunshine. I sprinted across the open courtyard, knowing the pill would buy me enough time to escape unnoticed. Well, I hoped unnoticed, since I was pretty sure my heart slammed against my rib cage loud enough for the entire Underworld to hear.

I jogged to the barrier wall behind the storage facility. The barrier was endless in length and height, and what it separated us from I never knew, only guessed. Sometimes my guesses were right. Sam's folder had explained everything to me. In different parts of the wall, there were keypads, and with the correct password, you could gain entry to other realms. I drew my breath, flipped down the keypad, and entered the code. From here on out, things would be even trickier.

An entrance opened before me, a door into the great unknown. I wished Nate were here so we could step through the entryway together, but his spirit went with me in my heart.

On the other side of the wall was a waterfall, the one Sam had written about in the folder he gave me. He said to throw my body into it with all my might, and that I wouldn't get wet since everything was a mirage. So I flung myself into the rushing water and at once, felt the thrilling sensation of going down one of those waterslides where the floor drops out beneath your feet. I once went on one of those when I was thirteen, when my parents forced me to go on the church's youth group trip to Noah's Ark Family Park in Wisconsin. Dropping out of that capsule reminded me of seeing people falling down elevator shafts in movies. They called the ride Scorpion's Tail, and the total height equaled ten stories with a length of four hundred feet. I hadn't been able to draw breath then, and I couldn't now.

Just when I thought I'd have a panic attack, the waterless waterfall hit a surface, and dumped me into the cool night. For a moment, I sunk into the blue darkness. Then terror froze in my chest, remembering the last time I'd willingly jumped into water. I'd been trying to rescue fake Conner, the one from my simulations as part of my spirit guide training. The thought was like a cup of ice water thrown in my face, even though I still couldn't feel any of the wetness in this lake. I swam toward the surface, kicking powerfully until I broke free of the water.

This time, there was no choking and gagging, no gasping for air. The only wetness came from my tears, dotting my vision as I climbed onto the riverbank. I clawed at the damp grass, realizing the blades were wetter than I was. I breathed a lungful of fresh air, more to calm myself than out of necessity. Turning around, I realized I'd just climbed out of a good-sized lake, though definitely no Lake Michigan. The water sparkled like sapphires, reflecting the many moons present in the sky.

From my place on the riverbank, I had a clear view of a two-story building lit up across the way. I wondered why the atmosphere was so dark outside though. Sam told me Juvie was twenty hours ahead of spirit guide headquarters official time, but that meant the time should be a little past eight in the morning, plenty of time for a sunrise to happen.

I unzipped my cell from the front pocket of my parka. Luckily, the phone still appeared to be in one piece despite the crazy whiplash ride. According to the map I'd snapped of Juvie, the lights coming from across the lake must be Camp Fusion High. My coordinates estimated the distance I needed to walk was three miles in either direction. Conner's tent would be a half mile farther than that. I tried to teleport across, but no luck.

A chilly breeze ruffled my curls as I looked out at the moonlit grounds. I set out at a quick walk, keeping to the thicket of bushes around the perimeter of the lake for an extra measure of security. Forty-five minutes later, my pace slowed as I arrived at the corner diagonally across from the path in front of Camp Fusion High. Leaning against a light post, I pretended to chat on my cell phone while surveying the area. The school grounds were beautiful, moss green with trees and flowers of every kind and color. Two no-nonsense patrols guarded the entrance, checking school ID's. I wondered if I should head over to Conner's tent, or just check inside Fusion High. My gut told me I'd find him inside.

Since my use of teleportation was down, I highly doubted I could walk through the walls of the high school to gain entrance. And by the looks of things, I couldn't just walk in through the front door. I kept to the shelter of the trees with my head down and followed the trail. The manicured brick path ran along the side of the building, the pristine lake on the other side, but the trail didn't continue around to the back of the school. There was no concrete at all there, but a looming forest with lots of oak trees instead, everything dark and quiet.

I scrutinized the building, weighing my options. Grand windows were situated on the bottom floor, all closed, all decorated with a large potted plant beneath them. Then I spotted an open French door on the second floor of a balcony. A tree led right up to it. I made sure no surveillance cameras watched me. Then, in a flash, I crossed the grounds, low and swift. I climbed the tree with confidence, knowing the limbs led me to my destiny. I grabbed hold of a branch, and then jumped, gripping the balcony railing. An executive looking office greeted me inside the door. Beyond another door, I spotted a stairwell.

Just as I was about to bolt for the stairs, a row of security monitors caught my attention on the wall. By luck or destiny, I instantly spied Conner talking to another boy who looked about his age, and they walked up a path looking strangely identical to the one I just left. My heart did a hopeful flip. I contemplated jumping back out the window, but figured I'd just walk down the stairs and meet up with him in a minute. I needed that minute to plan what I was going to say. The whole time I'd been figuring out how to get to Conner. But what I actually wanted to say when I found him wasn't a point I'd considered yet, and I needed a moment to bolster my nerve. The flutter of butterflies almost made me want to abort my mission entirely, but I'd come too close now. With my head down, I walked out of the room and tried to act normal.

Acting normal was a hard thing to do for someone like me. All the students wore their ID on a lanyard around their neck and before long, a guard spotted me, my heart dropping to my feet. *Crap. Whattodowhattodowhattodo.* The hallway dead-ended. If I turned back now, he'd probably ask for my ID badge and I'd be shipped back to… well, I wasn't sure. In any case, I couldn't let my mission be over before it even began.

Music that sounded like old hymnals played softly through the hallway speakers. The sound gave me an idea. Lightning quick, I pulled the fire alarm. The ringing pierced my ears. I waited for the hall to fill with more students, then followed them down the stairs. Just before I exited the lobby, someone announced over the loudspeaker the fire had been a false alarm, and we were free to go about our daily business. Unsure of where to go, I steered clear of the cafeteria and walked to the other wall, studying the announcements on the large bulletin board, hoping for clues as to what this place was exactly. One paper in particular caught my eye. Free guitar lessons from Conner Anderson every Thursday night from six to seven at campsite number one.

"Honey, I'm home!"

Instantly, I recognized Conner's voice. The way he spoke—in a somewhat quick, throwaway, carefree manner—was unmistakable.

I turned just in time to see him entering the cafeteria with the guy from the security monitor trailing behind him. Watching Conner take a seat at the picnic table and then devouring breakfast felt surreal. He seemed to enjoy his playful banter with his friend around bites of pancakes and sips of orange juice. This Conner looked more like my Conner than the pictures Sam showed me. His dreads were gone, replaced by a hairstyle that wasn't exactly long or short, more like Harry Potter during his fourth year at Hogwarts. As someone who liked to listen to punk rock and indie rock in equal doses, he was always a character who seemed at odds with himself. I just figured he hadn't made up his mind about the kind of person he wanted to be yet, and why should he? He had been seventeen and had every right to believe he had all the time in the world to figure things out. The burden of responsibility threatened to weigh me down again. But at the same time, this responsibility had given me purpose, and led me to Conner.

After one last sweep of the area, I decided the coast was clear for me to step inside the cafeteria. But after a few steps toward Conner's table, I stopped short. A girl pretty enough to stop traffic smoothed down his hair from across the table. My mouth hung open by its own accord, and I sunk down onto the nearest bench, thinking this was the end of me.

Things only deteriorated as I watched their interaction. She soon wrapped him in a hug before launching into a heated discussion. A spat between lovers? But there was Conner's trademark look of almost intimidating coolness, so perhaps this girl cared way more for him than he did about her. I gained some confidence back as I realized some things never changed, then stood to approach him once more. But I stopped short again when I saw him giving her a familiar peck on the lips.

Oh, this was a mistake. Why would I ever think he'd be lost without me? Tears blurred my vision as the words 'too late' echoed through my mind, everything within me turning to ice. 'Too late' seemed to be the story of my life. I wanted to run the other way and forget the past twenty-four hours.

But I told myself to be rational, to use the I.Q. God gifted me with to think things through. I decided whatever happened, for better or worse, I hadn't come this far to turn back now without even saying hello to my best friend. And that's all he ever was… my *friend.* No reason whatsoever to feel jealous of this girl right now. Except now might not be the time to let Conner know I was here, but—

"Olga?"

My heart stopped. For a moment, time seemed to stop as well, and my body froze in a strange position. Our last outing together flashed before my eyes, and joy finally settled in—I'd found my way to him again.

He ran to me, lifted me off the ground, and swung me around and around, letting me know he felt the same way.

So much for staying inconspicuous.

"Is it you? Is it really you, or am I dreaming?"

Our gazes met. I couldn't believe I was looking at Conner, staring into his blue eyes. He wore a pair of dark gray athletic shorts that rested on his knees and a plain white T-shirt revealing his muscled body quite well. I knew I shouldn't be thinking about his muscles or his flat, hard stomach, but old habits died hard. Already a familiar feeling hung between us, like no time was lost.

Pinching his stomach, I said, "It's really me."

His eyes filled with tears. "But, how?"

I stood on my tippy toes and reached up, placing my hands on his shoulders as I whispered into his ear. "Shh, not here."

He grabbed my hand, and I shuddered. For a moment, we both just stood there, studying each other again.

"Okay, let's go somewhere more private. Follow me."

CHAPTER SEVENTEEN

"There is no flaw or vacuum in the amount of the truth—
but that all is truth without exception."
—Walt Whitman

So, what have you been up to?" he asked, like this was completely normal.

Laughing, I held his gaze steadily. I couldn't stop looking at Conner sitting across from me on his military style cot inside his tent.

In the cafeteria, he'd quickly introduced me to his roommate Bo, then to Julia, who stood silently, looking from Conner to me and back again. She didn't give her stamp of approval on our alone time, but Conner didn't wait around for her judgment either.

Now we both laughed at his question, and then there was silence for a moment. "Oh, you know, the usual stuff. Drinking coffee, joining the cheerleading squad with Tammy, winning karaoke contests with Sean, breaking world records at Grand Haven High School."

He nodded, rubbing the stubble on his chin, and I could see a question on its way, one that would prove hard to answer. "Uh, you didn't die? Are you visiting me by… by the power of the Force, and now you're here to try to dead Yoda me?"

"Did I detect some classic Conner sarcasm in that question?"

"Um, yeah. Because I'm not sure I want to hear the truth. I want you to be alive, and you spent the last year with our friends, but that doesn't explain how you're here right now."

My eyes traveled up to his forehead, where both eyebrows were still singed from the accident, and I sighed.

Conner plugged his ears.

"What are you doing?"

"It's just that sigh you let loose. Seriously, I think you busted my eardrum. This must be one hell of a story you're getting ready to tell."

I shoved him sideways, and he fell off the cot. We both laughed again, and I felt all the history between us returning, putting me at ease as if we still lived back in those simpler times. I spent the next hour or so telling him about Limbo, about Nate in Limbo with me, because how could I leave Nate out of my story? I told him about a year of grief, sympathy, hardship, loss, atonement, and even love. I told him about leaving behind the person I'd been and moving on to the person I wanted to be.

He sat back, leaning on his palms. "Okay, number one. The person you had been was awesome. And num"—he stopped and shook his head—"so, what do you remember about the accident?"

"I…" *I remember your gorgeous eyes, looking over the lake, and then I remember you falling into nothingness.* The grief from the memory washed over me, and I couldn't get any words out. I stared at the tent, at the bed, anywhere but Conner's face. Our lives as we knew it were gone, and I still couldn't get over that fact. Before I realized what was happening, I sniffled. "I'm so sorry."

"Sorry for what? It wasn't your fault I got struck by lightning."

"No." More sniffling. "But I was the one who introduced you to sailing. I was the one who asked you to go with me that day because I was jealous of Tammy. I was supposed to be the responsible one, but I didn't make you put on your lifejacket or wear mine. I didn't notice until it was too late that you stopped breathing." Suddenly, I felt dizzy, my vision swimming.

"Come here," Conner said, sitting next to me and drawing me close. "Don't play the blame game. You'll frickin' kill yourself with those kinds of thoughts."

I recoiled at his comment. *Yeah, no kidding.* Still, I was grateful for his last sentence because I could use his choice of swear words to avoid the subject at hand.

"What, are you too classy to say the real bad words now? Taking a page from Nic?"

Nicole always used the fake swear words while we worked at The Bookman. Since her parents were always around as the store owners, they wouldn't have appreciated the things she really wanted to say when relaying the daily high school drama to me while we stocked the shelves. Instead, she started saying frick, fudge, shoot, and darn, and then the PG words just stuck to the point where she never muttered the real swear words anymore.

Conner nodded. "I'm trying to work on having better language. I figured it couldn't hurt my situation here."

I raised one eyebrow. "Yeah? Call me impressed."

"Well, not cursing is considerably easier to do without GTA to play. I was thinking of going British style with the swear words. You know, wanker, bugger, bloody hell. Figured that might be a step up from before. I feel like I may need a twelve step program or something."

I covered my mouth, trying not to laugh at his absurd thought process. "Whatever you want. I just think you may be missing the whole point though."

His jaw twitched. "How's that?"

I shrugged. "God wants us to care about what He cares about, and He always cares about people more than rules. The stories we read about Jesus demonstrated that over and over again. If you say more than five hundred thousand people die of cancer every year in America, but most people don't give a flying—insert chosen expletive here—Jesus will take more offense to people dying and us not doing anything to help than saying a 'bad word,' ya know?"

He looked at me. "I hear ya, but if that's how you feel, why have I never heard you say a *real* cuss word."

"Because I'm perfect." I winked at him. "Besides, I used to get a whipping for saying the 's' word all the time as a kid."

His mouth fell open. "You did? I never heard any type of potty language from you. Well, except crap."

"No, the 's' word to my mom was stupid or shut up."

"Right? I do remember her looking at me like I'd killed her parents whenever I said those words around her, too."

"Oh, you remember that, do you?"

"A couple things about my time with you stuck." He remained silent for a moment, and I heard birds calling out somewhere. "But I can't remember when you died."

My eyes went wide. "I'm sorry?"

He sighed. "I mean, I must've died quickly. I hardly remember a thing. Just us joking around, then blinding rain, then the strike, then you screaming my name, then someone trying to save me. I thought that someone was probably you, but now… were you hit by the lightning, too?"

I shifted uncomfortably out of his arms. "No, Conner." I tiptoed around the subject like it was dynamite. Any minute now, I would explode. "The lightning strike flung you from the boat. I dove in after you. The water was freezing. It took me a while, too long, to get you and swim back to the boat, and hypothermia set in. Eventually, I draped you over the lifebuoy and dialed 9-1-1. I should've noticed sooner you weren't breathing, should've pulled you on board sooner to administer the rescue breaths. I kept repeating the CPR steps over and over again. It was maybe five or six times before the boom of the sailboat swung in the wind and knocked me unconscious."

Conner had been completely still while I spoke, but he groaned now, stomping his foot before standing. Sadness and anger clouded his features like the thunderstorm that had darkened the sky that fateful night. He picked up a lantern and flung it across the room, away from me. The light bulb inside exploded, a fitting metaphor for what my heart was doing.

"I can't believe this! I'm the reason you're dead!"

My entire body went cold. "What? No, Conner, let me finish."

"Please," he sobbed. "Don't tell me anything more. I was right about not wanting to know the truth."

I picked at a loose thread on the blanket covering his cot, tears streaming down my face. In my experience, knowing the truth tended to get you into a lot of trouble. I bent a lot of rules to come here. Actually, forget bending. I smashed them to the ground and made my own. And for what? To make Conner feel guilty about something he wasn't responsible for? I still hadn't informed him about becoming a spirit guide. Now I thought maybe not telling him anything else was the best plan of action.

He sat next to me, reached out and touched my hand. At first, the notion summoned a thousand other times he'd done the same thing for a number of reasons. But none of those reasons felt like this. This hand on my hand felt strange.

"Do you think everything happens for a reason?" He swept a tear off my cheek.

I stared at the ground, praying I could give a right answer for once, an answer that would bring comfort. "Yes. I mean, I'm sure we'd all love a perfect life. But like it or not, everything serves a purpose."

He glanced uneasily at me. "Yeah, Leo always touches on that point at our weekly service. He says you can't be triumphant without going through trials first." He squeezed my hand. "Why did you come here, Olga?"

The same familiar blue eyes from my childhood bore into mine.

"The truth?"

He nodded.

"To see you. I just needed to see my friend." I squeezed his hand back, harder than I meant to. "Even though I felt more alive this past year as a dead person, how could I ever be happy after learning the truth from Dr. Judy? After knowing in my heart someone I deeply cared for wasn't there with me, but was within my grasp somewhere. At times, I tried to fight how I felt. But I think God put us in each other's lives for a reason, and I thought I needed to use my situation to help you. And maybe you don't need my help, but you're a real part of me and for me as a whole to ever be saved, you would have to be there, as much as my own body has to be with my soul."

He scooted closer and put both arms around me, hugging me as we both sobbed some more. Despite our sadness, I basked in the feeling of his warm arms around my shoulders, of the stubble of his chin on my scalp, of the closeness of us as my head rested on his chest. There was a long silence before he asked another question.

"What was your reaction when, when you found out you had been dead that whole year?"

I sat up, displacing his head. "I thought the news was the most absurd thing I'd ever heard. Wouldn't you?"

He tugged at the blond hair falling into his eyes. He needed another haircut, and the thought struck me as odd, that his hair was still growing. Mine didn't anymore.

"Remember my Aunt Tricia?" He grabbed a box from the shelf in-between his and Bo's cots and passed me a tissue. "The nutty family member everyone has? She believed in ghosts, went to psychics, and had a Ouija board. I thought all of her superstitions were insane, but she was smarter than all of us."

I laughed. Of course, only Conner could make me grin with one of his remarks at a time like this.

"You look really pretty when you laugh."

An awkward silence pierced the air like a cannonball. I wasn't used to compliments from Conner. I was used to a boy who thought of me as the nerdy best friend he loved to tease.

I cleared my throat. "Well, this isn't weird at all."

"Do you want to hear a corny joke?" His voice was unsteady. I didn't think I'd ever heard his voice sound unsteady until today.

Shooting him a fake-annoyed look, I said, "Is the sky blue, the grass green?"

He smiled. "How do you make a hormone?"

I threw my pillow at him. "Conner! Don't tell that kind of joke here."

He lifted his shoulders and shrugged. "What? The only dirty mind here is you. All I was thinking is you like science, and it's a science joke."

"Oh, you remember *that*, do you?" I twisted my hands in his blanket.

"Olga, I remember everything about you."

Suddenly, a lump rose in my throat. "Mhmm. Where'd you hear this joke?"

"Sean told it to me in ninth grade."

Swallowing over the lump, I blinked hard. "Then I definitely don't want to hear the punch line. You wouldn't believe the amount of totally inappropriate jokes he passed on to Nate."

I blushed, forgetting I probably shouldn't mention He-Who-Must-Not-Be-Named.

"Ah, him again." He spoke in a harsh tone, one I'd hardly ever heard him use before. "So how serious is this relationship?"

I didn't know how to answer this, so I deflected, like usual. "You know a nap sounds really good about now. Aren't you tired? It looks late outside."

"It always looks late outside. But we can climb underneath the covers if you want. I just wouldn't get too comfortable because I'll sit on top of you and fart until you tell me everything."

"Back to your old dirty bag of tricks already? I figured an experience like this would've made you a little more mature."

"I'm still just a rocker who likes to have fun."

"And I'm still the quirky geek girl, except I'm dead and met my first boyfriend in an alternate universe. When you get beyond that, not much has changed."

He gave me an incredulous look, and even in the darkness, I could see myself reflected in his eyes. "Everything changed today. For the past year, all I saw was your face. Your freckles scattered across your cheeks. You're untamable red hair. Your moody eyes—always shifting from green to blue. Your nose—always in a book. Your lips—always pressed together in thought." He lifted his hand and outlined the shape of my mouth with the tip of his finger.

I held my breath as my heart pounded. Him touching me this way, THE guy I'd always loved, felt intimate. No, not intimate. We'd been intimate friends for a long time. This felt a hundred times better than intimate, this felt… sexy.

"Now you're here. And I really want to do something with you, even some things I shouldn't want to do since you have a boyfriend, not to mention my girlfriend."

I swallowed, then took a breath while glancing around the tent and trying not to blush, my hands shaking. "Wow, you're not holding back anything, huh?"

As if his confession hadn't thrown me for a loop already, the thought occurred to me that I hadn't known for sure if the girl with him earlier, Julia, was his girlfriend. Now my brain shouted, *Newsflash, Katie Couric! Of course, he has a girlfriend! He's probably had a million of them here! This is Conner!*

"I know this must all seem confusing. But I promised myself if I ever got to see you again, I'd tell you the truth. No more secrets… my new words to live by, or die by."

I wasn't sure I was ready for his truths. For sure, I wasn't ready to tell mine; including the fact that Nate technically wasn't my boyfriend anymore, so I tried to lighten the mood. "Hmm, no more secrets. Conner, once when I was in second grade, I told everyone Jon Bon Jovi was my boyfriend."

"You know what I mean."

I did. His words tugged at my heart. I knew I had to explain the entire situation about how I got here. Not just about the deal with the demon, but also how I ended my own life. Right now, he believed I died alongside him, even because of him. I wished I had the guts to tell him everything. But no matter how much I knew what I should do, I just couldn't bring myself to get the words out. I was stressed enough about figuring out how to corrupt the Alpha File 120, so Sam wouldn't really get the information, and about finding a way to stay with Conner for longer than twenty-four hours. Rehashing the events of my death in detail would only add to my growing list of problems. We'd need to cross that bridge later.

Out of the corner of my eye, I saw Conner giving me a look, waiting for me to respond.

I stood. "Are you gonna show me around this place or not? It's not every day a girl gets to travel to another dimension."

For a moment, he just sat there, a flabbergasted expression on his face. "Right then. Time to change the subject." He stood, and then grabbed his guitar. "Follow me. It's about time I took you out on our first date."

Without meaning to, I let a smile slip across my face, remembering so many other days and nights I had wished for Conner to say those exact words to me.

CHAPTER EIGHTEEN

"This above all: to thine own self be true,
And it must follow, as the night the day,
Thou canst not then be false to any man."
—William Shakespeare, Hamlet

Once outside the tent, Conner took my hand in his and led the way with a tiny flashlight. Feeling the warmth of his hand over mine made my heart feel like it was sky diving as he showed me around the mazelike forest.

"So, what is there to do here?"

He craned his head to look back at me. "We really just have the usual camp stuff. There are bikes to ride. The lake water is always warm for swimming, and it's ultimate sailing weather here year round, never any storms. Inside the school, there's a rec room with a television and couches to watch movies, nothing over PG-13 of course. There's also some pool tables, air hockey, dartboards, and two bowling lanes. Oh, and we have a massive library spanning the two floors, with a coffee shop inside. When I can't stand missing you for one more second, I'll go there and read your favorite classics. I'll even drink a coffee in your honor, despite still loathing the stuff."

I pushed away the tiny voice in my head telling me I wasn't here to flirt. "Is that where you're taking me for our first date? Plenty of opportunities in the library to woo me with some poetry and pour some Bailey's into my coffee."

He blinked at me. "Are you implying I need to get you liquored up to be interested in me? If so, I'm seriously gonna have to work on my skills. And wooing? Sounds like your mom's vernacular finally rubbed off on you. I see we're back to the turn of the century."

"Yeah," I said, my voice dropping to a whisper, thinking about how much I missed my mom. "She'd want a proper courtship for her one and only daughter, so you better make our trip to the rec room or the library spectacular."

He grinned. "Any of those options would be fine for another girl, but not for you."

His voice lacked the seductive tone he'd used on other girls. This tone felt genuine.

We made our way along a deep green canal, our usual banter leaving little room for quiet. He held my hand firmly the whole time too, and I couldn't help but think how right it felt, his hand in mine. Eventually, we came to a crossing bridge at the foot of a large leafy tree. The bridge led to a set of wooden stairs, lots of them, winding up to a simple platform surrounding a rather large Swiss Family Robinson like habitat.

I tightened my grip on Conner's hand. "What is this place?"

"A tree house. When I first stumbled upon this place, the kid in me got so jacked up. I have so many good memories of playing with you in my backyard fort. It just made being here in Juvie seem more like home."

I could feel his gaze on me as I stared up at the top. "How many stairs do we need to climb?"

He laughed. "One hundred thirty-three, but the panoramic view from the wrap-around porch at the top is better than anything I've seen here. Well, until you showed up today."

Guilt washed over me. I had begun to enjoy myself way too much. I still hadn't told Conner the truth about how I died or how I got here. Determination set in, and I decided I had to tell him soon, before this 'date' went any further.

"Race you to the top!" I yelled, dropping his hand before sprinting up the first set of stairs.

Squinting in the darkness, I realized this might not have been the best of challenges. But being dead had its advantages. Being fast or getting tired or having an asthma attack wasn't a concern anymore. Instead, I focused on how it felt to be here, for the moment, acting like a kid again with Conner.

Soon, he sprinted next to me, laughing as the wind whipped around us. This was what my entire life had been about. Moments like this with my best friend. Romantic or not, Conner was my soul mate. My love for him was innocent and tied to every nostalgic memory I had of my childhood. We'd always be connected because what we had went beyond romance or friendship.

I didn't know what kind of soul mate Nate was anymore, but I counted myself lucky to have two soul mates in the span of my short 'life,' three if I counted Nic, and I did. To me, a soul mate went way beyond romance. Soul mates were the people I could share my life with on a deeper level; all the things, truths, thoughts, hopes, fears, disappointments, and dreams that my life encompassed. They were with me, and I was with them, for the long run. If we didn't see each other for a year, we could pick right up where we left off and not miss a beat, like Conner and I did today.

I knew I still loved Nate, but our time together only spanned the past year. Maybe there wasn't enough history to keep us together forever. Maybe I was too quick to lump him into the soul-mate category.

Whatever the case, I knew I'd made the right choice by coming here. I owed Conner coming here, no matter what Nate thought. With peace in my heart, I knew the first thing I needed to do was just enjoy the moment. Putting off telling him all the gory details could wait another hour or so.

We climbed a plain wooden ladder one rung at a time for the last leg of our journey, so racing wasn't an option. He let me go first. Dying must've turned him into a gentleman. At the top, Conner laid his guitar case against a tree, and then pushed the hair out of his eyes before taking my shoulders and turning me gently, so we both faced the same way.

Ever since I started sailing, I learned I'm a better person outdoors. Something about the way the moons and stars shone here on the lake below, the musky smell of the ash tree, and the fresh breeze lifting the wisps of hair around my face made me feel like I was home again, too.

I walked to the edge of the platform, surrounded by ropes for safety, and looked down. "This view is breathtaking."

"Yeah, when I feel like this stuff is just too big to comprehend, I come up here. There's something about a tree house that feels just my size. You want to look inside?"

I turned to him, and heard his gasp of breath as I kissed his cheek. All the times of spending as many hours as possible out in the sunshine, running through sprinklers, digging in the dirt, having picnics on the beach together, flashed in my mind.

"I'd be delighted to."

"Delighted?" He lifted his chin, a smile tugging at the edge of his mouth. "Well, come on then."

Conner stopped before the entrance and nudged aside a pile of leaves with his foot. He held the door open for me, and I stepped in. After blinking and giving my eyes time to adjust, the first things I noticed about the tree house were the glass walls with window seats lining the entire inside. In each corner, there was a large basket, one filled with *The Chronicles of Narnia* books, another filled with typical camping snacks, another filled with lanterns and flashlights, and the last one filled with games like cards and dominoes. A large rug covered the floor, a few blankets stacked off to the side, and I wondered if campers sometimes spent the night in here.

"So this is it?"

"This is it. You sound disappointed."

"Not disappointed. It's just from the outside the tree house seemed more fancy."

"It's got the only thing I need inside." He reached out to touch my hand. "Do you always wear the Morticia Addams ring I gave you, or did you just put it on for this trip?"

I shrugged. "Sometimes for luck. Sometimes wearing the ring was too hard."

Conner grabbed his guitar from the side of the tree. "I wrote a song about you. Would you like to hear it?"

Laughter bubbled up from deep inside me. "If you're referring to *Ode to a Septic Tank*, Nate already sang me that hit."

His blue eyes blazed, looking thoroughly pissed. "*He* sang you *my* song?"

Twisting the ring around my finger, I said, "The band found your songbook. They were all just trying to cheer me up after you died."

"How did they find my *real* songbook if you were dead and everything that happened to you was *fake*?" His nostrils flared like a raging bull. "Are you playing with me or something? Because it's not funny."

"Conner, would you seriously think I would mess with you like that? Life—death—ugh!" I screamed, my body trembling. "Limbo just mimicked everything about our life exactly. You don't understand how real the entire experience felt, and I can't explain it. I can barely comprehend the past year myself. But I would never, ever play such a cruel joke on you, on anyone."

He ducked his head. "I'm sorry. I just… wanted to be the one to sing that song to you on your birthday. It's not like I thought you wouldn't move on or anything, but I'm still jealous that you did. Does that make sense?"

"Yes," I whispered. "Being jealous makes total sense because that's exactly how I felt when I saw you this morning with Julia. But you should know, I never really moved on. Otherwise, I wouldn't be here with you. After I found out Nate and I were dead this past year, almost every single second was spent thinking about how to find you. I never would've stopped trying either."

His eyes lit up. "Really?"

I nodded. "We can do the secret handshake swear if you don't believe me."

He laughed my favorite laugh from childhood, one filled with the giddiness of innocence that makes a person want to giggle with him. "I believe you, but I still want to do the handshake."

We both put our own hands together, then hit them back and forth three times before stopping and hi-fiving above and underneath our left hands. Then we shook with one hand while using the other to shake each other's foot.

When we finished, he pulled me against him and dropped a kiss on my forehead, and I remembered the last time he kissed me on the forehead. It was the last day he'd been alive, after I learned he was attending prom with Tammy. I invited him to go sailing that afternoon to prove to her I could go on a date with him whenever I wanted. He'd said yes, then the bell rang, announcing the last period of the day. He kissed me quickly and hurried away, Tammy scowling from afar. At the time, I attributed every cruel stereotype I could imagine to her personality. But during my Limbo, she became one of my best friends. Thinking about how none of that was real could quickly cause me to have a whack attack, so I was thankful for Conner holding me now.

"What are you thinking about?" he whispered.

"About the last day you were alive."

"The last day *we* were alive you mean. Do you know what I remember most about that day?"

I tipped my head back to look up at him. "Tell me."

"When you told me *Home* by Edward Sharpe and the Magnetic Zeroes was the song that most reminded you of me."

My arms around his neck slid down his shoulders and arms, the tips of my fingers brushing the warm, hard muscle of his biceps. "That's because home is wherever I'm with you."

He stepped free of me, blushing, just like he'd done the last time I told him that. "Come, sit on the rug. I want to play you that song I wrote."

I rumpled his blond hair as we walked to the center of the tree house together. "So there is a different song than the one about the septic tank?"

Bending over his guitar, he placed his fingers on the cords. "Oh, that song was total crap compared to this one. It's called *Your Love,* and this one is from my perspective during the past year while I pined away for you."

My heart leaped, despite my surprise at another bold pronouncement. His gaze met mine, and when he began singing the soft melody, I felt like we were the only two people in the world.

"Your love is a drug controlling me/ Desire so bad I can't even see/ I wish I didn't know what I know/ I wish that I could just let you go/ It's the very thing I neglected saying I told you so/ Demonstrating I really was as lost as my afterlife shows/ It looks like lightning in the sky tonight/ Storm clouds fill my thoughts and nothing's all right/ There's only your love to run to in the theater of my mind/ When I wish I could leave this world behind/ Looking back on my life not so long ago/ I was living as a care-free soul/ Doing all the things Mom told me not to do/ Like kissing all those girls but now I wish they were all you/ Looking back on my life I see the truth now/ You were the best thing that I found/ It looks like lightning in the sky tonight/ Storm clouds fill my thoughts and nothing's all right/ There's only your love to run to in the theater of my mind/ When I wish I could leave this world behind/ I hope that unlike me you're not torn/ I never want to see you mourn/ Deep inside my restless soul/ It's only you I want to hold/ In my heart you're forever mine/ And we stay together until the end of time/ I wish I could leave this world behind."

My mouth opened, and then closed, words failing me. My mind flashed to the only other time Conner directly sang to me. The Cantankerous Monkey Squad had been performing at the Grand Haven Music Walk event downtown. It was the first time I saw them perform at an actual venue. Previously, I'd only seen them play in Conner's basement or at school since my mom wouldn't let me travel to the bigger places like Grand Rapids and Detroit to see the gigs they'd booked that year. Nic and I danced and mosh-pitted at the front of the stage during their whole show. At the end of their set, they played *Return*, a huge crowd-pleaser, the audience chanting the chorus with Conner: *So don't be afraid, I will return/ After my life lessons I have learned/ I will return/ Return. Return.*

The whole crowd howled with excitement, so Conner just kept playing, pulling me on stage and repeating the lines over and over. He even turned the mic on me, encouraging me to take over, but I wouldn't give in to his whims for once. None of that mattered though, because the audience still sang the words for me. The set was done, so Conner said his *Thank you and goodnight* and walked off the stage, his arm around my waist, the rest of the band following in our wake as Kyle threw his drumsticks into the mob. For the first time in my life, I felt like I walked a moment in Conner's shoes, the rock star, the popular one. Even better, I felt like his girlfriend as he kept singing the song into my ear backstage, all smiles, like he'd written the song for me.

And now it felt like history being rewritten, because he had been returned to me, something I didn't think possible for so long.

So no need to cry/ This isn't goodbye/ For you I will always sing/ Like eagles we will soar with our new wings/ When the curtain tears in two at the end of the day/ My love for you will never fade away/I will return.

Conner exhaled a loud breath, clearing the song out of my head.

"Do you think you made the right decision in coming here to see me?"

I scooted closer to him on the rug. "If I think about it, then no. But if I go by how I feel, then yes."

"How do you feel?" He reached out and pushed a strand of hair behind my ear, then let his index finger trail down my cheek.

His light touch made me shiver. "I feel happy. Like searching for you was the right thing to do, even if it technically wasn't."

His hand fell into his own lap, but my face still burned from the path of his touch. He put his hands on my waist and pulled me even closer. "What about kissing me? Does that feel like the right thing to do? Because I love you. I've been in love with you for a long time, and I've spent the last year regretting not doing anything about it."

My heart pounded, and I swallowed, trying to think of what to say. Could it be that just yesterday I broke up with Nate? And now what? I was just gonna go straight into Conner's arms, like the past few months with Nate didn't even matter? Making rash decisions wasn't my calling card. Decisions that were thought out ahead of time, the results tallied in good or bad columns, that were beneficial to everyone involved, that was how I rolled. Rash decisions were often the downfall of even the best of people, and in the long haul, rash decisions usually proved regrettable, sometimes painful, and very hard to undo. I'd already hypnotized Dr. Judy, conspired to commit acts of treason with a demon, and broken up with a guy I truly loved.

If I looked in a mirror, I wouldn't be able to recognize the girl I'd become. My faith had become a doubting Thomas. At times, I thought my faith gave me the courage to do the things that needed to be done. Mom had this magnet on our fridge at home that said, 'Courage is fear that has said its prayers.' But now, I was reminded of all the ways this situation didn't fit. Conner had been my *friend* for years. We shouldn't mess with a good thing.

And that's when it hit me. All this time, hadn't that been my second biggest regret? Number one was I'd tried to rescue Conner and he died anyway, then I died from the guilt. But number two was never getting to tell him I loved him and seeing if our friendship could've been more. I'd been wanting Conner for so long. I knew I still loved Nate, but he didn't love me anymore, and I owed it to myself to see if there could be anything with Conner. After all, I'd thought it would be him and me forever from the moment I didn't think boys had cooties.

Opening my mouth to tell him all of this, I realized something else. I'd been wrapped up in the three little words I never got to say to him, but sometimes words weren't enough. Sometimes the actions, the execution of *showing* someone how you felt was what mattered. Just like faith, love without actions was dead.

So I let my body answer for me. Once again, he was a magnet drawing me near. I had never kissed him on the lips, only soft brushes on the cheek in goodbye or hello. This kiss felt like many goodbyes and hellos rolled into one. Immediately, all my doubts floated away as he pulled me down next to him. I wanted to remember everything: the slant of his mouth over mine, the shape of his body under my hands. His fingers seemed to multiply: stroking my back, smoothing my hair, tickling my sides, all at once.

A million years might've gone by, Earth might've stopped turning, and I might've drifted into another dimension, because time and space seemed to disappear when he held me.

I kissed him like I was the one drowning this time, and he was my air supply. Then Nate's face flashed in my mind, and I couldn't help comparing. If the kisses Nate had for me were all sweetness, Conner's kiss was pure desperation, and I could taste the difference. I'd been waiting for this kiss my whole life.

I brushed my lips against his ear. "I always loved you, too, Conner."

It felt like I had something else to say, maybe something about our timing always being off and if he thought it was a sign that we weren't 'meant to be'? But then he half groaned my name and kissed me again, and I forgot my words.

"I can't believe we were both in love with each other, and it took this long for us to say anything." His lips whispered against mine, gentle and careful.

But I didn't want gentle and careful anymore, because those things just reminded me of Nate, and I wanted to forget him now. I pulled Conner on top of me, gathering all of his body against mine, and kissed him with a fierceness I hadn't even known I was capable of.

When we finally drew apart, his eyes were glassy. "So, you liked the song then?"

I traced the line of his jaw with my finger. "Much better than *Ode to a Septic Tank*."

His mouth crooked up at the corner as he rolled off me. "That was going to be the breakout hit of Cantankerous Monkey Squad. The internet would've thought it was hilarious, and then Ellen would've had us on her show and signed us to her record label."

Leaning in, I rested my head on his shoulder, my face against the crook of his neck. "Well, the internet did think it was hilarious in my Limbo state. Nic filmed Nate and Sean doing the song and posted the video on You Tube, and it got a lot of hits."

My heart pounded, as if just now remembering Nate and all the things I still needed to confess to Conner. He kissed me on the forehead, then moved to set his mouth over mine before noticing how still I'd become.

"What's wrong?"

I wasn't ready to face all the heavy yet, so I put off the truths a little while longer. "Well, it's just I've told you all about what I've been up to this past year, but I don't know anything about your life here."

He propped himself on one elbow and looked down at me. "I was wondering when you were gonna ask me how I've been. You're incredibly rude, you know?"

I slammed my palm against his shoulder and he fell backward, a twisted smile on his face. Before I had time to think of a comeback, he pulled me on top of him.

"Do you really think I care about updating you on the past twelve months? All I want to do is kiss you. That's all I've ever wanted to do."

"And there will be plenty of that coming, after you tell me about your time in Juvie."

"Fine, but can we stay like this as I tell you?"

Resting my head on his chest, I said, "Deal."

He worked on undoing my braid and ran his fingers through my hair. "Well, when I first arrived at Juvie, Leo met me at the gate and explained the situation. They offered me counseling sessions, too, but I refused. I figured talking about what I'd missed, mainly you… I didn't see how that would be therapeutic. So for the first two months, Juvie felt like prison. I didn't eat or leave my tent, except when Bo made me."

"Since when could anybody make you do anything?"

"He's my roommate, my accountability partner. It's like a brotherhood, and we can influence each other a bit more than others can. So he made me attend my Intro to Juvie class at Camp Fusion High, made sure I came with him to the weekly Sunday service, helped me with my chores."

"There are chores, too?"

"Yep. It's a lot like being a teenager on Earth, except more sheltered, and dark. Eventually, I started to see there was no point in my moping around. I was going to be stuck here for a long time, probably longer than I lived on Earth, so I might as well make the most of things. After that reality check, I went back to what I knew and started to do what I did best."

"Flirting?" I teased, but the thought made my heart shrink inside my chest.

"Hahaha. Not too far off. Socializing, just to keep my mind off you. At first, I was just *fakin' it till I made it* type of thing. But I also wrote tons of music during that time. That's when I finally started crying over everything that had happened, crying mainly over having to let you go. Leo saw I needed something to keep me going, so he suggested I start weekly guitar lessons in exchange for one of my chores, and then I became kind of popular, and more at ease here."

I looked up at him. "Are there not many guitar players in this camp?"

He laughed. "There are, just none that play as good as me. Or sing well for that matter, so I've kinda thrown in voice lessons as an extra bonus."

Raising an eyebrow, I said, "Looks like death has managed to humble you."

"What? It's not my fault I rock to Holy Heaven! God gives us gifts, and I'm just trying to use mine. And by the way, music isn't the only gift I have."

I took the bait. "Oh, really? What's your other gift?"

"Haven't you noticed tonight? This," he whispered, brushing his lips against mine, sending shivers down my spine. "Can I stop telling stories now, and do more of this?"

His mouth brushed against the spot just behind my ear, leaving me trembling. Part of me wanted to ask about Julia, who he was in fact, still dating. That also made me think of Nate, who I wasn't dating anymore, but that didn't mean I was over him. As Conner's lips made their way to mine again, I pressed a finger to his mouth.

"Conner, stop. We're moving too fast."

"On the contrary. It's taken us thirteen *years* to get here."

I squeezed my eyes shut, forcing some self-control. "You know what I mean."

The tips of his fingers trailed down my back, finally coming to rest in the back pocket of my jeans. "What do you suggest we do instead?"

"Why don't you show me around Juvie some more?"

He smiled at me, his eyes growing wide. "I know the perfect thing to do with you. Come on."

Chapter Nineteen

"Know that the true worth of your travels
lies not just in where you've come to be,
but in who you became along the way."
—Linda Staten

Conner hauled the sailboat out onto the lake.

"She's a nice boat," I said, hopping aboard.

Conner jumped on behind me, then flipped on a navigation light so we could see in the darkness. "Yep. All of them are a standard fifteen feet. I give sailing lessons here, too."

"So, he can sing, he can play guitar, he can sail, he—"

"Is incredibly insightful and freakishly good-looking. I know, I know. The list goes on and on."

I clicked my tongue. "Yup, and humble. Don't forget that."

He plunged around in a storage locker on the starboard side, dug out two life jackets, and then propped one in a corner. He sat down and leaned back before noticing my stare. "Oh, don't worry. No storms, remember?"

I pulled the other life jacket on. "I'd rather not tempt fate. Everything has the potential to be a test."

Wind parted Conner's hair. "Oh, okay. Even though we're dead, I'll wear one if it makes you feel better." He pulled the jacket over his shirt, and then saw my frozen face. "What? Too early to make a flippant remark about dying?"

"No, I was just wondering, why do you even have life jackets here then? Can you still get hurt?"

"Yeah, I mean nothing can kill us, but we still get hurt. Don't you?"

I thought back to my time on Limbo, when ramming head first into a sliding glass door and slicing my hand with a cutlery knife did nothing to me. "Nope. Not as a spirit—" *Crap. I almost forgot I didn't tell him that part yet.* "Not as a spirit during my alternative timeline. I guess each realm has its own set of regulations."

"Well, you may be operating under our rules now that you're here, so I wouldn't take up juggling machetes any time soon."

"Aw, but that's the sole purpose of my visit."

He threw his head back in laughter, and then went about setting a course, avoiding the jagged rocks along the shore.

"You ever walk along the rocks like we used to down by Lake Michigan?"

"I pretty much spend all my free time at this lake. In fact, sometimes when I can't sleep, I sneak out to come here and listen to the lapping of the water against the side of the boats. It's nice, being able to sail again."

I nodded. There was nothing that could beat the freedom I felt from sailing. Lake Michigan provided a wonderful thinking spot during my middle and high school days. Often the only sound interrupting my pondering was the occasional Coast Guard ship signaling their return to Grand Haven. One hour always faded into the next, and before I knew it, I'd neglected my entire to-do list for the freedom of the water. My parents managed a marina together, so I grew up around boats my whole life. The summer after fifth grade was when I taught Conner how to sail.

A tiny light flashed in the air, zapping me out of my trip down Memory Lane. "Are those fireflies?"

"Yep."

I shook my head. "It amazes me, all the stuff that's the same in the Underworld."

"You can find those little guys around the lake here 24/7." He scanned the darkness. "And you're right; we do have a lot of the comforts from home. There's also a floating dock we all like to do flips off and skip rocks from. Some campers are still afraid of the lake though, even in Juvie. I guess *Jaws* robbed the experience from them of ever swimming in anything that isn't chlorinated."

"Does Julia swim in the lake?" I hoped she didn't. I just couldn't help myself; I wanted her to be the type of prissy girl nobody from the Jedi Order would like.

Conner changed course abruptly, as if the question caught him off guard. "No, but she said it was actually the *Friday the 13th* movies that ruined freshwater swimming for her. By the way, as soon as I see her again, I'm breaking up with her."

We headed toward the tip of something, a small island from the looks of it, but seeing in the dark still proved difficult for me. "How'd you guys get together anyway?"

The sound of the wind multiplied, as if somehow protesting my question.

"Bo's girlfriend, Cheri, hooked us up. We'd all been hanging out quite a bit, just doing the usual stuff. About a month ago, Cheri asked if I wanted to see a movie with her and Bo. When I got to the rec room, Cheri shoved me ahead of them and shut the door. Julia waited on the couch, *A Walk to Remember* starting to play. There were candles and everything. When I sat down, she informed me we were on our first date. The girl doesn't ask permission, she just does what she wants."

I felt my cheeks flame. "Sounds like your kind of girl."

He reached out and held my hand. "You're my type, nobody else even comes close."

My gaze traveled out over the lake, the boat approaching a narrow strip of island. "So was she your first girlfriend in Juvie?"

His eyes searched my face, as if looking for judgment. "Yes and no. My first *girlfriend* I suppose, but I've been on dates with three other girls."

"Three?" I couldn't hold back the surprise in my voice, and the hurt.

He took a deep breath, bringing the boat beside the island. "No second dates followed with those. And like I said, Julia and I have only been together for a month; hardly compares to the thirteen years we've been together."

Conner jumped out of the boat and secured the line to a post in the sand.

I clambered after him, seizing my backpack. "A month is a long time though, for you."

He nodded. "How long have you and Nate been dating?"

"Two months."

We were both quiet for a moment. "So your first relationship has lasted longer than almost all of mine put together."

I looked up at him, meeting his eyes, and realized I still hadn't told him Nate and I weren't together anymore. "I guess. But it's over. We broke up right before I came to Juvie."

"Was it because of me?" His voice was low, like he felt bad.

Shrugging, I said, "Maybe. I mean you factored into our decision, but the truth is, a lot of things were off with us these past couple of weeks."

Moonlight flickered against the water and I shivered, but it wasn't because of the temperature. Cold radiated through me at the memory of losing Nate.

Conner misread my reaction and snaked his arm around my waist. We walked along the beach, silence filling the air. Finally, he knelt down in the sand and grabbed a handful. "There's this passage I read in the Bible recently that talks about God's thoughts for us. The verse says that if we were to count them, it would be like trying to count the grains of sand, and even then, His thoughts would outnumber the vast sum of them. These grains of sand in my hand represent the number of thoughts I had about you in just one hour. No matter where I went, no matter who I was with, I never stopped thinking about you."

I caught his hand, released the grains of sand, and laughed softly. "Okay, Mr. Casanova. I expect to hear this in a song dedicated to me later."

"I've been called far worse. And anything for you. If there were any way for me to know that you were coming back, I would've waited. Believe me; our past was very much alive in my head. But I thought whole-heartedly our future was dead." His lips gently brushed my cheek. "Come here, I want to do something with you."

My steps were a little shaky, wondering what that something was. A question remained in my mind, one I'd always wanted to ask him, but never had the guts to do so. "Conner, did you die a virgin?"

Conner snapped to attention like a solider. "Did you?"

I kicked at his foot lightly. "I asked you first."

He sauntered forward a few steps without me, then turned around. "Yes. Does that surprise you? Did you and Nate ever—"

"Yes."

Conner looked as if I had slapped him. His lips parted, but said nothing for a moment. Even in the almost pitch-black, I could see his eyes shining. "Which question are you saying yes to?" he asked breathlessly.

"Oh!" My voice squealed. "To the first one."

He smiled; his hand seeking and finding mine once more. We strode to the center of the small island where a single oak tree stood.

I frowned, the subject still nagging at me. "Are you still?"

He took a deep breath. "Yes. I mean, I want to tell you the truth. I'm no saint."

A snort escaped my lips. "I think that's well documented."

"True, true. But I just want to be honest with you. I've done many things I'm not proud of, even here, at the beginning, with those girls. I don't know why they just let us roam around Juvie with our free will and hormones intact. They should utilize shock therapy or something. It would make being a guy a lot easier."

"It's okay. I don't think I want to hear anymore." Feeling my face start to burn, I looked up. "Are we gonna climb another tree?"

From the corner of my eye, I saw him raise his head. "Nah. I just remembered the tree as we approached the island, and I got to thinking about your bucket list thing, and I realized not once did we ever carve our initials into a tree. I know tree carving is nothing big, but it just seems like we should claim a spot as our own, right?"

I stroked his back. "Nothing could seem more fitting. I actually have a Swiss army knife in my bag."

Bending low over my backpack, I felt him drop a kiss on the back of my head. "Oh, good. I actually hadn't thought that far ahead about needing something to carve with." When I stood, he kissed my mouth. "I'll take it from here. You just sit back and relax."

"That's what she said."

"The Office! Did you get to watch shows in real time during Limbo? I want to know all about the finale!"

I spent the next ten minutes updating Conner on all the foolish and poignant moments of the last season of our favorite documentary style comedy show. By the time I finished, so did he.

"All right, what do you think?"

I moved to stand in front of him, studying the 'CA+OW=TLF' with the heart around the initials. "TLF? The Espanol abbreviation for telephone?"

"What? No!" he said impatiently.

"No? Total Loan Financing then?"

He took a step away from me, studying my backside. "It actually stands for 'Tight Little Fanny.' I thought if the shoe fits—"

I seized a handful of sand and flung it at him. He ducked, and then tackled me to the ground, his arms circling me. We rolled over the sand, tangled together, until we hit the water's edge. Shells dug into my back, but I didn't care. All that mattered was this moment between us.

His hands slide down to my waist, and he lifted me up against him. I gasped in surprise.

Conner held me still. "What's wrong?"

"Nothing. It's just you bumped against my phone and it dug into me the wrong way."

I thought of my phone, the one issued to me by headquarters, the one I used to download files from a secret document. Sudden cold flooded my veins, ruining the moment, even as his lips tried to part mine. Using all of my self-control, I turned away.

"Conner, we need to focus for a minute. I only have a few hours left here with you, and—"

"What? So this visit was just closure for you or something? Your chance to say goodbye?"

My eyes met his and I saw the anger brewing there. "No. I mean yes, part of coming here was closure, to know what happened to you and to make sure you were all right. But now that I'm here, I know that's not enough. So we need a plan. I've had my fun, Sherlock Holmes style, but I'm out of ideas. I'm gonna need your help."

"What do you mean? You *have* to leave soon? But you just got here."

I proceeded to tell him all about becoming a spirit guide and making the deal with Sam to get here. I left out the part about how I really died, tackling one confession at a time. First things first.

If Conner was surprised to hear all this, he didn't reveal it. "I don't know what to do to help. All I know is not to let go of you. Thinking of you is the only thing that got me through the past year. The idea that I'd have to let you go again is inconceivable."

"Okay, when you say things like that, *I* can't focus."

He leaned back, throwing one arm casually across my stomach. "Come on, can't you think of something? You're a journalist. You're trained to hound people until they give you what you want."

"Is that a good character trait, or an annoying one?"

His mouth crooked up on one side. "Never annoying to me. Maybe to living creatures, but not to dead people."

I hit him lightly on the shoulder. "Good to know."

"I'm kidding! But you are a reporter, and you're good at it. And the reason you're good at it is that justice matters to you. Shedding light on things matters to you, and you make others care because they see your heart. And it just so happens when you're on the right path, the universe rewards you by meeting the right people."

"Meaning you?"

He raised his eyebrows. "Me and my roommate Bo. The kid is a computer genius. He already had a dozen Microsoft certifications from his high school before his untimely death."

I smiled. "I think it's time I got to know this guy."

CHAPTER TWENTY

I sat beside Conner, spinning the Morticia Addams ring on my finger.

"What a day, huh?" he asked, breaking the silence as we watched Bo trying to decipher the Alpha File 120 on my phone.

Bo's slight, five-foot-five frame hunched over my screen, and I noticed he probably weighed less than I did. He scrolled rapidly through the contents, searching for a weakness in the code. I was so wrapped up in seeing Conner again this morning; I hadn't even noticed that Bo was Asian. More specifically, I knew now he originated from the Philippines. He looked handsome in a very clean-cut kind of way, but in a way suggesting he could never pull off cool no matter how hard he tried. Personally, I thought it was funny that even in death Conner attracted a geeky sidekick. How Conner restrained himself from telling a bunch of jokes about the stereotype of Asians being techies was beyond me. He'd probably gotten all the punch lines out of his system sometime during the past year.

I smiled and answered Conner's question. "You can say that again. You want to go get drunk or something? I never added that one to my life list, and now I think I should've."

Conner laughed. "Well, welcome to Camp Fusion. Unfortunately, there are no alcoholic beverages allowed. I can tell you some more jokes to help pass the time though."

Bo made a noise, suggesting he was familiar with Conner's offensive joke telling.

"How do you know an Asian has robbed your house?"

I elbowed Conner. "Have you ever heard silence is golden?"

He crossed his arms over his chest and ignored me. "Your homework is done, your computer is upgraded, and the thief is still trying to back out of your driveway two hours later."

Bo glared at him for a second, but couldn't hold his laughter in for long. "I can see why you were best friends with this guy for thirteen years," he said to me. "There's no way to ever stay mad at him."

"Yeah, it's one of his many *annoying* traits," I said, my gaze on Conner.

When Conner and I had arrived back to the tent, he formally introduced me to Bo, who had no qualms about helping me with the Alpha File. So, I immediately liked Bo. But first, he wanted to eat, so he asked his girlfriend if I could borrow her ID. The security guard only mildly glanced at the badge when we entered Camp Fusion High. Her skin was as white as mine, and she even had red hair, though hers wasn't as bright or as frizzy. Apparently, cross-dimensional visits weren't common, so flashing her badge was all I needed as a pass to get in without arousing suspicion.

After dinner, the three of us had drifted into the large, wood-paneled library on the second floor to investigate the file. We thought having computer access would prove useful, and this was the only place in Juvie with laptops. The media center was large and drafty; its vaulted ceilings with hanging lanterns and the stone fireplaces with freshly built fires the only sources of light. We huddled together in a secluded corner, but even while sitting in a high-backed lounger, I felt exposed here.

Bo slumped in a brown leather armchair next to me, glowering repeatedly at the screen. Conner slouched back lazily on the black sofa across from us, smiling as he flipped through a leather-bound volume on the end times, hoping for any clues on what the Alpha File 120 could hold. Between us was a polished wooden coffee table with a laptop. The internet was restricted to ten sites here, all related to spirit-filled living.

Tight, panicky feelings fluttered in my stomach; I knew I had no real chance of escaping the predicament I'd gotten myself into. The worst thing I could do was panic now, but it seemed like all I could do. My fidgety hands wouldn't settle down, twisting in my lap. My eyes couldn't seem to stop blinking often enough to focus on anything. I kept looking over my shoulder, waiting for someone to bust us, jumping at the tiniest of sounds. More often than not, the sounds weren't even there when I investigated around corners, just a figment of my imagination. Each time Bo eyeballed me, I pasted a frozen smile on my face.

He put my phone down on the table. "Okay, I can't concentrate with your manic behavior." He turned to Conner, who was still reading calmly. "Why don't you two go bowling for a while?"

"Bowling?" I said, looking up at the clock on the wall. "We can't go bowling at a time like this."

Conner set the book down on the table. "No, Bo's right. He needs peace and quiet to work. Just thirty minutes. Then we'll come right back here. Deal?"

I gave him a look that I'm sure said I questioned their sanity, but he was already pushing me toward the door.

Conner and I used to go bowling at Starlite Lanes in Grand Haven with the Jedi Order all the time. For two years, we even joined a league with Nicole and Sean, who hadn't been dating yet. During that time, Conner bowled a perfect game. Once. Everybody made a huge deal about his three hundred, which he loved of course, but also made it out to be no big thing. He said bowling was a sport made for the laziest of "athletes," using air quotes on the last word. "Basically," he'd told the Grand Haven Tribune, "if you have three fingers and can walk four steps in a straight line, you can become a certified world-class athlete in the sport of bowling."

On our walk to the rec room, I thought about how we'd bowled every year on Conner's birthday for as long as I could remember. Then, just as Conner opened the door, I realized something very important. "Your nineteenth birthday is this week."

He looked down at me and smiled. "And you're my early present."

I let loose an exasperated exhale. "I can't believe I almost forgot! Time has gotten away from me this past month, with the news that I'm dead and all."

He nodded. "Good thing, too. Otherwise, we'd have nowhere to bowl tonight, seeing as Starlite Lanes is a few dimensions away."

Glancing around the room full of teens, I said, "I was just thinking about that. I wish we had a cake and some candles to celebrate like old times."

"I don't need cake to celebrate when I have you for my treat." He slid an arm around my waist, directing me toward the lanes. "Though technically, we don't age here, so I'm not sure if this birthday even counts."

"I say it does, and I'm always right."

He pulled me closer against him. "Can't argue with those words. Are you still a size seven shoe?"

"Last time I checked."

"Okay, I'll be right back. Why don't you go set us up on lane number two?"

The lights glared off the glossy linoleum as I made my way over. Funny how even in the Underworld the bowling alley managed to smell like a combination of stale nachos, sweaty shoes, and floor polish. Lane number one was full with five pretty girls, all plastic looking, sipping from their plastic cups and sitting in their plastic chairs, staring at me.

"Who are you?"

"Are you Conner's new girlfriend?"

"Do you know about Julia?"

"When did you get here? I've never seen you around Camp Fusion before."

"How'd you die?"

Each one took their turn firing a question my way, but never giving me a moment in-between to answer.

"Um, I'm just a friend of Conner's."

This only made them stare more.

Ignoring them, it took me a moment to come up with names to enter into the scoring computer. Usually, I'd just type in our real ones, but since I was incognito… *Kurt and Poncho.* Poncho was his nickname for me, based on an inside joke. I even used the word 'poncho' in my blog title when I started one last year.

When Conner came over with the shoes and saw my choice of names, he laughed. "Nice. Maybe when this whole after death life is over, God will reincarnate me in the Spirit of Kurt Cobain."

I didn't believe in reincarnation, and unsure if Conner really did, I was just about to ask him about his beliefs, but he already moved onto the next thing.

"Do you want a big ball or a small ball?"

"Big ball."

"That's what she said."

The plastics dropped their mouths open. When Conner returned with a red fourteen-pounder for me to bowl with a minute later, I whispered in his ear. "Why won't they stop staring at us?"

He shrugged. "Girls can't help but have that natural reaction to me. You put me to go first?"

I nodded. "It is your birthday week. But in the name of equality, I think you should bowl with your eyes closed."

"That would be dangerous."

"As if danger ever stopped you from doing anything before."

"Why do you think I never told you I loved you?" he deadpanned, stepping up to the line. He hurled the ball down the lane and knocked all ten pins down.

"Not bad, Mr. Anderson," I said, walking past him with my ball. I threw my red ball down the lane, but it veered left, and I only knocked down six pins.

Conner grinned as he stood by the ball return, waiting to go. "Ouch. Try not to suck at this, or it could get embarrassing for me. I have an image to maintain here, you know."

"You better shut your mouth before I crush you like an ant."

"You and what army?" He turned, and then proceeded to bowl another strike.

"I don't need big muscles like you. I'll use the Force and my powerful brain waves to take you down." I grabbed my ball and hurled it down the lane. At least I knocked down eight pins.

He grabbed me by the waist with his free hand when we passed each other. "I'm sorry you suck so badly at this, but I am available all night to ease your sorrows. You can take me down any time."

I looked past him. The plastics all huddled together, whispering. "Ha! I'm only letting you win because it's your birthday."

He took a step back. "I wonder what my parents will do on that day."

"Last year they still had a party for you. Your death was kind of a big deal in Grand Haven. I mean, the flags flew at half-mast the day of your funeral and everything. So your birthday celebration was packed. They did this whole bonfire in the back with s'mores and gave everyone sparklers in remembrance of you. They even played a Cantankerous Monkey Squad song on the radio in your honor." I recalled the entire thing before sadly realizing I wouldn't have been at Conner's eighteenth birthday party, because I was already dead. That had all happened in my limbo state.

"Sounds fun," he said, only picking off seven pins this time. "But that was only real to you, right? Or did your alternative timeline mimic real life for everything?"

He looked at me, waiting for my response, but suddenly, I felt too gutted to answer. Everything from the past day weighed me down—Nate and Grace, the Alpha File, the deal I made with Sam, my twenty-four hour time limit, the lies I'd let Conner believe since I'd arrived at Juvie, the threat of what might happen if I was caught for violating pretty much every single Spirit Guide law.

And I couldn't take it. It seemed I'd become an equal opportunity sinner, but I couldn't lie to Conner anymore. On his almost birthday, he deserved to know the truth, whether he wanted to or not.

CHAPTER TWENTY-ONE

"Man can embody truth,
but he cannot know it."
—W.B. Yeats

Conner kissed me, his hand winding into my hair, the other on my hip, pulling my chest to his. I wasn't sure why he was kissing me, but the touch of his lips on mine felt powerful. Even though this kiss was slow and deep, I felt it more than the ones filled with desire and passion back at the tree house. He felt the difference, too. I could tell by his breath, ragged and swift, the intensity growing, until Bo cleared his throat, reminding us we weren't alone.

I felt my cheeks blush, and twisted my hair back into a knot. "What was the purpose of kissing me just then?"

He raised his eyebrows. "It made you shut your mouth. You were getting too worked up."

We were back at the library now. I'd spent the last five minutes trying to tell him about my death, but couldn't find the right words.

"What the hell?" someone shouted behind us. We turned to see Julia moving forward through the stacks.

"What are you doing here?" Conner asked, backing away from me.

I tried not to take his distance personally.

"Tara was pissed she never got her ID back, so I told her I'd investigate and find you guys. You can imagine my surprise when my friends informed me that you and *Olga* were getting cozy during a game of bowling. I decided to lay low and figure out what was going on for myself when I saw you guys here in the library."

"How much have you heard?" I asked. We'd already discussed the Alpha File and Sam's twenty-four hour time limit with Bo.

"Everything." She had one of those high nasal voices that just set your teeth on edge.

"Well, this complicates things," Bo said. "You two should probably go talk somewhere."

"Too late for that, Bo. And I know Conner is your friend, and your responsibility as his accountability partner, but the pair of you should've never helped Olga with that file. I have to turn her in, and now you'll both be incriminated, too."

She headed toward the front doors of the library, but Conner blocked her way. "You can't just go barge into Leo's office and tell him about this."

Julia hit his chest with the flat of her hand. "I know you're in love with Olga. Thanks for the gentle breakup, by the way. All things considered, I'm certain you understand I don't give a damn about what you want me to do."

I practically flew across the room, helping Conner to block the entrance. Luckily, nobody else needed to go in or out. The library remained empty at this hour.

Julia didn't look pleased. "Did I stutter?"

My shoulders tensed. "I don't care if you did."

Conner sucked in a deep breath and grabbed her hand as if to implore her. "Listen, Julia. You may have already stopped caring about what I think, but it's not just me. Bo is your friend, and your best friend's boyfriend."

Julia rolled her eyes.

"Look, we're working on a plan. This whole thing will be over soon. Nobody else needs to know, unless you tell them."

Julia looked from Conner to Bo, and then glared at me like I was the devil. "Well, what's in it for me, Conner?" She sung his name like a love song, and I could hear her desperation, her need to cling to him.

"Um, eternal glory?"

She cleared her throat. "I'm being serious."

"I am, too. Isn't it enough to just get a pat on the back and know in your heart that you did the right thing? Isn't that what being in Juvie is all about?"

She took a step closer to Conner. "You tell me. Is it about doing the right thing, or about loving people? None of us here were good at either of those things. But it seems at times like these you can't do both. It's one or the other."

He straightened his body to full height. "I really don't know what you're getting at, so why don't you just spell it out for me, sweetheart."

Julia leaned into Conner. "I mean, I could do the *right* thing according to you, and I would only do it because of my love for you. But then I would lose you in the process to Olga. Every coin has two sides, so let's look at things from your perspective. You can keep on loving Olga, or you can do the right thing for all of us. Let her go when she leaves, and don't try to find a way to be with her. Promise to stay with me and commit, and I won't tell anyone."

I stared at her. "Conner, you don't need to make any deals with Julia. We're wasting time. So please, let me give her an object lesson in the abuse of power. That's one thing I never added to my life list and I should've. Number nineteen, kick someone's a—"

Her eyes widened, and she made a clean sweep for the gold chain around my neck with one hand, jolting me forward. "You probably know this, but just to be clear; I hate you."

My nails dug into her flesh, holding her hand in place. I prayed for the crucifix to burn her hand, but no such luck. "You've got spunk; I'll give you that. But FYI, I don't care if you do hate me. Look around. Does this look like middle school to you? Do you see braces and pimples on my face? There's much more at stake here than winning a catfight." I leaned forward. "I'm your worst enemy, sister. I've already risked everything, so I've got nothing to lose. This is my destiny, and I'll be the one telling *you* how it's gonna go down."

She let go of my chain and shoved my hand away, visibly shaken now. "Geez, someone forgot to take their happy pills this morning."

Her words were hard and cold. My expression must've given away some pain at the mention of pills, because it seemed to give her the strength to continue, a twisted half smile on her face.

"Although, I can't say I'd be a ball of sunshine if I had to look in the mirror every morning and see that big frizzy hair, those ugly freckles, and now a broken nose."

"Wh—"

Julia drew back her right hand and drove her fist into my face, knocking the breath out of me. I flew backward from the force of her punch and hit my head. Stars swam in my vision for a second before darkness enveloped me.

When I came to on the floor, I saw stars again and Conner hovering over me. "What happened?"

He met my gaze, but his voice was oddly flat when he answered. "My actions knocked you unconscious for a second time. First the boat, now this. I'm sorry I can't seem to protect you, Olga."

Running a hand over my face, I inspected for injuries. There didn't seem to be any blood, and I felt fine, just a little dizzy. I jumped up and lunged for Julia. "You little bi—"

"Olga, stop." The words struggled through Conner's vocal cords as he yanked me backward against him. "Julia's right."

For one horrible lucid second, my mind flashed back to the last thing she said and thought he agreed with her about me being ugly.

"She already knows too much. Without her help, we can't finish this. And if you don't make it back in a few hours, we're all in a lot of trouble. Maybe we only have twenty-four hours now, but we'll both make it to Heaven someday, and then we'll have an eternity. It's all about perspective. You've got to see the big picture."

A look of dark glee spread across Julia's face.

"What?" I practically hissed. I took his hand and pulled him a safe distance away from Julia and Bo. "I know we're all freaked out right now, but I thought we agreed we're staying together from now on," I whispered into his ear.

"We will. I'm just buying us some time." His hot breath seared across my cheek. "But there is something I need to ask you about. When you were out of it for a minute, you kept mumbling something about 'Don't tell Conner the truth, the pills.' And some other stuff about suicide. What was that all about?"

I couldn't look him in the eyes, but I knew I needed to come clean now. I sighed. "Okay, the truth is, I felt so guilty over your accident that it killed me."

The word "killed" came out broken, tasting of guilt and loss.

"What do you mean guilt killed you? Didn't you die from hypothermia and your head injury?"

How could I answer that question? My voice seemed to have fled; I said nothing. I had hoped to spare him from the truth–or spare myself from his reaction to it. Now I watched the color drain from his face, as realization dawned on him.

"That's how you're here, isn't it? You weren't sent to Limbo to deal with… me?" He took a step back, shaking his head. "What did you do?"

I reached out my hand to him, and he grasped my fingers automatically, but with no feeling behind the gesture. "Conner—I felt so incredibly guilty for not being able to save you. After your funeral, I went back to school. There was this memorial at your locker with notes overflowing out of the tiny slots. When I got to my locker, there were notes in mine, too. I couldn't even stay until second period. I called my dad to pick me up, and while home by myself, I made the mistake of reading the letters. They were hate letters, blaming me for your death, confirming my suspicions about everyone's true feelings about the accident. Guilt already plagued my heart. Then I read your obituary online and listened to your song, *Haunted.* Everything just felt like too much to handle. I was tired of the hurt, tired of not knowing why I survived when you didn't. I had a bottle of pain pills from the hospital that I hadn't touched yet."

His hand trembled in mine. "No, no, no. I don't want to hear anymore. If you don't say it, then, then…"

"I'm sorry," I whispered.

His face crumpled. "You're sorry for killing yourself?"

"Not exactly. I didn't mean to commit suicide. I swallowed the bottle of pills without thinking. I just wanted to numb the pain."

He turned away from me and paced the floor, all the while muttering, "This is crazy," to himself over and over again.

I slowly stood up and watched him for a few minutes, then I grabbed him by the shoulders and looked him in the eye. "I'm so sorry," I said again, because I didn't know what else to say.

His gaze intensified, like he was jerking himself out of a trance. "Okay, okay. So you didn't die from hypothermia, and you thought they just pumped your stomach and you were okay. Then…"

Sometimes, when we were in middle school, we'd play Manhunt at night. While trying to find the hunted, Conner and I would set up squad teams to search the perimeter, each of us stationed in a tree, him in the front yard and me in his backyard. We'd call out updates to each other and his voice always seemed farther away than a few hundred feet, like it was coming from a faraway mountain somewhere. That's how he sounded now, and this was one update I didn't want to give. But I owed him closure. I only hoped it wasn't 'game over' after I explained everything.

"Then I unknowingly entered Limbo. That's when I started seeing Dr. Judy for counseling. I spent the last year thinking I was still alive, and I met Nate. He saved me when I couldn't save myself." I'd told Conner about Limbo when I first got here, but I could tell he needed to hear the explanation again. Limbo was a lot to take in. "And I'm sorry for the pain I'm causing you now, but I don't regret my actions as much as you might think. Ultimately, everything led me back to you. I don't regret that, not even for a second."

"Limbo," he repeated. He looked like he was trying to hold back tears. "Then maybe *this* isn't real. *This* isn't happening right now. You're really still alive and one of those angels is testing me, seeing if I'm ready to move onto Heaven or something. I mean, that has to be it, that—"

"Hey!" I stumbled forward and grabbed onto him frantically. "I wish that were the case. I wish I could take away the pain you're feeling right now. But listen to me, you know what I wouldn't take back? I wouldn't take back the only thing keeping me going these past few weeks since I found out the truth. And that's finding you. In fact, I'd die a thousand times over just to find you again."

He gaped at me for a long moment, then finally dropped to his knees and wept.

What had I done? I came here to save him, but instead of saving him, I only succeeded in imparting more hurt. Hell spared him only for me to bring its fury straight to his heart.

I kneeled down in front of him, tears gathering in my eyes. I wanted to collapse, but I couldn't. Right now, I needed to focus on getting out the words. "I'm so sorry," I repeated again and again. "I was hurting. I didn't save you. I didn't get the chance to tell you I loved you. In a twisted way, maybe this is how things were supposed to turn out. Maybe—"

"Shut up, Olga! Just shut up!" He bared his teeth like an animal, his nostrils flaring. "This isn't how things were supposed to turn out! Quit trying to make your suicide an act of fate instead of calling it what it is, an act of cowardice."

Anger bubbled inside me. *How could he say that?* "You're calling me a coward?"

He drew back, his gaze looking me over in disgust. "Yep. You're a coward. I just didn't realize before. You're not the best friend I used to know. You're just her shadow. An empty, hollow shadow."

There was always that one thing. A particular action you couldn't ever forgive. I knew for Conner, the thing was suicide. He'd lost one of his good friends to a bottle of pills in middle school, and he always talked about how stupid it was to take your own life. Now I had taken mine, and he was too angry to hear my excuses. Once again, I yearned for a cosmic do-over, the chance to do everything again differently.

He looked up, his face streaked with tears, the perfect wisps of blond hair framing his features, making him look like an angel. I wanted to reach out and touch him, but I felt so useless. I wanted to punch Julia, kick the wall, something. None of this was fair. Mom's voice popped in my head, reminding me: *Life isn't fair. Put your big girl panties on and deal with it.*

"Conner," I said, shuffling toward him.

He backed away from me again. "Did I stutter?" It hurt how he quoted Julia to me. "I said, *shut up*!"

A sinking feeling of terror rooted my feet to the floor. "Let me explain some more, please. If you could understand the guilt I suffered. Please try to see things from my perspective. After I got you out of the water, I didn't realize you weren't breathing at first, but you had this pulse, and—"

"I don't care," he said. His complexion drained of all color, and he spoke without any emotion now. "I don't want to know. I don't care about the details, your excuses. What you did… I can't even look at you right now. And I don't know if I can ever look at you the same again. The damage you've done."

"The damage I've done?" I snapped at him, suddenly furious. "Yeah, you know what? You have no right to judge me! I said I was sorry. And really, what am I apologizing for anyway? For loving you too much? You have no idea what I went through! You can call me a coward if you want, but I remember the day you died, even if you don't. I remember it like it was yesterday! I'd never been more scared than when that lightning struck you. But I jumped in the water to save you. Then I jumped again at the chance to save you here, even if it meant making deals with demons. So I don't know why you're acting like I'm the one who betrayed you."

"I know *exactly* what you went through!" he shouted back. "You don't think I've been going crazy for the past year? But I died of a freak accident, not by choice! How dare you take your own life after all our friends and family were already dealing with my death? You stupid, selfish, self-entitled brat! I've been your best friend since kindergarten, and suddenly, I feel like I don't know you at all and I—"

"Don't *want* to know me? Is that right?" I spat the words at him. "Well, that'd be the second time I've heard that in the past twenty-four hours from a boy who I thought loved me. But I guess your love and Nate's love are more conditional than you both claimed."

His expression looked naked and horrified. "How can you even speak of love right now? I don't think you love me at all, and if you think you do, then you don't know what love is. You lied to me this whole time you've been back about how you're here. You haven't been true to me or yourself. I can't even believe a single thing you've said to me in the past few hours."

I reached out and held his hand, trying to implore him to see reason. "I didn't lie. I just didn't tell you the whole truth."

At that, Conner jerked his hand out of my grasp. "The girl I loved wouldn't see the distinction. A half-truth is a lie in disguise. The sin of omission."

Sniffling, I noticed he already used the past tense of love. "Fine. But does that give you the right to just turn your back on me so quickly, after twelve years? It's not like I've been much of a liar during the course of our friendship. I think you owe me another chance to make things right at least."

"I just need some time away from you to think, to figure out how I feel."

Scrubbing a hand over my face until my skin felt raw, I said, "Conner, you could potentially have all the time in the world. I have to go back and deliver the file, and I don't know if I'll be able to come here again. I can ask Riel for a transfer, and he might give it to me. But if that's something you want, I need to know before I leave." I didn't want to think about never seeing him again.

Tears touched his cheeks. "If I go by how I feel now, then I don't want you to come back. Maybe forever isn't in the cards for us. This just doesn't feel right."

Looking at him, I didn't see love anymore, only anger. "Fine, I get it. I'll go." I turned to retrieve my things.

"Olga…

"Yes?" I asked.

For a moment, I thought he'd take back what he just said and tell me he loved me again. Instead, he grabbed a hold of my hands in his and said, "Be safe. I'll always be here if you ever truly need me."

Then he walked out the door, taking his hurt and Julia with him. But of course Julia couldn't leave without some parting words of wisdom.

"Don't worry, Olga. I'm sure Hell has a nice padded room for you. I'll warn the devil not to give you any pills." She gave me a look of absolute hatred.

I probably should've let bygones be bygones, but I said, "Touché."

That one little word seemed to shut her up for some reason. She went out of the room, slamming the door behind her.

Pride comes before a fall. The Bible verse echoed in my mind. The truth was my own stubborn pride kept me from opening up my heart to Conner. First, worrying I'd make a fool of myself if I told him I loved him all those years. And now, worried I'd ruin his perfect image of me if I told him about the suicide. I used to be happy and smiling, but now I felt like I'd lost everything.

I turned to Bo. "I suppose you're gonna leave me now, too?" My voice came out a half whisper, already hoarse from the screaming of the past few minutes.

"Yes."

Right. I guess he didn't see any point in lying.

"While your little drama unfolded, I tried to make a copy of the file and corrupt the contents." He looked at me with dark sorrow. "The file is read-only though, and I can't crack the code for you to see what the real file says, but I probably shouldn't get more involved in this anyway. I'm hoping to be sprung of this place one day for my good behavior. Plus, I'm really tired. And I should check on Conner, and my girlfriend. Oh, hey, can I have her ID card back now?"

For a moment, I stood there silently, the shock of what just happened settling in. Bo didn't meet my eyes now. I slid the badge out of my jeans pocket, walking toward him. "Thanks for trying to help. It was nice meeting you. Please look after Conner for me. Make sure he doesn't do anything stupid."

Something in Bo's face changed as he stood and took the ID. Maybe it was the total desperation in my tone. He stepped forward and wrapped me in a hug, lasting longer than any normal hug. When he pulled away, he squeezed my shoulder and offered me a sad smile. "Things will work out. I can tell your heart is in the right place. And at least you know what happened to Conner. Just remember, you're never alone." He pointed upward, and then saluted me before sliding the badge into his own pocket.

I watched him walk toward the exit, anxiety in his steps. Then, I watched him turn around abruptly.

"Olga, did I hear you mention a Nate?"

I crossed my arms against the chilling feeling building inside of me. "Yes, he's—was—my boyfriend. We met during our time in Limbo."

His face looked like misery, the skin bunching around his dark narrow eyes in a pained stare. "So, that means this Nate died around the same time as you and Conner did last year, right?"

Silently, I commanded myself to answer despite the terror making me quake. "Yes."

"And your Limbo took place in the same town that Conner was from? Grand Haven, Michigan? Because the guy I drag raced home from school was named Nate, and he was upset about moving to that town. I thought it was a very strange coincidence when I learned Conner lived there, too."

A few seconds ticked by before I really understood what Bo was saying. He was the one drag racing Nate on the last day of school, which meant I stood alone in a room with Nate's biggest regret.

I caught his gaze and held onto it. "Coincidence? Yup, God is very big on those."

"It's the same Nate, then?"

I nodded. We both stood in silence for a few minutes. I couldn't read his mind, but I assumed he was taking it all in just as I did. I felt like fainting, like I should lay down or something. Like all the blood left my body or something. I didn't know why the coincidence was so difficult for me to believe after everything else I'd learned in the past month. Finally, I managed to choke out an explanation.

"He died drag racing another student, just like you. I'm sorry I didn't realize the connection. He never told me your name. The accident is too painful for him to talk about. He feels responsible for your death."

Bo rubbed a hand over his face before sliding it into his hair, tearing at his dark locks. "I figured, because I feel responsible for his death, too."

"You're not… angry at him?" I held my breath, waiting for his answer.

He let out a deep sigh. "No, not at all. We were equal in our stupidity that day. Will you tell him that for me?"

Brushing my eyes with my fingers, I nodded. "If I see him again, yes. Absolutely."

Bo smiled. "I think you'll see him again. You're good at finding lots of things, that's how you got here. And maybe God had more to do with your plan than you even know."

He turned on his heel and strode away. My gaze followed him until I couldn't see him anymore. Yeah, I knew lots of things, except where to find a box of tissues and a good cup of coffee. What I wouldn't give for that knowledge right now.

I shuffled to the couch and slouched down. My lungs felt like they couldn't get enough air. Considering everything that just went down, a lot of emotions should've been running through me. Instead, I felt dead inside. That's when I remembered, I was dead inside. Funny how I kept forgetting that unforgettable fact, like I could change things.

My eyes burned, and I told myself not to cry. Tears wouldn't help anything. One thing I did know was I didn't want to stay here anymore. After all, I accomplished what I'd set out to do. I made sure Conner was safe. I told him I loved him. Maybe it would've been better to let sleeping dogs lie, but I also knew that no matter how much I loved Nate, my mind would've always wondered how things might've been with Conner if we had our chance. I could tell myself all I wanted that I wasn't in love with two guys, but nothing changed the fact that I was. How I wished I wasn't!

I kept thinking and thinking of the last year I spent with Nate though and how I remembered every second of it like it was yesterday, and think it was probably the most fulfilling year of my life. I never thought my senior year had the potential to be so perfect without Conner there, but Nate made it happen. So now I was confused as to why I felt such an urge to come see Conner, but I also knew in my heart of hearts that I needed to tell him I loved him in order for me to move on. I mean, I obsessed over him for twelve years. That's not something that disappears overnight. What if I'd spent forever with Nate and wondered the whole time about how it could've been with Conner? I knew these were the thoughts of a crazy person because Nate is like the perfect guy for me, but love made me do crazy things, apparently.

Thinking about crazy made me remember how I still needed to encrypt the file, but Bo couldn't help me now. There was nothing left for me here. Part of me wanted to go after Conner, to fight for us even though he wouldn't. But the other part of me, the part that'd been exhausted from the trying weeks, wanted to lay the day to rest because I knew I couldn't take his rejection twice. Plus, if we couldn't stay together for more than a few hours, then it was easy to chicken out with the excuse that we weren't really meant to be.

After gathering my things, I scrambled out the door and down the hallway, thankful that God never changes and that no matter what, He would never leave me. The power of faith was by my side, and I felt that somehow everything was leading to His purpose for me. The words of Jeremiah 29:13 echoed in my head: "You will seek me and find me when you seek me with all your heart." I'd sought and found Conner, and ultimately, both of us were let down. Maybe the thrill was only in the chase for us. Only God could fulfill me in this difficult time. I knew that didn't mean I'd be spared pain, suffering, and hardship for my actions, but He would still see me through if I seeked Him whole-heartedly. Neither strange dimensions, sorrows, or frustrations would break up my relationship with Christ.

Figuring I should leave the same way I came so I wouldn't alert any guards, I blindly turned around a corner—I couldn't remember which direction I'd come in. The only thing I knew was I entered on the second floor. When I spotted a fire alarm, I stopped and leaned against the wall, studying the hallway. The open door up ahead looked like the one I had come through yesterday, considering I could spot what looked like a row of security cameras on the wall just through its entry.

Something inside me twisted. Disappointment. I couldn't believe I was leaving without saying goodbye to Conner, but I also couldn't focus on that, or I'd hurl. Without giving him another thought, I found my feet carrying me down the hall, my hands holding my book bag in place on my back so it wouldn't make too much noise as I ran. Willing myself to swallow my terror, I tiptoed into the room. I squinted against the fluorescents and found the room occupied, a guard sitting behind a desk. *Crap!* Stepping away immediately, I thought of what to do. I ducked around the nearest dark corner and noiselessly opened my backpack and retrieved the other invisibility pill I hadn't used yet. Just outside the door, I swallowed the magical tablet. Within seconds, I'd already leaped off the balcony onto the tree branch and climbed down the trunk, my visibility not returning until I stood at the lake's perimeter. I ignored the tears in my eyes the whole way to the wormhole.

Luckily, since the hour approached midnight, the lake stood empty. Sam's instructions stated that to everyone else in Juvie, the portal was nonexistent because you had to know about its existence to see it. But to me, I could see the magic there in the form of a mist over the lake, trailing like a cloud from the riverbank to a spot about eight feet away. The damp Earth, still churned up from where I clawed my way out yesterday morning, clearly marked my point of entry.

I didn't wait long to dive into the water, or I might've chickened out. Just beneath the surface, a faint light gleamed. I plunged deeper in the water, swimming swiftly toward the glow. As soon as I reached the wormhole, a whiplash current caught me, sending me spinning like a tornado into an abyss. There was a sense of flying through space, weightless and dizzy, until I broke through a surface and suddenly, I arrived at the base of a waterfall. I climbed out, woozy but dry, and took in the nighttime sky dotted with a million stars.

Before I could take in my surroundings, a pair of hands gripped my shoulders from behind.

CHAPTER TWENTY-TWO

"Love is the voice under all silences,
the hope which has no opposite in fear;
the strength so strong mere force is feebleness:
the truth more first than sun, more last than star."
—E.E. Cummings

"Olga!"

The voice sounded anxious and familiar, and I spun around to face Nate. My eyes met his, and I expected anger, but I didn't see any. Instead, he reached his hand up to my face and rubbed my cheek lightly.

"You're all right?" His voice was soft now. "I've been sick with worry."

I felt a burst of love for him, just like I had when I saw Conner in Juvie. *What is wrong with me? I can't be in love with two people at once, can I?*

"Nate, what are you doing here? I thought you…" *Hated me*, I thought, but was unable to speak the words aloud.

"You thought I hated you," he said, like he was trying to keep his voice even. "Olga, I was in a jealous rage the last time we spoke."

"Yeah, well, I know what that feels like."

"You mean Grace and me, right?" With a heavy sigh, he scrubbed a hand over his face. "Look, I'm sorry about that. I only tried to shut you out because I was following orders."

My head jerked back. "Following orders? From who?"

"Riel." His lip curled a little bit when he said the name.

I took a step closer to him. "I don't understand. Why would Riel tell you to shut me out? She was *our* assignment."

"Because there's something about Grace you don't know. Something Riel told me. And he didn't want you getting involved with Grace's case because he thought it was too dangerous. He wanted to protect you."

"What? Why would he want to protect me? Riel doesn't care about us. We're just humans." Although I knew that wasn't totally true. Despite his rough exterior, he had shown he cared a little bit about me.

Nate hesitated a split second before replying. "He does care about one of us. I think he's in love with you."

I scoffed. "You think he's in love with me?" The thought was so absurd, I actually laughed.

He shook his head. "Yes. Think about it. He made our realities when we were in Limbo. He got to know you. How could he not fall in love with you, with your vulnerability?"

I rolled my eyes. "You're acting like I'm special. Riel does that for everyone, sees vulnerability all the time. Besides, he's an angel. They can't fall in love with humans."

Even as the words flew out of my mouth, I thought back to the conversation I had with him before I went rogue. He'd said an angel falling in love with a human wasn't common, but not unheard of either.

Nate took my hands in his, giving them a squeeze. "First of all, you are very special. You're also humble, so you don't see it. Secondly, apparently angels do fall in love with humans sometimes, even if it is forbidden. That's the secret Riel told me about Grace. Dr. Judy had an affair with an angel, and Grace is their child. Saving Grace is really important. Even though Riel thought you were competent, he didn't want you to face the circumstances if we failed, so he told me to push you away."

I straightened, dropping my hands to my sides. All the mumbo jumbo Dr. Judy said during her hypnosis kind of made sense now. "But they said our failures and successes are tied to one another, so if you failed, wouldn't I still fail, too?"

He gave me a cautious look, biting his lip. "Only if we're in a romantic relationship."

I drew in a long breath. "So why are you telling me about Grace now?"

His eyes were red, like he'd been crying the whole night. "Because after you left, I started thinking about the past three weeks. There's a reason we're supposed to be working as a team. We're better together than we are apart. Riel took our greatest strength and manipulated the situation to convince me it was a weakness. Maybe he made the argument because he was genuinely scared for you, but my gut tells me the whole reason behind his little speech to me was he wanted you for himself. "

My gaze narrowed. "I can't believe you didn't tell me about Grace before now!"

"Riel told me we'd all be better off if we weren't together and if I didn't tell you anything, at least until Grace moved on. I was a brand-new spirit guide, and my boss was a freakin' angel. Can you really blame me for listening to him?"

I pressed my hands against his chest. "Yes, I can! I don't care who he is and if he thinks our connection can be severed. This mission could've meant suicide for both of us."

He held my hands at his chest and angled his body closer to me. "Do you know what time it is?"

"Huh?"

He took my face between his hands. "Time for you to stop being a hypocrite and forgive me."

I thought about how I pushed Nate away for his own good, and the whole time, he did the same for me. He was right on in calling me a hypocrite. Then I flinched, remembering my desperate kisses with Conner. I'd been so broken by the way Nate walked away from me, I'd ran headfirst into kissing Conner, the very thing I told Nate I wasn't going to do. If I learned anything in the past twenty-four hours, it was that I needed to tell Nate the truth now. But I wasn't quite sure how to do that yet.

A cluster of trees moved with the wind, and I watched a few leaves drift to the ground out of the corner of my eye. "So what now? Do we demand Riel let us work together on the Grace assignment again?"

"Shouldn't be too difficult. I'm failing miserably without you, and I'm really scared of what might happen to Grace if I can't help her have a breakthrough soon." He dropped his hands to his side and sniffed, like he was trying not to cry, and I couldn't help but feel jealous over how much he cared for another girl.

I opened my mouth, but a moment passed before I could form words. "Do you think she has super powers we could help her tap into somehow? You know, because she's part angel?"

Nate laughed. "I don't know. What super powers does Riel have, other than being one cocky SOB?"

"Oh, I dunno. He can fly and teleport anywhere faster than the speed of light, he can manipulate our perceptions of reality. He can probably transform into others, too. If Dr. Judy had an affair with an angel, then that angel must've taken on a human form, right?"

"I guess so." He kicked at a rock. "You don't want to be with Riel, do you?"

"Of course not."

My mind spun in a million different directions, trying to decipher everything Nate told me. What had he said? He followed orders from Riel? "Are you still in love with me?"

He stared, like my question shocked him. "Olga, of course I'm still in love with you. There's no chance of ever falling *out* of love with you. I'll always love you. I'll always want you and nobody else."

I took a step closer to him. "You still l-l-love me?" After all I said to him, the idea that he still loved me seemed impossible.

"With everything that I am."

I mentally cursed, wishing for the millionth time I had a cosmic do-over button. *How could I have made out with Conner within twenty-four hours of breaking up with Nate?*

I sighed. "Well, add everything you've just told me to the long list of things I never thought I'd hear but have in the past twenty-four hours." I thought of Conner, how he gave up on me so easily, and I already missed him horribly.

Nate tilted his head to the side, studying me as if I were an alien species, and maybe I'd become one somewhere along this journey. "Olga, I'm sorry for not fighting for you, for us. There was a quote by Ralph Emerson that I tried to live by, when I was still alive. He said to, 'Live everyday as if it is the best day of your life.' Somewhere in death, I forgot about all of that. I should've been putting my trust in God, but I didn't."

His words should have made me happy, but they didn't. Instead, I felt this giant void inside of me. I knew I had to come clean with him about what happened, but I'd already broken one heart today, and I didn't know if I had what it took inside of me to break another.

He drew me forward until our lips brushed. His mouth trembled. My own body shook against his, but I didn't pull away. I knew I shouldn't kiss him, shouldn't take back up with Nate at the first sign of his remorse. We needed to *talk*, not kiss. But I couldn't stop him either, and I didn't want to. We were a gravitational force, our desire for each other too powerful.

I took in a breath as his hands smoothed down my shoulders, dropping my book bag to the ground. His hands rested on my hips, pressing me against the back of a tree. A shiver passed through me, and I molded my lips to his.

This kiss wasn't like our other ones. I couldn't help myself from comparing them. This kiss was sharp with all the hopelessness we felt the past twenty-four hours, maybe even the past year, almost painful. No restraint existed here, and I was thankful for that. We couldn't stop touching each other. His hands grazed over my shoulders and down my arms; I fisted mine in his hair then in his shirt until finding the slope of his hard stomach. Somehow, I didn't know if he pulled me down on top of him or I pushed him down, but our bodies collided on the grass as we continued to devour each other.

I sucked on his bottom lip; he nuzzled my neck; I trailed kisses along his ear and down his throat; he pulled at my shirt. Not to be outdone, I copied him. But then, the feel of skin on skin sedated us. The intimacy of the gesture awakened us to the knowledge that we moved too fast. Our breaths, soft and hot, began to slow. His hands traced up and down my back, and I laid my head on his shoulder, a feeling of peace washing over me, like I floated on a cloud somewhere far away from all my troubles.

The desire for more answers pounded my brain, despite just wanting to enjoy the moment. "How did you know how to find me by the wormhole?"

He gently rolled me off him, then rested his elbow on the Earth as he looked at me. "When you came to me about Conner, my anger and jealousy was genuine. Later, I regretted what I said to you, but I knew I couldn't keep you from going after Conner. No matter what I did or said, you weren't going to stop until you had your answers. But I couldn't abandon Grace, and I thought someone who knew what was going on should stay at headquarters in case you needed some help. I actually contemplated turning you in to Riel or Ash or Dr. Judy for a good hour, but then I remembered I promised you I wouldn't, and I feared you'd hate me forever if I did."

I looked down at our hands, intertwined, and felt a surge of guilt when my eyes fell on the Morticia Addams ring. Feeling sick to my stomach, I pressed on, "So, what did you do instead?"

He fixed his eyes on me, and I could feel his intense longing to touch me again and put all this unpleasantness behind us, but he pressed on with the explanation. "I snuck into your room at night. I made sure you were asleep first, and then—"

"Wait a minute." I held up my hand. "How could you make sure I was asleep before you entered?"

A smile flickered across his face. "I listened at your door for snoring."

I poked him in the stomach. "I do not snore!"

"Yes, you do."

I threw myself on top of him again, pinning his arms above his head on the soft ground with my hands in fake indignation. "Take it back."

"What are you going to do if I don't?"

I ducked my head down to his face, pressing our noses together, which was about the only part of our bodies not already pressed together. "Kiss you to death."

He arched up against me, lips brushing mine. "I demand you carry out this sentence immediately."

Slipping my hands behind his neck, I smiled against his mouth. "Not until you tell me the rest of your story."

He groaned. "You evil woman, can't you tell not kissing you is killing me?"

The desire nudged at me, too, but I needed to know what happened to plan my next move. Noon approached too quickly; I still needed to figure out what to do about the Alpha File.

"One quick kiss then." I pulled him toward me and pressed my lips to his, just for a moment, thinking what an idiot I'd been to let him go, then rolled off him. "Now talk."

He took a ragged breath. "I had seen you meeting with Sam at The Morning Glory Café and at the park."

"You saw me?"

His lips parted, but he said nothing for a few seconds. "I always see you."

Always. The word sat in the air between us for a heartbeat or two or ten. His word echoed in my mind, resonated like a fact, and I didn't know how to respond.

"I knew he'd given you a folder. When I searched your room, I found the file and read the information there about the wormhole. But I didn't feel like that was enough, just having the details. So I injected a tracking device into your arm."

Gah! What? I bolted upright. "You did what?"

"Yeah, I wasn't sure what your reaction would be when I told you about that."

I could feel my eye twitching like it always did when I flew right past mad and became irate. "So, you seriously injected me with a tracking device against my will?"

Nate's face turned ashen. "It wasn't exactly against your will if you didn't know about the device."

Now I was *way* past irate. I was pissed! "Oh, okay then… you implanted a tracking device *without my knowledge*. Yup, that sounds so much better." I crossed my arms over my chest. "What the hell were you thinking?"

Eyes widening, his brows remained furrowed. "I'm sure you mean that in the nicest way."

I shook my head. "I don't, actually. What if the security scanners in the storage facility or in Juvie picked up on my tracker? I was on a rogue mission where I broke at least twenty spirit guide laws. You could've gotten me killed!"

Nate bit his lip. "Olga, you're already dead."

"Fine! You could've landed me in a nice cell in Hell."

He sat up and retracted his arms from behind his head as he did, bringing them to his torso, and I tried not to get distracted by the hardness of his stomach. "Look, you said it yourself. You were going rogue! It wasn't as if you were off to see a parade of fluffy unicorns and peppermint puppies."

Surprising even myself, I let out a gasp of laughter despite my anger. "Fine, you made your point. But know this, I will send you straight to Hell in a hand basket if you ever pull a stunt like that again."

He squinted at me, his eyes quizzical. "Are you planning more dangerous missions in the near future? Maybe to infiltrate the enemy's headquarters next?"

"Shut up. I should still be mad at you." I studied my arm, but didn't notice anything different. "Where would you get a tracking device anyway?"

His mouth quirked up slightly. "Have you explored headquarters at all? We have an entire room of gadgets at our disposal. That book bag Riel and Ash issued us was just for starters. All that stuff is child's play."

"Wow, I had no idea. That would've been helpful to know before I went all rogue. Where did you inject me exactly?"

He bent his head and kissed my right arm, just below my shoulder. "Right there."

I wound my fingers into his hair. "Okay, you have to stop kissing me, or we'll never finish this conversation. And I really want to know how this tracker works." I tilted my head to the side, a terrifying thought seizing me. "Could you hear everything going on, or just track my whereabouts?"

He gently brushed my arm with his index finger. "I wish I could've heard everything. Definitely would've put my heart at ease."

Probably not.

"I could follow the tracker through the GPS app on my phone. It showed me coordinates, although I had no idea what those points on the grid meant since you were in another dimension. I just figured they'd come in handy if I needed to get you help, knowing Riel would know what they meant. Although traveling across dimensions must've delayed the signal a bit. It took a full hour after you left for the signal to pop up. Those sixty minutes took about ten years off my life, or after-life."

I grabbed his finger and held his hand to my heart. "How did you know I was alive? I mean, couldn't you have just been tracking my dead body being transported around the Underworld?"

He poked me in the side. "Geez, you're a morbid little thing, aren't you?"

Nodding, I said, "I just want to understand how these gadgets work. My mission isn't over yet, and now that I think about it, something like a tracker could come in handy. Can I track the file somehow?"

He grinned. "So, best worst idea ever? All is forgiven?"

I shrugged. "Maybe."

"Oh, come on. I'm gonna have a Star Wars marathon by myself and cry my eyes out if we don't kiss and make up soon."

"I will beat the crap out of you if you dare to watch Star Wars without me. But first things first, focus please."

"Sorry, what was the question again?"

I pushed a piece of hair out of my face and sighed. "Can I track the file?"

"Um, no. The tracker interacts with your bloodstream. Oh, and I think you're forgetting you're already dead, so that's how I knew you were okay."

I stiffened and drew back a little. "You're right. I keep forgetting that little detail. I can't believe I'm such a doofus."

A slow smile spread across his face. "Hey, even freaky genius girls have their gifted moments sometimes. Makes the rest of us not feel so dumb." He cupped my face gently in his hand and brushed his lips across mine. "I wasn't worried you'd end up in a ditch somewhere or anything, but if you weren't back within twenty-four hours, I was finding out where that tracker led to. Even giving you that much time killed me. After I spent the day with Grace…"

His voice trailed off when my body tensed. Of course, he felt it; his hands had barely left my body since the second we reunited.

"I was only doing my job, Olga, nothing more."

I winced, wishing he had done something more, a little kiss even. Then maybe the thought of kissing Conner behind his back wouldn't sting so much. But deep down I knew that wasn't true. Secretly, I craved some time alone to think through everything that happened.

"We had dinner together and saw a movie, and the whole time I was chomping at the bit to explore the portal. I would've been here all night, trying to find a way to break in, if I hadn't been summoned by Riel to report on my progress with Grace. I rushed back here as soon as I could, and then you showed up. I'm so glad you came back early."

"Me too."

"So why did you come back early? I thought you'd want the full twenty-four hour excursion with Conner. Is everything okay?"

The brilliance of the sun peeked above the horizon, brightness touching my face. Usually, I loved the early sunrise of five-thirty at headquarters, but not this morning, when all I wanted to do in this moment was hide.

Shutting my eyes, I said, "Yes, and no. I mean, Conner's okay, physically speaking. But not emotionally, and it's all my fault. He didn't take the news of my suicide very well, especially since I let him believe I died in the accident with him for most of our day together."

Nate swallowed, and I watched his Adam's apple bob up and down. "That jerk-hole. You spend a year of your life grieving over his death, you give up Heaven, and you risk your entire status as a spirit guide just to check on him, and he has the nerve to hold your one moment of weakness against you?" He slammed the ground with his fist so hard I thought a long crack might appear in the dirt. "He better hope I never have the pleasure of meeting him face-to-face, because if he does, I'm going to—"

I pulled him toward me and kissed him. I didn't know what else to do. A million thoughts raced through my mind, and maybe Nate could sense my anxiety because he remained tense. Was it okay for me to go back to Nate, the only love I'd ever truly known, as soon as Conner gave up on me? Should I tell Nate about Conner now or wait? With the file needing delivery, it seemed we still had more pressing matters to take care of. And Nate did say he loved me and wanted me no matter what, and of course, I never stopped loving him either. I decided telling him about me and Conner kissing could wait. Wanting to enjoy every moment with Nate and put this whole mess behind us, my body melted like butter into his and he relaxed too. It was the sort of kiss that turned my limbs to spaghetti and made me forget about all the wrong things I'd done. With my whole heart, I thanked God for His faithfulness and His love. I knew I'd never find another love to match what the Lord freely gives, but I also felt like Nate's love for me came in at a close second. All these thoughts made me stop our little love fest though.

"Nate," I said, getting up. "We seriously have work to do. I want to drop the file off at the dead drop. I have a feeling if I'm even a millisecond late, there'll be literal hell to pay."

Nate stood, brushing the dirt off his jeans. He bent down to grab his shirt and yanked it back on. "You can't actually give them the file they wanted."

I slipped my own shirt over my head, and then slid my phone out of my pocket. "That's why I wanted Conner's friend in Juvie to make me an encrypted file, hoping they'd never be able to decode it. But the file was read only, and he couldn't mess with the contents at all. We weren't even able to read what the Alpha File 120 says. The whole thing is written in language and symbols Earth has never seen before, so I don't think handing over the file will do any harm."

He brushed a hand through his hair. "What if the demons have a way to read the file though? We can't take that chance. Let me take a look. We've still got time, right?"

I glanced at my watch. "Yeah, about six hours. But we need a computer."

Nate pulled my bag from beside the tree and grabbed my hand. "It just so happens I have one of those."

"Yeah, but still. What makes you think you can succeed where Bo failed?"

He cupped my face in his hands and smiled. "Faith."

CHAPTER TWENTY-THREE

"If you look for truth,
you may find comfort in the end."
—C.S. Lewis

Nate sauntered over to his desk and opened his laptop. "I'm just not sure if we have enough time for me to hack this file and translate the code for you. I mean, we'll want that knowledge to use for leverage with Riel and Ash if needed, but I think you'll agree it's more important for the demons not to get this file."

I watched Nate sitting in his desk chair perfectly while staring at his computer screen. I was worried for sure, but I couldn't help smiling at him, wishing I could touch him every moment.

"I can probably scramble the code and make a false file for your dead drop. The trick is making the code complicated enough to buy us some more time to hack the real file. Go ahead and hand me the power cord for your phone. I'll download this stuff to the laptop and get to work."

He took my phone from me while I rummaged through my bag to find the USB cable he needed. After he connected my phone and moved the file onto his computer, he gave my cell back to me. "You went shopping while you were away or something?" He pointed inside the opened front pocket of my backpack.

My gaze followed his finger and discovered the pair of sunglasses I picked up at the storage facility. I'd forgotten all about them until now. "Those are something I stole at the storage facility along with the file."

He gave a little gasp. "Be careful. You know what they say. First, the kids are stealing a pair of sunglasses. The next day they're stealing cars."

My lips curved. "I don't even know why I took the glasses. When I saw them lying on the counter, an impulse took over."

"Maybe women's intuition told you to take them. They could be important." Nate reached in and grabbed the glasses, then slipped them on.

"How do I look?" He made a duck face and flashed the peace sign.

I laughed. "Like a friendless thirteen-year-old girl taking a selfie for an online profile pic. Here, let's see what these do." I pressed one of the silver buttons on the side of the glasses, but nothing.

Then I saw the Alpha File 120 scrolling on its own on the screen.

"What's happening?" Nate asked, suddenly a wiry bundle of energy.

"The computer is indicating another transfer in progress. Crap! Is someone already hacking your laptop for the information?"

"No, I mean the glasses are sending a pulse through my body, like the code is transmitting to my brain through these glasses."

"What?"

A loud beep followed my question, and the computer monitor illuminated with wild, fluctuating images. Airplane crashes, young lovers on the beach, coal mining explosions, apple orchards, boats sinking, a sunrise, church fires, a royal wedding, bombs exploding, a baby being born, dolphins playing in the ocean, towers collapsing, a dog greeting its owner at the door, dams breaking, a parent hugging their child, a twister ripping through a city, moviegoers laughing at the screen, cars colliding, someone reading a book at the library, a tsunami flooding a city, a gathering of friends eating dinner, a drug addict overdosing, cookies baking in the oven, a lightning strike, children playing, a funeral.

After a minute of these flashing images, Nate's whole body began convulsing.

"Nate!"

He didn't answer me. I tried to rip the glasses off, but they were suctioned to his face. After another minute, he stopped shaking but remained unconscious. I wheeled his desk chair to his bed, laid him down on the comforter, and checked his pulse. It seemed stable, as though he merely slept. I checked his pulse every ten minutes for the next five hours. I didn't want to blow our mission or anything, so I just stayed with him in his room, and since his pulse remained steady, I trusted that he didn't need medical attention. Then I realized he was dead anyway and felt pretty foolish.

Nate's unconscious state aside, the good news was that putting on those glasses unlocked the file somehow, enabling me to scramble the contents. Even though I had no idea what the Alpha File 120 said, I felt certain the real code would be unreadable to Sam and his demon friends. Still, now I only had one hour left before the dead drop, and Nate still wouldn't wake up. *What if he never does?* Tears clouded my vision. I took out my pencil pouch and retrieved the glue stick Riel created.

Just as I was about to press the toggle switch that would signal for immediate help, Nate came to, sliding the glasses to his forehead and opening his eyes at last.

I crouched beside the bed. "Nate! Nate, are you all right?" I felt frozen with fear, but managed to lift his head and place my arm underneath, feeling his forehead for fever with my other hand.

He blinked rapidly and looked around. "Where am I? What happened? It feels like I've been electrocuted."

"You're still in your room. You've been out a long time. Five hours."

"Five hours! What time is it?"

"It's 10:43 a.m." I caressed his forehead, brushing his hair back from his pale face. "But I was seconds away from getting Riel."

"Riel?"

I nodded through my tears. "You know, the grumpy angel in charge of us?"

"Oh, right. I remember. I just feel so dizzy. Why didn't you wake me?"

Walking over to his computer, I slid the glue stick into the back pocket of my jeans and made a few clicks on the screen, closing down the file, then ejected the CD I'd burned the file onto. "I tried, but once you put those glasses on, you were out cold. I couldn't even pry the darn things off your face. I was worried sick. If I lost you again, it'd kill me a second time."

I darted back to Nate's bed, sat down, and pulled his head into my lap.

He grabbed my hand and held my fingers tight. "I'm sorry. I didn't mean to leave you all alone. As soon as you pressed that button on the glasses, a bunch of images flooded my mind. I was actually awake for the first few minutes, but paralyzed. All I could do was just sit there while the Alpha File 120 became comprehensible, a bunch of data overloading my brain. I got this massive headache and felt all light-headed and stuff. Then, a blinding yellow light flashed through my mind, the images came to an abrupt stop, and I guess I passed out."

I handed him a bottle of water from his nearby mini fridge. "Well, whatever those glasses did, the file changed from read only to something I could manipulate. I made an encrypted file, even though I still have no clue what the real file says." I held up my hand. "Wait, did you just say the Alpha File became comprehensible to you? Because you said something similar to that before passing out."

He glanced at the CD in my hand, then at me, and gave me a half smile. "I think these glasses are used to read the code, as in I know what the Alpha File 120 is now. It was like I became Eve, eating the forbidden fruit in the Garden of Eden. I saw every good and evil thing God sees."

I grabbed for his sleeve, felt him wince. "Holy crap! You're saying the entire Alpha File 120, the one all of Hell is after, is now encrypted into your memory somehow? You're saying you know every secret there ever was?"

Nate nodded. "Almost. This particular file only showed me things from the years 1950 until 2000." He rubbed his free hand over his face, scratching his palm over the stubble covering his chin.

My fingers curled tightly around Nate's left hand while sliding the CD into my book bag.

"Whatever the years, it's not beyond the realm of possibility that you may have just become exactly as God, even if you don't have all of his attributes, making you your own god in essence." I eased Nate's head out of my lap with one hand, then stood and tucked my shirt into my jeans before pacing back and forth. "Maybe that's what the demons wanted. Logic says that the result of cracking the Alpha File 120 is how someone could somehow become independent from God. In theory, you would no longer have the need for God once you understood good and evil as He understood those concepts." I shook my head. "Holy crap! This is far worse than I ever could've imagined. What would happen if the demons found out you have the file in your head? It could mean the end of you!"

"Just when I thought there was no way you could possibly get me into more trouble," he said, slowly sitting up, and then standing.

His words made me freeze, the panic swelling inside me, feeling like I would burst open at any second. It was like I'd been caught up in a tornado and fallen into an abyss very far away, nothing familiar, yet knowing too much information at the same time.

Nate touched the side of my face. "Hey, I'm only teasing. We'll figure this out together."

"There's no way a half hour will be enough time for us to discover what we're supposed to do with this new information. All the time in the world wouldn't be enough. I mean, why would Dr. Judy tell me to go after the Alpha Fi—"

Taking a breath, my gaze landed on the glasses still on top of Nate's forehead, reminding me he had the knowledge of God. I ripped them off his head and threw them on the ground. Then, I stomped on them until they were dozens of tiny pieces.

"What'd you do that for?" He looked at me with half-open eyes, his usual ocean color looking dull with exhaustion.

"Keeping the glasses would be too dangerous." I stooped down and swept the broken pieces under his bed. "What if the demons got hold of the real file somehow? They obviously don't know you need the glasses to comprehend the code, or they would've asked me to retrieve them, but we can't take the chance of letting the glasses fall into the wrong hands." I stood up, and a wave of satisfaction washed over me.

"Good idea," Nate said, his voice uneven.

I silently prayed he wouldn't pass out on me again. "Look, Dr. Judy wanted me to find the Alpha File 120 for a reason, a reason that could help Grace and all of us, she said. Can you find out what that reason was before I do the dead drop?"

"The problem is, I don't know how to access all the information now stored in my brain, but I'll try."

He closed his eyes, and I could tell he concentrated hard by his furrowed brow. "This isn't going to be easy. It's like a full volume set of Encyclopedia Britannica's exploded in my brain, and you're asking me to find one specific entry out of millions."

I shook my head. "Yeah, I know. Just try to focus only on memories of Dr. Judy and Grace, the way they look, the sound of their voices, everything you know about each of them. Maybe thinking those thoughts will make the information from the file somehow flash in your mind."

"Olga!" he squealed, sounding excited now. "It's working. I see something!"

I grabbed at his hands and held them. In the steadiest voice I could manage, I said, "Tell me what you see."

"I see a younger, gorgeous Dr. Judy. I'm talking Miss America material. A young man named Simon whispers to her about her beauty…but not just a man, an archangel, and a Heavenly kingdom transplant sent to Earth as a professor at Brown University to inspire young people to change the world. But instead, he got distracted by Judy and had an affair with her. She was only twenty-four, finishing her Master's degree and only married for a year when she found out she was pregnant. She didn't know if Grace was the daughter of her husband or Simon's, fully human or half angel. Simon couldn't stay. He was sent to the Underworld for duty as punishment. Working with delinquents seemed to suit him better than inspiring youth.

"He wanted to take Grace to Heaven to grow up, no matter if she was his or not. He was afraid if she stayed on Earth, she would be a big target for demons because of his affair with Judy. But if he took Grace with him, Judy wouldn't ever be able to see her again, so she wouldn't agree to his plan. She couldn't bear to lose Simon and her child all at once, the only child she'd ever have. The pregnancy and labor had been the hardest her doctor had ever seen, and didn't know how she made it through, but said she could never have children again. So she wanted to keep Grace close, but before Simon left, he vowed to come back.

"He mentioned something in passing about the Alpha File, about obtaining the knowledge of God so he could find a way back to Earth. But years passed and no word from Simon came. Dr. Judy spiraled into depression, ending in a band of demons killing her. As Grace matured, the demons could tell by her gifts and traits she was Simon's child. They bombarded Grace with negative thoughts after Dr. Judy's death, hoping her torture would lead to Simon's intervention, so they could convince him to work together to obtain the Alpha File. But they thought wrong. Simon was reformed. He never made a move. He was nothing like the demons. He serves out his punishment, watching over the Underworld for a century, and trusting God to unite him with Dr. Judy and Grace when his time is up."

I shook my head. *Crap, only I would have the luck of bailing on my first assignment, who just happens to be half archangel!*

Nate opened his eyes and stared at me. "Now what?"

I felt just as puzzled as he did. "I don't know why Dr. Judy thought that could help all of us, do you?"

Drawing his hand from mine, he said, "There's more. A genetic code flashed through my mind when I saw Grace being born. I wonder if that has anything to do with what the demons are after."

Shrugging my backpack on, I said, "Well, if it is, they won't be able to read it. I better get going."

He leaned forward and kissed me gently, and then I felt one hand gripping my waist, the other in my hair, his kiss deepening.

I leaned back. "I have to go."

He sighed. "I hate this."

"You think I don't?"

"Promise me you'll be careful and come back to me. Hey, should we make a Plan B in case something goes wrong? Who else knows about the Alpha File? I'd hate for someone to turn you in after all this trouble of covering things up."

I shook my head. "The only ones who know are you, me, Conner, and his roommate. They won't tell." Julia's name popped into my head. "Ah, I can't believe I keep forgetting some very important details."

He held up his hand. "What details?"

"There's also Julia. Conner's very jealous girlfriend," I whispered.

Nate took a step away from me, looking like I slapped him. "Why so jealous?"

I remained silent.

His mouth twitched like a cat's. "Olga, why so jealous?"

"I'd rather not have this conversation right now." An ache spread through me that felt like being sucked into that wormhole again, the floor dropping out from underneath me.

Nate looked like he felt the exact same way. "I don't think I want to have this conversation right now either. But I also don't think I can go forward with you until you explain why Julia is so jealous, and why you're suddenly so quiet about it."

My knees wobbled, the world collapsing in on me.

"Olga! Just tell me! You owe me the truth. Did something happen between you and Conner?"

I hesitated, my spirit feeling so weak and small from all my fears and challenges of the past days. The thought occurred to me now that maybe I was able to go see Conner not because of God's allowance, but Satan's. Wouldn't Satan want to distract me with the temptation of Conner's love, a detour trip from my true mission? But really, I knew Satan wasn't my biggest enemy, I was. Ever since I'd learned the truth about the last year, I couldn't stop worrying about Conner and all I'd left behind on Earth. Something always plagued at my mind and stole peace from my heart. Sure, I tried to go on the best I could, but I didn't allow God to calm my anxious thoughts and put my worries to rest. I didn't even give the spirit guide opportunity a chance to turn into the joyous experience I knew He meant it to be. My over-worrying and my need to be in control got the best of me again.

Now, I needed God's grace and wisdom to find just the right words for Nate. Because the truth was, I needed both of their love to help me to be the stronger and more secure person that I wanted to be.

But coming clean was agonizingly difficult, especially when I'd allowed one bad decision to lead to another until everything snowballed out of control. I'd wandered so far down the road of self-deception that I didn't even know how to turn around and tell the truth now.

Forcing myself to look Nate in the eye, I knew he was right. I owed him the truth, a thousand apologies, and so much more. I swallowed, praying for the right words to explain. "You have to understand, I loved Conner my whole life. I never thought he could love me back, not the romantic way I wanted him to. And I didn't go to him to seek that out. Part of me still regretted never telling him, but my heart belonged to you. Then you were so mad at me, or at least I thought you were. I thought you'd never want to see me again, and that you wanted Grace now. So when he confessed being in love with me all these years, too…" I had no idea how to break the next part gently, so I just spit the words out. "Kissing seemed like the natural thing to follow. Nate—"

"Is kissing all you did?"

I took a step toward him, trying to remember. The last day seemed like a blur. A flash of our hands on each other swept through my mind. "The kisses were passionate, but not like ours."

Nate's posture was stiff. "Meaning what? You managed to keep your clothes on?"

"Yes, of course." My voice sounded scratchy to my own ears. "I'm so sorry, Nate. I never meant to hurt you. You know I would never hurt you on purpose."

Nate raised his eyebrows. "The only thing I know for sure right now is that you don't *think*. I mean, it's the greatest of all ironies, isn't it? What is your I.Q.? One-forty-something? Yet you don't *think*, you just act! You don't have any foresight. You don't think of any consequences. Oh wait, you do think. Of yourself, and what you want. Not about what I think. Or what's right." His hands began to shake. "I'm tired of this. If you *think* you still love Conner, then you can *think* of a way out of this on your own."

He turned to walk away, but I gripped his arm, pulling him close. "I love *you*, and you love me. You're gonna let one little mistake ruin everything? Isn't that what you were just threatening to punch Conner over?"

Nate disentangled himself from my grip. "Don't say his name! And don't pretend this is my doing. This is all you." He spat the words with such hate I felt like someone knocked the wind out of me. "I love you, more than anything. But it's clear to me now that even if you do love me, it's not the same. Not with your whole body, soul, heart, mind, and your very breath. Because if you did, if you loved me like I loved you, you would've never been able to kiss someone else. I can't even look at someone else!"

"But you never had a best friend you loved your whole life. You don't understand how confusing the whole situation was."

"The fact you found it confusing is what I find confusing. Love is not the author of confusion. Indecisiveness is."

The empty void returned, threatening to swallow me whole. "Please, just give me another chance. I promise it won't happen again."

He laughed sharply. "Oh, sure, until Conner needs you. And if I could give you some advice? Don't go running to him the next time you *think* he needs you. There's a holy war going on here. I do love you. I don't want you to end up in Hell playing house with Sam."

And with that, he turned and teleported on the spot, too fast to grab onto him and see where he was going. Just when I thought all would be okay, things fell apart again. I'd lost Conner, gained Nate, then lost Nate, then gained Conner back, only to lose him again the same day, then got Nate back, only to lose him again within the span of six hours. How had I gone from the girl who never got chased to the girl constantly caught in the middle? I never should've opened my heart to love. I never should've gone to see Conner. All I did was open myself up to more pain and make things worse for everyone involved.

But I couldn't fix what I shouldn't have done, things that would haunt me forever. Everything had changed, and there wasn't a darn thing I could do about it.

Wetness streamed down my cheek like a waterfall, and I finally felt the courage to let the tears flow free, to feel the loss and heartbreak. The tears weren't just for not staying true to Nate, but for not staying true to myself. Maybe after I grieved properly, my true self would be waiting on the other side, so that I could come out whole and cleansed again. Maybe God wasn't through with me yet.

If I kept repeating this mantra over and over again, maybe faith would take hold of me before depression did.

CHAPTER TWENTY-FOUR

"I am certain of nothing but the holiness of the Heart's affection and the truth of the Imagination."
—John Keats

The dead drop was to take place on Grace's Limbo plane at Biltmore Estate, the same location where Grace conned her way into a date with Nate. I teleported there and made my way to the Housekeeper's Suite to drop the CD into a trash can in Mrs. King's room as instructed.

"Olga? What are you doing here? Have you seen Nate?"

I turned to see Grace coming toward me. Quickly, I jumped in front of her, blocking her path. I didn't want her anywhere near Sam. "Um, no, Nate isn't with me. What are you doing here?"

She grimaced. "He sent me a text early this morning, asking me to meet him here at noon."

"This specific spot?"

Grace nodded.

I took a deep breath, which didn't help calm my rising panic. I had to get her out of here, and fast. "Ah, I'm just messin' with you. My brother became suddenly ill, so he sent me here to tell you to go home, and he'll visit you later." *Did she buy it?*

"Why wouldn't he just call or text to tell me that himself? The drive out here cost me a lot of gas money."

Now I definitely felt ill. "Um, because…" *Holy freakin' crap, please just leave!*

"Because," Sam said, filling the doorway to Mrs. King's room as he glanced from Grace to me. "She's lying to you. But first things first, do you have the file, Ms. Worontzoff?"

I swallowed hard. "Sam? What are you doing here?" Even though this was only supposed to be a dead drop, I sensed the lie when I spotted Grace. Still, I needed to buy some time and asking questions was usually how I accomplished that task.

"The terms of our agreement have changed. My boss wants me to bring you and Grace back to our headquarters with the file."

"Tell your boss he can go screw himself. I did my job, now our business together is done, and there's no reason to involve Grace."

Sam shook his head and stared thoughtfully into the distance. "I figured you might say something like that. And the rules of these realms dictate we can't kidnap spirit guides. They have to come willingly to the dark side. But we can take subjects from Juvie after so many strikes. Which is why, at this very moment, my associate is kidnapping Conner." He held up his mobile device, a video displaying images of Conner being bound and gagged. "Still want me to deliver that message to my boss?"

Sam blocked all the light coming from the room, so I hoped he couldn't read the utter terror on my face. "Okay, fine. I'll come, but leave Grace out of this."

He sauntered up to Grace and me as if he knew something I didn't, and I'm sure he knew lots of things I didn't. Things I didn't want to know, but was about to find out. "Well, you see, I planned on leaving her alone, because I had to. But now *both* of her spirit guides have come to the dark side, so she belongs to me now, too."

"Spirit guides?" Grace mumbled. "What—who is this crazy person?"

"I'm your worst nightmare, sweetheart," Sam answered, gripping both of our arms and blinking us into darkness.

Seconds later, we followed Sam down a long tunnel, where he opened a metal door, then started down an impossible number of stairs.

"Where exactly is your headquarters?" I shivered, trailing my fingers along the cold stone wall to help guide me and Grace, who shuffled beside me in the darkness.

Sam nudged me from behind with a bony finger. "A dungeon. What did you expect for demon headquarters? Cinderella's castle? Now shut up and walk faster."

"Well, it's not like I don't want to hurry, this place reeks like rotting meat. But it's kinda hard to move quickly with these ankle chains you've shackled us in."

He didn't say anything in response, just pushed me farther into the darkness. The chain from my ankle cuffs clanked against each metal step, a reminder that there was no turning back, and no way to get out of this. I had to summon all my courage not to scream. I drew in a deep breath. Saving Conner and Grace was the only thing keeping me together. I couldn't fail them again.

Both of her spirit guides… what had Sam meant by that? I wished there was some way I could send a message to Nate or Dr. Judy.

At the bottom of the stairs, Sam took the lead. We followed him through a flickering corridor, wincing as grime-streaked arms reached for us through the steel bars of cells. I didn't want to look at the faces inside, but I had to find him.

"Where's Conner? I want to see him to make sure he's okay. Otherwise, your boss can forget about my cooperation."

"Why do you think we're down here, sweetheart?"

He dragged us for another moment, and then stopped in front of a brightly lit lair. Through the bars, I saw Conner huddled in a corner, naked and shaking. Fiery cuts swept across his back.

They'd beaten him because of me. Tears welled in my eyes.

"Conner?"

Conner turned his head, revealing three cuts across his cheek as well. "Olga, don't do it." His backside still facing me, he tried to lean on the wall to stand, but didn't seem to have enough strength. He groaned and squeezed his eyes shut. "Whatever it is they want from you, Olga, don't give in. My life isn't worth it."

I narrowed my eyes at Sam. "If you hurt him again, I'll—"

"You'll what?" A voice spat from behind me, a voice I'd know anywhere. *No, it can't be.*

I glanced over my shoulder and closed my eyes, unable to look at him.

"You'll kiss him and make him all better? It's too late for that." Nate's voice shook. "Hands up and come with me."

Turning slowly, I opened my eyes. He held a tranquillizer gun in his hand, the same one issued to us by angel headquarters.

"Nate? What is going on?" Grace shrieked. "Are you part of some satanic cult?"

He inclined his head and turned toward Grace. I could tell from the blank look on his face that his confusion was genuine as to why she was here with me.

"Nate, you don't want to do this." My plea was the desperate cry of an insecure spirit guide who didn't understand what the heck was going on.

He leaned forward, pressing his nose to mine. "You're right. What I wanted was loyalty from you, but we can't always get what we want, can we?"

"Well, that's what The Rolling Stones told us anyway," Conner answered, his voice hoarse. "Guess they were right."

"You think you're funny, Con-ner?"

Conner shrugged. "Olga did, N-ate." He lifted his finger and pointed at Nate, but looked at me. "This douche bag is your boyfriend?"

"Was," Nate answered. "And you'll shut your mouth if you know what's good for you. Or would you like me to beat you again?"

"Boyfriend?" Grace muttered. "I thought you were her brother? Oh. My. Gosh. You're part of an incestuous satanic cult! Gross!"

Any other day I would've laughed at the absurdity of her conclusion. But all I could do now was suck in a quick gasp of breath, everything hitting me at once. The world seemed to slow down as a million images flooded my mind. Nate—who helped me see the beauty inside myself, who I thought I'd spend eternity with, who pushed me away to protect me, who had always been kind and gentle—Nate, who now had the knowledge of good *and* evil. The shock of realizing he'd beaten Conner, of realizing I'd created a monster, made me want to scream, but what good would screaming do?

A door off to the left caught Nate's attention. Two demons approached in heavy, deliberate steps, their smiles a flash of black decay. A bloody apron covered the wide girth of one, and he carried an ice pick in his hand. Nate looked at me and Grace, then the demons nearing, then Conner. He trained the tranq gun on me and pulled the trigger, the dart sailing into my neck. My eyes drooped; my limbs felt like they were made out of spaghetti as warmness spread through me, then pain.

Once, when I was five years old, I stuck my finger into an outlet, just out of curiosity. The electricity pulsed through my skin, but the tingling subsided after a few seconds, barely raising an 'Ow' out of me. This pain felt three hundred times worse.

Finally, I dropped to the ground, sleepiness washing over me as Nate told the demons he had me. He scooped me up in his arms, our eyes meeting. I wanted to tear him apart, just like he was doing to me, metaphorically. But paralysis made the notion impossible. So I stared at those eyes with all the hatred I could muster, wishing he were dead. He opened his mouth to speak, but stopped short.

Then everything went dark.

CHAPTER TWENTY-FIVE

"I used to believe in forever,
but forever's too good to be true."
—Winnie The Pooh

I opened my eyes and looked directly into a bright light above my head. Groans escaped me as an explosion of pain erupted in the side of my neck. I tried to raise my hands, but they were clamped down at my sides. From the cold penetrating my clothing, I guessed I'd been strapped to some kind of metal slab. Squeezing my eyes shut, I waited for the pain and the stars to subside and opened them again and looked down, much more carefully. Turning my head from side to side, I discovered my instincts were correct.

I was strapped to a table in what looked like a medical laboratory. Worse, Grace lay unconscious, strapped to the table next to me. For what, I didn't know. Maybe they wanted to make sure we were okay after the tranquilizer gun had rendered us unconscious, but that was the least likely of the scenarios running through my mind.

I surveyed my surroundings a little better. A computer was set up on a cart about three feet away from me, the Alpha File 120 flashing on the screen. I swallowed hard and thought back to copying the files at the storage facility yesterday. Instinct now told me that my capture had been their plan all along. Pulling at my leg and arm restraints, I tried at least to make them looser, but struggling proved useless. I was bolted to the table, and the table was likely bolted to the floor.

The moments ticked by in silence, nothing but dead air. I felt dizzy, not just from the drug injected into my system with the tranquilizer, but with betrayal. As I digested the situation I'd put Grace and Conner and myself in, I felt like the ultimate failure.

My heart skipped a beat when the door at my feet opened and Nate walked in. He wore a different outfit than this morning, a casual pair of khaki shorts and a Super Mario Donkey Kong shirt that said 'Going Bananas.' I felt another surge of pure hatred for him flow through me, and I wished more than anything I could go ape on him. How could he turn on me like this just for an innocent kiss I had with someone I'd been in love with for most of my life?

"You're awake," he said.

"No dip, Observer of the Obvious."

"There's no need for name calling." Sam's face, nostrils flaring, appeared behind Nate's shoulder.

"Nate…"

I turned toward the sound of Grace's groggy voice, wishing she would stay asleep. The less she knew, the better.

Grace glanced down at her hands for a moment before looking at me as if I could give her answers, brows drawing together quizzically. "Olga?" She turned her gaze toward Sam, her eyes half-closing.

"Oh, don't go back to sleep now, sweetheart. You'll miss all the fun," Sam told her before studying me through his dark lashes. "My associate paid Juvie a visit not long after you left and questioned Julia. She told us you were trying to scramble the file. That's when we decided to grab Conner for insurance. I must say, I'm very disappointed in you."

"What do you want from me?" My words were barely a whisper, all I could muster, and even that caused black spots to cloud my vision.

"We were just going to throw you to Hell for your betrayal. No doubt, we could approach the Throne and build a solid case for your sentence. But Nate intervened on your behalf. He told us you have a perfect photographic memory and could recall what you saw on the original file. Now we can do this the easy way or the hard way. You can simply tell us what you saw. Of course, I understand any reluctance on your behalf, which is why we've concocted a truth serum. Sometimes, those serums don't work on a strong-willed subject, though. That's what Conner's here for. We can torture him, focusing on one body part at a time until you cave."

"And if I still don't tell you?"

I thought of Conner's words earlier, telling me not to give in to their demands. Before today, I would've never entertained the thought of sacrificing Conner. But I'd finally learned something in the past twenty-four hours. This wasn't about me, Nate, and Conner. In my journey to save us all, I'd sacrificed the greater good. I'd sacrificed Grace. God loves His children so much, and I just threw that love back in His face. My pride deceived me into thinking I knew what was best. I didn't listen to Riel or Dr. Judy or Nate, before he turned all evil. And now Conner and I would be damned right along with him. I guess I'd get my eternity with the two guys I loved beside me after all. But the Conner I knew would rather be beaten and thrown into Hell before betraying his honor anyway.

"What will happen if you don't tell us? Well, that's why you're in this laboratory." He craned his head back, nodding to the medical equipment. "We have scientists here ready to perform a lobotomy. The procedure is tricky, so we'd rather not, but if you don't cooperate—"

"We won't hesitate to hijack your brain," a man said in a deep voice, moving forward and standing beside Nate. A woman trailed behind him, but I couldn't get a good look at her. I could, however, get a good look at the guy. He was well dressed in a black suit, a buttoned down red shirt under his jacket. "Allow me to introduce myself. I'm Samuel's father." He clasped his hands at waist level and flashed me a welcoming smile.

I'd never seen him before, but he looked dashing, his face all shadowy angles and his dark hair slicked back into a ponytail. But I wouldn't let my eyes deceive me. I knew under all his good looks lay the coldest of hearts.

"Although you probably know me by another name," he said. "Perhaps Lucifer, Angel of Death, the Grim Reaper, the Devil—"

"You're Satan?" I spat.

He reached out and gently ran his fingers through my tangled red curls. "The one and only. And this is my bride, Lilith, Demon of Storms. This whole time, your friend Conner, and sometimes even you, blamed God for that lightning strike. But you really should've been bowing down to Lilith. God doesn't send storms like that, my Lilith does."

"You wanted us dead?"

"Well, at first you were nothing special. Just another pure spirit I sought to destroy. But now I can use you for my revenge."

"What revenge? You've already taken over the planet. The whole world is madness."

"This is an ancient war spanning the beginning of time, child. The world hasn't yet seen what I am capable of. Most of the world doesn't even believe I exist, the greatest trick I've ever played. But now they will know just how grave the consequences are when a man doesn't follow me."

What the heck is he talking about? "What does any of this have to do with me?"

Lucifer chuckled. "It's your reward for retrieving The Alpha File 120 for me earlier. You see, for years I've sent in my demons, disguised as the best looking men of this world, to impregnate the women and bare my spawn to raise up an army. But the women and demon children always died before completion of the first trimester, unable to take the more powerful physical changes.

"I realized I was going about my plans all wrong. I looked at the other realms. I knew I couldn't get access to Heaven, and Hell was already bound. So I studied Purgatory, Limbo, and Juvie. Perfect subjects for my experiment. But first, I needed the chemical makeup of the people residing there. God's angels had obviously changed the DNA of the deceased to become immortal, even though they retained most of their human characteristics in those realms. They're half breeds, just like Grace, and she holds the key to unlocking the genetic code."

I looked at Grace, and her gaze was on me, too, wide and dark with horror. Here the devil was, confirming the suspicions Nate announced earlier to me about why the demons wanted the file. *Was he a double agent the whole time?* I fixed my gaze on God's Public Enemy Number One. He smirked down at me like a television evangelist who had just swindled me out of all my money in exchange for false hope.

"Now I have Grace's genetic code and the Alpha File 120. I will be able to see what God sees in Dr. Judy's mutant spawn, and I will replicate it. Then my greater demons can begin impregnating the women of the Underworld, creating an army more powerful than the angels, uprising from within."

I expected him to end his little speech with an evil laugh, but he didn't. A fit of rage took over, my body thrashing against the restraints. "You sick bastard! You're going to order your demons to force themselves onto the vulnerable souls of the Underworld?"

He laughed, throwing his head back. "Relax. We're living in the modern age now. We'll accomplish the whole thing through an in vitro fertilization process to control the super powers we want to impart to each subject. I assume you're familiar with IVF?"

I snorted through my nose. "Even with God's genetic codes, there's no way anybody remotely human would accept your demonic fertility treatment plan." I tried to sound bold, but my voice cracked on the last few words.

"We'll see soon enough, my dear, for you will be our little guinea pig today to get this whole ball rolling. First, we'll feed you the truth serum. Then, you'll get dibs on carrying *my* first half-breed spawn. Aren't you glad you stopped by?" His tone served to patronize me. "And no worries, if at first we don't succeed, we can try again with this second little piggy you've brought us." He nodded toward Grace.

"You're psychotic. You know that, don't you?"

He leaned closer to me, looking me in the eye. "That may very well be true. I've certainly been called worse. But ask yourself, which one of us stands here a free man, holding all the cards, and which one of us is strapped to a metal table? Look where all your good deeds have landed you. Where is your all-powerful God now?"

His words caused my stomach to turn violently, but I wouldn't look away. "Don't worry. I'm sure He'll be here soon." *God, you won't let this happen, right?*

Lucifer looked at his watch, then turned toward the door. "Oh, I do hope you're right. I've been waiting to see him for a long time now. But in any case, I doubt you're correct in your assumption. He cares about free will far too much to intervene in most circumstances. Now, I must go meet our other prisoner. I do hope this Conner was worth all the fuss."

As he walked out, the others followed. Nate turned and gave me a long hard stare before flipping the light switch, and once again, Grace and I were left in complete darkness.

"Grace, listen. No matter what happens, if you get the chance to run, take it. Don't worry about me dying or anything else. I'm already dead. You're dead, too, in case you hadn't figured that out yet. And I'm really sorry about deceiving you, but I was under your mother's orders." I waited a moment for her to ask questions, but she didn't. "Are you okay, Grace?" I wished I could see her.

"What are you going to do?"

"Right now there's nothing to do but pray. Pray hard, Grace. Pray very, very hard."

CHAPTER TWENTY-SIX

It could've been minutes or hours later that the door burst open, blinding me with brightness when the light switch flipped on. The same demon from earlier came in, still wearing his bloody apron and carrying a glass of water in one hand and some sort of kit in the other. I struggled in vain to sit up.

"No use in trying, Olga," he said, stepping up to my side. "Don't make this harder on yourself than it needs to be. I'll have to use my ice pick if you don't cooperate, and believe me, you don't want that. You saw what it did to Conner's back, didn't you?"

My insides twisted as I remembered Conner in his cell, bloody and beaten.

"First things first. We'll need to do a blood test before I give you any drugs to help our DNA study."

He pushed up the shirtsleeve on my left arm, then retrieved some gauze and antiseptic spray from his kit. Terror built inside me at the sight of him putting on sterile gloves before he held my arm in place so he could clean the filth off my flesh.

I tried to make small talk while we waited for the spray to dry. "You should really rethink your path in life. I have this boss named Riel, maybe you've heard of him? He's a pretty powerful angel, and he is gonna be very pissed when he finds out about this."

The demon ripped a sterile needle from its package. "You want to know what I think? I think you're just a little girl who's too stupid to realize the honor being done to her." He stabbed my arm with the needle, harder than necessary, and drew blood into a syringe.

"Stupid is as stupid does," I said, watching him prepare a second syringe for Grace as he stood between our tables.

"What's that supposed to mean?" He transferred my blood to a bottle and scribbled my name in black marker on the label, then repeated the process for Grace.

Stars swam before my eyes. *I will not pass out, I will not pass out, I will not pass out.* "It means I'm agreeing with you. Even an intelligent person is stupid if she does stupid things."

He shut his medical kit with a bang. "Perhaps you'd like to stop acting stupid then? Are you ready to tell me what was in that Alpha File, or shall I proceed with the truth serum?"

"You got a pen and paper?" I whispered, still feeling woozy from the blood work.

He picked up the black marker and heaved himself across the room to grab a piece of paper off the counter. "Go ahead."

"Olga, don't," Grace warned, writhing and kicking as much as the straps would allow.

Spots still clouded my vision as I spoke. "It started with a series of letters. E, W, S, C, R, A, Y. You got that so far?"

"Yes."

"Good. O, U, Y, A, Y. You'll have to decode the letters to read what it says. Are you familiar with the rules of Pig Latin?"

"No."

I was buying myself some time, but having a little fun, too. "Okay, in Pig Latin you take the first consonant of each word, then move the letter to the end and suffix an 'ay' at the end."

There was a long silence before the demon stared straight into my eyes and chuckled. "A pity such talent is wasted on always trying to be the hero. But we'll fix that soon enough."

I held my breath while he brought the rim of the cup toward my lips. My mouth wanted to scream, but all I could do was press my lips together and thrash. To what avail, I didn't know, since I was sure he'd just bring another glass if I knocked this one out of his hands. Or worse, get his ice pick.

"You're only hurting yourself," he said, grabbing my chin between his fingers. His grip was like a vise. "Come on; drink up like a good little girl for daddy." He grunted from the effort of trying to hold me still, but then he pressed his fingers together, forcing my lips into a pucker.

I clamped my jaw shut and tried to kick my legs, fighting to free my hands or feet. But then, forced by muscles beyond my control, my lips started to part. Try as I might, I couldn't struggle against his grip any longer. I wanted to yell, appeal to anyone who might hear me and still have a heart, but that would be the end of me. If the truth serum worked, they'd discover I didn't know how to read the Alpha File, and then what? Conner and I wouldn't have any leverage, and what about Nate? That thought blurred into another. If Nate had gone all evil on me and wanted to help the dark side, why hadn't he told Sam he knew what the file said? I couldn't make heads or tails of it, and I didn't have enough time to try to work through the convoluted thought process.

Help me, God, Jesus, Riel, Ash, Dr. Judy. Anybody, please help—

My mouth opened. The glass tilted toward my lips. The demon smiled. In my mind, I saw Conner's smiling face, sweet Conner. His face was what I wanted to take with me during my last moment of being myself, before I changed into some truth-telling robot. And for one brief exhilarating moment, I was rewarded with the memory of racing him down the sand dunes of Grand Haven State Park before jumping into the frothy waters of Lake Michigan.

Then suddenly, the demon's hand jerked. His beady eyes went wide. I turned my head when he dropped the cup, the sound of it clattering on the concrete. The demon slouched over my body before slipping to the floor.

Carefully, since I still felt dizzy, I turned my head sideways.

"Grace!" I squealed.

She shushed me, and drew the tranquilizer gun from the front pocket of the demon's apron, her chest heaving. I closed my eyes slowly, then opened them again in disbelief.

"How'd you get out of the restraints?"

"I have no idea." She holstered the gun in the back of her pants as she walked over to my side and then loosened the restraints. "I was struggling against them with all my might, so afraid for you, and they just came loose."

"But—" I thought about her unique biological background. "Grace, your father was an archangel. You probably inherited some of his more powerful chromosomes."

She snorted, then squinted her eyes at me, a twinkle of mischief lighting her face with an inner glow. "Perfect. Let's use my powers to get us the heck outta here."

She helped me sit, then I jumped off the table, wincing as another wave of dizziness washed over me. I was bone-weary. My neck ached where Nate had shot me, my arm was sore from the needle, and my ankles were in agony from the shackles.

"Um, do you think extraordinary strength is part of your superpower abilities? Because you might need to carry me." I only half-joked with her.

"You can't walk?"

I shrugged.

"Okay then, let's try this." She scooped me into her arms. "Grab the tranq gun from my back pocket. You'll need to play the role of bouncer if we run into anyone out there."

She didn't need to tell me twice. I snatched the gun as she raced to the door. Within seconds, we were down the first hallway. My body still felt sore, and I clenched my teeth to keep from crying out as her movements jostled me. Supersonic speed seemed to be another power she accessed quickly now that she knew about the angel blood running through her veins.

"Doing okay?" She must've noticed my grimacing. "Aren't you dead? I thought there was no more pain after death."

I nodded. "Nate used the tranq gun issued by our spirit guide headquarters, so they must be able to cause pain to us and other spiritual beings."

Her mouth fell open as she let out a gasp. "Makes sense, I guess. But… no, none of this really makes sense."

We'd come to the hallway with the row of cells. "Conner!" My voice quivered; half-afraid for the state we might find him in, and half-afraid we'd have to fight Nate to get to him.

Grace slowed and I scanned the small rooms, blowing out a series of short breaths, trying to squelch my panic attack as cell after cell showed no sign of Conner. Equally odd was the lack of guards.

I frowned. "Where did everyone go?"

"They're in the computer lab," came a familiar voice from behind us.

Grace swung us around.

"They're still trying to crack the encrypted Alpha File on their own," Nate said. "Hopefully that'll keep them busy until we're long gone. Come on, I'll show you the rest of the way out."

I trained the gun on him. "We're not going anywhere with you. Hands in the air, traitor!"

He threw his arms up. "Olga and Grace, I owe you a thousand apologies, but I'll start with one. I'm so, so sorry. I had no choice but to act like I was on their side."

"Yeah, right. My kiss with Conner made you snap, and now you're just trying to buy some time. You have until the count of zero to tell me where Conner is, or I swear to God I'll shoot."

"You're not supposed to swear to God," Nate said, shuffling two steps toward us. "And do you honestly believe you have it in you to shoot me?"

His taunt scorched my ears, fueling my anger "You showed me how, remember? Now, where was I? Oh yeah, the countdown. Three, two, one, zer—"

"No, don't! I moved his body outside." Nate's breaths were labored, heavy, as he waited for my response.

My own breath caught in horror. *His body? He'd already killed him, and now he had to bury him?* An echo of rage bounced across the corridor, and I thought the sound might be an animal before I realized it came from my own lips. *I'll make him pay dearly for this.*

"Show me. Now."

Nate slowly shuffled in front of us and led the way. I trained the gun on his back the whole time, my finger feeling as trigger-happy as a gangster. We continued to follow him—Grace carrying me easily up the steps—but I felt like I was the one carrying her, as the weight of more guilt settled upon my chest.

I glanced over my shoulder when we approached the exit, making sure we weren't being pursued. "Grace, I'm sorry for involving you in this fight. I've made a ridiculous mess of things since I've been dead."

Grace chuckled. "Oh, come on, some of it was fun. Right, Grace?"

I found it odd that her tone still held humor after all this. *Was she being condescending*? Her demeanor didn't look patronizing, but that didn't stop her statement from cutting me like a knife. I guess I deserved any hurtful words she wanted to throw my way though.

Nate kicked the door open with a surprising intensity, a raw look on his face. Everything in me wanted to believe he was good, but if he had turned evil and I let my guard down for even a second, then I would ruin everything again.

We stepped outside to a sterile moonscape, a waiting forest a few hundred feet in the distance, a glowing yellow lake about a mile wide at its entrance. The lake might've looked beautiful if it weren't for the black clouds swirling above the surface, carrying the screams of death. I lifted my face to the sky, searching for light, but there was none. The whole area held the sickly stench of rotting animal carcasses. Grace's shoes crunched over leaves as we followed Nate around the building. I wanted to ask him what was in the lake, but my mouth felt full of cotton. The wind wailed between us anyway, making hearing difficult while coating my skin with the dampness of terror.

"Hurry up," Grace ordered him, human pace apparently much too slow for her now.

Nate held up a hand, checking around the corner, making a show of actually caring if the coast was clear. He motioned for us to come, stepping into a clearing and pointing ahead to a clump of trees in desperate need of some rain, their bare branches beating against each other in the violent wind.

"He's behind those bushes over there."

My gaze followed the direction of his index finger.

"Put me down, Grace." I half-closed my eyes, trying to ignore the dizziness making the whole forest in front of me spin when she released me.

I moved past Nate, ignoring him, too, and ignoring the briars catching on my jeans. Hidden beneath a pile of dead leaves, I saw him. Conner. My breath caught at the sight of him. Time seemed to stop, stretching itself out as my feet remained frozen to the ground, my mind returning to the scene of the lightning strike.

Once again, I was too late to save him.

I turned, threw the gun to Grace, and hurriedly brushed the foliage off Conner's body. Though my head throbbed, and parts of my body still felt numb, my injuries were nothing compared to Conner's wounds. He wasn't naked anymore, but only a thin pair of hospital scrub pants covered his lower half. His shirtless form revealed lots of dried blood—way too much blood—crusted to his side, his back, his abdomen, his arms. With closed eyes, his body lay motionless on the cold, hard dirt.

I choked on a sob.

"Conner!" I whispered, hoping he was still alive. *Could someone die twice?*

I turned to Nate, horror gripping my chest. "What have you done to him, you monster?" Hands still up in a defensive stance, he spoke in a placating voice. "Olga, I'm sorry. I—"

"Shut up! Both of you!" Grace's look of fury almost frightened me more than the sight of Conner's bloody body. "You can sort out your sick little love triangle later. Right now, we need to focus on getting out of here. Olga, take the gun. I'll get Conner."

In a flash, Grace moved to Conner's side, sliding her arms beneath him. His clouded blue eyes fluttered open.

"Conner! Thank God. Can you move at all?"

He attempted to smile. "Of course; I have the moves like Jagger, baby."

I sighed; relieved his sense of humor wasn't lost in all the beatings. "Okay, we're gonna get out of here. We—"

Branches crackled loudly behind us. The two demons from earlier rounded the corner, their angry steps shaking the ground beneath our feet.

"Olga! Take Grace and get help!" Nate yelled. "I'll guard Conner." He pulled a small hand grenade from his pocket.

For a split second, I wondered where he would've secured such a weapon. *Did he find it in the spirit guide headquarters, or did the demons give to him? And why hadn't he blown us all to bits if he had that in his pocket the whole time?*

I shook my head. "I'm not leaving Conner with y—"

But there was no time to argue. Grace grabbed my hand and slid down the hill behind us. At the bottom, my knee grated against the rough bark of a tree, but the pain was distant compared to my mind playing the 'what if' game as I was laid flat on my back. What if the demons got a hold of Conner again? This whole thing about traipsing around the Underworld had been my idea, but now my brain filled with Nate's words of warning. I pictured him in my mind with his arms crossed, giving me his sexy knowing smirk. *Jerk.*

Crap. Maybe I should just surrender in exchange for Conner's freedom. And I wouldn't let Nate get away either. I'd find a way to exact my revenge on him.

The sound of a deafening explosion pierced my ears, snatching me from my thoughts. Behind me, smoke rose toward the sky. Nate must've thrown the grenade, but did he and Conner survive the blast? I couldn't stand this fight any longer.

"Are you okay?" Grace yelled.

I sat up slowly, my eardrums still ringing, but I was ready to give up and tell her to save herself, when I felt something protruding in my back pocket. Reaching into my jeans, my heart pounded faster when I realized I'd held onto the glue stick this whole time! I threw the cap off, ready to hit the toggle switch when I realized it was already down, signaling *Angel 9-1-1*.

Two things I was certain of in that moment: one, I'd just brought butt dialing to a whole 'nother level; and two, I was about to have my butt handed to me by one very powerful angel.

Chapter Twenty-Seven

"No man dies for what he knows to be true.
Men die for what they want to be true,
for what some terror in their hearts
tells them is not true."
—Oscar Wilde

Grace grabbed my hand again and we began sprinting, cutting through the woods, buying some time. I could hear at least one demon chasing after us. The knee-high briar patches snatched at my pants as I tore through the forest. Over my panting breath, I heard the demons whispering, "You'll never escape. You're mine. You're mine."

Their shrill warnings were a hammer in my head, beating against my brain. I'd come so far on my journey, and now I was about to lose everything. The frigid air burned my lungs, but I kept running with Grace. We cleared a patch of distorted tree trunks, passed a mangy lone wolf, and raced around the side of a cave to find a path leading to the right.

Grace bolted into the thick of trees toward the left instead. A demon jumped out at us, only a foot in front of my face. I darted around him, quickly moving to the left as he continued his hot pursuit. I could tell Grace ran as hard as she could while practically dragging my human butt along, everything around me a blur.

My childhood dog used to suffer from unfortunate epileptic seizures. I shook more now than he ever did. I heard the demon behind me, and hid us behind a wide tree. Breathing heavily but silently, I searched for a way out, my mind racing. My gaze settled on a huge rock a couple feet in front of me, and I lifted it, throwing the heavy stone in another direction. The distraction worked, sending the demon sprinting the other way.

The second demon strayed behind and stood directly in front of me—his back to us. Eyes wide, I tried to control my panic as I watched Grace quickly break off a branch and whip crack him on top of the head before slamming him to the ground. He fought back, but after a fourth punch to his face, he disappeared. What had I been thinking when I made a deal with these creatures? They were pure evil. Had I actually thought I was such a great spirit guide that I could trick them?

Well, I labored under no such delusion now, that was for sure. And even though I was supposed to be the one helping Grace, I was thankful for her assistance.

With loud snapping wings, Riel materialized in front of us. "Come with me!" His eyes glowed with urgency.

"Grace, come on!"

She hesitated, her lower lip trembling. "What about Nate?"

I couldn't believe she still cared for that little traitor. My concern was only for one person now. Nate had made that choice easy. "Conner's out here, too." Tears spilled over my cheeks, and I could feel them making tracks on my dirty face.

Suddenly, another demon popped in front of us. I sucked in a breath and turned away from it, my gaze pleading with Riel to destroy the disgusting creature.

"Now!" Riel barked.

My mind tumbling, I grabbed hold of his hand while Grace took the other. We were back at headquarters in another blink. I looked at Nate sitting in the chair, eyes wide, his face racked with confusion.

"You okay?" Grace asked him.

Nate only gave a slight nod. His eyes drooped, looking like a wounded basset hound, his gaze flickering back to Grace and Riel.

Ash flew into the room, his eyes wild.

"Take Grace to her mother," Riel ordered. "I'll deal with these two."

Ash nodded, grabbed Grace, and off they went.

Terror washed over me when I caught a glimpse of Riel. "Nate was responsible for this. He—"

"Sit down, Olga." Riel gestured toward the chair next to Nate, who dropped his gaze to the floor.

I didn't want to sit next to that piece of pond scum, but Riel's eyes remained focused on mine with a look that said 'do not disobey me.'

"What I'm going to say will be hard, so listen carefully because I don't want to repeat myself. You are going to have to accept there are many things you won't understand and have little control over. The one thing you must understand is the Angel Council doesn't trust you anymore—"

"The Angel Council?" Nate said, a low urgency in his voice.

Riel blinked at him, his eyes black. "Oh, honestly. Did you read your Spirit Guide handbook at all? There are Nine Choirs of Angels. The Angel Council is made up of special warriors against evil who are the staunch defenders of justice. And they will send Olga and you straight to Hell unless you do exactly as I say."

I pointed to Nate. "He *should* go to Hell. He's working with the demons!"

Fury flashed across Riel's face. "Did I give you permission to open your mouth? I swear a dog has better obedience than you do."

A sudden coldness hit my core. Riel's words knocked something loose in me and before I even realized I was crying, I tasted the salty tears.

"You've put us into a complicated position. You haven't just put yourself at risk—you've compromised our whole operation! As of tonight, you are no longer spirit guides. You will never again step inside headquarters. I've arranged for a Purgatory passport for you and Nate for the next forty-eight hours while you await your sentence concerning your crimes. You've read in your Spirit Guide Handbook, or *should have* at least, the verses from the sixth chapter of Proverbs: 'There are six things the Lord hates, yes; seven are an abomination to Him. A proud look, a lying tongue, hands that shed innocent blood, a heart that devises wicked plans, feet that are swift in running to evil, a false witness who speaks lies, and one who sows discord among brethren.' You've acted with no regard for veracity. You've made excuses for not doing the right thing. Told yourself lies for your abhorrent actions. You've deceived others, but not God. He sees all and will not be mocked. His council of seven angels will judge if you've broken the deadly sin they rule judgment over, and then will determine your sentence if you have. They convene tonight."

My heart thudded, a sick sensation rolling through my stomach. "What about Conner?"

In a flash of fire, he hovered above me. "He. Is. Not. Your. Concern. It's not your place to question God's justice and use it to rationalize your unfaithful actions. What's it to you where Conner is? Your job is to trust that God is in control." Each distinct word was like thunder, shaking the ground beneath me, the lights flashing with volts of electricity.

"You should be asking about Grace, or did you forget about your real assignment?" Ash returned, his rebuke filling every corner of the room.

I'd never heard his voice sound so powerful. I wished his tone would shake some sense into me, but my thoughts still drifted toward Conner.

What was he doing? Was he safe? In trouble? Mad at me? Worried? Brainwashed? I only hoped I could keep myself together long enough to find out.

Ash snapped his fingers, and the door burst open. "Put them with the others."

Others? As in prisoners?

Two guards half dragged, half carried Nate and me down the long corridors of headquarters, and then deposited us into an elevator. Nate's guard pressed the down button. The elevator dinged a few seconds later when the door slid open, and the guards shoved both of us out into a carpeted area. The room looked to be a lobby of some sort. A desk sat in the middle of a series of doors, three on each side. Each door was made of marble and featured a hand carved stone sign in the middle.

"Juvie, Limbo, Purgatory." I read aloud the door signs on my left.

"Celestial Court, Heaven, Hell," Nate said, reading aloud the door signs on our right.

"Where are these transports going?" The secretary behind the desk scrutinized us, scrunching up her face at me.

"Purgatory, same cell as the others," my guard answered, placing a rough hand on my arm.

I extracted myself from his grip and shuffled to the labeled door. Nate tried to grab my hand from beside me, but I yanked my arm away in disgust.

My guard snorted. "Erin, buzz these two kids in."

The secretary nodded, and then the Purgatory door opened automatically. We stepped into a room no bigger than a storage unit, only emptiness inside, just like me.

"Enjoy your stay." With those parting words, the guard slammed the door behind us.

I limped toward a corner in the darkened room before bumping into a form curled into a ball on the floor.

"Conner?"

To have him here right now, safe with me, seemed impossible. But there he laid, blond hair matted to his face with dried blood, his blue eyes staring blankly at me, his cheeks bruised, his lip swollen.

"Fancy meeting you here."

I dropped next to him, trailing a finger along his jaw line, smearing a trail of his sweat. "Conner, I'm so sorry for everything. Can you ever forgive me?"

Nate bent down. "I'll go talk to Dr. Judy and Grace, give you two some time."

I was about to tell him I didn't care what he did when my mind replayed the words. *Dr. Judy and Grace?* My face twisted in confusion until my eyes found the mother and daughter reunited in an opposite corner of the room.

"In case I die again soon," Conner said, and my gaze met his. "I want to tell you I love you. My heart is in your hands. It belongs to you, always has, and always will. I'm not gonna let death or demons or angels or"—he tilted his head toward Nate—"other guys change that."

My mouth went dry, and I licked my lips. "I love you, too. But, you're not still mad at me?"

The warmth of his body permeated my skin, my mind full from the memory of our short time in Juvie together. "There's no room for holding onto grudges against you in my heart."

I planted a soft kiss on his lips and snuggled up next to him, but we didn't talk, though there were a million things I wanted to tell him. For whatever reason, it felt like my humanity had been handed back to me. My knee throbbed, and I was so tired. Maybe it had something to do with being stripped of my spirit guide license. Conner moved his head to my shoulder, and I closed my eyes and quickly passed out.

I awakened on a cloud, the pain gone for the moment.

"Why didn't you tell me?" The deep voice didn't surprise me. Somehow, I'd already sensed Riel manipulating my dream.

Looking at his sad eyes, I sighed heavily. "Because I was instructed not to tell anyone."

"Since when do you follow orders?"

Ouch, that burned. I turned away, feeling like he slapped me in the face. When I turned to look at him again, a deep suspicion grabbed hold of me, because pure devotion seeped from his gaze. I hadn't warranted that kind of devotion. Maybe Nate was right, maybe Riel did love me.

"Who are you?" he whispered, his eyes trained on me.

"I'm someone you should've never let inside headquarters."

"Do you ever regret being born?"

I hissed out a breath through my teeth. "I think everybody does at some point. I didn't… until I lost Conner. Heartache. It's a real heavy thing to experience. I think I'd take Hell over heartache if the choice was condemnation or to go through that again."

"Be careful what you wish for. That's borderline blasphemy."

"What? Is the truth too much for God to handle? He sees all and knows all, right?"

"Yes," he whispered, exhaling a slow breath. "And He loves you, as do Nate and I… yet you act like you don't know it. Do you know who you are?"

My heart beat faster at the realization that he'd already asked me this question. Perhaps there was one last truth he needed to impart to me. "I was a human, then a spirit guide."

His fingers gently grabbed my chin and turned my face toward his. "I didn't ask *what* you are, but *who* you are. There's a difference. Don't you see that?"

I nodded slowly. "I'm a forgiven daughter of the Most High God. I'm a friend to the Kingdom of Heaven."

He smiled, lighting the sky with his brilliance. "Then it's time you start acting like it. Do you hear that?"

The faintest of sounds touched my ears. "It sounds like singing."

"Yes. Nate could join the choir of angels."

I blanched at his comment. "You mean, our Father will even forgive *his* treason? Does God's mercy know no bounds?" Frankly, Nate wouldn't even still be here if I were God. I would've delighted at the sight of Nate being struck by lightning at this point.

"Humans make a lot of mistakes. So yes, God's mercy is boundless for those who repent. But Nate didn't commit treason, silly girl. He was trying to protect you, again. If you listened to his heart, you'd know there is no wickedness in him. In fact, he's finally following his heart and that's why he's singing. He has caught on to the secret of life."

My breath caught. "What's that?"

Riel laughed. "Well, it really isn't a secret. The Dr. Judy's of the world would go out of business if humans would just remember two simple words. Look up."

CHAPTER TWENTY-EIGHT

I blinked, and then looked down at Conner's hand enclosing mine.

He smiled. "Welcome back. You've been out for a while."

"Were you singing?"

"Yeah. Nate started it. I just figured I could wallow in self-pity and fear, or I could join him. He's not a half-bad vocalist either. I can see why he took my place in that fake timeline of yours."

I looked around the dimly lit room, barely able to make out the shadows of my friends. "I want to sit closer to them. Can you move okay?" Eyeing the thick bandage taped to the bare skin of his back, I mentally kicked myself for even asking. But then his hand gripped mine and with a jaw set with determination, he stood, taking me with him.

For a long moment, all of us just stared at each other around the Kumbaya circle, until Dr. Judy finally broke the silence.

"Well, it's probably time we all had a little talk, yes?"

Sighing, I nodded in agreement. My throat felt too tight to talk, but I swallowed and pressed on. "First off, I want to say I'm so sorry to you, Dr. Judy. I went behind your back and let you down. And Grace, I let you down too, even though you didn't know I was supposed to help you. And Nate"—I glanced at Conner—"it's probably best we discuss some things in private."

Nate gave me a nod, and I knew he understood.

"No matter what happens," Grace said. "I never thought I'd see my mom again. I dreamed, wished, and even prayed about it every night. So I forgive you, thank you even."

Dr. Judy wrapped Grace in a hug. "I think we can all learn something good from this bad experience. We have to remain truthful to ourselves. I never told Grace the truth about her father her entire life because I was afraid, and look where that landed the both of us. And Nate, you weren't honest with your feelings because you didn't want to add any stress to Olga's life, and look where that got you. It got you a jealous, insecure girlfriend who was willing to rebel and work with demons because of the unhappy situation she found herself in. Isn't that right, Olga? And Conner…well, I don't really know you, but I heard a lot about you this past year. And for Olga's sake, I'm glad to see you."

A flush crept across Conner's cheeks. "Thanks. I'm glad you got to be reunited with someone you love, too."

"I'm just relieved my daughter doesn't hate me."

Grace turned toward her mom. "I could never hate you, maybe strongly dislike you sometimes, but that's my right as a teenager."

They both giggled together.

"I tried so hard to protect you by hiding the truth from you, but I should've told you about your strength. If you knew the power within you, the demons could've never captured you tonight."

My mind flashed back to the conversation I had earlier with Nate, when we wondered if Grace possessed any angel powers. In the end, she saved us all.

Grace sucked in a breath. "What exactly are my powers, Mom?"

"Your father wasn't an ordinary angel… he was an archangel."

"Right, so what does that mean?"

"That you have angel power in your blood," Dr. Judy explained matter-of-factly. "For years, I didn't know if Simon was your biological father, or if your earthly dad was, but by the time you turned thirteen, I was fairly certain you were half angel. You were smarter, wiser, stronger, and faster than other girls your age. I was convinced Simon was watching us from afar, would see your gifts, and come to get us."

Even now, the sorrow in Dr. Judy's voice was raw. I knew from experience there were some kinds of grief you never recovered from, no matter how much time passed.

"When another year passed and Simon still didn't come for us on your fourteenth birthday, I fell into a deep pit of depression, drinking all the time. And well, you know the rest of the story. The drinking opened the gateway for the demons to torture me. I'd wake up in the middle of the night and black-hooded, faceless figures would be standing at the foot of my bed, and I'd be paralyzed. After a year, they came and got me for good."

A long silence fell over us, and I wondered what would happen to Grace now. Surely, as a half archangel, she wouldn't receive the same sentence as the rest of us. At least, I hoped she wouldn't. She didn't do anything wrong. It wasn't her fault she couldn't continue to live out in Limbo now that she knew the truth. For a second, I wondered what Dr. Judy was even doing here. Then my mind flashed to her telling me to hypnotize her. Like a trail of breadcrumbs, the truths I learned in Dr. Judy's office that fateful day caused the demons to take notice of me, setting me on a path of deceit, and ultimately culminated in me breaking every rule in the book and attempting a dangerous journey on my own. I supposed Dr. Judy would be tried as an accomplice, but that didn't take away the cold-hearted fact that I was the one to blame for the situation we now found ourselves in.

I sighed. Half of my conclusions just brought more questions. Studying a familiar outline in the darkness, I decided it was about time I got some answers, because mental prison? That was the worst kind to be in.

As if sensing my mood, Nate looked over at me. He reached across our small circle and took my hand. "Can I talk to you for a moment? Alone."

Nodding, I said, "I was just about to ask you the same thing." I stood, sneaking a glance at Conner. He didn't smile. I stopped mid-step, feeling awkward holding Nate's hand in front of Conner, but then Nate tugged me and I started again, lacking the strength to decipher what I should do right now.

He led me to the farthest distance we could manage in the tiny room. "So…" He trailed off, letting a breath go out of him.

"So, has this whole experience pretty much been your perfect idea of the afterlife?"

Half choking on a laugh, he said, "Well, I was hoping for unicorns."

"Yeah, I always hope for unicorns." I nodded toward Grace. "We saw some pretty crazy stuff tonight, eh?"

"Crazy doesn't even begin to describe the state of things." His joking demeanor vanished. "Speaking of the state of things, where do you and I stand? You know I'm not a traitor, right?"

I gave him a slight grin. "Yes, Riel visited me in a dream when I fell asleep in here." Shivering, I hugged myself and nodded toward Grace. "You really had nothing going on with her?"

He made an impatient noise. "Gosh, my act was more convincing than I thought. No, Olga, no, there was nothing ever going on with Grace and me outside of a spirit guide relationship. I was going the extra mile because I doubted my abilities to help anyone after learning I killed that kid in the car accident. I just wanted to do the best I could for Grace to make up for the life I lost. And"—he paused for a few seconds, like he was searching for the right words to say—"because Grace was a welcome distraction in our relationship. I knew something was up, could tell you were trying to hide your feelings from me. I ignored my thoughts in the hope it was nothing, in the hopes that if it was something, I wouldn't add to your stress by pressuring you to be with me in your already fragile state. So when I got assigned to Grace—"

"*We* got assigned," I reminded him.

"Okay, we. In any event, I already doubted my abilities as a spirit guide, and I didn't want my failure to be your failure. That's why I went the extra mile and spent all my time with Grace, to be the best I could be for her, and for you. And part of me felt relieved when Riel told me to distance myself from you because that meant you wouldn't have the chance to break up with me."

I reached up, caressing his cheek. "Seriously? You're always putting my needs first, protecting me. How do you do that all the time?" *God, help me to be like that. I don't want to love two people at once.* If Nate was a traitor, things almost would've been easier for me.

He shrugged. "Well, if I'm being totally honest about my feelings, the day when you said you wanted to look for Conner… it just hurt so badly. It's like you didn't become a spirit guide to be around me, you stayed with me just to find him."

I didn't know what to say to this, so I sat there for a moment, my head down. "Why didn't you tell me all of this before? Have you just been angry at me, holding a grudge?" That didn't seem like him, but I'd also never seen him jealous before.

"I thought I should be angry with you, but when I searched deep down inside myself, I didn't find anger at all. I just found sadness and misery." He reached his hand to my chin and tilted my face toward him. "And I was going to tell you all of this later that day when you first brought up Conner. But if I had, you'd hear all the sorrow in my voice, and I still wanted to give you the space to figure things out for yourself without guilting you into something you didn't want."

Taking his hand and laying his palm against my cheek, I said, "Well, now I'm sorry. I love you. Wanting to find Conner never changed that for me."

"I know, and I wanted you to have that closure with him. That's why I did all that nonsense with the poem in the courtyard."

"You provided a distraction," I cried out, sitting bolt upright. "So I could sneak in? Why?"

"Because I'd do anything for you. Because I love you with all my heart," he answered in a voice much calmer than I felt. "I would never leave you, Olga, but I'm not sure if I know that about you."

I felt the breath go out of me. "How can you even say that?"

"Because you did leave me. Look, there are just certain truths I believe in." He ran a hand over his face, and then ticked the truths off his fingers. "I know we never know where life, even afterlife, might lead. I know God created you to do great things. I also know you're still dealing with a lot of problems in your head and your heart right now, and I hope you'll let me help you figure everything out. I'm so scared you'll lose heart because of everything we've been through, and without heart, we have nothing. In our hearts is where God lives and where we keep our fondest memories, the ones that will always stay with us. I truly know my heart's filled with nothing but you. Can you say the same?"

Even in the darkness, I could see the look on his face when I didn't answer—surprise and hurt—and it made me want to throw up.

"I believe God orchestrates our paths to meet specific people along the way, and that He brought us together for a certain time in our lives." Judging by his vulnerability, getting the next words out was difficult, but he rushed through them anyway. "I guess what I'm really trying to ask is do you believe that means me and you forever, or the purpose for our relationship has ended, and now you need to move on to write the next chapter of your life, afterlife… you know what I mean."

Shaking my head, I offered a sad smile. "Nate, I don't want to break up, but I also don't know what to do. Just like when Conner told me he loved me, I didn't know what to do."

There was a long, awkward pause. I thought about the first day I met him at Dr. Judy's office. He'd had perfect posture back then: shoulders back, straight neck, a warm hand extended, instantly trying to get to know me. Now he held his legs and knees together tightly, rocking back and forth, and I wondered if he regretted that eagerness he approached me with, that side of him that drew me in from day one. He hadn't known when he introduced himself how much pain I would cause him.

"I don't want to break up either. But"—he broke off and searched for my hand, like groping for a light switch in the darkness—"I don't know what I'm trying to say to you. I just want to tell you I'm sorry, and I love you. Even if you want to be with Conner, nothing will ever change my love for you. If you ever need me, even if it's just to talk to someone, about anything, I want you to."

My heart beat so fast I found myself wishing I still had that tranq gun just so I could rest for a minute. "After that speech, I must be the stupidest girl in the world to not pick you here and now."

He laughed. "You totally should. But as for being stupid, don't say that. I'm the only one allowed to call you that."

I snorted. "Jerk."

He kissed me on the forehead. "Kidding. Seriously though, I'm here for you from now until forever."

Squeezing him in a hug, I said, "Thanks, Nate, really. Speaking of forever, when do you think we're getting out of here?"

CHAPTER TWENTY-NINE

Nate scooped me into his lap and fastened his gaze on my face, daring me to look away. "You're deflecting again, Olga. Please, just tell me the truth about how you feel. I can handle it."

I bit my lip, thinking about what I wanted to say. "I don't *want* to lie to you anymore, never did. Like Dr. Judy said, if we'd all just been truthful with one another, we wouldn't be in this big mess. The truth is I'm in love with you, but brace yourself… I'm in love with Conner, too, and I have no idea how to choose between you. I know loving two people sounds insane, like I'm not really in love with either one of you, but I swear that I am. I also know I can only be with one of you, and I'll break one heart in the process. But, no matter how badly we needed to clear the air tonight, I still think we should wait to hear our sentence before discussing the matter of us any further."

Nate smiled unevenly. "Well, that would be convenient for you, wouldn't it? Riel would swoop in and make the decision for you. Guess what? I'm not gonna let you take the easy way out this time. I want you to imagine that somehow, some way, you're able to go someplace where you're able to be around both Conner and me." He grabbed my hand and pressed my palm over my chest, holding it there for a moment. "In your heart of hearts, who do you picture yourself being with?"

I stiffened, shocked at his sudden forwardness, but I also felt so much love for him. He was still so young, but before me sat a man with strong integrity, a guy any girl would be lucky to call her own. But I still didn't feel up to making that decision right now.

"I don't picture either of you."

He squeezed his eyes shut. "I was afraid you'd say that if I pushed you."

I hugged him close. "Nate, it's just that I'm still trying to wrap my head around Satan trying to plant his evil spawn in me, and Dr. Judy's history, and Grace being half archangel, and seeing Conner again, and getting stripped of our spirit guide titles, and the very real probability that we'll be sent straight to Hell any minute now. I mean, no offense, but our little love triangle, or love pentagon if you consider the parts Grace and Riel played in our lives the past month… it just feels really trivial right now. I'm sorry if saying that hurts your feelings, but you wanted the truth."

Lacing his fingers through mine, he said, "I guess we just think differently. To me, in the end, and this could very well be the end, all that matters is love, so nothing but us could be more important right now." He cocked his head to the side. "You know, I remember the valedictorian of my graduating class gave this great speech, where she said life would have pain, but in the end love would be worth the pain. I know we haven't arrived to the place where we've learned all the life lessons we need to." He paused, then tapped the side of his head. "Well, maybe I have, because I do have the knowledge of God now."

I wished I could shove him playfully, but I couldn't move. My body felt frozen, because I knew where he was going with his speech. Nothing that happened to us as spirit guides voided out all the lessons we'd learned from our time in Limbo. The Beatles had it right when they sang *All You Need Is Love.* No matter what decision the Angel Council made, they couldn't take away the love I felt for my two… *soul mates*? I'd used that term interchangeably to describe Nate and Conner during the past month. My love for both of them felt so strong, but only one could be my soul mate in the truest sense of the word. And in this moment, my heart pulled more toward Nate. A part of me thought the tug was weird because my heart belonged to Conner for so long, but honestly, Nate seemed like he loved me more than anybody. Maybe that was why I pushed him away before. We hurt the ones we love the most. None of these conclusions meant I was in the right frame of mind to make any decisions about my love life though.

"If you have the knowledge of God, then use it to tell me what our verdict will be."

His brow furrowed. "We hit the play button on our lives a year ago, always moving forward and doing what we thought was right. It's a choice we make every day, to live or die. Luckily, God isn't ruled by emotions like us. He sees our heart and shows us mercy, even when we don't deserve it."

I tucked my head against his chest. "I sure hope so. Hey, you never even told me how you got into demon headquarters anyway. I thought after my confession about Conner, you'd walked out of my life for good."

He gathered me more closely in the circle of his arms. "It took all of five minutes for me to think about things from your perspective. I mean, it still hurt to think of you kissing Conner. But you had some good points, and I did start to think about how I would feel and how I might behave if I lost my best friend who I was in love with for so many years, and I was the only person there to try to save their life and then was reunited with them after believing I'd never see them again. I knew I needed to find you. I didn't know where the dead drop was taking place, but I was afraid you'd do something crazy like try to go back to Juvie. I went back to the portal and overheard Sam talking to a demon there. Sam was about to go meet you, and he explained the plan to kidnap you and Conner and throw you both in Hell. The demon Sam was with had already visited Juvie and spoken to Julia, who told him everything. I knew I didn't have time to alert anyone, and I had to act fast. I approached them, explaining how you betrayed me, and I told them I wanted to come to the dark side."

"Well, they do have cookies."

He nuzzled me closer. "That's true. But it was all just a story, of course. I didn't want to reveal I was the one with the file in my head, and I didn't want them to hurt you. So I told them how you had a photographic memory in the hopes they wouldn't destroy you because they'd think they needed you."

I smiled. "It was a good plan. Were you really the one who tortured Conner?"

He cupped the side of my face in his hand. "I didn't want to. But I had to prove my loyalty to the demons, and I knew if I did the beating, I'd have control over how much he got hurt."

A shudder ran through me. "Well, it looked like he got hurt quite a bit."

His fingers traced a slow line along the bottom of my chin. "I'll be honest. I was angry with him, but I never meant to hurt him that badly. Do you believe me?"

I thought of all my moments with Nate over the past thirteen months. Thirteen was said to be an unlucky number; was even the number of the sailboat Conner and I were on when the lightning struck him. But I felt like a lucky girl to have Nate in my life, and part of that was because of his honesty with me. "I'll do you one better," I whispered. "I'll forgive you."

He bent his head down, touching his forehead to mine and smiling. "Thank you."

Suddenly, I remembered something I couldn't believe I'd forgotten until now. "And you know who else forgives you? Bo."

"What?" He scowled. "I never told you his name."

"I know, but I met him in Juvie. Bo was Conner's roommate."

"What?" he repeated.

I nodded. "Listen, Nate. Bo doesn't hold you responsible. He told me to tell you that there was nothing to forgive on his part because you weren't to blame."

Nate's eyes shone. He put his hands over his mouth, like he was trying not to cry. "Are you just trying to make me feel better, or did he really say that?"

"He really said that. Bo doesn't hold one ounce of anger toward you, I swear."

He slumped against the wall, a slow smile spreading across his face. For the first time, Nate looked like he believed the truth of those words. In his happy tears, he shook like a child.

I put my arms around him for a long time, marveling at how God brought us around full circle. "What do you think happens to the Alpha File now? To those demons and Satan's plans?"

He looked down at me and gasped, then grinned. "I thought you knew. I blew up their headquarters with that hand grenade. As for the file in my head, I'm certain Riel has some program he'll use to erase it from my brain. And I'm sure Satan is still out there plotting somewhere, but as for what he does next, I think I'll let the people in charge take care of things from now on. With everything that has happened though, I don't think the demons will be bothering you with their plans of Underworld domination any time soon."

I gave a shaky laugh. "Yeah, now that they see who they're messing with."

We sat in complete silence for a while. Finally, he asked, "What do you think we should do now?"

I stood up so quickly, I nearly tripped over my own two feet. I could always count on my lack of coordination to bring some comic relief. Releasing a sigh, I said, "Sing. I think we should sing."

Nate scrambled to his feet and intertwined his hands with mine. "I wish I had Breedlove with me. I left the guitar in Dr. Judy's office that one day she told us we were dead, remember that?"

"Yeah, kinda hard to forget that day." I grinned. "Let's ask her about it, maybe you can get Breedlove back from her."

We only took one step forward before he stopped me. "I just thought of something."

"What?"

"Breedlove belonged to Conner. Kyle and Sean gifted it to me in Limbo, but only because Conner wasn't there."

"So, who gets the guitar now?"

He shrugged. "How would I know? Geez, you'd think I had the knowledge of God or something the way you ask me questions."

I gestured toward Conner. "Well, maybe you can explain things to him and the two of you can share Breedlove… start your own band."

"Oh, I can't wait to hear his ideas for a new band name. Let's go ask him."

The thought of them arguing over band names made me laugh out loud, and I was thankful for Nate's sense of humor in the most serious of situations.

My gaze fell on Conner, who seemed to be waking up from a nap and noticing mine and Nate's hands intertwined, his eyes widening. The color drained from his face, and he lowered his head. I broke away from Nate and sat next to Conner.

"Hey, you okay?"

He smoothed a hand over my red curls. "With you by my side, why wouldn't I be? Still no word from your angels?"

Shaking my head no, I looked toward Dr. Judy and Grace huddled together, Nate sitting beside them. "You guys up for a little music?"

Dr. Judy smiled. "I think some praise and worship would do all of us some good."

Hour after hour, we did nothing but belt out old hymns I grew up singing in mass.

How Great Thou Art.

Rock of Ages.

Joyful, Joyful, We Adore Thee.

It was my first glimpse of Conner's developing faith. He never attended church when he lived on Earth, but he seemed to know the words, so he must've picked up some of the praise tunes from his time in Juvie.

When we sang *Amazing Grace*, I realized there had been very little music in my life the past month. Usually, I sang to celebrate. There was no celebration here, but the songs and their words flowed naturally, like water to my soul. My voice was rough and broken, but Nate and Conner's voices were warm and displayed the splendor of God's love.

Maybe, if God hadn't yet revoked the natural talent he given both of them, then maybe there was still some hope left for all of us.

CHAPTER THIRTY

"Then you will know the truth,
and the truth will set you free."
—John 8:32

Our time was up—a truth I realized when Riel opened the door, shedding light inside the dim room. It also occurred to me that it was now Conner's nineteenth birthday, even if he didn't exactly age anymore. Unable to stop myself, I planted a quick kiss on his lips, in case now was the last time I could do so.

"Happy Birthday."

"Thanks," he said with a smile.

"Your trial is over," Riel announced. "Come with me. All of you."

Nate stood first, then glanced down at me, and offered his hand to pull me up.

We all shuffled out of the room in a single file line like it was the first day of kindergarten. After standing briefly in the foyer for a moment, Nate gestured to the walls. "Well, I'd like door number two on the right, please."

Riel's face glowed. "*You* aren't going through any of these doors."

My blood chilled in my veins. "Then, what did the Angel Council decide to do with us?"

Riel explained they called on a multitude of witnesses before they made their decision. He personally testified on our behalf, as did Ash, as surprising as that was.

The Council even called Sam in to testify, who broke numerous peace agreement laws during this whole debacle. They sentenced him to roam Earth as a lesser demon, separated from Hell and his dear old dad until the Day of Judgment.

They brought in Leo, the angel in charge of Camp Fusion in Juvie, who'd spoken to Bo and Julia to make sure the leak of top-secret information had been contained. Since Conner's friends really didn't know anything, they were kept out of the trial.

The council also agreed that stronger security measures were needed at their storage facility.

Given the situation, Grace was allowed a reprieve from her time in Limbo. She would be sent to Heaven, and hopefully, she'd reunite with her parents there when their one hundred year term of service ended. Dr. Judy would remain a spirit guide, but would not keep her title as the head of that department anymore, and her travels to Earth would be limited for a probation period of one year.

"I hope that means you can continue to counsel my and Conner's parents."

She nodded. "For as long as they need me."

Riel's smug expression returned. "They won't."

I narrowed my eyes. "What's that supposed to mean?"

He sighed. "You'll all see soon enough. Now hurry up, say your goodbyes. I've got somewhere to be soon."

Dr. Judy waved a dismissive hand. "Oh, Riel, can't you swallow your ego for one minute and just admit the reason you want to rush this goodbye is because you'll actually miss Olga?"

Riel gritted his teeth, then looked at me. "I will, actually."

My eyes watered. "Why? Where am I going?"

He paced the floor before opening Heaven's door. "We'll get to you in a moment. Come on, Grace."

Grace eyed me with a frown.

"Are you trying to figure out if you should thank me or slap me?"

She laughed. "At this point, I think I should simply thank you. Both of you." She gestured to Nate and me. "I am going to Heaven after all, and what's better than that?"

Dr. Judy smiled. "Let me walk you out."

We gave each of them a quick hug goodbye and watched Ash escort them through the appropriate door.

Finally, it was just me and three men who claimed to love me left in the room. *Awkward!*

Riel informed us that the angels decided my actions weren't inherently evil since I never intended to give the demons the file, but my actions were unfortunate for many involved, especially Nate and Conner.

He paused at the end of his explanation, and I froze. "So, what does that mean? They don't know what to do with us or something?"

"God sees and judges the heart, not just the actions, and God will use every possible means to save us. Many of those means are unknown and unexpected. No one dare limit the mercy, the cleverness, or the power of God. He never tears up His plan for us. He fulfills and transforms it. He weeps over those sent to Hell, but not over ashes. He weeps over the souls that existed before they were burned, the souls who could've chosen good but chose evil instead. He delights in those who believe the most strongly in Heaven, because they make the greatest difference on Earth. To many, your plan sounded crazy when laid out bare in testimonies, but it also made perfect sense."

My hand went to my heart. "It did?"

"Yes, for God is pure love. Pure love gives itself. God gave Himself, so we might have membership in His family. He made us partakers in His divine nature because pure love has no stinginess to it. In the end, your love for Nate *and* Conner mimicked the love of God, as did their love for you. You were all persistent in your spiritual journeys, and your strong character developed as you struggled through tough conditions. You didn't always make the right choices, but only God is perfect. He doesn't expect you to be perfect, only that you try, and try you did."

Nate looked at me, then back at Riel. "So, that means what exactly?"

He shrugged. "That means the Angel Council has been given the approval by the Man upstairs to send you back to Earth."

Nate gasped. "You're sending us back?"

Riel nodded. "I know. God help us all."

I shook my head. "What do you mean we're going back to Earth? To roam as ghosts?"

"No," he said, just as the door labeled Juvie opened, and an angel looking like he was made of fire and brimstone—there was no other way to describe him—stepped out.

"Leo?" Conner's eyes widened.

"Who else would it be?"

I instantly understood why Conner said Leo had no trouble controlling two thousand teenagers at Camp Fusion. And I was extremely grateful Julia hadn't stepped out of that Juvie door. Half of the teenage girls in Grand Haven were already in love with Conner… I didn't need one more to compete with.

"Papers ready for the transport?" Riel asked, his expression flat.

"Yep, I have them right here." Leo stepped forward, clipboard in hand, and instructed Conner on where to sign.

"What is this for?" Conner asked.

"Your release from Juvie… just tying up some loose ends. If you die again before the age of twenty, you won't be able to come back to Camp Fusion. So do me a favor and stay safe, kid, all right?"

Conner finished signing with a flourish, then stepped back a few steps, like he was scared Leo might change his mind.

But Leo just handed the paper to Riel, who turned to Conner. "You understand what you just signed?"

Conner nodded.

"I can't hear your head shake. Please say the words."

"Yes, I understand."

"Okay then. I guess that confused look on your face is standard."

Nate chuckled. "You know, there was seldom enough time to enjoy your humor while I was here."

Riel ignored him and blew on the paper.

"What are you doing?" I asked him.

"Bearing witness to the contract." He handed the paper back to Leo and nodded. "Thank you. See you at the leader picnic tomorrow?"

Leo nodded, and Riel waited until he made his exit before addressing us again. "You three amigos are returning to Earth, where it will be the first day of April, when lightning struck Conner. Nate will return to his hometown and make his way to Grand Haven eventually."

"God can orchestrate all that?" Nate whispered.

Riel popped his wings out, momentarily blinding us with his greatness. "Do you not yet recognize the power of God? He is God! He is in the past, present, and future. He is not limited by time and space. And God *acts* and *intervenes* in history to accomplish His ends."

Curiosity glinted in Nate's soulful eyes as he whispered, "But does God often send dead people back to Earth to live their life?"

"No, your situations are quite unusual," Riel stated casually. "I can only recall five other times that this has happened in the last six thousand years or so."

Nate seemed to let this truth settle into him before opening his mouth again. "So God gives a free pass once every millennia or something?"

Riel laughed, a sound reminiscent of church bells chiming; rich, complex, loud, and rhythmic. But there was no trace of humor in the gesture. "I do not make the mistake of deciphering God's actions. He is not a secret code that can be translated. But remember, the fact that you two chose to become spirit guides instead of entering Heaven was an anomaly in our system to begin with."

I took a deep breath and pushed aside my guilt over stealing the Alpha File because I still wanted clarification while I could have it. "But Nate and Conner's accidents will still happen?"

He held out his palm, and I slid my free hand in his. "Yes. But their outcomes will be different. You will all live, though I can only pray you don't make the same mistakes twice. All your memories of this past year will be wiped clean upon re-entry to Earth. So Nate, I'm afraid you won't have that full knowledge of God to help you out, although you will have a side effect." He leaned forward, releasing my hand to give Nate a pat on his back. "I do hope you'll put your supernatural talent to good use. I know I would."

"What is it?"

"You'll see soon enough."

Despite my overwhelming happiness about being sent to Earth for a second chance, the thought of Satan's son roaming around freely sent waves of terror through me. "What about Sam? Won't he be out to get me?"

"Yes, though demons have always roamed the Earth, out to get people. If you stay on the straight and narrow path, then you'll be fine."

"But I won't remember any of my life lessons… I'll be starting over from day one?"

Riel nodded. "A part of your spiritual being will be aware of the journey you've taken, but only in the subconscious of your mind."

I sucked in a deep breath, my eyes watering at the thought of leaving Riel. "Any parting words of wisdom from my angel, then?"

A smile ghosted across his face. "Remember when I asked you who you were?"

I nodded. I knew he had been hijacking my dreams!

"Your name means holy, Olga. Remember, God consecrated you for His purpose. He is giving you a new beginning. Don't waste a minute of your new life and take nothing for granted. Love yourself, believe in yourself, and fight for yourself; then God will give His faith to you and success will take on a new meaning in all the areas of your life. Nathan"—Nate startled at hearing his full name—"your name means to give. Because you freely gave your love to Olga and Grace, you have been given a second chance at life." He placed his palm on Nate's forehead. "Use it wisely. God has given you maturity beyond your years.

"And Conner, not surprisingly, your name means strong willed. God loves you, but He is tired of butting heads with you. Olga's compassion for you has motivated our Father to allow you to return to Earth with her and Nate. *You* did not earn this second chance at life as they have, but your return demonstrates more clearly the message that none can truly *earn* our place in God's Kingdom because it is given freely to all who seek it. But He *will* test you as He has done with countless others, to see if you believe that God can help you, to see if you *really* want His help. He will use this lightning strike as a wakeup call, and I pray you answer it before it's too late."

I reached out to Conner then and put my hand in his.

He half-closed his eyes. "I hope I answer it, too."

Riel took a deep breath. "Olga, I feel I owe you an apology before you leave."

"Me?" I croaked, my throat thick with emotion.

"Yes. I am to blame for the whole mix-up between you and Nate. I should not have told Nate to take on Grace as a solo assignment. I should have had faith in your abilities, but I let my feelings for you cloud my judgment. I was so concentrated in my efforts to keep you from Hell by pushing you away from Nate and Grace that I neglected to realize I almost led you straight there by taking away your sense of purpose. The thought of you going after Conner never occurred to me. Your love for Nate kept you grounded, and I robbed you of that. There is no excuse for what I left you to face on your own. Please know I am deeply sorry for everything. An archangel should, and does, know better."

I looked down at my hand intertwined with Conner's. "Riel, we have a saying on Earth. Hindsight is 20/20. Even if you would've done things differently, please know I always had my sights on going after Conner. Sometimes you can't stop people from making bad decisions, no matter what you do."

Shaking my head, I let go of Conner, in more ways than one. "My mistakes are mine to bear, and mine alone. You must understand that during the year in Limbo, my whole existence was a carefully made list, a fabrication suggested by Dr. Judy as a way of making me put one foot in front of the other toward a path of healing. But once I learned I was dead and realized Conner must be in the Underworld somewhere within my reach, the whole experience seemed pointless. Because I could have Conner again. But I couldn't, not really, but I had to discover those things on my own. Going to find him by myself was the only *real* thing I've done in the past year, and thankfully, God kept me from harm and is delivering me safely home now, where I belong." I took a long, deep breath. "Please know there's nothing to apologize for. Your very nature demands that you protect vulnerable souls. You were only trying to do what you thought was best for everyone."

He stared into my eyes with such an intense gaze, I was certain he could see into the window of my soul. "Olga Gay Worontzoff, I think you're laboring under the misinterpretation that I would go to such lengths to safeguard everyone I have charge over. Everything I did is because I love you. No matter how inappropriate my feelings were for you, they were there. So don't try to sugarcoat the scenario my actions created, and please just answer my one question before you leave. Can you accept my apology now that you know the truth?"

Leaning back on my heels, I stared at him darkly in the silence that followed. Finally, I stepped into the space between us and wrapped him in an awkward hug, since his wings were still popped out. Thankfully, he'd dimmed their brightness, but I still closed my eyes as I stroked the curves of his muscular feathers. "Of course. If you were only trying to protect someone you love"—my heart pounded as I repeated back his absurd admission—"then how could I hold that against you, when I broke about every spirit guide law in the book to do the same thing?" I pulled back. "And I hope you'll still watch over me, even if you're not my boss anymore."

"Always," Riel answered, looking at the three of us. "Now that we've said our goodbyes, it's time to get going. I have an appointment at the Throne after this."

Conner turned to Nate, a struggle to remain civil clear on his face. "I'd say it was nice to meet you, but—"

"Oh, save it." Riel scowled at him. "Your paths will cross again soon."

Nate nodded. "And FYI, I'm not giving up. May the best man win."

And right then, I knew I had problems. My best friend was in love with me and counted my boyfriend as his enemy. Sam would still be on the loose somewhere on Earth, and I had a feeling he'd move close to Grand Haven so he could torture me for getting him kicked out of the Underworld. Plus, Nate would have some sort of side effect that made even Riel chuckle with delight.

Problems for sure. If being a spirit guide didn't almost kill me, the drama that lay ahead for my senior year of high school just might. But the thought that I even had a senior year of high school to look forward to made any possible drama seem so beyond *worth it.*

Riel gathered us in his arms and prayed in a tongue I didn't recognize.

I decided I should end my journey the same way I started, with a prayer. Except this time, I wasn't ready to die, I was ready to live.

God, thank you for being my companion through everything. So many emotions pulled me in all directions this past year, but even though I strayed off course, You never left me. Help me find my safe harbor in Your grace. Help me to awaken to a bright new day in the comfort of Your love, no matter what lies ahead with the two guys standing next to me. There are so many thoughts running through my head about what I want to do with my life now that I have a second chance, but help me to know everything will turn out okay if You have other plans. After all, You are the protector of my heart and my soul, the One I can always count on for a perfect ending.

Thin tears seeped from the corners of my eyes when I whispered 'Amen.' Raising my arms out to the sides, I'd never felt so much peace as I enjoyed the sensation of pure weightlessness and infinite space for a brief moment.

Suddenly, coldness washed over me as rain pelted my skin. *What had I just been worrying about?* A flash caught my eye, and I watched something fly off the sailboat.

"*Conner!*"

I took a deep breath, and then dove in, feeling more alive than I ever had before.

ACKNOWLEDGEMENTS

I'd like to give thanks to:

First and foremost, Jesus, for my salvation, for transforming my despair into hope, and for giving me the desires of my heart.

My family: My husband, Dan, for inadvertently supplying me with lots of funny one-liners to use in my writing, along with too many pop culture references.To Kaylee, for your invaluable insights into the life of a teenage girl and for simultaneously being my toughest critic and biggest fan.To Ashley, for supplying me with daily fun facts, around the clock laughs, and supersized hugs.Thank you for sacrificing so much (the crazy hours, sharing me with imaginary people, piles of unfinished projects around the house) so my dreams could become reality. Without the three of you by my side, all of this would mean nothing.

The two BEE's this side of the galaxy, Jessa and Krystal. Jessa, you're like my own Han Solo, a rogue who doesn't play by the rules but has my back with any problem, adding humor to any crisis with your quirky and witty ways and often holding me together with duct tape and bubble gum. And Krystal, you're like my own mixture of Yoda and Obi-Wan Kenobi whispering sound advice in my ear. Somewhere in the middle, I always find my perfect solution. And to everyone else at Curiosity Quills, I could not have come this far without your dazzling collective know-how.

My own personal Jedi Order, my family and friends, your encouragement and support continually spurs me on. A special shout out to Deana Barnhart, Jenny Keller Ford, and Kelly Seaton, whose insights on the first reading of this book were invaluable.Marisa Cleveland, thanks for being my first writer friend who believed in this series! Also to all the bloggers out there who helped with blog tours, blogfests, giveaways, and reviews. I would be very remiss not to mention the Insecure Writer's Support Group and Writers Helping Writers specifically. To all of my pastors over the years for preaching messages that helped inspire the heart of this book: God has a plan for our lives. Going through hell is worth it to arrive at the place He has for us.

The teachers, librarians, booksellers, and loyal fans who gave my little series wings to fly. An extra heartfelt thanks goes out to the students and staff at Gulf Middle School for continuing on this journey with me. And to all my students, present and past, you've taught me so much more than I'll ever teach you.

My readers, because you are A*W*E*S*O*M*E! Even though this is a work of fiction, I hope you walked away with at least one truth to carry with you on your own journey.

I wish I could personally thank every person, book, movie, television show, and song that inspired my muse, but to do so would be an act of tree homicide, and that would not be cool. But please know that the voices whispering in the dark corners of my mind are eternally grateful.

LITERATURE CIRCLE QUESTIONS FOR *18 TRUTHS*

1. The events of *18 Truths* take place in the Underworld. What do you imagine the afterlife to be like? Do you think it could resemble the different regions described in this book?
2. Olga says: "To me, a soul mate went way beyond romance. Soul mates were the people I could share my life with on a deeper level; all the things, truths, thoughts, hopes, fears, disappointments, and dreams that my life encompassed. They were with me, and I was with them, for the long run." Talk about the idea of a soul mate and compare your definition with Olga's. Make a friendship tree for yourself, separating people by who you consider Acquaintances, Companions, and Soul Mates.
3. What do their relationships with Grace and Riel mean to Nate and Olga? Was it surprising how quickly Grace and Nate bonded knowing the truth of his relationship with Olga? What did you think of Riel when he was first introduced? Did your opinion of Riel change throughout the book? If so, how?
4. Not being truthful is one of the larger themes in *18 Truths*. What does being "untruthful" mean for Olga, Nate, Riel, and Conner? What do you think it says about Olga's character that she's willing to fight for everyone around her except herself? How do you stay true to yourself?

5. What other themes are present in *18 Truths?* Consider how the themes of trust and faith occur throughout the story and play out in several relationships. Discuss the meanings of "trust" and "faith." Compare and contrast the two.
6. What would *18 Truths* be like if Conner or Nate narrated the book? If you had to pick a character other than Olga to narrate, who would it be and why?
7. Why do you think Olga felt the need to try to 'save' Conner again in *18 Truths,* despite being healed of her guilt over not saving him in the first book, *18 Things,*?
8. Out of all the tools and electronics Olga and Nate are issued by Spirit Guide Headquarters, which one would you most like to have and why?
9. What do you think is the significance surroundingthe book's title? What do the "18 Truths" refer to?
10. *18 Truths* is the second installment of a trilogy. What do you think is in store for Olga, Nate, and Conner in the last book of the series, *18 Thoughts*?
11. At its core, the *18 Things* trilogy is a coming of age love story. Who would you choose for Olga's one and only? Why?
12. The first book, *18 Things*, ended in an unexpected way for many readers. What were some of the plot twists woven into the storyline of *18 Truths*? Do you like a book riddled with twists and turns? Why or why not?
13. Olga says: "Like a trail of breadcrumbs, the truths I learned in Dr. Judy's office that fateful day caused the demons to take notice of me, setting me on a path of deceit, and ultimately culminated in me breaking every rule in the book and attempting a dangerous journey on my own." Describe the untruths, actions, and feelings that led Olga to the decision to finally go after Conner.
14. *18 Things* was a very serious book set on Earth. *18 Truths* is set in the Underworld, an environment that causes Olga and Nate to focus more on their faith. Do you feel the second book was just as serious as the first one, or did you sense a lighter tone? Cite evidence for your argument.
15. Angels are considered heavenly beings entrusted by God to help guide His children. With this definition, what do you think guided Riel in his decisions concerning Olga? Do you think his actions were honorable?

16. Do you think Olga was right in her assertion at the end of *18 Truths* that there were more pressing matters than the state of her love life, or do you side more with Nate when he said love was all that mattered in the end? Support your argument.
17. *18 Truths* is a strong example of internal conflict. Cite passages from the novel that speak the strongest to Olga's struggle with herself.
18. Think of the indelible truths that guide your way of life. Write them down. Can you come up with eighteen?

Thank You For Reading

© 2014 Jamie Ayres

http://jamieayres.com

Curiosity Quills Press

http://curiosityquills.com

Please visit http://curiosityquills.com/reader-survey/ to share your reading experience with the author of this book!

About The Author

Jamie Ayres writes young adult paranormal love stories by night and teaches young adults as a Language Arts middle school teacher by day. When not at home on her laptop or at school, she can often be found at a local book store grabbing random children and reading to them. So far, she has not been arrested for this. Although she spent her youthful summers around Lake Michigan, she now lives in Florida with her prince charming, two children (sometimes three based on how Mr. Ayres is acting), and a basset hound. She really does have grandmothers named Olga and Gay but unlike her heroine, she's thankfully not named after either one of them. She loves lazy pajama days, the first page of a good book, stupid funny movies, and sharing stories with fantastic people like you. Her previous works include the first installment of her trilogy, *18 Things*. Visit her online via Twitter, Facebook, or at www.jamieayres.com.

Photo Credit: *Owl Sisters Photography*

TURN THE PAGE FOR A PREVIEW OF JAMIE AYRES' NEXT BOOK...

18 THOUGHTS

Olga Gay Worontzoff left the Underworld anxious to return to normal, but fate had other plans.

Now she's caught in a world that's a mix of familiar and supernatural, torn between past and present. All sorts of bizarre events has her senior year of high school becoming increasingly odd with every passing hour. Things like the new hottie at school reading her thoughts but nobody else's and her best friend waking up from his coma acting like a completely different person. Now she must confront what she will—or won't—do to save the lost soul her childhood friend has become and stare down her own perceived inadequacies to face a couple of tenacious demons, figurative and literal.

Everything she thought she knew about real will require suspension of her disbelief as she walks the line between fear and faith, love and loyalty.

In the end, she'll realize "normal" in the conventional sense of the word is the one thing she could never achieve.

PROLOGUE

"Every heart sings a song incomplete,
until another heart whispers back."
—Plato

All it took was one quick glance away from the road, one look at the guy racing me, one second of distraction… a slow veering of the steering wheel to the left that sent me skidding in the wrong direction.

As our cars collided, a loud thud vibrated through the air, and the car I drove jerked sideways. I lurched forward at the swaying of the vehicle's weight, slamming my head against the steering wheel before the airbag deployed and punched me in the face. The sun glared off the hood of the car, blinding me as I groped for the wheel, trying to break. Breaking too hard, breaking too late, the car going airborne.

For one split second, I was flying, my shaggy hair whipping back from my head, the trees on the side of the road waving to me in the peripheral of my vision. I screamed, yelled a prayer for help. Then Dad's Monte Carlo landed, flipped on its side, and ejected me from my seat. A shattering of glass pierced my skin in the process, and then I was flying again, all on my own. As I sailed through the air this time, I squeezed my eyes shut.

No seatbelt ever strained against my chest.

I hadn't meant to forget that safety feature when I decided to drag race another student home from school today. Suffice it to say, I wasn't in the right frame of mind for making wise decisions. Being forced to move to a small town three hours away the summer before my senior year would suck, but this was a gazillion times worse. If I didn't die now, my parents just might kill me.

The asphalt slapped me hard as I skidded across the road before landing in a heap of weeds and rocks. The atmosphere smelled of smoke, metal, hay, and freshly turned graves. Lying in the field, my blood oozed out faster than a waterfall. Dad's car looked like one giant, crushed soda can. Bo, the other kid racing me, remained in the driver's seat of his car, unconscious, seatbelt securely fastened. His vehicle was still in one piece, but completely turned upside down.

I tried getting up to help him, but winced instead. The shock of the accident wore off and panic set in with the pain. Every part of me hurt. *My nose must be broken.* I cried out as if my heart were broken, too, and maybe it was.

How long will it be until I bleed to death? I looked at my skin, now a red body suit, patches of it missing, ripped off by the pavement. Blood covered every single inch of me, and I sensed more oozing out, gaining speed just like the car had before I wrecked.

I cried now, screaming for anyone to help, but no one came. We were on a deserted highway. No cars rushed past, no screeching sirens heralded our rescue. Instead, wild sunflowers lined the dusty road; their heads nodding in the wake of our car crash like a cheerful welcoming committee to the afterlife.

Using all my strength, I slid my hand into my jean's pocket, praying my cell phone hadn't fallen out. Trembling, I painfully dialed 9-1-1. When the operator asked what my emergency was, I opened my mouth to speak but gagged on the words instead. I couldn't remember who I was, or why I called, or anything. I just stared up at the fluffy clouds dotting the perfect blue sky, and drifted away into the subconscious of my mind.

I'd always been a thinker. Confucius, Plato, Aristotle… those were my heroes. One day, I hoped to join the ranks of the greatest philosophers of all time. But all the thoughts I needed eluded me now.

In my English III class this year, our teacher had us create a list of personal belief statements for one of our journal entries. Most of the students scoffed, complaining the assignment was a total waste of time. I think they just didn't know what they believed yet, and were afraid of producing anything that couldn't be summed up in a text message.

For whatever reason, the thoughts I wrote down for Mrs. Seaton scrolled through my mind now, like a playlist, as I ignored the emergency operator's pleas for me to answer her.

I believe you can do something in an instant that will give you heartache for life. I believe it'll take me a long time to become the person I want to be. I believe you should always leave loved ones with loving words because you never know when your time is up. I believe you can keep going long after you think you can't. I believe we are responsible for what we do, no matter how we feel. I believe either you control your attitude, or it controls you. I believe that sometimes the people you expect to kick you when you are down will be the ones to help you get back up. I believe sometimes I have the right to be mad, but that doesn't give me the right to be cruel. I believe just because someone doesn't love you the way you want them to, doesn't mean they don't love you with all they have. I believe maturity has more to do with what types of experiences you've had and what you've learned from them and less to do with how many birthdays you've celebrated. I believe it isn't always enough to be forgiven by others; sometimes you have to learn to forgive yourself. I believe that no matter how bad your heart is broken, the world doesn't stop for your grief.

I believe our background and circumstances may have influenced who we are, but we are responsible for who we become. I believe you shouldn't be so eager to find out a secret because it could change your life forever. I believe two people can look at the exact same thing and see something totally different. I believe people who don't even know you can change your life in a matter of seconds. I believe even when you think you have no more to give, when a friend cries out to you, you will find the strength to help. I believe the people you care about most in life are taken from you too soon.

A light blinded me, forcing my eyes into a squint. My face pressed against the few warm blades of grass surrounding my pounding head. Time slowed, and darkness began to close in on me like the heavy curtains that signaled the end of a performance. I pulled in a final reedy breath.

I believed I might be dead now.

In the end, my thoughts were all I had to take with me.

A TV played quietly in the corner of my hospital room… not that it mattered, since I couldn't *see* the screen. An optic nerve slammed against my brain in the car accident, resulting in some serious damage. The doctors thought my blindness to be temporary, but after five full days of total darkness, I was losing hope fast.

This was my first day of being stuck in North Ottawa Community Hospital. My drag racing earned me a total of twenty-four stitches across my left leg and abdomen, staples in the top of my head, a broken nose, temporary blindness—*fingers crossed*—a major blood transfusion, four broken ribs, and deep bruises and cuts covering the entire length of my body.

Despite all of my injuries, I took a three-hour ambulance ride to Grand Haven today because Dad had to start work at his new job here. What's worse is they set me up in a room with some kid who's been in a coma for two months, so now I had nothing to watch and nobody to talk to. Mom did her best to keep me company, but the way I constantly felt her swarming my bed made me nervous. Claiming fatigue, I encouraged her to go set up our new house while I rested.

I heard the door swoosh open.

"Lunch time already?"

Someone yelped in surprise. "Oh, sorry. I didn't realize Conner had a new roommate." A girl laughed nervously.

Oh my gosh. New roomie is h-o-t, even if he is all bandaged up. With my luck, he's probably gay… What am I even saying? My best friend is in a coma! Who cares about Mr. Hottie? Ugh, what's wrong with me these days?

"Whoa, take it easy. You okay?"

She cleared her throat. "Um, yeah."

I forced myself to smile. "I'm Nate, new in town. They just transferred me to this hospital today."

Nate, that has a nice ring to it. "Nice to meet you. I'm Olga."

"Olga has a nice ring to it, too. I'd shake your hand, but obviously, I can't see a thing with these bandages. I've got this temporary blindness thing going on right now."

And that would be why he's still talking to me. Oh well, bonus! I can stare at him all day, and he won't even know I'm being a creeper! I hope he can't hear my heart pounding. "Wow, that… stinks."

Okay, this girl is kind of… different. "Pretty much sums up the situation. I drag raced another kid on my way home from the last day of school. I'm the one who wasn't wearing a seatbelt and flew through my windshield, but the other kid is the one who died. Can you believe that twist of fate?"

And I thought I had problems. "I'm sorry to hear that. Sounds like you're lucky to be alive."

"Am I?"

How should I know? I just met you. "Um, yes, I think so." *Great, everyone ignores me on a daily basis, but the one day, one day, I want to be left alone, the nurses give Conner Mr. Talkative as a roomie.*

I laughed at the girl's honesty. "Oh, sorry. My mom says I suffer from verbal diarrhea. But Helen Keller said character cannot be developed in ease and quiet. Only through experience of trial and suffering can the soul be strengthened, ambition inspired, and success achieved. Anyway, you probably want to visit with your friend. I'll shut up now."

"Um, yeah, thanks." *Who do you think you are anyway, the town troubadour?*

I let out another laugh. "Ha! That's a good one. Most people don't even know what that word means. You must've rocked the Verbal on your SAT."

"Huh? What word? Thanks?" *As if I don't get enough mocking at school already.*

"No, troubadour. Is Grand Haven looking for one of those?"

The room dissolved into silence for a minute. "I didn't *say* anything about a troubadour." She said the words slowly, cautiously.

"Yes, you did. I heard you loud and clear, even if I can't see a thing."

I heard her drag a chair to her friend's bedside. I could feel her looking at me even though I couldn't look at her.

"Sorry, I didn't realize I said that out loud. That sailboat boom must've hit my head harder than I thought. I've been in such a daze these past two months, I can't tell if it's sadness over Conner's coma, or if I've suffered permanent damage myself." *Just shut up, Olga! Or Mr. Hottie will suggest a nice padded room for you the next time the nurse walks in.*

Adrenaline pumped through my veins as she referred to me as Mr. Hottie again, and I decided to call her out on my new nickname. "You think I'm hot?"

"What? No!"

My body tensed up. "So I'm ugly?"

"Uh." She cleared her throat. "I think I'm gonna try to read a book to Conner." I heard her fumbling through a bag.

"What book did you bring?"

"It's a novel by Timothy Zahn called *Dark Force Rising*. It's the second volume of a Star Wars trilogy he wrote. I just finished reading volume one to him last week."

"Hmm, Star Wars, aye? I don't know why, but I pictured something completely different, like some bodice ripping cover."

She snorted. "Oh, great. So your first impression of me is I'm some bimbo incapable of stringing more than three words together without giggling?"

Although I have to admit, I'd pick up a bodice ripping novel if this guy was half naked on the cover. Oh my gosh, why did I just think that? What is wrong with me? Conner's not even out of the woods yet, and I'm crushing on the new kid in town?

I expertly felt around for my glass of water and took a sip, trying to figure this chick out. "Why do you keep talking about me, to me, in the third person?"

"Huh?"

"You just said you're crushing on the new kid in town, and I know I can't see and all, but the only new kid in here is me, right?"

She sucked in a breath. "What? Are you high on hospital meds or something? Is this some kind of twisted joke?"

Olga sounded just as confused as I was. "No and no."

"Look, I don't know why you're messing with me, but you're starting to freak me out."

Freaking her out? What did I do? Goosebumps broke out all over my body. "Sorry." I angled my face in her direction and tried to sound sincere because it was clear to me now I was dealing with one huge batch of crazysauce. "I'll really shut up now."

Yeah, you do that, and don't forget to take your dose of Ritalin tonight! Oh, great. I need to pee. But if I walk down the hall, there's the chance of running into Toe-touch Tammy visiting her dad, and I already had enough of her at school today. Thank God it was the last day of actual classes. Ugh, I should not have drank that second cup of coffee from the hospital cafeteria on the way in. I really do need to get a grip on my caffeine addiction.

I shook my head in frustration. "Look, Olga. I'm all for shutting up, but that's gonna have to work both ways, all right?"

"What are you talking about? I haven't said a word." Her voice was quiet.

Why is it that if there's a freak within a mile radius, they find me? Maybe he'll die before I get back. Oh, why do I think things like that? I'm sorry, God. I'm a horrible, horrible person. Please forgive me. But oh, man. What's that funky smell? Is that Nate? If he's not gonna die, somebody should really come in to give him a sponge bath soon. I could offer to help. Ugh! Seriously. What's wrong with me? Yes, he's hot, but he's also a freak. You're at the top of the class, Olga. Doesn't take a genius girl to figure out you should stay away from him. Just read to Conner, and forget about Nate already. Or maybe I should get another coffee first. I must be suffering from sugar withdrawal. That's why I'm having all these thoughts. Or maybe I need therapy like Mom suggested.

I placed my hands over my ears, longing for the hours of quiet boredom I had this morning. The walls felt like they were closing in on me, the room getting smaller by the second. "Go to therapy, visit Conner, drink some coffee, or go to the bathroom. Just whatever you do, try to shut up for like two seconds. I can't believe I apologized to you for talking too much."

"Excuse me?" I heard her suck in a deep breath, but she hesitated before saying anything else for a few seconds, and I basked in the silence. "Do you need me to get a doctor for you? Or some pills?"

I crossed my arms over my chest, my stance of defiance, and winced from the pain instantly shooting up my ribs. "You're the one who needs pills! You never shut up!"

"I haven't even said one word!" *I better get out of here.*

Was this girl a special ed student or something? I heard her chair scraping against the floor, gathering her things to leave. I wished I could see her. "Oh, really? I suppose that was some other girl who sounds exactly like you rambling on about giving me a sponge bath?"

On second thought, maybe he needs an exorcist. Can he read my mind or something?

I couldn't believe what I was hearing! I laughed, bitterly, and winced in pain again. "Read your mind? Are you messing with me? Because I'll have you know that teasing a blind man like that has got to be on a top ten list somewhere for how you know you're a douche bag."

"I'm not messing with you! I didn't say anything about a sponge bath." *I just thought it. I swear, this guy must be the devil or something. Get me out of here now! But is it safe for me to leave Conner unattended with him in the room? Maybe I should just press the nurse call button instead. But what would I say? Maybe I am the one who's crazy. Maybe I'm imagining things. I'll call Mom when I'm done here, tell her I need to see that shrink after all.*

I didn't know if she spoke out loud and was still messing with me, or if I really could somehow read her mind. Her voice sounded frightened, sincere, even if she was crazy. Before I could offer a reply, I heard the door swish open again. "Ready to get those bandages off your eyes?" the doctor asked.

I sat up straighter in bed, too fast, and dizziness washed over me. "Are you kidding? I've been counting the seconds." And honestly, I couldn't wait to look this Olga chick in the eyes the next time we crossed paths and see if she really was as crazy as she sounded.

"Hello, Olga. How are you today?" my doc asked, gently guiding my body into a wheelchair.

"Oh, you know, the usual. How's the fam doing? Did your wife like the book you bought for her birthday?" Her voice was jumpy, her words quick and high-pitched.

I felt movement, and I only hoped it was taking me far away from the weird girl in my room.

"Yes, she loved it! Already read the whole thing though, so I'll have to stop by The Bookman again soon for another recommendation."

"Any time, Joe. Take care."

Her words echoed off the walls, and I could tell we were passing right by her now. I tried to ignore the goose bumps reappearing all over my body, the feel of my heartbeat speeding up. Weird. Suddenly, I didn't want to leave her anymore. The desire to reach out and touch her hit me harder than the impact of Bo's car, but I swallowed the urge.

"You, too. See you soon," Dr. Joe answered.

After I heard the door shut behind us, I asked, "What happened to that girl in there? She said something about a sailboat boom knocking her in the head." I kept my voice calm, uninterested, even though I was far from it.

"I don't know if that's any of your business."

I held up my hands in surrender. "Fine, but whatever happened, you might want to do a brain scan. She was acting really strange."

"Well, if I had to give a brain scan for every person I thought was strange, I'd be a very rich man."

"Aren't you?"

He chuckled. "Well, I guess that depends on what you define as rich."

"I define rich by counting all the things I have that money can't buy."

The doctor snorted. "That's a deep thought, kid."

I shrugged. "That's just how I roll." One thing I knew for sure. After today, all my thoughts would center on this new mystery girl. And something told me she'd make a bigger fool out of me yet.

18 Thoughts
Jamie Ayres

Coming Soon from
Curiosity Quills Press

18 Things, by Jamie Ayres

A young girl struggles to live again after a lightning strike kills the best friend she was secretly in love with.

Her therapist suggests she write a life list of eighteen things to complete the year of her eighteenth birthday, sending her and her friends, including the new hottie in town, on an unexpected journey they'll never forget.

As she crosses each item off her list, she must risk her own heart, but if she fails, she risks losing herself and her true soul-mate forever

Gifts of the Blood (Angel's Edge, Book 1), by Vicki Keire

Before her world tilts towards impossible, Caspia Chastain thinks the only strange thing about her is that she sometimes draws the future. Only her brother Logan, fighting his cancer diagnosis, knows what she can do.

But when a stranger named Ethan appears, determined to protect Caspia and her brother from dangers he won't explain, she's not sure what to think. Strangers almost never come to Whitfield. They certainly don't follow her around, frightening her one moment and treating her like glass the next. And they certainly don't look exactly like the subject of her most violent drawing.

Please visit CuriosityQuills.com for more great books!

The Devil's Flower, by Lisa Collicutt

Killing isn't exactly on Rosalie Lockwood's list of things to do when she runs away from home. But despite her search for peace; guns and motorcycles become her latest fashion accessories as Divine interference leads her to Steele, co-leader of the Fallen Paladins motorcycle club.

Rosalie is immediately drawn into the dangers of his biker world—and into Steele's heart. But he guards a secret that if Rosalie knew, could shatter their new love—along with the human race. The Dark and Light Realms collide as Rosalie chooses between life, death, and the ever-after to become that which she is fated to destroy.

The Charge, by Sharon Bayliss

Warren never lets bullies mess with his family, no matter now big or bad–so when the King of the Texas Empire kidnaps his brother, Warren embarks into a still-wild West to save him. On his journey, he makes a discovery that changes his life forever – he and his brother are estranged members of the Texas royal family and the King wants them both dead!

Warren soon learns that a legacy of violence isn't all he inherited from the brutal Kings of Texas - the myths of their supernatural powers may not be myth at all. Warren must save his brother and choose whether or not to be King, follow a King, or die before he can retire his fake ID.

Please visit CuriosityQuills.com for more great books!

Five: Out of the Dark, by Holli Anderson

Five teenagers who've recently discovered they have magical powers and are living in the Seattle underground feel it's their responsibility to protect unsuspecting humans from otherworldly foes. Things are going well until Johnathan, their unofficial leader and the boy sixteen year old Paige is in love with, is bitten by a changeling. Page vows to find a cure, no matter the cost.

If that's not enough, the Five are also gearing up to face their toughest and most dangerous enemy yet—a powerful and ruthless Warlock who will go to any means, including high school, to build his Dark Army.

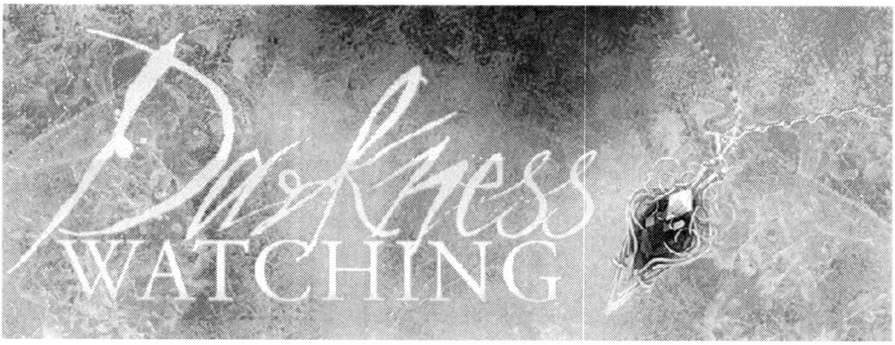

Darkness Watching, by Emma Adams

Eighteen-year-old Ashlyn is one interview away from her future when she first sees the demons. Having withdrawn from the outside world out of fear that she's going mad, Ash is thrown back into reality when she moves away to university.

New friendships, bizarre flatmates and all-night pirate-themed parties are part of the package of student life. But when she meets Aquila, a reckless party-goer with a secret, Ash learns that there's something else that drew her to the small village of Blackstone: the presence of the Venantium, gatekeepers of the barrier between our world and the Darkworld - the source of magic and the home of demons.

CPSIA information can be obtained at www.ICGtesting.com
Printed in the USA
LVOW12s2106080215

426169LV00005B/7/P

9 781620 074473